BATTERED JUSTICE

Center Point
Large Print

Also by Linda J. White and available from
Center Point Large Print:

Words of Conviction
Bloody Point

BATTERED JUSTICE

Linda J. White

CENTER POINT LARGE PRINT
THORNDIKE, MAINE

Library of Congress Cataloging-in-Publication Data

Names: White, Linda J., 1949– author.
Title: Battered justice / Linda J. White.
Description: Center Point Large Print edition. | Thorndike, Maine :
Center Point Large Print, 2016.
Identifiers: LCCN 2016023877 | ISBN 9781683241034
   (hardcover : alk. paper)
Subjects: LCSH: Government investigators—Fiction. | Large type
books. | GSAFD: Mystery fiction.
Classification: LCC PS3623.H5786 B38 2016 | DDC 813/.6—dc23
LC record available at https://lccn.loc.gov/2016023877

For Pam and Dru, who share a passion for justice and for Christ

Character List

Jake Tucker, an FBI agent, late 30s; divorced with two kids. He's trying very hard to be a good agent and a good dad.

Craig Campbell, Jake's supervisor.

Cassidy McKenna, Jake's FBI partner and good friend. Her great love is sailing; her great loss was the death of her husband, Mike, also an agent.

Danny Stewart, an FBI agent on the verge of retirement. He and his wife, **Lavonda**, have been close friends with Jake for many years.

Sylvester Grounds, a fugitive wanted by the Detroit FBI office.

Robert T. Carter, a short, wiry agent from New York known for his bristly temperament. When he transferred to Baltimore, Jake dubbed him "Moose," a nickname that, curiously, stuck.

Manny, a Latino kid from Glen Burnie. He ran from the scene when Danny got shot, but had nothing to do with the shooting. Jake befriends him.

Tamara (Tam) Westfield, Jake's ex-wife and the mother of his children.

Chase Westfield, an influential Maryland state senator and Tam's new husband.

Travis Lowery, an Anne Arundel County, Md. detective and a sailor. He's been dating Cass, and is working on gangs.

Carlotta and **Dan, Jr.**, Danny and Lavonda Stewart's grown kids.

Nick, owner and bartender at Nick's Bar and Grill.

Rudy Glass, an Anne Arundel County police officer. He knows Jake from the gym, and spots him outside the Westfields' house one night.

Maria, a young Latina who has become an informant. She's dating an abusive guy named **Renaldo**. Later, she gets involved with **Tomas Bandillo**.

Aunt Trudy, Cassie's father's sister. Trudy is a widow and lives on the Eastern Shore. She helped Jake recover from a head injury that left him with seizures (see "Bloody Point"). Nurturing and wise, she is like a mother to Jake.

Jasmine (Jazz), Trudy's Springer spaniel.

Justin and **Caitlin**, Jake's kids.

Ramon Garza, Senator Westfield's assistant.

Juan, a low-level drug user who becomes an informant for Jake and Moose.

Cesar Cisneros, mid-30s, a deliveryman for Wright Fresh Seafood and a low-level drug dealer.

Richard Maxwell, killed Cassie's husband, Mike, and later, abducted her (See "Bloody Point"). Jake chased down Maxwell's boat on the Chesapeake Bay, saving Cass and killing Maxwell.

Dr. Snowden, a psychologist who consults with the FBI. Cass talked to her about domestic abuse.

Sam Fico, owner of the Lucky Leaf Casino.

Jim Davison, Cassie's dad. He's a widower, and a retired biology professor. He lives in a small cottage on the western shore of the Chesapeake Bay.

Frank D'Angelo, a casino developer from New Jersey. He'd been connected to some shady dealings in NJ, but is now associated with Lucky Leaf.

Bruce Kilgore, a county homicide detective. He investigates Tam's murder.

Jaime Gonzalez, an undercover cop with Anne Arundel County.

Butch, a guard at the Maryland Senate Office Building and a friend of Jake.

Mrs. Lowery, 70. Travis' mom from Atlanta.

Pete Brown and **Chuck Thomas**, homicide detectives investigating a triple murder.

Len Boyette, editor of the *Bay Area Beacon* (see "Bloody Point").

Josh Willis, Jake's lawyer.

Consuela Hernandez, the Westfields' maid.

Stoddard Hughes, prosecutor for Anne Arundel County.

Mr. and **Mrs. Anderson**, Tam's parents.

Frank Teller, Maryland state police officer who lives in Montgomery County. He and his wife took in Maria, trying to help her get away from the gang.

Luis Molino, limo driver for Chase Westfield. Deals in cocaine.

Alejandro Escobar, aka "Salamander Man," aka *La Sangre.*

Judge Morganthal, hearing the case on Tam's murder.

Meg Harrison, **Angela Parker**, agents brought in to interview Escobar.

Dr. Albert Stockton, medical examiner.

Chapter 1

FBI Special Agent Jake Tucker ended the call on his cell phone and locked eyes with his squad supervisor, Craig Campbell. "It's tonight," he said. A rush of adrenaline coursed through his body.

Craig's bright blue eyes narrowed slightly. "Finally. Where's Cass? Why isn't she with you?"

"She's in Annapolis," Jake said, glancing at his watch. "I'll call her."

Spray from a cresting wave bounced off the starboard rail and splashed Special Agent Cassidy McKenna. She stood at the helm of her sailboat, headed for the second turn in what would be the last race of the weekly fall series. The water was surprisingly warm, a contrast to the nippy air of late October. Cassie's Alberg 30, *Time Out*, sliced through the waves, heeled over at fifteen degrees, sails gleaming as they caught the waning rays of sunlight. "Prepare to tack!" she yelled to her crew.

Cass almost didn't hear her cell phone. When its ring finally registered in her brain, she grabbed the phone off her belt. "McKenna," she said, answering it. "Yes? Not tonight! Jake, for crying out loud! I waited seven days for him to show up!" The buoy marking the turn lay just ahead. "All right," she said. "Give me the where and when."

"Tacking, Captain?" the port grinder called.

"Yes," Cass snapped. At least they could do one more tack.

Minutes later, Jake called back. Another agent would take her place. Thank you, Danny.

Special Agent Danny Stewart pulled his Bureau car to the curb across from a cemetery on a darkening street in Glen Burnie, Maryland, just outside Baltimore. He was two weeks from retirement, and by all rights he shouldn't have gotten this ticket. But when he'd heard that Cassidy was out on the Chesapeake Bay on her boat, he'd volunteered to sub for her. After all, he'd been pulling surveillance for 25 years. One more night wouldn't kill him.

Jake had assigned him an easy job: rear guard two blocks away from the action—backup in case the fugitive tried to flee south on Route 2. Cutting his headlights, he put the car in park and turned off the ignition. Then he reached into his breast pocket and pulled out a picture of his brand new granddaughter and propped it on the dash.

Danny glanced at his watch. He was ten minutes early. He had time. The front right wheel of his Bureau car had felt a little odd on the drive over. He wondered if the tire had developed a bubble. He unbuckled his seat belt, opened his car door, and got out.

· · ·

Inhaling the chilly night air, Jake mentally checked his body along with his ballistic gear. He felt good, strong—something he didn't take for granted any more.

Sylvester Grounds, age 34, was wanted for pulling a series of bank robberies in Detroit. The guy was a desperate ex-con, a cokehead looking for cash. Tonight, based on a tip from his girlfriend, they should get Grounds behind bars.

Jake went over the game plan with Craig again. "He walks through the gate, and up the sidewalk and we wait until he's on the first step, then we go," he said to Craig, adjusting his holster.

"Right," Craig replied. "That way . . ."

The sound of a gunshot split the night. Campbell stopped mid-sentence. His eyes met Jake's. Automatically, they turned toward the sound. Then they heard four more shots—boom, boom, boom, boom—in a staccato burst.

"Danny!" the two agents said in unison.

The two men jumped in their cars and raced toward the agent's position. From half a block away Jake could see a body on the sidewalk next to a Bureau car. He heard Craig on the radio calling for an ambulance and backup. Jake screeched to a stop, leaped out, and raced to the fallen man.

"Danny!" Jake's heart beat hard. Danny lay on

the sidewalk, his arm stretched out before him, his gun still in his hand. A widening pool of blood darkened the concrete. Jake moved the gun away then touched Danny's neck. He found a pulse. Then he tried to find the source of the blood. His stomach turned as his hand felt the warmth of a throbbing stream. "Hold on, Danny. I got you!" He pulled a clean handkerchief out of his back pocket, pressed it over the wound, and shot up a desperate prayer.

Craig barked into his cell phone. A crowd of agents and cops gathered around them.

"I've got you, Danny." Jake wished he could hear an ambulance. Blood glistened in the night. "Don't leave me, man!"

"We're losing him!" someone said.

Sirens in the distance. Finally, the EMTs arrived.

"You all right?" Craig asked as Jake stood up and stepped away.

He shook his head, watching as the EMTs compressed the wound and started an IV. "How'd this happen?" Someone handed him a bunch of wipes for his hands.

"We need to contact his wife."

"You want me to go?"

Craig shook his head. "You take charge here and I'll go."

Jake nodded. Craig was definitely taking the tougher job. "We have a perimeter set?"

"Eight blocks. Everyone going in or out is being checked. A helo is on the way."

"Okay, then. I got it."

The red, blue, and white lights from the emergency vehicles bounced off the houses, trees, and cars in a kaleidoscope of color. The ambulance pulled away as Jake gave orders. Sounds seemed amplified: the rasping of radios, the slamming of car doors, voices. And the images—Danny lying on the ground, the pool of blood, the stretcher being placed in the back of an ambulance—remained burned in his mind. "Moose!" Jake yelled.

Special Agent Robert T. Carter, aka "Moose," walked away from a small cluster of agents standing in the middle of the street. Small and wiry, from New York, he'd joined the squad just six months ago.

"Moose, you stick with the car," Jake began.

The commanding shouts of an agent interrupted him. "Stop! FBI! Stop!" But the runner who emerged from between two houses didn't stop. Instead, he dodged between the parked cars and across the street just thirty yards from Jake. Then he jumped a short, stone wall and disappeared into the cemetery.

Jake began running as soon as he saw him. He was a kid! A teenager!

"Don't shoot!" Jake yelled. He followed the kid

into the dark graveyard, watching the figure dash around the upright headstones. As Jake ran he was aware of Moose on his left, breathing hard, and other agents and cops close behind. The kid ran into an area of large, above-ground tombs. Momentarily, Jake lost sight of him.

He motioned for the others to slow down, to fan out to his left. The kid had to be hiding. There was no gate at this end, and no one had gone over the wall. He'd been watching the wall. Flashlights played across the stones forming crazy shadows and more than once Jake jumped.

"C'mon kid," an agent shouted. "You don't want to get hurt."

Suddenly, Jake saw motion behind a large tomb on his right. The boy took off running again. Jake yelled at him, then followed him over the cemetery wall and onto a side street. The kid was fast! But Jake put on speed and was nearly close enough to grab him when the kid turned into an alley, stepped onto a metal trashcan, and jumped over a six-foot wooden fence.

Jake followed. Later, he would remember grabbing the top of the fence and scrambling over. A better memory was the look of shock on the boy's face when he realized he was still being pursued. Jake tackled him and the two landed in a heap in the small backyard of a row house.

"Ow, ow, ow!" the kid squirmed underneath him.

"Stop!" Jake said, as he wrestled with the kid. He jerked his handcuffs off his belt and began cuffing him. "Stop fighting!"

"What's going on?" someone shouted as the back door of the house opened and a snarling brown dog raced out. A pit bull! The kid screamed louder. A jolt of searing pain ran up Jake's leg as the dog latched on to him. He snapped the cuffs shut, then yelled and tried kicking the dog off, but its vise-like jaws just gripped harder.

"Caesar, get off him!" the owner shouted. He grabbed the dog by the collar and tugged. "Caesar!" but the dog would not loosen his jaws. The owner grabbed a bucket of water, and doused the dog—and Jake. The shock made Caesar release his grip. His owner dragged him away.

"FBI, control that dog!" Moose yelled, scrambling over the fence.

Dripping wet, Jake stared up at Moose. "You're a little late."

Moose extended his hand and helped Jake up. A sharp pain knifed through Jake's ankle as he put weight on it. He reached down and pulled the kid, who was crying, to his feet. "You okay?" he asked, shaking the kid gently. His own leg hurt like crazy. "Why'd you run, kid?" Jake asked. "Why'd you run?"

Chapter 2

Like pieces of a puzzle, the evidence began falling into place over the next few hours. The perpetrator, an "unknown subject" or UNSUB in Bureau parlance, had shot Danny with a nine-millimeter handgun. They'd found the shell casing thirty feet away, in the grass. One of Danny's shots, fired in return, lay embedded in a tree. The other three were still missing.

Medics transported the kid, Manny, to a hospital. Protocol required he be checked. Manny was thirteen years old and said he had just come out to see what was going on. Jake tended to believe him. Still, he'd have to be questioned, and his parents called, and juvenile justice brought into it. Was he the UNSUB? Jake sincerely doubted it.

The question remained, why was Danny shot? Was it an attempted carjacking? A robbery? Was he an intentional target?

"Hey, Tucker!" someone yelled.

"What?"

"We got the guy!"

Jake's heart thumped.

"Sylvester Grounds. We got him."

The bank robber. Jake had almost forgotten about him. "Where? Which direction was he headed?" Had Grounds shot Danny?

"He was four blocks away, coming southbound and headed for his girlfriend's house. Got close, and saw all the blue lights. He tried to turn around and get away, but we nabbed him."

Jake blew out a breath. "That's great, Smitty. Detroit will be happy."

"What do you want us to do with him?"

"Take him downtown. I'll deal with him later." Jake ran his hand through his hair. Glancing at his watch he noted the time: 10:15.

"Jake, look at this." Another squad member stood in front of him, her gloved palm open, holding a bag full of tiny, folded papers.

Jake flipped on his flashlight. "Where'd you find that?"

"In the grass, near the bullet casing."

"Tag it and test it," he said. "Be sure you document everything."

"Okay, Jake. Will do. This was near it." She held out a matchbook with the name of a bar on it: *Nick's Bar and Grill.*

"Document it." His cell phone rang.

"Jake, where have you been? Why didn't you call me?" Cassie's voice sounded upbeat. "Guess what? We won, Jake! First time ever! We won and then we went out to dinner and celebrated. It was great. You should have been there." She took a breath. "So how'd it go, Jake? Did you get him? Where are you? I expected a message."

He took a deep breath. "We had a problem."

21

"He got away? Oh, please, don't tell me . . ."

"No, no, he didn't get away." Jake tried to relax. "Danny got shot."

"What?"

"Danny got shot."

"Shot? By Grounds?"

"No, an UNSUB."

"Oh, Jake!" Cass said. "Where is he now?"

"Shock Trauma."

"He's alive, then?"

"So far. Shot in the hip. Lost a lot of blood."

"What can I do?"

"Pray for him."

"Where are you? Jake, can I help?"

He touched the scar on his head with his hand. "We're covered."

"I'm going to the hospital, then."

"No, don't. Just . . ."

"I'm going." Cass hung up.

Cassidy McKenna stripped off her sailing clothes and threw on navy blue slacks, a light blue blouse, and a blazer. She brushed her hair and caught it up in a ponytail. Then she grabbed her gun bag, and headed out the door. For the third time in four years, she was racing to the University of Maryland Shock Trauma Center in Baltimore because an agent had been injured. First, her husband Mike, then Jake, now Danny. Why, God?

Danny had taken her place. She should have

22

been there, by all rights. She should have taken that bullet.

But what bullet? It was a simple fugitive grab! How did it go so wrong?

Jake meticulously documented the crime scene with photos, maps, and video. Evidence techs loaded Danny's car onto a truck and took it to an FBI garage. Agents conducted the initial door-to-door of the neighborhood as well as a preliminary interview with Sylvester Grounds. At midnight, Jake drove to the hospital. Bone-weary, his ankle aching, he felt like a dead man walking.

Victims of stabbings, shootings, car accidents, and burns populated the hospital's waiting area, a microcosm of the world's misery. Jake showed his credentials to an information clerk, who directed him to a surgical waiting room.

Four agents looked up as Jake walked in. Lavonda, Danny's wife, sat in a blue chair, her eyes teary. Cass sat beside her. Jake met Cass's eyes. He knew immediately what she was feeling.

Jake limped up to Danny's wife, leaned down and took her hand. "How are you doing, Lavonda?" he asked.

"I'm all right. I'm just sitting here, talking to the Lord, Jake. Just talking to the Lord."

He squeezed her hand. "How's Danny?"

"The doctors are working on him now. They say he's lost a lot of blood." Lavonda looked up toward the ceiling, her brown eyes brimming. She was a beautiful woman, with smooth, cafe-au-lait skin and short hair, stylishly cut. She wore large gold earrings, each inlaid with a deep red stone, and a cream-colored sweater and dark slacks. Jake had known her for years, had had dinner at her house, had talked to her many times when he was going through his divorce.

"You called the kids?"

Lavonda nodded. "They're on the way. Carlotta is, anyway. Dan Junior is down at Lejeune, trying to get leave. The Marines don't cut first lieutenants much slack."

"He'll get here." Jake tilted his head. "You need anything? Something to drink? A soda, maybe?"

"I'm fine, Jake."

"Danny's strong. He's going to make it. I'm sure of that. He will make it."

"He's a child of God. And I know he's in God's hands. I know that from the bottom of my heart." The way she said it, it was almost a hymn. A tear dripped out of her eye and slipped down the side of her face, leaving a shiny trail. She wiped it away.

"I'm praying for him. You know that, don't you?"

She nodded.

Jake stood up. He was aware of agents watching him intently. The whole room throbbed with tension.

Craig Campbell moved from his seat. "Would you excuse us, Lavonda?"

"Sure."

Craig signaled Cass to follow as he and Jake walked out of the room. Out in the quiet hallway, he looked at Jake. "How's the leg? Did you get it taken care of?"

Jake took a deep breath.

"What leg?" Cass demanded.

"It's nothing," Jake said.

"He was bitten by a dog," Craig said to Cassie. "It needs treatment."

"I'll take care of it on the way out," Jake responded.

Craig looked at him skeptically. "Make sure he does," he said to Cass. Then he turned back to Jake. "Update me."

Jake took a deep breath. "We found a nine-millimeter casing thirty feet away. We're running that through the ATF database. Near that, in the grass, Jen found a small packet of drugs and a matchbook from a bar."

"What kind of drugs?"

"Heroin, I think. She's sending it to the lab." Jake took a deep breath.

"What bar?"

"Nick's Bar and Grill."

"I've heard of that bar," Cass said. "It's in a pretty bad area."

"We're going to check that out."

25

Craig took a deep breath. Nearly forty-five years old, he had lines around the corners of his eyes and gray at his temples. "And the kid?"

Jake shrugged. "He said he just wanted to see what was going on. I'm guessing that's all there is to that. He was just stupid to run."

"What kid?" Cass demanded.

Jake told her a short version of the story.

"I want to see the crime scene," she said.

"I'll take you, Cass," Jake responded. "Oh, by the way, we got our suspect, Grounds," he added. Six hours ago, getting the fugitive bank robber would have made it a successful night.

Craig's eyebrows rose.

"He just kind of got caught up in the confusion. I've talked with him. He had nothing to do with the shooting."

He nodded. "Look, Jake, bring Cassidy up to speed on all you found, okay? I'm sure you'll have plenty of time waiting to get that leg treated."

Jake rolled his eyes.

Craig checked his watch. "It's almost one a.m. If everything is stable here, let's plan to meet in my office, all of us, at ten this morning. Can you have this stuff written up by then?" he asked Jake.

"Most of it."

"I've notified the Shooting Review Board. They'll want to meet with you ASAP," Craig continued. "You guys better plan to work the weekend."

"Sure," Cass said.

Jake tightened his jaw. "Yes, sir." Out of the corner of his eye, he saw Cass's eyes cut toward him.

After saying goodbye to Lavonda, Jake and Cass walked down the hospital corridor. "What's wrong?" Cass asked.

He didn't answer.

She pressed the point. "Why'd you call Craig 'sir'? We never call him sir."

Her eyes felt like heat on the side of his face. "It's my weekend to have the kids."

"Why didn't you tell him?"

"What can he do? It's not like you can schedule this stuff." He gestured in frustration. He hadn't wanted the divorce and he was determined to stay active in his kids' lives. The job, which he loved, made it real hard sometimes. So did his ex-wife's new husband.

"So what are you going to do?" she asked.

He shrugged. "Whatever I have to do."

"Maybe she'll switch with you. Let you have them next weekend."

"Tam?" He shook his head slowly. "Nope, I think I'm outta luck." Uncomfortable, he switched topics. "How are you doing, Cass?"

She looked away quickly. "I should have been there. That should have been me."

"It wasn't meant to be you."

"I mean, it kills me . . ."

He turned toward her, taking her arm. "Look, Cass, you didn't do anything wrong, going sailing after work."

"I wasn't at my job! I wasn't where I was supposed to be."

"No one thinks you're a slacker. This job," he said, raising his hand in frustration, "can eat up your whole life. Everybody deserves a little time out."

She smiled wanly. "Is that a pun?" she said, referring to the name of her boat.

"If it makes you think I'm exceedingly clever, sure, it's a pun." He motioned toward the elevator with his head. "Let's go. My car's in the garage. You can follow me."

Cass stopped walking. "No."

"What?"

"Not until you see a doctor."

Jake rolled his eyes.

"C'mon, Tucker," she said, pulling him by the arm. "Let's go see if you have distemper."

Chapter 3

At 10 a.m., after a nearly sleepless night, Jake walked into Craig Campbell's office where Cassie, Moose, and three other agents had already assembled. His leg hurt like crazy and he was trying to avoid thinking about the phone call he had made to his ex-wife that morning, and the argument that followed.

He looked at Cass. She was dressed in a black suit and a cream-colored shirt, and she looked sharply professional, despite her lack of sleep. He caught her eye. She smiled. Sometimes he thought she could melt stone with that smile.

Craig started them out with an update on Danny's condition. "He had surgery six hours ago. The bullet fractured his hip and went through an artery, but Jake's quick action kept him from bleeding to death." He nodded toward Jake. "He's in intensive care. The doctors are hopeful. I'll update you as I get the information." He shuffled some papers. "I don't need to tell you an assault on a federal officer is high priority with the boss, and with all of us. Jake, you're the case agent. Take it."

Jake nodded. "Look, I want to wrap this up quick. I have other agents and uniformed officers checking all the hospitals, ERs, and urgent care centers looking for anyone reporting a gunshot wound. Moose, you follow the evidence techs. Cass, you look at Danny's personal life. I'll go out in the neighborhood, ..."

"Wait," Cass interrupted, "your leg?"

Jake closed his eyes and blew out a breath. "You're right. I'll take Danny's computer and go through his case files." He continued handing out assignments to the other agents. "Some mope is out there bragging about shooting someone. Let's try to nail him this weekend, all right?"

Cass spoke up. "I know a detective who's been working on the gangs in the area. It might help to consult with him, since we found drugs on the scene."

A detective? The guy she'd been dating, Jake figured. What was his name? Travis.

His mind shifted. After his divorce had gone through, he and Cass had talked about dating but had never gotten around to it. Truthfully, he had felt funny at first about asking his best friend's widow out on a date. So his relationship with Cass had fallen into the "friends and partners" category. Which felt fine. Comfortable, in fact. And then along came Travis.

Jake forced his thoughts back to the present. "Sure," he said to Cass. "Set that up."

The others left. Cass approached him. "How's the leg?"

Deep blue and purple bruises covered his ankle

and lower calf. "It's fine," he said. "Did you get any sleep?"

She shook her head. "Did you talk to Tam about the kids?" she asked.

He stretched the tight muscles in his neck. "Yeah."

"How'd that go?"

"Not good."

"I'm sorry, Jake." She touched his arm.

He stood up, wincing in pain. "It is what it is."

For the rest of the day Friday and all morning on Saturday, Jake sat in the office with his leg propped up, scrolling through Danny's case files, tracking down criminals Danny had investigated, most of whom were in jail or dead. Danny's computer was a small universe for a guy like Jake. He'd much prefer chasing bad guys down an alley or kicking in doors. Instead, here he was, staring at a fifteen-inch screen.

By late Saturday morning, his frustration had peaked. He had to move! So he decided to check in on Danny.

As he walked into the hospital, his neck felt tight. This place held too many memories.

Lavonda sat by her husband's bed in ICU, her Bible open on her lap. "How is he?" Jake asked, bending down and giving her a quick kiss on the cheek.

"Better," she said. "His vitals look good. I'll be

31

happy when he wakes up." She nodded toward Danny. "Go ahead. Talk to him. Maybe he's just ignoring me." She smiled.

Jake moved to the other side of Danny's bed and took his hand. "Hey, Danny. It's Jake. Time to get up. We need you, man." He cleared his throat. "Wake up and tell me who shot you so I can go play golf or something." He glanced at Lavonda. "First, I'd have to learn to play golf."

She laughed.

But Danny didn't move. Jake tried again. "I know. You're tired. So, let me just pray for you, okay?" He laid his hand on his friend's head and closed his eyes and his words flowed.

"Thank you, Jake," Lavonda said when he was finished. Her eyes welled with tears.

He stood up. "How about a cup of coffee?"

By the time they'd gotten to the cafeteria, he'd talked her into having lunch. "My Danny and I ate many a meal here," she said softly, "when Mike was hurt, then you." Special Agent Mike McKenna, Cassie's husband, had died in what had first looked like an accident on a rain-slick road. In actuality, he'd been murdered by the man who then assaulted and nearly killed Jake.

"We've been friends for a long time." Jake handed her the napkins and silverware he'd collected for them. Then he unwrapped his burger. The smell made him realize how hungry he was. "Where are the kids?"

"Carlotta took the baby over to the hotel for a nap. Dan Junior went with them."

Jake nodded and took a bite, savoring the meaty burger.

"How are your children, Jake?" Lavonda toyed with her salad.

"Good." Jake shared a little about Justin, his son, age nine, and Caitlin, his six-year-old daughter.

"When we get down to our house in Virginia, I want you to bring them. Danny will teach them to fish. I'll feed them cookies and just love on them." She sounded so positive.

"I hope we can do that."

Lavonda put down her fork. "I believe we will." She reached over and opened her Bible. "Can I share with you what I been leaning on?"

Jake nodded.

" 'Fear not, for I am with you; Be not dismayed, for I am your God; I will strengthen you, I will help you, I will uphold you with my righteous right hand.' Isaiah 41:10. That is the foundation of the truth I'm standing on. You remember that old hymn?"

"No."

She sang a few bars of "How Firm a Foundation." "That song's been going 'round and 'round in my head. Sometimes I sing it to Danny; sometimes I sing it to the Lord. And I remind him, I'm counting on that verse to be true. True for me, and true for Danny." She looked at Jake, her big brown eyes wide. "Oh, don't go thinking I'm naïve. I know what can happen. All I'm saying is God is in this. He's promised to uphold us, whatever happens. And he will."

By the time Jake left half an hour later, he felt like he'd been to church.

Jake drove back to the office, checked in with the others working the case, and then picked up where he'd left off. Late that afternoon, he got another break: Manny, the kid, wanted to talk. To him.

Manny lived with his mother and aunt in a second-floor apartment a block away from where Danny was shot. Jake parked his car and limped up the stairs. He knocked on the door and a middle-aged Latina invited him in and offered him a chair at the table in the kitchen as she called the boy.

Jake sat down with his back to the cluttered countertop, taking a position that allowed him to see both the door he'd come in and the adjacent living room. He could see a box of boy's clothes in the corner of that room, and a backpack, and a bed pillow on the worn couch. He wondered if that's where Manny slept.

"What's up, kid?" he said, rising as Manny entered the room.

The kid had on jeans and a purple Ravens shirt

that was way too big for him. He shook Jake's hand and then they both sat down.

"So what were you doing the other night? It was a school night, right?"

Manny looked down. "Yes, sir. But I heard the sirens and," he shrugged, "I had to see what was going on."

"So what'd you see?"

The kid's eyes met Jake's. "A lot of lights! And the guy on the ground. Is he dead?"

Jake shook his head. "No. So why'd you run?"

"I got scared. I wasn't s'posed to be out."

"Do you know you could have been shot?"

"Yes, sir." Manny shivered. "I was stupid to run."

"So next time a cop yells at you, don't run."

"Yes, sir. I won't do that again." He lifted his eyes and grinned. "I didn't expect an old guy to keep up with me."

An old guy! Jake smiled. "Hey! We old guys still have legs."

"Can I see it?"

Jake raised his eyebrows.

"Your leg. Where Caesar bit you."

"You know that dog?"

Manny nodded. "Since he was a pup."

"No wonder he came after me." Jake pulled up his pants and pushed his sock down revealing the deep purple bruises.

"Wow!"

"Yeah, that dog would've crushed your skinny bones." Jake looked around. "Your dad live here, too?"

"No, sir. Just my mom and my aunt."

"Where's dad?"

The kid shrugged.

Another fatherless boy. Jake eyed the backpack. "How's school?"

"Good! All As and Bs."

"Good job. What do you want to be when you grow up?"

"A cop! That's why I like to see what's going on!"

"So what'd you learn?"

"Don't ever run. Even if you're scared."

"Good." Jake smiled. "So what'd you want to tell me?"

"Can I show it to you? Over in the cemetery?"

"Ask your mom."

After getting permission from his mother to leave, Manny led Jake down the stairs and one block over to the cemetery. The kid kept glancing over his shoulder as he walked. "You go out a lot at night?" Jake asked him.

"I'm not s'posed to, but I do."

"Curiosity kills more than cats."

"Yes, sir."

"Cops always have backup when they go out."

Manny looked around. "Where's yours?" He grinned.

Jake laughed. The kid had moxie. He followed Manny through the cemetery, stopping at an above-ground crypt with the name "THOMAS" carved on it.

"I've seen some guys putting stuff in here," Manny said.

"Have you ever opened it?"

"No, sir."

"Let's do it."

Manny put his shoulder to the crypt's door and pushed.

Jake helped him. The stone swung away and cool, stale air rushed out. Jake took a small flashlight and shined it inside. A raised concrete box held the casket. Around it, the floor of the crypt was empty.

"I swear! I've seen guys putting packages in here."

Jake shined the flashlight around on the floor. And then he saw places where the dust had been disturbed. Rectangular places. Like packages of drugs had been left there.

Chapter 4

"If dealers are using the crypt as a drug drop, and we can nail them, we may get our shooter," Jake said in a conference call with Craig Campbell and Cass.

"So, in addition to surveillance, we need to bring in the locals on this. Or DEA," Craig said, "whoever's working the drug scene."

"Cass is setting up a meeting with the locals. I'll get with DEA."

"Good."

But the meeting with the county police couldn't happen until Monday. He'd spend Sunday reviewing more of Danny's files and meeting with representatives of the Shooting Incident Review Board. That left the rest of Saturday for Jake to fill. He asked Cass if she wanted to grab a quick bite but she had other plans—plans that apparently included Travis, the boyfriend-detective.

That didn't bother him. No.

With Cass busy, he tried calling his kids, but they weren't home. So he chose another idea: Follow the lead provided by the matchbook found at the crime scene. Check out that bar in Glen Burnie.

. . .

A concrete block building with bars in the windows housed Nick's Bar and Grill. Flanked by an adult bookstore and an abandoned storefront, the bar looked rundown, like a tattered old sweater. On the wall outside, graffiti proclaimed, "Shorty: Rest in Peace" and "11th Street Clique."

The graffiti, Jake knew, could give a savvy investigator a lot of information. Who was Shorty? And who were the members of the 11th Street Clique? And did they have any connection to Danny's shooting? Any drug ties? Would Cass's friend know?

He had changed into jeans and a T-shirt. The chill in the air required a jacket, which was good. It was an easy way to cover the Glock pistol he wore in a holster on his belt. He'd put his backup weapon in an ankle holster on his unbitten leg.

The bar was smoky and loud, filled with half-drunk men, mostly Latinos, swearing and laughing. A few women were there. Most were hookers, Jake was sure. The music was blaring, the dancing hot, the drinks plentiful. It was a fun Saturday night at Nick's.

Jake limped up to the bar and sat down on one of the red vinyl-covered barstools. No way should he have come on his own—there were rules about backups and surveillance, all of which he was violating, plus his leg hurt like crazy. But tonight, he'd rather beg for forgiveness than ask permission.

The bartender was a big guy with tattoos on his arms and one gold front tooth. He didn't look like somebody to mess with. Jake ordered a soft drink and stealthily tipped the guy ten bucks. He put a few cherries in his glass from the bowl on the bar to make it look like a mixed drink. Then he sat and just listened to the conversations around him, picking up as much of the Spanish as he could and trying to look nonchalant. The gun under his jacket pressed comfortably into his hip.

A young woman approached him. He smelled her perfume even before she slid onto the bar stool next to him. She was young, with bronze skin, brown hair, and a very low-cut red blouse. She placed her hand on his thigh.

He didn't move, didn't even turn to acknowledge her. He could see the bartender out of the corner of his eye, staring at them, but the guy didn't try to shoo the girl away. That was a good thing—Jake figured the guy had made him as law enforcement. If he'd wanted to let everyone in the bar know Jake was a cop, this was his chance. Tip off the hooker.

"Hey, guy," she said.

Jake turned toward her.

"You want some company?"

"Not tonight, sweetheart," he said, "I'm not in the mood."

She stuck her lower lip out like a little kid, slipped off the barstool and walked away, swaying her hips and glancing once over her shoulder.

Jake watched her in the mirror behind the bar, glad she'd left so easily.

The bartender walked over and began wiping down the bar near Jake. He had dark, small eyes and a narrow face. A scar ran from his right ear down his neck. "You from here?" he asked.

Jake shook his head. "Came here for a job."

The bartender nodded. He moved past Jake, and then worked his way back. Jake, meanwhile, turned around with his back to the bar, and leaned back, resting his elbows on the wood.

"These guys in the corner," the bartender said softly when he was right behind Jake, "you see their names around. Painted on the walls. Pinky. Ugly. Rascal. The Eleventh Street Clique. I'm sick of them messin' up the place. Sellin' drugs in the alley. I complain to the cops, but they ain't doing nothing."

"They're never around when you need 'em, right?" Nonchalantly Jake looked at the table in the corner, memorizing the young men's faces while he worked at being casual. "You own this place?" he asked the bartender.

"Yep. Fifteen years. Name's Nick."

Jake nodded.

"Retired from the Navy and bought this bar to

41

put my kid through college. But the neighbor-hood's changed and I'm getting too old for this."

Jake motioned for another drink. "Did you hear a cop got shot?"

The bartender shook his head.

"FBI agent. Up on Ninth, near the cemetery."

The man nodded and refilled Jake's glass, and this time Jake slipped him a specially folded twenty dollar bill on which he'd written the phone number he used for informants. Nick slipped it into his pocket.

Jake finished his drink and when the woman started eyeing him again, he slid off the bar stool and left. Stepping out into the cool night, he took a deep breath, filling his lungs with fresh air. Then he walked toward his car, alert to sounds behind him.

His Bureau car was just ahead of him when he heard footsteps. So he walked past it, then crossed the street and pretended to put keys in a similar vehicle, a parked Ford. The car's alarm went off, its shrieks piercing the night. The men following him took off running.

Jake smiled.

So what had he learned? Nick's had become the hang-out for a small street gang. He knew small gangs did most of the crime and drug trafficking in the Baltimore area—the big organized-crime families had never gained a foothold. Would a small gang have taken on the FBI by shooting an agent? That seemed unlikely. Of course, they didn't know Danny was FBI. So why'd they shoot him? Because he was a potential witness to their drug transactions? As a gang initiation? Or just for fun?

Jake checked his watch. It was late. He should have just driven home. But the sodas he'd been drinking had him wired up. He decided to make a detour.

Shortly after her re-marriage, Tam's new husband had moved their family closer to Annapolis. The Maryland legislature met for only three months, but state Senator Chase Westfield said it was important that he live near the capital. Was he intentionally making it hard for Jake to connect with his kids? Chase wanted control and Jake was a threat to that.

Jake had countered Chase's move by breaking his lease on the townhouse near Baltimore and moving further south, nearer to Annapolis.

Chase was not pleased.

A classic Georgian colonial with pillars on the front porch and boxwoods lining the walk, Jake knew the house must have cost a bundle. But then, he'd heard Chase had made a fortune as a personal injury lawyer before he was elected to the Maryland Senate.

As Jake approached the darkened home, he slowed, then pulled over to the curb and turned off his engine. The night was black and cold. The streetlights created little islands of brightness on the tree-lined street.

He tried to imagine what it was like for his kids, living inside that big house. Tam had a maid. And a gardener. And occasionally, a butler. Jake had never ventured farther than the foyer, but from what the kids said, there was plenty of room. A game room. A family room with a bar. A breakfast nook. A finished playroom in the basement. Five bedrooms. An office for Chase.

When the kids come to the apartment, Jake thought, it must be a real step down for them. Did that bother him? Maybe. Still, he had to believe he had the kids' hearts, at least until the materialism of the teen years took over. Jake's heart had swelled when Justin had told him he'd refused to call Chase "Dad."

He started praying for his kids, sitting there in that car, praying for them hard. Sometimes it seemed like all he could do for them. Just pray.

Headlights appeared in Jake's rear view mirror. The car moved slowly down the street. On the top was a rack of lights—it was an Anne Arundel County police car. Jake reached down to turn on the ignition.

But as the cop car passed, it slowed down, and the officer must have seen him, because he shined a flashlight into Jake's car. Jake squinted in the bright light, and then got irritated. The cruiser pulled in front of him, and an officer got out.

It was Rudy Glass. Jake knew him from the gym. Better meet him head on.

He rolled down the window and turned off the ignition. "Rudy!"

"Jake! What are you doing here, man?"

Now that he'd been recognized, he stepped out of the car. "How's it going?" Jake kept his tone light, his jaw loose.

Rudy shook hands with him. He was an African-American, about six feet tall, and built like a rock. "It's fine, brother, fine." He stuck his hands in his pockets. "Say, that's too bad about that agent up in Glen Burnie."

"Danny Stewart. He's getting better."

"Good, good." The officer took a toothpick out of his pocket and began chewing on it. He looked around at the night sky, then back at Jake. "So what brings you out?"

"On my way home. Thought I'd drive by and see if my kids were back in town yet. They live with my ex." Jake motioned with his head toward Tam's house.

"The senator's wife? She's your ex?" Rudy exclaimed. "Man, how'd you get a woman that looks that good?"

"Getting her wasn't hard. Keeping her was the problem." Jake grinned.

Rudy laughed. "We've been told to drive by here now and then. The senator's had some threats. That's why I stopped when I saw you sitting here. Except I didn't know it was you."

"I hadn't heard about any threats," Jake said.

"That's politics these days."

Rudy left. As Jake started his car he wondered, were his kids in danger?

Chapter 5

On Monday, Cass and Jake drove together to Detective Travis Lowery's office in the Anne Arundel County police station. Travis was the guy she'd been dating.

The building was a typical modern police station, blocky and secured with bullet-proof glass. The desk sergeant buzzed them in when Travis arrived to escort them.

As Cass introduced him to Travis, Jake automatically sized him up. Blond. Blue-eyed. Athletic build. An inch or so shorter than Jake. Bearing an uncanny resemblance to Mike, Cassie's deceased husband. Did Cass realize that?

A rush of emotions blindsided Jake. He shook hands with Travis, then followed him down a hallway.

Travis led them to an interview room and sat down at the table with Cass on one side and Jake on the other. Cassie had on a black pinstriped pantsuit, and a white blouse. She looked good. She always looked good. And Jake could tell that Travis thought so too.

"What we have in the Eleventh Street Clique," Travis began, "is a group of Latinos—a dozen, maybe fourteen, men and women between the ages of fourteen and twenty-four. So far, we've had the usual arrests: marijuana possession, coke, a couple of break-ins, and several assaults. The assaults have been fights with a rival gang connected with MS-13. Got ugly once, but for the most part it's been knives, baseball bats, that sort of thing."

Jake tried to concentrate. "So how are you targeting them?"

"I've been working with the schools, counselors from the community, and the DA, of course. We're trying to decide on a particular methodology. There've been a lot of drug overdoses coming into emergency rooms lately, so I think we're going that direction, working with the medical community, and trying to educate the public."

"Are you working with DEA? ATF?"

"Not yet." Travis leaned back. "A lot of them are just kids, and frankly, they're mostly into petty crimes."

"An assault on a federal officer isn't petty."

"And that's the question isn't it? Did they have anything to do with assaulting your officer? Was the shooting an aberration? A chance meeting? Or are these street gangs becoming more violent?" He stroked his chin. "He didn't have on a raid jacket, right?"

"Correct."

"So whoever shot him may not have known what they were doing," Cass added.

"Here," Travis handed them folders. "This is

some information I've put together for you. Mugs of all the gang members, arrests we've made, graffiti, tattoos, and a chart that puts it all together."

Jake flipped his folder open and immediately spotted some of the men he'd seen at the bar. "Yeah, I saw some of these guys."

Cass stared at him. "When?"

He glanced at her but didn't respond.

"Now," Travis said, "it's up to you. How would you like to proceed?"

This guy was thorough. On paper, anyway. Jake shifted in his chair. "Our primary interest is in finding out who shot Danny. So the question is, what's the best way to do that? We want to wrap this up quickly."

Travis took a deep breath. "We've been working on this gang for two years. I'd hate for that to be blown away by hasty action."

Jake raised his eyebrows. "Two years?" His inference was clear.

Travis's face remained impassive. "You want to claim jurisdiction?"

"No, of course not. Not unless we link the shooting to them." Jake continued leafing through the folder. He stopped at the picture of a young Latina. "Who's this?"

"That's Maria," Travis said. "She got stopped for speeding. When she rustled through the glove box looking for the registration a couple of joints and some coke fell out. She says it was her boyfriend's, and the cops believe her, but still, they've got her. So she's helping out to avoid prosecution."

"She's Mexican?"

"Yes. She has no family. She's basically been on her own since she was sixteen."

"Tell me something unusual."

"She's beautiful and very musically gifted."

"So why's she hanging out with these losers?"

"A guy, what else?" Travis tapped on her picture. "She's scared, now. She doesn't want trouble. If her boyfriend finds out she's helping us, he'll hurt her. So we're taking it slowly. Basically, we're using her to identify the gang members."

"So she might tell us if anyone is bragging about shooting a cop."

Travis nodded.

"I'd like to meet her," Cass suggested.

"I think it would be good for her to talk to a woman. We can work together." He smiled at her.

Jake could not miss the look in the detective's eyes. He shifted his weight and tried to relax his jaw. "You said the gang was into coke and heroin. What about meth?"

"I haven't seen it. But they may be changing what they're selling." Travis stretched back.

Jake closed the folder. "Okay, let's try working with Maria."

"Cass, I can introduce you to her tomorrow

morning," Travis said. "We were going to meet anyway."

"Wonderful. Text me the time and place."

"What was that all about?" Cass asked Jake a few minutes later as they left the building.

"What? Nothing!"

"You were squaring off with him."

"Me? No!" Jake sighed. "He's very nice, Cass. Smart. Deliberate. No doubt a good cop. I'm glad you like him. I just want to find Danny's shooter." Dropping into the driver's seat, he slammed his door for emphasis.

The next day, Cass pulled her Bureau car onto busy Maryland Route 2, and headed south, toward Annapolis and a restaurant where she was meeting Travis and Maria for breakfast. He'd chosen a spot far away from Glen Burnie so there'd be no chance of being recognized. He'd picked up Maria a few miles from her house.

The day had dawned clear and bright, and a high of 65 was expected. It was November, the month of Thanksgiving, but for Cass, it was the month of mourning. Three years ago, her FBI agent-husband Mike had died when his car was run off a rain-slick road. Devastated, Cass had left her job. She'd nearly succumbed to the deceptive advances of a man who turned out to be Mike's killer. Shame still flooded her when she thought about it. If it hadn't been for Jake . . .

After that, she'd sworn off dating for a long time. Then she'd met Travis through a mutual acquaintance. He crewed for her through two racing seasons. Gradually, they'd begun to see each other socially.

Her Aunt Trudy had expressed surprise when Cass had told her about Travis. "Why aren't you dating Jake?" her aunt asked with uncharacteristic directness.

"Being with Jake is like riding a roller coaster blindfolded and handcuffed," she'd replied, laughing. "My stomach couldn't take it."

Cass left Route 2 and drove into the parking lot of Fair Winds, a restaurant at a marina on the Magothy River. Inside the dark, quiet restaurant she spotted Travis and walked over to his table. A young woman sat on his left.

Travis rose. "Cassie, this is Maria. Maria, my friend Cass."

Maria had long, chestnut brown hair, huge brown eyes, and a trim nose. Her even features were highlighted by perfect makeup. Cass noted the sable eyeliner, the subtle blush, her outlined lips. The girl was beautiful, as Travis had claimed.

Maria held out her hand timidly. Cass shook it, reflexively looking for gang tattoos. There were none. No tattoos. No piercings. No colors. No outward signs of the life. She sat down, intrigued.

"Well, what are we eating?" Travis said,

opening up a menu. He didn't look like a detective, dressed in jeans and a chambray shirt, his blond hair hanging over his collar.

A waitress arrived and they ordered, then Cass opened the conversation with a question to which she already knew the answer. "Where are you from?"

"Guadalajara, Mexico," Maria responded.

"How old were you when you came here?"

"Eleven. My mother worked cleaning houses. We live in an apartment with my uncle." Maria looked down quickly. "Then my mother, she was murdered."

Cass sat very still. She saw Maria glance at Travis.

"Officially, they say it was a suicide," he said.

"I don't believe it. I don't believe my mother would leave me." Maria's voice was passionate.

"She loved you," Cass said softly.

"Yes. She loved me."

Travis cleared his throat. "It was two years ago. The medical examiner said she shot herself."

"That's unusual," Cass remarked. "Women don't usually shoot themselves." She changed the subject, initiating small talk about school and jobs. Then the food came, and Cass let the conversation slide for a few moments. "My mother died also, when I was three," she said, hoping for a connection.

Maria leaned forward. "Your mother?"

"Yes, in a traffic accident on the Washington Beltway. I only remember her a little." Cass saw the girl stop chewing. "It's hard, growing up without a mother."

Maria swallowed. She stared down at her drink.

"There is no one to bring your papers home to, no one to talk to, no one," Cass switched to Spanish, "to *enseñarle arreglar el pelo.*" Teach you to fix your hair.

Maria smiled. "You speak Spanish?"

"A little."

Cass fingered her coffee cup. "You still live with your uncle?"

"No, a cousin."

"Maria," Travis said, "Cass had a friend who was shot a few days ago."

The girl bit her lower lip.

"On a street in Glen Burnie," said Cass. "He was this little baby's grandfather." Cass held out a picture of Danny's grandchild.

"He is dead?"

"No, still alive. But badly hurt."

Maria's brown eyes met Cassie's, then quickly flickered away.

"I'd like to find out who shot him."

Maria's cell phone rang. The girl jumped and answered it, speaking quickly in Spanish. Cass picked up most of it. "Yes. Yes. I'll be there soon, Renaldo. I had to run an errand. Yes, I promise. I'm sorry, Renaldo, I had to do it. Okay. Okay."

Maria clicked off the phone and said to Travis, "I have to go."

He signaled the waiter for the check, and paid the bill.

The three walked out into the bright sunshine. Cass slipped Maria a business card. "Call me, okay, Maria? If you hear anything about my friend. Or," she added impulsively, "if you just want to talk."

Quickly, Maria handed back the card. "I can't take this. If he finds it . . ."

"Okay, look," Cass said, pulling her cell phone off her belt. "What's your cell phone number? I'll call you, and then you'll have my number in your log."

"No! No! He will see it. He checks it!" Alarm lit Maria's eyes.

Cass exchanged glances with Travis. Was Renaldo that possessive? "Maria, I'd like to talk with you some more. How about we meet at the mall? If anyone wants to know, I'm a social worker. How about that?"

Maria hesitated, then agreed.

Cass clarified the time and place. Travis and Maria turned to leave. Suddenly the girl said to Cass. "The grandfather . . . he will live?"

"Yes."

"I think it was not our boys. But I find out."

Travis shot Cass a glance over his shoulder.

Chapter 6

"Hey, Partner." Cassie's voice cut through Jake's thoughts. He raised his head. She was standing next to his desk, dressed in her khakis and a burgundy shirt, her leather jacket slung over her arm.

Cass sat down and began telling him about her breakfast with Maria that morning. "She's an enigma," she said, "beautiful, talented, and stuck in a relationship with an abusive boyfriend. I think I want to work with her."

Jake played with his pen. "Did you get any hard information?"

"No."

"Then what's your purpose?"

"It was our first meeting! But I think she can help us."

"We don't have time for a rescue mission."

"I know!"

"I'm just saying, we can't get involved."

Cass's mouth twisted into a smile. She tapped her finger on his desk. "Wait—didn't I hear you calling that kid, Manny, the other day?"

"That's different. I had to warn him to stay away from that cemetery." Jake stretched back and studied her face. "You like this guy, Travis?"

"He's a very nice guy."

"You've known him for how long?"

Cass shrugged. "Two sailing seasons. So fifteen months, maybe."

"And he treats you right."

She nodded.

"Because he knows you have a friend who will beat the stuffing out of him if he doesn't."

Cass rolled her eyes. "Yes, Jake. You're my own personal brute squad."

"That's right." He didn't smile. "So when do you see this Maria again?"

"At the mall tomorrow afternoon at four. Can you back me up?"

"Absolutely."

"So how were the kids last night?" She took a piece of gum from the pack that Jake was offering her and stuck it in her mouth.

Jake threw the pack of gum back onto his desk. He took a long, deep breath, and relayed what the kids had told him.

Cass stopped chewing as he got into the story. Her eyes were focused straight on him. "So you're telling me," she said, "Chase took them to some sitter they'd never seen before? They spent the weekend with strangers?"

"That's right." The anger felt like scissors in his gut. "He told Tam any weekend I couldn't take them, she'd have to find a sitter for them. If she didn't, he would." He felt sick. "This time it was some friend, or relative, of his assistant, Ramon."

"Those poor kids!"

"Tell me about it. They'd never seen these people before. Half of them spoke only Spanish. Justin and Caitlin spent the whole weekend huddled together watching TV trying to avoid them."

"Have you talked to Tam?"

"I went over there this morning, after they'd gone to school."

"You confronted her?"

Jake nodded.

"How'd that go?"

He looked away. "I got too loud."

Cass stopped chewing. "Oh, Jake."

"I couldn't help it!" he exploded. "I couldn't believe she'd let him do that!" Jake shook his head. "Don't ever get divorced."

"No problem. I'm never getting married again."

"Does Travis know that?"

Her eyes flickered. "So what are you going to do?"

He tightened his hand into a fist and relaxed it, then did it again, a habit he'd developed following the brain injury he'd sustained in the assault a few years back. "I talked to my lawyer. He said I have no recourse unless and until a kid is hurt or abused. I can't dictate who Tam gets to babysit the kids when they're in her custody."

"That's stupid," Cass replied.

"You're telling me!"

At 3:45 the next day, Jake, dressed in jeans, a black golf shirt, and a Ravens jacket strolled into the Heritage Mall food court, a newspaper under his arm. He ordered orange chicken and lo mein from the Chinese booth, then found a table and sat down. He spread the sports page out in front of him, uncapped his water, and pretended to be busy reading.

Cass came in at 3:55, Maria shortly after that. Together, they walked to Chick-fil-A, and within a few minutes, sat down at a table near where Jake was sitting. Cass had changed into jeans and a navy sweater. She looked like any other young suburban woman, but Jake knew she'd have a gun on her hip, under her clothes.

Maria was, as Cass had said, beautiful. Jake watched her as she spoke, her hands gesturing, her eyes bright. Her cheekbones were perfect, her eyebrows plucked to arching lines, her lips were full. She would purse them like a little girl, then smile, then frown, her emotions playing freely on her face. Any man, Jake thought, would find her attractive. Any man.

Cass had told him they'd only have about thirty minutes to talk. At 4:20, Jake took a big drink of water, and noticed a Latino standing off in the shadows, behind Maria, in a hallway that leads to the bathrooms. What Jake noticed most about him was his clothing. He had a blue bandanna around his head, and was wearing a blue-and-white Dallas Cowboys jacket. Blue and white: gang colors.

Yawning, Jake cleaned up his tray, folded his newspaper and put it under his arm, then rose and dumped his trash. Careful not to make eye contact, he walked straight past the Latino and into the restroom in the hallway behind him. When Jake emerged a few minutes later the young man was still there. He was drinking a soda, and as he lifted it to his mouth, Jake saw tattoos on his knuckles. He couldn't quite read them. Another gang sign.

Jake walked to a nearby kiosk, the one with the biggest line. He stood there, looking bored. He pulled his cell phone off his belt, and pretended to key in some numbers, as if he was making a call, while he took a picture of the man in the jacket. Then he put the phone to his ear, left a fake voice mail message, clicked off the phone and put it back on his belt. When he got to the counter, he ordered a tall Kenya, black. And as he walked away, his coffee in his hand, he noticed the man disappearing into the main part of the mall. Cass and Maria finished their conversation. He dumped his newspaper in the trash, and left the food court.

"You were being watched," Jake told her later.

"What?" Cass asked. "What are you talking about?"

"Did you see the guy in the Cowboys jacket? Near the restrooms?"

Cass shook her head.

"He must have been behind the pillar from where you were." Jake pulled out his cell phone and showed her the picture. "I'll text it to you."

Cass frowned. "Why a Cowboys jacket?"

"Blue and white. Gang colors."

"Mara Salvatrucha?"

"Could be or the Mexican gang, either one. They both use blue and white." Jake narrowed his eyes. "I checked: He's not in Travis's folder."

"Why would he be watching us?"

"Maybe they're worried about Maria. Who are you supposed to be?"

"A social worker."

Jake nodded. "Just be aware, okay? They may have ID'd you as a threat."

On Thursday, Jake went to see Danny. He was well enough to be interviewed, doctors said.

Lavonda stood and kissed Jake on the cheek when he entered the room. Danny was sitting up in a chair with a food tray in front of him.

"Nice gown," Jake said, grinning.

Danny held up his hand and Jake grasped it. "Better than a shroud. I understand you kept me alive."

"I didn't think that ambulance would ever get there. You look good!"

"Another day or two and I'll be out of here."

"You feel like talking?" Jake said.

"Sure."

Lavonda moved to the door and said, "I'll leave you two alone."

Danny didn't have a lot to report. "I got out to check a tire," he said. "Shot literally came out of the dark. I drew and fired, but I don't think I hit anything."

Jake asked him more questions, about any threats he'd received and cases he'd worked. Strange phone calls. Anything that might be a lead.

"I've been wrapping things up for a year now. Honestly, this came out of the blue," Danny reported. "I've thought and thought about the cases I've had, and who might be wanting to take me out. Seriously, I'm coming up dry."

Half an hour later, sensing Danny's fatigue, Jake rose to leave.

Danny stopped him. "You watch your back, son."

Jake frowned. "What do you mean?"

"A couple of years ago, you started looking into Mike McKenna's death. Next thing we know, you're lying in a park with your head bashed in. Sometimes a thin thread leads to a knot of trouble. So watch your back. Don't let this turn on you."

Chapter 7

Jake puzzled over Danny's statements while he followed up on what thin leads they had. A canvass of the neighborhood had turned up no witnesses to Danny's shooting. Nick the bartender had heard nothing the last time Jake checked with him. And DEA was so tied up with a newly discovered meth ring that they were no help at all.

Restless, Jake came up with a plan to try to stir up what he called the "mud at the bottom." He pitched Moose on it, then showed him the maps he had asked an analyst to create of the Glen Burnie and Brooklyn areas south of Baltimore. Green dots marked arrests of gang members. Red dots showed reports of shots fired. Yellow dots showed drug deals.

"Someone spent a lot of time on these," Moose said to Jake.

"We have to know where to go fishing." Jake stood up. "Let's go."

"Where's Cass?"

"She's got an appointment. She doesn't need to be in on this."

The two agents, dressed in jeans and sweatshirts, drove to the street where Danny had been shot and then turned onto Route 2 and headed north to a commercial area. A collection of rundown buildings and small businesses lined the street: a carry-out Chinese food restaurant, a tattoo parlor, a couple of used-furniture shops, a fortune teller, a vacuum cleaner store, and a liquor store. The area was racially mixed. Jake noted an elderly black woman, several Hispanics, and a beautiful Asian girl walking down the sidewalk. A young man with his name on his shirt leaving a sandwich shop nearly ran into her.

Graffiti marred everything. The 11th Street Clique, Los Bravos . . . each gang left its mark in curly, spray-painted messages and impressive murals. Suddenly, Moose unbuckled his seat belt and exclaimed, "Here . . . here . . . stop!" As Jake slammed on the brakes, he bolted from the car.

Jake saw Moose follow a young Latino who ducked into a narrow alley between two brick buildings. He had his hand to his mouth, as if he were drawing on a cigarette, but tobacco was not what he was puffing. The guy looked up, saw Moose, and immediately dropped the joint.

Jake quickly parked the car. By the time he got to the alley, Moose had the guy up against the wall. A still-smoking joint lay on the ground. "Doesn't smell like a Marlboro," Jake said. "What do you think, partner?" Carefully stepping on the lit edge to extinguish it, he pulled a small sandwich bag out of his pocket, took a file card, and scooped the joint into the bag. "What's your name, buddy?" he asked the smoker.

The guy resisted until Moose pressed him a little. "Juan," he said, gasping.

Moose began patting him down. He pulled a packet from Juan's front right pocket. "Look at this!" he said. "What do you figure this is, partner?"

"A ticket to downtown, I'd say," Jake responded, looking at what he guessed was two grams of cocaine.

Then Moose pulled out a wad of bills from another pocket. "Intent to distribute?" he mused. "Okay, Juan," Moose said. "You and me got a date." He flipped cuffs on the young man. "We're going for a ride."

"Aw, man, please, c'mon . . ."

Jake opened the back door of the Bucar and Moose put him in. Jake got in the driver's seat, but before he did, he caught Moose's eye and wordlessly initiated the plan.

"You know what, partner?" Jake said, settling into his seat. "I don't feel like going all the way back downtown."

"Don't give me that!" Moose responded angrily. "Man, you did this to me last week."

"He's a two-bit player. I don't feel like filling out all that paperwork for a man that's hardly done anything." He glanced at the man in the back seat. "What do you say, Pancho?"

"Juan. His name is Juan," Moose said. "And we are going downtown!"

"What do you say, Juan? You want to go downtown or should we let you go?"

"Man, I'm telling you, it ain't nothing. It's a few joints and a little coke, y'know?" Juan's face was full of hope.

"Partner, I'm tellin' you, you do this to me again and . . ." Moose began.

"All right, all right!" Jake started the engine.

"Wait!" Juan yelled from the back seat. "Look, you'll make me lose my job, man. I didn't do nothing, man, nothing! It was just a little something over lunch hour, you know?"

Jake turned the engine off. He looked over at Moose. "Listen to him. He's a working man. You want to ruin his life?" Turning to Juan, he said, "My friend is grouchy, today. You got anything to make him happy?"

The suspect squirmed. "Just take the money, man!"

Jake grimaced. "I'm not talking money! I'm talking help, like information, you know?"

Juan slouched back in the seat. "I don't know, man."

Jake started the engine. "Fine. Mr. Grumpy gets his way."

"No, wait! Wait!" Juan sat up. "What do you want to know?"

Twenty minutes later, Jake and Moose had the name of the dealer Juan had bought from, the places where the 11th Street boys hung out, the names of five members of a rival gang, Los Bravos, and Juan's cell phone number along with a promise that he would try to help them find who shot Danny.

"Two weeks," Moose said, holding up the baggie full of joints and coke. "I'm keeping these for two weeks. We'll see how much you help us. No calls from you, you're gonna get burned. I'm gonna burn you. You got that?"

He did.

"Let's move away from here," Moose said to Jake.

Jake drove down two blocks, then cut over to a quiet area behind a store. Moose opened the door and uncuffed Juan, and like an animal sprung from a trap, Juan scooted off.

Jubilant, Moose got back in the car. "Now, that was fun!"

Jake's ex-wife, Tam, called an hour later and asked him to meet her at a McDonald's halfway between Baltimore and Annapolis. What did she want, he wondered as he drove to the restaurant. More child support? Less time for him with the kids? He braced himself for a conflict.

"What's up?" Jake asked, fighting to sound casual as Tam slid into the booth seat across from him. He had a half-empty cup of coffee in front of him. She was late. Very late. "What can I get you?" he asked. "Soda? Coffee? A hamburger?"

Tam waved him off. "Nothing." She had deep

circles under her eyes, Jake noticed, and her hair was slightly disheveled, like she'd been rushing. He still wasn't used to her as a blonde. Her natural hair color was a reddish brown. She'd bleached it right after she'd met Chase Westfield.

Tam glanced around. "Look," his ex-wife said, leaning toward him. "I need your help. We need to do something about Justin."

He tilted his head. "Justin? What's wrong?"

"He got into a fight at school."

"What? When?"

"Two days ago."

"Over what?" Why hadn't Tam mentioned this to him sooner? Tension arrowed up his spine.

"That was never clear to me. The point is, he bloodied some kid's nose and I had to go in and speak to the vice principal. He was almost suspended, Jake."

"For the first offense? That's rough." Jake took another sip of his coffee. It was getting cold. "Look, all kids, boys anyway, get into a fight now and then. I don't see what the big deal is."

"No, of course, of course you wouldn't." Tam's eyes flashed. "You don't have to live with it. You get to be the weekend dad."

Get to be? A blaze of anger streaked through him. He started flexing his hand, over and over. "Look, Tam: That happens again, you call me. I'll go talk to the principal." Jake had to work to keep his voice calm.

"It's not just that. He and Chase clash. Justin talks back to him and doesn't do what Chase says."

"Give me an example."

"The other day, Chase told him to go to his room. He didn't, he just hung around, sneaking around the kitchen and the family room. We were trying to talk. I could hear him. The floor was creaking, but I didn't want to say anything."

"You were afraid Chase would get mad at him."

She didn't confirm that. "Then, all of a sudden, the car alarm went off on the BMW in the garage! Justin had taken my keys and set off the alarm! Chase was so angry, and I don't blame him. He had told Justin to go to his room!"

Jake took a deep breath. He was trying to read Tam's eyes, but she wasn't meeting his gaze. "Was Chase angry with you?"

Tam's eyes flashed. "That's none of your . . ."

Jake held up his hand. "I know, I know. It's none of my business. I was just wondering." He was already playing out a scenario in his head. Chase was angry, and Justin didn't want to leave his mother alone with him. Was that it? Had Justin used the car alarm to deflect Chase's attention?

Tam nervously twisted her hands. The diamond on her ring finger had to be at least two carats, Jake thought. Much bigger than the one he'd bought her. The ring turned easily. He wondered how much weight she'd lost.

"Jake, you have to talk to him," she said. "It's causing problems, big problems." She took a deep breath. "Chase is talking about boarding school."

"Boarding school!" Jake exploded. Two old men on the other side of the room looked over at him. "No, Tam, no. Listen, if you can't handle the kids . . ."

"I can handle them! I can!" She closed her eyes momentarily. "It's just . . . Justin is so stubborn!"

"And Caitlin?"

Tam shrugged. "She's okay. It doesn't help," she said, "it doesn't help that all they talk about is you."

He raised his eyebrows.

Tam twisted the tissue in her hand. "Jake, would you talk to him, please? Would you tell him he needs to mind Chase? Respect him as a father?"

"He's not his father!" Jake replied, his heart pounding. Then he saw tears spring to her eyes. His jaw softened. "I'll talk to him."

"Thank you." And with a quick nod, Tam rose to her feet. As she did, her scarf caught on the table and pulled away from her neck. And there were bruises on her neck, marks left by fingers. She froze, her eyes met Jake's, and she blushed deeply. Before he could say anything, she flipped the scarf around her neck once again and left, leaving only the barest trace of her expensive perfume lingering in the air.

Chapter 8

It was noise, that's all. The six o'clock news was just noise to fill his quiet apartment while he fixed some dinner for himself and tried to quell the fury raging inside. Chase was abusing Tam. He'd seen proof.

A steak sizzled in the grill pan. Jake threw part of a bagged salad in a bowl and chopped up some carrots, peppers, and celery and put them on top.

He wanted to talk to Cass. No, he needed to talk to Cass. He'd left a message on her office phone and called her cell but had gotten no answer. He had even called Travis to see if he'd heard from her. He hadn't but they were supposed to meet for dinner, Travis said, at 6:30. He'd be sure to have Cass call Jake back.

Travis's answer to his question had not improved Jake's mood.

The broadcasters droned on in the background. A murder. An attempted carjacking. A kid who was protesting having to say the Pledge of Allegiance in school. A fire. Then the anchor changed her tone. "Today in Annapolis, Senator Chase Westfield held a news conference . . ."

Jake turned to look at the TV.

". . . to announce a new domestic violence initiative . . ."

Jake left the kitchen and walked over to the television.

". . . designed to help educate the public about the signs and symptoms of what is often called a hidden plague." They cut away to a picture of the senator at a lectern. "Our goal," the senator intoned, "is to protect every woman, every child, from this scourge."

"You hypocrite," Jake muttered.

"Someone you know could be the victim of abuse," he said, "an innocent soul caught in the deadly trap of domestic violence."

Jake snapped off the television. Then he turned off the stove, left the steak in the pan, laced up his running shoes, and went out to pound his frustration into the pavement.

The next day, Jake was working at his desk when Cassie dropped into the seat next to it. "I'm sorry I didn't get to call you back last night."

"Out late?" Jake said, more sharply than he intended.

Her eyes searched his. "So what did you want?"

Jake sat back in his chair. His neck felt tight. "Tell me what you got first."

"That guy in the Cowboys jacket? He's MS-13, Los Bravos. His name is Tomas Bandillo. He asked Maria out."

"That's going to go over big with her boy-friend." He shifted his jaw. "Still, if she gets

involved with them it could widen our information pool."

Cass raised her eyebrows. "That's all she is—a
source?"

Jake grimaced. "I'm sorry. I'm edgy."

"So I see. What did you need last night, Jake?
Why did you call me?"

He looked around. No one was nearby. Then he
told her about Tam.

"You think he's abusing her?"

"Yes," Jake replied. His stomach felt like he'd
eaten fishhooks for breakfast.

"So what are you going to do?" she said.

"What can I do? She's an adult!" Jake threw a
pen down on his desk. "If he touches my kids . . ."

"You'll take them to court," Cass suggested.
"Go for custody again."

"That's right. Absolutely." Jake's eyes drifted
as he became lost in thought.

"What are you thinking about, Jake? Right
now."

He hesitated, then turned back to Cass. "How
I can help her," he admitted.

Cass leaned forward. "Don't do it, Jake. Don't
go there."

"Why? Why shouldn't I try to help her?"

"Because you can't. Chase already hates you.
The more you get involved, the more he's going
to feel threatened, and the more controlling
he'll become. It's not your job to rescue her."

"Sometimes," he said, his stomach knotted, "I wonder whether anything I did set her up." Eight years of marriage. Arguments. Tensions. Tears. His anger. Hers. How do you sort that stuff out?

"Set her up for what? Being abused by Chase?"

He nodded imperceptibly.

"Did you ever hit Tam?"

"No."

"Push her?"

"Never."

"Verbally abuse her?"

"I hope not." Jake sighed.

"But you have a temper."

He nodded.

Cass bit her lip, her eyes lost in thought. Then she looked at him. "I don't see it, Jake. I don't recall ever hearing you speak dismissively or abusively to Tam when the two of you and Mike and I went out together. If I had, I don't think I could be friends with you."

"I'm glad we're friends."

"It's more than that," she said.

His heart thumped.

"You saved me literally and figuratively. I was drowning and you held me up. I was dying and you gave me life. I will never, ever forget that, Jake. Never." She touched his hand briefly. "I should have called you back, even though it was late. I'm sorry I didn't."

• • •

All day, his conversation with Cass played over and over in his head. He'd never forget that stormy night on the Chesapeake Bay when he had rescued her from Richard Maxwell. Both of them had nearly drowned in those cold waters. Thoughts of it still made him shiver.

Thankfully, Moose showed up with just the distraction Jake needed.

Juan, the guy Moose and Jake busted in the alley, had provided the first real break in Danny's case. He heard a man named Cesar Cisneros talking in a bar about a shooting, possibly Danny's. Moose discovered Cisneros worked as a delivery man for Wright Fresh Seafood.

The next morning, Jake met Moose at the office at six. Together, they drove to Wright Fresh Seafood's distribution center, located in an industrial park in Jessup, south of Baltimore.

Moose, apparently, had done his homework on the seafood industry. "Used to be these distributors haggled with captains at the dock," he told Jake. "Now, you got buyers tracking fishing boats using GPS so they can see when they're coming in. They negotiate deals over the Internet, for cryin' out loud. For fish!"

Moose parked where they could see the rear of the company's building, and watched as small, white, refrigerated trucks pulled up to the dock and loaders filled them with cartons.

75

After half an hour, Moose sat straight up. "That's it," he said. "That's the last truck."

"What are we doing?" Jake asked.

Moose drove over to the front of the building and parked the car. "I'm going to see if I can find out more about Cisneros. You watch, okay? Give me ten minutes."

"Got it," Jake said, and he slumped down in the seat. Bored, he started to think about what he was going to do with the kids this weekend. Something fun. Something unusual. Something that would help ease the stress of the talk Jake would have to have with Justin.

A few minutes later he texted Cass. *What's up for this weekend? Can we take kids out on your boat?*

A few minutes later, she texted back. *Are you kidding?*

No, he responded. He hated boats, but his son was inexplicably drawn to the water.

Will Sunday work? Cass asked.

Sure.

Justin would be so happy. He'd been bugging Jake about going out on the boat all fall. Pretty soon, it would be too cold. Jake settled back in his seat and began planning it out while he waited for Moose.

A young woman staffed the front counter of the seafood company. Moose glanced around as he entered. The floor was covered with blue indoor-outdoor carpeting and a stuffed swordfish hung on the wall next to a stopped clock. Behind the counter was a pin-up calendar and a huge whiteboard with the day's fish prices written in black marker.

"Can I help you?" the young woman asked. She was probably in her early twenties, brown hair, blue eyes, and perky for so early in the morning.

"Yeah, I'm looking for a guy, Cesar Cisneros."

She frowned. "A driver, right?"

"Yep."

She checked her computer screen. "Oh, he's picked up already. He's on his route. Won't be back 'til two or later."

Moose cursed softly.

"Is there anything I can help you with?"

He decided to flirt with her. Moose leaned forward over the counter. "Ordinarily, I'd say yes."

She blushed.

"I need to deliver something to him." Moose pulled an envelope out of his breast pocket. "It's pretty urgent, you know what I mean?" He winked and tapped the envelope on the counter.

The girl cocked her head.

"Any way, I could, like, figure out which way he went? Maybe I could catch up to him."

"Sure." She walked over to a map of Baltimore

hanging on the wall. Moose followed her. All of the routes were highlighted on the map in different colors. "He's on Route Eight, down here." She traced a pencil down a blue line. Moose noted that the route ran right through 11th Street's turf. "First stop is the Sea King restaurant on Route Two. The rest are marked, see?"

"Okay, got it!" he said, jotting down the delivery man's stops on the envelope.

A radio squawked in the background. "You want me to call him?" she suggested. "Tell him to wait for you?"

"Naw," Moose said. "Let's let it be a surprise, okay, sweetheart?"

"We're in business," Moose said as he got back into the car.

"Terrific," Jake said. Headed south, the sun cast a blinding glare off the other vehicles on the congested road. Jake felt a headache coming on like a freight train, another remnant from his head injury three years ago. At least the seizures were gone. He felt grateful for that. And he had regained use of his hand. "You sure this guy is the one?" he asked Moose.

"Name's right." Moose motioned down the back alley of a parking lot. "Look, look, there's the truck! And that's got to be him." A mid-thirties Hispanic man, short, swarthy, and lean was rolling a stack of boxes on a dolly into the back of a grocery store.

Jake sat up straight. "There could be more in those cartons than cod." He looked over at Moose. "We need to confirm his identity."

Moose eased the car halfway down the block. "Get out here."

"What are you doing?"

"Just go do something for a few minutes."

Jake rolled his eyes and complied. "I'll get coffee." He pointed to a coffee shop down the street."

"Good. Hazelnut, extra cream and sugar."

"You should be fat."

Ten minutes later, Moose pulled up out front. Jake emerged with two cups in his hands. "What'd you do?" he asked, climbing in and handing Moose his coffee.

"Checked the bill of lading. The market had to sign off on that delivery. Cisneros had to sign, too. It was easy." Moose smiled. "I identified myself to the manager as quality control for the fish company."

"Okay, so now we check wants and warrants for Cisneros. But we've still got to connect him with Danny."

"Okay, okay. Cool your jets. We're getting there! Let's go one more round with this guy." He pulled into traffic half a block behind the fish truck and followed him to his next delivery.

Two restaurants later, Moose looked at his notes. "This is it, his last stop. He should head back home now."

But he didn't. In fact, he went the opposite direction. Jake sat up straight. "Where's he headed?"

"Man, I don't know."

Jake tapped the dash. "Go, go!"

"I lost him!"

"No! Take a right!"

Moose swung the car on to Patapsco Drive just in time to see Cisneros drive his truck up to the delivery dock of the Lucky Leaf Casino.

Chapter 9

What was the fish man, Cesar Cisneros, doing making a stop at the casino when it wasn't part of his route? Moose would pursue that question, but Jake was still puzzling it out as he drove the kids to the marina on Sunday.

"Cassie!" Justin yelled. He ran to Cass, who had *Time Out*'s engine warming up in the slip.

"Justin, my man!" she said, and held up her hand for a high five.

"Oh my gosh, where's Caitlin?" Jake said, faking alarm as he walked down the dock with the little girl on his shoulders. He spun around as if he were looking for her behind him. "Where'd Caitlin go?" he asked, spinning again.

His daughter giggled. "I'm here, Daddy! I'm up here!" she exclaimed.

He kept it up. "Caitlin? Caitlin? Where's Caitlin?" he said, spinning round and around.

"Daddy! Daddy!" Caitlin put her hands on the side of his head and tried to make him look up. "I'm up here, Daddy!"

Finally Jake reached up, grabbed Caitlin by the waist, and flipped her, so she was in front of him, face to face, but upside down. "There you are! I thought you'd gotten lost!"

"Da-addy!" she responded.

He set her on the dock and steadied her with his hands as she found her balance. He looked over to Cass, who was smiling.

"Cassie!" Caitlin cried.

Cass reached over and plucked Caitlin from the dock. "How's my little Cat?" she exclaimed, hugging her.

"Cass and Cat. You get it, Dad?" Justin asked. "The girls are Cs and the boys are Js."

"I'd rather be a J any day," his dad said, grinning. Cass shot him a look over Caitlin's shoulder. He tousled Justin's hair. "Who's ready to go out on Cassie's boat?"

"We are!" the kids said.

"What do you need?"

"Life jackets!" they both responded.

While maneuvering out through the channel, into the Chesapeake Bay, Cass pointed out ospreys to the kids, and ducks, and cormorants. She wore shorts and a gray University of Maryland sweatshirt. Jake thought she looked especially happy.

"Who wants to help put up sails?" Cass asked. Justin did and Jake helped him with the mainsail and then the jib. Then they headed north.

"Look, Dad!" Justin said, pointing to a huge container ship.

"Cool." Jake said. Caitlin huddled next to him in the cockpit.

"In a little while," Cass said, "we'll go under the Bay Bridge."

"Is that the one we take to get to Aunt Trudy's?" Justin asked.

"That's the one."

Justin wanted to do it all. He steered the boat, he studied the GPS and the chartbook Cass used to navigate, and he shut down the engine when it was time to use just the sails. Jake just shook his head. "You're stealing my kid," he said to Cass. "He's so into this."

"He just knows what's fun."

Caitlin, though, sat huddled in the cockpit looking scared. "You okay if I take her up front?" Jake asked Cass.

"Sure."

"C'mon, Caitlin. Let's go!" Jake took his little girl's hand and walked her forward. He sat down with his legs over the bow, Caitlin in front of him. As the boat crested each wave, the bow rose and fell. "Look," Jake said, "it's like riding a horse!" Periodically, water splashed them. Soon Caitlin was giggling, then laughing. By the time Jake brought her back to the cockpit, her blue eyes were shining.

"That was fun!" she said.

Cass laughed. "You doing okay, Jake?" she asked.

He nodded. "Yeah. Not too bad." He squinted out over the water. Images of the night he and Cass nearly drowned filled his mind again. Would he ever get used to being out on the water? "You ever think about it?"

"That night?" Cass said. "Yes, I do."

"But it doesn't bother you."

"Richard Maxwell took half my life from me. I won't let him take my love for sailing."

Jake nodded. "Mike loved the fight in you."

Cass laughed. "I'm not sure Travis understands it."

They sailed north, then south again. When the sun began dropping in the western sky, it was time to go home. Soon they had joined a procession of sailboats motoring back into port, their masts bare, gliding alongside assorted powerboats in the no-wake zone. They'd passed the Red 4 channel marker and were headed for Red 2 when Justin suddenly cried out, "Dad. Dad!" and came scurrying back to the cockpit, his eyes wide. "That's his boat," he said, pointing to a large powerboat off the port stern rail. "That's Chase's boat!"

"How do you know, Jus?" Jake said. As far as he knew, the kids had not been allowed on the boat.

"I've seen pictures of it. And look! Is that Mom?"

Jake stood up quickly. There were six, maybe seven adults visible on the boat, a large, sleek yacht. Sure enough, Tam was standing in the bow, dressed in a bright pink jumpsuit and a white jacket, a drink in her hand.

He glanced at Cass.

"Mommy, it's Mommy!" Caitlin cried.

"Shh, shh." Jake put his hand on her shoulder. The boat was fifty yards from them, passing on their left. He could see Chase at the wheel, Chase, in his white shirt and captain's hat. He could see five, maybe six other people on the boat. Then he saw Tam move over next to Chase, and the sound of laughter and loud music carried across the waves.

Suddenly, Jake's stomach tightened. There she was, the senator's trophy wife, his social bling, and in private, his punching bag. If only people could see it!

As he turned away, his eyes met Cassie's. She understood.

Caitlin was waving. She started to call to her mom. Justin hushed her. "Be quiet. He might see us."

Jake blew out a breath. "Come here, kids," he said, trying to distract them, "let's see how we can help Cass."

Cass played along. "Okay, I'll need help coming into the slip. Jake, can you go forward and catch the bow line with the boat hook?"

"The what?"

"Boat hook. This." She handed the pole with the hook on the end to him. "Go up there and get ready to grab the rope on the dock."

"Sure. Cat, you stay put!" He walked to the

bow as Cass eased the boat into the marina.

"After I pull into the slip," Cass called after him, "you catch the bow line on the dock with the boat hook, and wrap it around a cleat. Justin, you help me back here."

"Got it."

"And Caitlin, you sit right there and watch for birds, okay? Tell me if you see any."

Ten minutes later, they were secure in the slip. "Good job, everyone!" Cass said.

"Kids, can you thank Cassie?"

They did, throwing in hugs for good measure.

"You have time for a quick dinner?" he asked Cass.

She hesitated. "Sure."

"Let me run the kids back to Tam's. She's expecting them at six. Meet you at The Blue Goose?"

"Perfect."

"I'm buying," Jake told Cass as she looked over the menu forty-five minutes later.

"You don't need to do that."

"I want to."

"I had fun today." She peered at him over the top of her menu.

"You always have fun on the water."

"I love your kids."

Emotions swirled up like dust devils. He forced himself to stare at the menu.

"Did it bother you to see Tam out there?" she asked.

Cass always did know how to cut to the chase. Jake put down his menu. "Yeah, yeah it did. You know, it's all so phony. I know what's going on. I know he's abusive. But you can't see it from the way they appear in public." Jake felt his anger rise. "And the thing that gets me is, why does she put up with it? Why doesn't she leave? Why is she letting him get away with it?"

The waitress came and took their orders. Then Cass leaned forward. "I had the same questions about Maria. Every time I've been with her, she's been hyper if Renaldo calls. He's so possessive! So on Friday, when you and Moose were out chasing that fish guy, I went to talk to an expert who consults with the Bureau on domestic abuse."

"And . . ."

"She told me what we already know: Relationships are a strong pull for people, but especially for women. After losing her mother, Maria was looking for an anchor."

"A substitute family."

"Which is why she got hooked up with the gang."

Jake nodded. "Okay, I can see that as an initial draw. But the thing is, when the guy starts treating her badly, when he's disrespectful or becomes physically abusive, why would she put up with that? Why not just go find some other guy?"

"Abusive men tend to be very controlling. They isolate these women, cut them off from their family and friends. Then, once the abuse starts, the women are often too embarrassed to tell anyone what's going on. Or, maybe they don't even recognize it themselves."

"How can that be?"

"Dr. Snowden says it sneaks up on them. Typically, an abusive man goes through cycles. He can be very sweet and charming. Then, as the tension builds inside him, he gets edgy and irritable. The woman senses there's this head of steam building and tries to diffuse it. She may try to satisfy all of his whims, make him a special dinner, or have sex with him. But eventually there's an outburst. The man blows up. Afterwards, he becomes contrite."

"He sends her flowers, right?" Jake's face was hot. "I've seen huge bouquets in the foyer when I've picked up the kids."

Cass nodded. "That's right. Women usually say, 'He's so sweet when he's not violent.' That's what seduces them into staying. He loves her. He's so sorry. He'll never hit her again. If only she didn't 'make him mad.' In actuality, he's simply externalizing the insecurity he feels inside. And the cycle goes on."

Jake raised his eyebrows. "The *guy's* insecurity drives it?"

"That's what she said. Cyclical abusers are

fighting to compensate for a terrible insecurity. They may come off as outgoing and confident but they're not. They have a real terror of being abandoned or, on the contrary, of being engulfed by the woman with whom they are involved, of losing control in the relationship. So they become very controlling. Sometimes morbidly jealous. They imagine she's seeing another man or getting ready to leave him. They feel they absolutely must control her."

"Because controlling her has become their definition of being secure," Jake said.

"Exactly." Cass glanced around. "She said anyone, given the right situation, can get hooked in an abusive relationship. Anyone."

"So why doesn't the victim defend herself?"

"When the actual abuse is going on, she may dissociate. She'll report later she felt like she was outside her body, watching the whole experience. The cyclical abuser is releasing his emotional tension. His blows will continue until he's exhausted, or until he kills her. Assuming she survives the attack, once it stops, she's often in shock. How could he do this, she wonders. What just happened? Then she collapses emotionally. She becomes depressed and despondent, and can't muster the emotional strength to walk away."

"He blames her, saying she made him angry. And because he's isolated her," Jake added, "and she's embarrassed, she doesn't get help."

"Exactly," Cass said. "That's exactly right."

The waitress came with their orders, placing a plate loaded with two crab cakes in front of Cass, and another with flounder stuffed with crab meat in front of Jake. "Anything else?" she asked.

"More water, please," Jake said, "and bread. Could we have some more bread?"

Cass smiled.

"What?" he asked her.

She shook her head.

He shrugged. "Grace?"

"Go ahead."

They bowed their heads and he gave thanks for the meal, and prayed for wisdom as they dealt with both Maria and Tam.

Then, as they picked up forks and began to eat, Jake changed the subject. He *needed* to change the subject—his stomach was in a knot.

"So, what'd you do yesterday?"

Cass leaned forward, her face glowing in the candlelight. "We sailed up to the Sassafras River. Travis wanted to spend the night." She grimaced. "I'm not okay with that. Guess I'm old-fashioned."

"I think that's called honoring God."

Her eyes flickered. "What'd you guys do?"

"I took the kids to see your aunt." Cassie's Aunt Trudy had taken Jake in a couple of years before, after he'd been assaulted. Seizures had nearly incapacitated him and left him despairing

90

of life. Trudy had sheltered and cared for him. More than that, she'd given him hope. With his own parents long dead, Jake felt determined to stay connected.

"You saw Trudy?"

"Yeah, I try to get over there once a month to help her with whatever needs to be done. The kids like to come. We raked the yard."

"You take better care of Aunt Trudy than I do. How is she?" Cass asked.

"Trudy? She's fine. She's taking a pottery class. Did you know that?"

"No," Cass admitted ruefully.

"She showed me some of the things she's done—some mugs and bowls. They're pretty good!" Jake sat forward. "She said something to me that was, I don't know, different. I'm not sure how to take it."

"What's that?" Cass said, tilting her head.

Jake took a deep breath. He frowned, measuring his words. "She said she was making a piece of pottery one day, a pitcher," Jake said, lowering his voice. "She was working the clay on the wheel and a flaw developed, and neither she nor her teacher could fix it no matter what they tried. Finally, she had to smash the piece and start again, and as she did, as she brought the pitcher down on the wheel and destroyed it, she said she felt like God spoke to her and said, 'That's Jake Tucker.' " Jake shifted in his seat. "How weird is that?"

Cassie frowned. "That is strange."

"I don't understand what that means."

"I don't either."

"Your aunt's not crazy. I mean, she doesn't go in for a lot of bizarre stuff. So this was kind of out of the blue." Jake stared at the candle on the table, as if it could shed light on the puzzle. Then he looked at Cass. "I asked her what she thought it meant. And she said she's prayed about it and studied on it. Jeremiah eighteen, she told me. She's guessing God is about to do something big that's going to change me somehow." He shook his head. "I asked her, why would God tell you this? 'So I could warn you,' she said, 'and remind you that whatever happens, Jesus is Lord. Trust him.' " Jake shook his head.

Cass frowned. "That's pretty heavy."

"I don't know what to make of it. And I didn't want to tell you in front of the kids." Jake sighed. "I don't understand a lot about what's going on in my life."

The waitress came with the check and Jake paid the bill. They said goodbye in the parking lot under a full moon and a sky full of stars. "Thanks for everything, Cass," Jake said. "The kids had so much fun."

"You bet, partner."

She hugged him and the feel of her arms and the smell of her hair lingered with him for the rest of the night.

Chapter 10

Late Tuesday afternoon, Jake, Cass, and Moose sat around the office comparing notes on the investigation into Danny's shooting. "Maria thinks it was someone associated with Los Bravos who shot Danny. Or at least, they've bragged about it," Cass said.

"Who has bragged? I need names," Jake said.

"She hasn't told me yet."

"Have we confirmed Cisneros is with that group?"

"Travis is working on confirming that."

Jake checked himself before he said what he was thinking. Travis was the slowest, most deliberate cop he'd ever worked with. He hoped it wasn't rubbing off on Cass. He turned to Moose. "We still don't have a match on the slug?"

"Nope. It's not in the system. We got no DNA off the car, either."

"All right, well, look, if we can get the evidence that Cisneros is supplying drugs to the casino, we can bring him in on that."

"I'm saying go bust him now," Moose said. "We saw him delivering to the casino. It wasn't on his delivery list."

"I want to find out more first. I mean, maybe

that was just fish. Maybe he got a call to do a special delivery. Besides, I know practically nothing about the casino."

"What do you need to know? It's a lot of sad people losing a lot of money," Cass said. "It's brought an increase in crime, the divorce rate, domestic violence, and gambling addiction in the community. It's a lose-lose. Except for the owners, and maybe some politicians." Cass slid into her blazer and pulled her hair out from under the collar.

Moose looked at his phone. "I gotta run," he said. "See you tomorrow."

Jake turned to Cass. "I really want to see the casino. I've never been in it. Be my date, will you?"

"I already have a date! I'm going out to dinner with Travis."

"Well, how long will that take?"

She rolled her eyes at him.

"I don't want to go alone!" Jake said. "And I sure don't want to go with Moose." He began following her toward the elevator.

Cass pushed the down button, then looked at him.

Her eyes told Jake he had a chance. "Ten o'clock. How about that? I'll pick you up. We'll just stay a couple of hours." He smiled.

She sighed. The doors opened. She stepped on and turned around. "Okay, I'll bring Travis."

"You're kidding, right?"

"Yes, I'm kidding. Make it eleven," Cass said with a wry smile as the doors began closing. "Wear something slinky!"

Chapter 11

The Lucky Leaf Casino had brought 24/7 gambling to the Annapolis area. Politicians who supported legalized gambling were quick to point out the superficial results—increased tax revenues and tourism dollars. Law enforcement and social service officials were more likely to note the human misery.

"You know, even if the politicians are blind to the social consequences," Cass said, "you'd think they'd notice the collapse of the gambling industry in Atlantic City and see casinos as the bad bet that they are." Some spectacular failures had recently captured the news.

Jake pulled into the three-story casino parking lot. "I know, you hate this place."

"I do! I hate what casinos are doing to Maryland, and especially to the Bay area."

"You can thank Chase Westfield for that." Chase was one of the main proponents of gambling in the legislature. Jake pulled into a parking space. He looked over at her. She had on a sleek black dress with tiny sequins that looked like stars on a black night sky. Her blonde hair brushed her shoulders. Her spiked heels looked lethal. She looked like a date. A real date. "Thanks again for coming with me," he said. "I promise I'll behave."

"Let's just go." She opened her door.

The lights and noise inside the casino belied the late hour and assaulted Jake's senses. He knew that was part of the plan: By keeping things bright and stimulating in the windowless environment, casinos encouraged gamblers to lose track of time—and the money they were losing. Cass gripped his arm. The jangle of slot machines, the tick-tick-tick of the roulette wheel, the click of chips, and the bright, flashing lights gave the illusion of busyness, of hope, of possibility. The dour faces on slot machine players told a different story.

A cocktail waitress in a tiny black dress approached them offering alcohol to lubricate their willingness to part with their money. "No thanks," Jake said. He patted Cass's hand on his arm and said in a low voice, "Let's go over to the bar."

Cass slid up onto a bar stool and Jake sat next to her. He ordered drinks for them, sodas with fruit. Cass eyed him as she took a sip. "You look good."

He was wearing his black suit. The last time he'd had it on was for Mike's funeral. He doubted she'd remember that. "You look spectacular," he responded. "You ought to wear that more often."

"Where? To the office?"

He grinned at her.

"So, why are we here?" Cass asked. "What are we doing?"

"I just wanted to get a feel for this place." He motioned to the bartender. "Could we get some shrimp? And maybe a couple of crab cakes?"

The food came quickly. "It's all so hedonistic," Cass said, biting into a shrimp, "the liquor, the promise of riches, the food, the glamour."

"Some people would say you don't know how to have fun."

Cass gestured toward a roulette wheel. A young man stood before it. "Look at him," she said. "He's plunking down twenty dollars at a shot."

As the wheel came to a stop, a young, very pregnant woman emerged from the shadows. She touched the young man's arm. He jerked it away.

"Now you tell me," Cass said, "if that is fun."

"Look, I agree with you!" Jake said, putting a forkful of crab cake in his mouth. "But you have to admit, the food is good."

Twenty minutes later, he said, "Let's check out the slots," and he walked her in that direction.

"I hate this!" Cass said, squeezing his arm.

Jake laughed. "I know, I know! Just hang out with me, okay? I'm playing to the cameras." He sat down and began inserting coins. If the whirring and jangling weren't irritating enough, the music track put the hype over the top.

Cass leaned over him like a girlfriend would and whispered in his ear, "If you win anything, you're donating it to charity."

He grinned. "I love it when you talk to me that way."

Twenty dollars later, Jake stood up. "That's it. Let's take a walk."

Cass took his arm and they strolled back toward the arched entrance of the high-stakes area. Suddenly, she released his arm and pulled him around toward her. "Kiss me!" she said softly, stepping back toward a wall. When he hesitated, she reached up and drew his head toward her.

She was serious. As her lips pressed his, Jake felt a shockwave run through him. "Wow," he whispered, looking into her eyes. "I am so glad I didn't come with Moose!"

"Don't look. It's Chase."

Chase! What was he doing here? Jake started to turn around. Cass put her hand on his face to stop him. "I said, don't look! Listen to me!"

His heart beat hard.

"They just walked past us. He's with a man. Wait, I recognize him. He's with the casino owner, Sam Fico, his legislative assistant—what's his name? Garza?—and a fourth man. They're going into the high-stakes area."

"Who's the fourth man?" Jake whispered in her ear.

"I don't know."

"Memorize his face." Then he said, "Should I kiss you again? I'm willing if it's absolutely necessary."

"Very funny. They're gone. Look at me!" She took his arm and walked him over toward the bar area, keeping him engaged with her eyes. "Right about here," Cass said, guiding him to a small table. "We can see them, and Chase has his back to us."

Jake sat down and casually looked toward the high-stakes room. He spotted Chase, then Ramon Garza, his assistant, and then the casino owner, Sam Fico. But who was the Fourth Man?

A waitress came over. Jake ordered a couple of drinks.

"Is that why you wanted to come here?" Cass asked. "Are you stalking Chase?"

"No! I had no clue he'd be here!" Jake casually took a drink as he looked to the right. "Hey, let me take a picture of you." He positioned himself so that it looked like he was shooting Cass. In reality, he was aiming for Chase and the other men.

Jake brought his cell phone up to take a picture. But a waitress put her hand in front of the lens.

"Sorry, sir. No pictures inside the casino."

Jake blinked. "Not even of my girl?"

"No, sir."

Jake slid his cell phone back into his pocket. "That's ridiculous."

"Sorry, sir, it's the rule." The waitress left.

"Bet there's no rule against supplying women," Jake said under his breath.

Cass followed his gaze.

Four young women, dressed in shimmery dresses and spiked heels, approached the four men in the high-stakes area, their intentions clear. The whole party drifted toward the back of the area.

"And that's how the high rollers play," Cass said.

That thought set Jake's teeth on edge. Tam. Was he abusing her *and* cheating on her?

"I've seen enough," Jake said abruptly.

Cass raised her eyebrows. "You ready to go?"

"Yes."

She took his arm and they began walking out. "Maybe this wasn't such a great idea."

"Who knew he'd be here?" Jake said under his breath. "Who knew?"

As they walked out of the main entrance, they saw a young Latino approach a security guard and hand him a small package. The guard pulled an envelope out of his jacket and handed it to the kid.

Jake and Cass pretended to be preoccupied with each other, but the interaction wasn't lost on them.

"You know what's a good bet?" Cass said, as they closed the doors to their car. "What's in that package isn't sold in stores."

Jake's tires squealed as he wheeled the car out of the lot. "Exactly."

The identity of the Fourth Man at the casino bugged Jake. The next day, Cass found him staring at computer images of the casino opening on news websites. "I know I've seen him before, but I can't place him," Jake complained.

"Stop, Jake. What's this got to do with our case?"

Jake furrowed his brow. "I'm not sure." He clicked away from that website. "You're probably right. I'm being obsessive." Then he ran his hand over his head.

Cass smoothed her hair behind her ear. "You know the guy who delivered the package to the security guard? I described the tattoos on his face to Travis."

Jake nodded.

"I'm going over to look at some new photos he has. Maybe I can pick him out."

"That security guard knew that package was coming," Jake said. "He had an envelope ready. If the package contained drugs, then there's some official channel for contraband at that casino."

Cass crossed her arms. "It's pretty bold to receive a package like that through the front door. That could indicate high-level management is involved. And then we have Cesar Cisneros possibly making deliveries through the loading dock."

"I thought they were pretty strict about enforcing drug laws at these casinos."

"And prostitution and organized crime involvement. That's how they sold them, anyway. They'd keep out the wiseguys and it would be just good, clean fun." Cass bit her cheek as she thought. "Jake, this feels like DEA territory."

"They say their budget's been cut. They don't have the money right now to send an undercover agent in."

"You've talked to them?"

"Yes." Jake sat back. "I don't know, Cass. It's just not right. I have a feeling this is tied in to our case."

Cass sighed. "We have no proof of that. And it's taking time away from what we should be investigating." She stood up. "I've got to go. Travis is expecting me." She looked at Jake. "You're coming a week from Thursday, right? My aunt asked me."

Thursday. Thanksgiving at Trudy's. Jake's kids would be with Tam, and Trudy had invited him. "Yes."

"Good! So is Travis."

Chapter 12

"I told Travis it was time for an undercover officer to connect with the gang." On the Monday before Thanksgiving, Jake and Cass stood in the office planning out their week.

"What'd he say?" Jake asked.

"He said he'd look into the possibilities."

Jake sighed and put his hands on his hips.

She sipped her coffee. "By the way, how are the kids? Did they have a good weekend?"

Jake blew out a breath. How could he say this? "Tam promised to have the kids back by two o'clock on Sunday, so they could make a three o'clock rehearsal for that Christmas play they're in."

"At your church?"

Jake nodded. "They were late. So I had to rush them. We're driving over there and Justin starts calling his sister 'stupid.' That's not normal for him." Jake stood up and put his hands on his hips. "After the rehearsal, I took them to dinner, and the same stuff is going on. So I say, 'Jus, what's up with you? Why are you calling your sister stupid?' His head went down and he got all red. I realized he was crying!" Jake turned toward Cass. "So finally Justin says, 'Chase calls me stupid.' I was furious. 'What do you mean?' I asked him. 'Chase says I'm stupid.' 'Why?' 'Because, I forgot my homework again.' Then Caitlin pipes up, 'And he lost his soccer schedule, too!' "

"That's infuriating!" Cass said. "Why would Chase say that to a kid?"

Jake took a deep breath. The anger began pounding in his head again, like dull hammer blows. "He's a jerk! Anyway, I got the kids back to Tam's and we're standing there in the foyer, and they're clinging on to me and I'm trying to say goodbye, and Tam is there. Then he walks in."

"Chase?"

"Yeah, Chase. Along with his buddy, that guy, Ramon Garza." In his mind's eye, he could picture the scene. Chase, with his dark, styled hair and good looks. He was dressed in a black suit, a starched white shirt, and a gray tie. His face held a perpetual tan and his eyes were a clear light blue. He was as tall as Jake, slim and fit. But lighter. Jake figured he could take him in less than a minute. Behind Chase stood Garza, his middle-aged assistant, a Latino from Los Angeles with a reputation for charming ladies and being ruthless with political opponents.

Jake clenched his fists as he continued his story. "Chase and I nodded to each other and I gave the kids one more hug. Then I looked at him and said, 'Chase. Don't call Justin stupid. He's not stupid, and I don't want you to call him that anymore.' "

"Oh, Jake!" Cassie's eyes widened. "What did he do?"

"He got mad. I saw it in his face. Then it was gone, and that PR mask was on again."

"Good grief! What did Tam say?"

"She was horrified." Jake shook his head.

"I'll bet."

"Here's the thing, I had to put him on notice that I was watching him. And I had to let Justin know he doesn't have to be afraid of that man. I *will* protect him. I will protect my kids." He jabbed the air with his forefinger to make his point.

Cass remained quiet.

Jake waited for a positive reaction, then threw up his hands. "What was I supposed to do?"

She shook her head. "I don't know. I guess you did the right thing. It's just . . ."

"I don't get points for diplomacy."

She nodded.

He jutted out his chin. "Well, you know what? I don't care."

Under pressure from Jake to get good information from Maria or cut her loose, Cass arranged to meet the young woman at a coffee bar a few days later. The Java Connection was nearly empty when she got there. In fact, it closed in just an hour, at seven, she discovered. "Let's sit here," Cass said, motioning toward a table in the back. Jake had agreed to back her up. He would be outside somewhere.

The young women sat down. They ordered coffee, and then Cass brought up the reason she'd wanted to meet. "Maria, how much do you know about Los Bravos?"

"I know them, some. I see them around. Our boys, they don't like them."

"Tomas Bandillo is with them, right?"

"Yes, but Cass, he's not a bad guy. The others, they are older. Tomas," Maria blushed, "he is a boy."

"Would he talk to me?"

Maria's eyes widened. "Tomas? Oh no! That would be dangerous!"

Cass shifted topics. "How's Renaldo's new job?" The boyfriend was working at the casino now, Cass had discovered.

The young woman brightened. "He loves it! He just got a big bonus! He's so happy."

"A big bonus?"

"He's going to buy a new car!"

A red flag. "That must have been some bonus," Cass said. She sipped her coffee. Through the front window she could see Jake in his personal car on the street. "Tomas asked you out, right? What happened with that?"

Maria laughed. "Renaldo, he was so mad!"

"You told him?"

"I wanted him to be jealous. He was ignoring me!"

Cassie arched her eyebrows.

"He was so angry!" Maria waved her hand. "That's just Latinos, you know? They are protective of their women. He wants me to be thin, he wants me to be beautiful, he wants me to be all his." She laughed again. "I tease him. I tell him maybe I meet this other boy tonight."

Cass blinked. "You said that to him? Was that wise?"

Maria shrugged. "He tells me about all the beautiful women at work. Then he tells me I am getting fat. I have to do something. So I play the game, too."

A thought crossed Cassie's mind. "Do the boys sell cocaine? Or heroin?"

Maria inspected her nails. She looked at Cass. "They don't tell me what they sell."

Cass continued. "Remember I told you about my friend who was shot? I need to know who was talking about that, Maria, who was bragging."

The girl shrugged. "Just guys. They talk."

"Names, Maria. I need names."

The young woman pursed her lips.

Cass tried to jog the information out of her. "Where were you when you heard them?"

"At a club." Maria's eyes flickered. "It was a guy named Cesar."

"Describe him."

"Middle-age. Maybe thirty-eight or -nine. Dark hair. Short, stocky. Not good looking."

Cass pulled a photo of Cesar Cisneros out of her bag. "Is this him?"

Maria studied it. "I'm not sure."

"Think, Maria! Is this the man?"

The young woman got a text. She glanced at it. The expression on her face changed. "I don't know."

Cass tapped the table. "Who was that, Maria? Who are you afraid of?"

"I think I need to go," Maria said, rising from her seat.

"Did Renaldo ask you where you were going?"

Maria nodded.

"And you told him?"

Maria nodded again. Her cell phone buzzed again. She read it, then looked at Cass, her eyes wide. "I need to go now."

Both irritated and concerned, Cass walked Maria out of the coffee shop. "You need a cab?"

"My cousin, she lend me her car."

"Where is it?"

"Around the corner. In a parking garage."

"You want me to walk you to it?"

"No. No! I am fine." She walked away, her head bent over the phone in her hands.

The cold night air took Cass's breath away. She pulled her coat around her, a signal to Jake, and turned and began walking toward her own car, lost in thought. Had she learned anything? Was

Maria reliable? Or was she, Cass, just spinning her wheels?

Three minutes later, she heard a scream. She turned, and raced back in the direction Maria had walked.

Chapter 13

Something told Jake to just hang around for a minute or two after Cass left the coffee shop. Maybe it was the red light he caught just after pulling away from his parking spot. Maybe it was the look on a Latino's face as the young man crossed the street. Maybe it was instinct.

Jake pulled through the intersection and parked again, then got out of his car. He walked toward the three-story parking garage that he saw the kid enter. When he heard screams, he started running.

Maria lay on the ground beside her car. The man hovered over her, screaming at her, his arm raised. Then he hit her.

"Stop! Hold it right there!" Cass yelled. Jake saw her running toward the angry man.

Adrenaline pumping, Jake barreled around a parked car, slammed into the Latino, and drove him to the ground. The younger man squirmed underneath him, but Jake had him under control. He could feel it. He wrapped his left arm around the guy's neck and tightened it, and heard a gasping, choking sound, and then he drove his fist into the man's kidneys. "Stop fighting, stop!"

From somewhere a woman screamed and screamed. Then, in Jake's mind, the screams became Tam's and the man underneath him became Chase, and rage poured into him, tightening his muscles, and deadening his ears.

His fury made him impervious to Cassie's voice. Only when she touched him, grabbing his shoulder, and yelling, "You got him! Stop, Jake!" did he relent.

Breathing hard, Jake relaxed his chokehold. He staggered to his feet, pulling the terrified young man up with him, pinning his arm behind his back and slammed him against a parked car. Jake's blood vessels pulsed with anger. "Call the cops!" he yelled at Cass.

"No, oh please, no!" Maria cried. "Renaldo!"

Cass hesitated.

Renaldo? Maria's boyfriend? "It's a domestic," Jake snarled. "You call the cops!"

"Oh, no! They take him to jail. Renaldo, oh, Renaldo!"

"Cass!"

Cass brushed her hair back out of her face. "Let him go. She won't testify."

"Are you serious?"

"Yes. Jake, please. She's eighteen. And she won't press charges."

Jake glared at her. He blew out a breath, then turned back to the kid. He twisted the kid's arm up until Renaldo screamed in pain. He flipped Renaldo around and pinned him to the car, grabbing him by the collar. "Don't you ever touch her again," Jake snarled. "Understand?" He shook Renaldo. "You get it? Don't touch her!"

Jake twisted the kid's collar until he gasped for breath. "You got that?"

The boy, clearly terrified, nodded.

"Now, get out of here, you punk!" Jake growled and he threw Renaldo away from the two women. Renaldo fell hard, on the cement floor. "Get out!" Renaldo rose, stumbled, and then began running away, blood streaming out of his nose. "Go!" Jake yelled. "Go!"

That night, Jake didn't sleep at all. His anger kept his eyes wide open while scenes of conflict flashed through his mind. It was Maria, then it was Tam; it was Renaldo, then it was Chase. Over and over the scene replayed in his mind.

Worst of all was the question that haunted him in the face of his rage—was he, Jake, any different from these thugs?

Wednesday morning, first thing, Cass plopped down into the seat beside Jake's desk. She straightened her black wool jacket as she sat down. "Hey," she said to her partner, "I'm sorry. I should have called you yesterday to make sure you were okay, but all I could focus on was Maria."

"I can't believe you didn't call the cops," Jake snapped.

"She wouldn't have testified! There would have been no purpose! In fact," Cass said, "it wouldn't have surprised me if they turned on you for assaulting Renaldo!"

Jake's jaw shifted. He shook his head.

"I don't know if this will help," Cass said, taking a deep breath, "but at about three this morning, I convinced Maria to go into witness protection. She's gone, Jake. Travis is driving her to Rockville. She's going to live with a state trooper, take her GED, go to Montgomery College. She's gone, Jake. Away from the gang."

He looked at her. "That's great, Cass. Good job," he said, and then he got up and walked away.

Ten times Jake started to call Trudy and cancel for Thanksgiving. Nine times he stopped himself. On the tenth, the disappointment in her voice made him change his mind.

Just as he expected, Trudy's felt like something out of a Norman Rockwell painting: a warm house, lots of food, good conversation, a dog to play with. There was just one catch.

Jake stood in the kitchen, helping Cassie's aunt lift a huge, golden brown turkey out of the oven. He grabbed the handles of the black roasting pan and lifted it to the stovetop, the smell of the savory bird filling his nose. Trudy closed the oven door. "I think I could eat the whole thing," Jake said, putting the potholders down.

"You'd have to fight me for it," Trudy joked. "Thank you, Jake." She wiggled the turkey's leg, looking it over to be sure it was done.

"What's next?" Jake asked.

"Let's lift it out of the pan. You get that platter over there," Trudy motioned with the fork in her hand, "and I'll get the lifters."

Working together, they got the bird on the platter and the platter on the table. As they were finishing, Cass walked in. Travis followed. And there was the catch.

"There's no football game on?" Cass asked, staring at Jake. Her face was flushed from the chill November air. She had on khakis and an emerald green sweater. Her hair and clothes smelled faintly of wood smoke.

"Jake's been keeping me company," Trudy said. "Did you give Travis the tour?"

"Yes, she did," Travis responded, moving aside as Trudy's dog, Jazz, pushed past him to get to her water bowl.

The bowl was nearly empty, so Jake picked it up and filled it at the sink. It gave him something to do. Why did he feel so awkward? Seeing Travis at Trudy's house was weird. It just felt wrong.

"Okay, folks, we're ready. Jim?" Trudy said, calling for her brother, who was in the sunroom.

Jim, Cassie's dad, ambled in while Cass and Travis went off to wash their hands. They all sat down at the big farm table in the kitchen, Jim at the end, Jake and Trudy on one side, Travis and Cass on the other. A pumpkin cut and filled with flowers sat in the middle, flanked by dark red candles in wooden candleholders. Trudy said grace, and the feast began, conversation and food flowing in abundance, and all the time a dissonant refrain ran through the back of Jake's mind.

Was it seeing Cass sitting next to this guy who looked so much like Mike, but wasn't Mike, here, in a family setting? Was it the way Travis so casually draped his arm around Cassie, stroking her shoulder with his thumb? Or the way she laughed, leaning toward him and resting her head momentarily on him?

Whatever it was, by the end of the meal, Jake was uncomfortable. More than uncomfortable.

After dinner, Jake made it a point to seek out Cassie's dad. Jim was in the sunroom, sitting in front of a warm fire. Following Cisneros around on his route had raised a lot of questions about the seafood industry. This would be a good time to get some answers.

As he had suspected, Jim knew a lot. "Seafood's gone international," he said. "Those guys you see making the rounds to restaurants and small grocery stores, they're buying from all over. Fish get freighted in by truck, even UPS and FedEx from Asia, Latin America, all over."

Drugs were brought in that way, too, Jake knew.

"With the flash freezing that's available, quality holds up pretty good," Jim said.

Jake was about to ask him about the casino when Cass entered the room and sat down on the sofa next to her dad. Jake braced himself, expecting Travis to follow her, but he didn't.

"Are you guys talking shop?" Cass said as her dad put his arm around her.

"We're talking fish," Jim replied.

"Anybody up for a game?" Trudy asked, emerging from the kitchen.

"Sure," Jim and Cassie both responded.

"You all go ahead," Jake said, rising to his feet. Jazz, who had been asleep next to his chair, jumped up and grabbed a ball. "I'll take the dog out."

Stepping out the back door, Jake took a deep breath. Smoke from wood stoves in the area scented the air. The bright yellow leaves of a maple, the red from dogwoods, and brown oak leaves lay scattered over Trudy's lawn. Jake picked up a rake and began raking the lawn. While he worked, he thought, and too much thinking was not good, at least for Jake. He knew Trudy would invite him to spend the night, and in fact, he had a gear bag in the back of his car anticipating that. But Jake decided he would decline.

He didn't fit anymore. He could feel it. Travis and Cass were a couple. Time to exit, stage right. Jake made a phone call, then whistled for Jazz and walked back to the house, propping the rake outside the back door.

In the kitchen, the others were in the middle of a wild game of Wahoo. He forced a smile, gave

Trudy a kiss, shook hands with the men and said goodbye. Cass followed him out to the car.

"I'm sorry you're leaving, Jake." She touched his arm. "Are you all right?"

"Of course! Moose and I have a hot date tomorrow." That wasn't exactly true, but after Moose returned his phone call it would be. The waning sunlight caught the edge of Cassie's hair, and Jake suddenly wanted to touch it, to feel it between his fingers, to run his hand through her hair, to take her in his arms, to kiss her once more. His heart trembled.

Why now?

Cass glanced up at the sky. "I took tomorrow off. The wind's due to pick up. Travis wants to go sailing in the morning."

"Great! Have fun," Jake said.

Cass looked down at the crushed oyster shells paving the driveway. She moved some loose fragments with the side of her foot. Then she looked back at Jake, her face golden in the light. He felt a sudden weakness. Words gathered in his throat.

"It was good to have you here," Cass said, a funny catch in her voice. "I'm glad you came."

"Yeah, me, too."

"I guess I'll see you Monday." Then she raised herself up on tiptoes and kissed him on the cheek.

And Jake drove off, emotions churning in his gut.

Chapter 14

The wind was stiff, out of the southeast, as Cass and Travis edged their way out of the marina on the day after Thanksgiving. The Alberg 30 seemed ready to run. Cass was at the helm, while Travis busied himself taking off the sail cover and securing the lifelines.

Cass watched him as he worked. He was slimmer than Jake, about Mike's build. He had his sunglasses on and he was wearing khaki cargo pants and a bright yellow windbreaker and brown, worn-in boat shoes. She didn't have to tell him anything about the boat. Travis automatically knew what to do.

The plan was to run south, toward Bloody Point Light, close-hauled, sailing for a few hours before heading back on a broad reach. The late November day would be short, the temperature, in the mid-fifties, chilly. Aunt Trudy had packed enough food for a lunch and dinner for them, turkey sandwiches on whole wheat bread with cranberry sauce and a touch of wasabi mayonnaise. An insulated Thermos held coffee.

Cass negotiated the channel slowly, taking her time. Her mind shifted back to the day before, Thanksgiving. Her aunt was so gracious, agreeing to let her bring Travis.

Over a sink full of dirty dishes, after Jim and Travis had gone on a walk, Trudy had asked her about him, what she was feeling, and where the relationship was going. "He's a nice guy, a really nice guy," Cass had responded. Her aunt had raised her eyebrows at that, and Cass was quick to add, "I like him a lot." Where was the relationship going? She said she thought he was getting serious. And was he a Christian? "Yes, I'm sure he is." A committed Christian? "I don't know . . . we haven't really talked about that," Cass had replied, immediately shaking off a stab of guilt.

Now, watching him standing on the deck, waiting for the right time to raise the mainsail, Cass wondered what it would be like to be married to him. He was kind and considerate, methodical, and patient. Trustworthy. Honest. A little fussy sometimes with details. But a good guy. Steady.

What would she say if he asked her?

"You ready?" Travis shouted, looking back at her. They were nearing the end of the channel. The gray waters of the Chesapeake were before them.

"Let's go!" Cass agreed. She turned *Time Out* to starboard, bringing the boat into the wind, while Travis pulled on the main halyard, raising the white sail up the mast. The canvas flapped back and forth. Travis winched the halyard tight and cleated it off. Travis came back to the cockpit.

He adjusted the mainsheet, and then Cass cut the engine back as the sail filled with air.

The Alberg sliced through the two-foot waves, heeling slightly, as Travis pulled out the jib. The winch made a racheting sound as he tightened the jib sheet for sailing close-hauled. The foresail formed into a gentle curve, heeling the Alberg over even more. Then Travis sat down on the cockpit seat, on the high side, and grinned at Cass. "She's looking good," he said. "How much are we getting?" He leaned over to read the knotmeter. "Four, four-and-a half, five . . ." he read. "Let's see if we can get more." He played with the sails, adjusting their trim. The boat heeled over at twenty degrees and the knotmeter edged up.

Cass braced herself behind the wheel. "All right!" she said.

Ahead, a tug pushing a barge loaded with sand edged northward. It reminded Cass of the night Jake had rescued her from Richard Maxwell's catamaran. The cat had gotten caught on a tug's tow line and capsized, throwing both of them into the cold Bay. She shivered just thinking about it.

"You cold?" Travis asked.

"No," she said. She had never told him that story. In fact, he'd never really asked her about Mike, about her relationship with Jake, about her career even. There were huge chunks of her life that Travis knew nothing about.

They were sailing on a straight course to Bloody

Point, the wind pushing the sails hard. Travis kept fiddling with the sheets, working to get the maximum drive. "Why don't you just relax, so we can talk?" Cass said.

He smiled and moved back, taking a seat on the high-side gunnel. "You're right. I'm a bit compulsive."

She asked him about his childhood. His favorite TV shows as a kid. How his family celebrated Christmas. And when he knew he wanted to be a cop. He responded with funny stories and self-deprecating humor, but afterward, after they'd had lunch and turned back toward Annapolis, she realized he hadn't asked her the same questions in return. It was like a big part of her life was a void he didn't want to enter.

Travis was funny and bright and he sure knew a lot about sailing. And that, Cass told herself, was enough.

Black Friday, 10 p.m. Moose, it turned out, had plenty of experience with casinos, and was happy to give Jake a primer as they drove toward Lucky Leaf. "I spent more time in Atlantic City than I did in my apartment when I worked in New York," he told Jake. "I been up to Foxwoods, Mohegan Sun, the Sands Casino in Bethlehem, Pennsylvania—fun times. I can't believe you've never been. Except for that time with Cass, of course."

Yes, that time with Cass. Jake had to push those thoughts away, hard, like he'd had to push Cassie's boat away from the dock to keep it from crashing into the pilings.

"So, what's your favorite casino game?" Jake asked. Questions about the possible link between the 11th Street Clique, or Los Bravos, and the casino filled his mind. Were drugs being trafficked illegally? Women? And was Danny's shooting even part of it?

Jake had talked to Danny just the other night. The now-retired agent sounded good, relaxed even. He and Lavonda were settled in their Virginia home. But there was still his shooting to resolve.

So, did a gang member see Danny on that dark night and decide to take him out? But how would they know he was law enforcement?

If he could connect Cisneros to drugs at the casino, could he flip him and find out who shot Danny? Or was he, Jake, just chasing his own tail? Worse, was he chasing Chase?

Chase was the major force in the Maryland Senate behind legalized betting. He'd argued passionately for the tax revenue it would bring in, the tourism dollars, and the opportunities being missed as nearby states legalized gambling and drew customers from Maryland. He'd won the hearts of Marylanders over to his position. Now Jake had seen him hanging out at the casino with the owner. That was to be expected. But was more going on?

And tonight, was he, Jake, being driven by his passion for justice or his anger toward the man abusing Tam and belittling his son?

Moose was talking. Jake forced himself to tune back in.

"So yeah, craps is my favorite. It moves fast. The house edge is low. It gets my blood pumping almost as good as chasing down some thug." Moose looked over at him. "It can be a complex game, but you can play it simple, too. I'll show you!"

"Can't wait."

"No seriously. You can make a passline bet, a simple bet—the shooter rolls seven or eleven and you win."

"And what makes me lose?"

"Two, three, or twelve."

"So two numbers make me win, three make me lose."

"Yeah, but seven's the easiest number to throw!" Moose gestured toward him. "Aw, man. You'll see. It's fun!"

Fun if you're not gambling away your kid's lunch money, Jake thought. He pulled into a space in the underground parking garage. A security guard in a car with a flashing yellow light drove past. Cass would have pointed out that people who lose money in the casino are sometimes desperate enough to steal from others, especially if the raucous jangling of a slot machine paying off had helped identify a likely mark.

Inside, the brighter-than-daylight lighting jolted Jake, as it had before. And the noise! Between the cacophony of the slots, the yelling and laughing of some people around the tables, and the jangle of coins, Jake's ears were ringing.

Moose led the way to the cashier's booth, bought a hundred dollars worth of chips, and paced over to the craps table. "Let's play a little."

Jake stood behind him as Moose joined the game. Indeed, Jake could see how the fast action and the auctioneer-like patter of the stickman announcing the results of the throws could be entrancing, almost addictive. The gamblers in the game seemed adrenalized, whooping and cheering and groaning with each roll of the dice.

Half an hour later, Moose's hundred was gone. "My luck was just about to turn," he complained as Jake led him away from the table.

They walked up to the bar, and ordered drinks and hot wings. "Let's go over there," Jake said, nodding toward a table with a good view of the floor. He could smell the spice of the hot wings. His stomach growled.

"So tell me how this works," he said to Moose, nodding toward the casino floor.

"Crime wise?" Moose glanced around. The

tables near them were empty. "A bunch of ways. You want to launder some dirty money? You use it to buy a bunch of chips, play a little, then cash the rest of them in. Voila, clean money."

"What else?" Jake asked, dipping a wing in the ranch dressing and taking a big bite.

"Well, you got to keep things under ten thousand dollars, because anything above that has to be reported. So sometimes, gamblers will try using cashiers on different sides of the room, cashing in six thousand dollars on one side and six on the other. The casinos should have software to prevent anyone from doing that. They're also supposed to file suspicious activity reports if they think someone's being hinky." Moose waved his hand in front of his mouth. "Whoo, hot!"

"I told you to get the medium!"

Moose shrugged. "Then there's another thing: Sometimes a gambler will work with a team and pass chips or winning stubs to a buddy so they stay under the ten thousand dollars. That's called 'structuring' and yeah, it's illegal, too."

"What about drugs?"

"Drugs, girls, I don't care what they say. They're available. I could go over there right now," he nodded toward a man in a casino blazer, "and I'd be in a room with a girl in twenty minutes." Moose took a bite of a wing. "So, did you spot him yet?" he asked with his mouth full.

"Who?"

"Your nemesis."

Jake had been watching for Chase all night. He certainly didn't want to be surprised by him. "Who says I'm looking for him?"

"You're kidding me, right?" Moose said. "Who's that guy?" He nodded toward the hallway leading to the restrooms. "He looks familiar."

"He's a cop, moonlighting. I saw him when I was here with Cass."

Moose nodded. "It's good pay. I've thought about it."

Jake raised his eyebrows.

"Okay, look, look!" Moose nodded toward the end of a row of slot machines. Three guys were talking. One passed some paper to the others. "I'll bet you anything those guys are working together." Moose looked at Jake. "Now if I can see that, don't you think the casino can?" He polished off his last wing, licked his fingers, then wiped his hands and mouth on a napkin. "I'm telling you, all these places are corrupt."

Jake took a deep breath. So many opportunities. Then he straightened his back. "Look there!" He nodded toward a man at the cashier's cage on the far side. "I think I recognize him. Let's go take a look!" But as he rose to his feet and turned to leave, he came face to face with a man in a dark suit he'd seen at his church. His eyes were strikingly blue, his face clean-shaven, his hair cut stylishly, and his suit more expensive than anything Jake had ever owned.

Jake pretended he hadn't recognized him. "How 'bout some slots?" he asked Moose, hoping to convey the message he was there to have fun.

"Yeah, man, I thought you . . ."

Jake shut him up with a look. "Let's go!"

Later, driving home, he told Moose about the man.

"So what?" Moose said. "You don't think people from your church gamble?"

What could Jake say to that? "People from church" included new believers, lazy believers, people pretending to be believers, as well as true believers. "It just feels wrong to me, Moose. I can't explain it."

Chapter 15

The rest of the weekend seemed to crawl by. Finally, Sunday came, and church, and Tam got the kids back in time for the church play rehearsal. And things felt better. On Monday night, Jake rattled around in his kitchen, looking for something he felt like eating. His refrigerator was nearly empty. One lone pizza occupied the freezer.

Alone. Just like him. Sometimes it got old.

Jake's mind drifted to a young woman at his church. Beth. She was a helper in Caitlin's Sunday School class. Every once in a while, she'd sit next to him in church. Somehow, Jake knew she'd respond if he began making overtures. She was attractive enough, long dark hair and a trim figure. And she had a good heart. She seemed to love kids. Maybe he should ask her out.

But no, Jake thought, stopping his own thoughts. No. There just wasn't anything there. Nothing.

And then his phone rang.

"Hey! You got a football game on that I can watch?" Cass said.

"What's the matter? TV broken?"

"No, it's just that, you know, we haven't done Monday night for a while. And I have this homemade lasagna and it looks so huge! I'll have leftovers forever."

Jake jumped at her suggestion. He'd missed her company on Monday nights. And he was hungry. "I can help you with that!"

"Come in, come in!" Jake said fifteen minutes later. He swung the door open so wide it bounced against the wall.

Cassie burst out laughing. "Jake, calm down! It's just me."

He grinned and shook his head. "Sorry. I guess it's been a little quiet around here tonight. Gosh, that smells good! I'm starving! Let me take that!" Jake took the lasagna out to the kitchen. On the TV, the New England Patriots were about to score. Cass dished up the lasagna, garlic bread and salad, and Jake poured drinks. Then the two sat down to watch the game, side-by-side on Jake's tattered couch. He analyzed the plays. She cheered on the Pats. And every fiber of Jake's soul said, this is good. This is so good.

But then the stark reality hit: She's still with Travis.

Why had she come? He would ask her at halftime, he decided.

When the second quarter ended, Cass stood up to stretch. Jake took their dishes to the kitchen. She followed him. "That was delicious," Jake said.

"I'm glad you liked it."

He rinsed off the plates and placed them in the dishwasher and she put leftovers away. "Your fridge is empty!" she said.

"I'm not much for keeping house," Jake responded. How should he ask her? Start somewhere else. "Hey, I haven't had a chance to tell you, but I'm sorry about that night with Maria and Renaldo."

Cass cocked her head, her brow furrowed.

"I lost it. And afterwards, I was harsh with you. And I'm sorry."

"It's okay. I understand. It's kind of a hot button with you."

"Yes." Jake dried his hands on a dishtowel and draped it over the handle of the oven. He wanted to say more. He wanted to tell her that, in his rage, Renaldo had become Chase, and that he could have killed him. And the intensity of his own emotions had scared him. "Cass, let me ask you something. Why'd you come over? After all these weeks?"

She shrugged. "I missed watching these games with you, and Travis isn't much for Monday Night Football." She straightened up a countertop. "He isn't much for football at all."

She was avoiding his eyes. He picked up on that. But before he could press her further, she announced, "Game's back on!" and they retreated to the couch. Like she was pulling back from the edge, too.

The Pats had the win clearly in hand by the end of the third quarter. That's when Jake heard a knock at the door.

Jake looked at his watch. 10:30. "What is this, a party?" he joked.

"You expecting someone?" Cass asked. "Moose?"

Jake looked through the peephole, then quickly opened the door. Tam stood in the hallway. She had Caitlin in her arms. Justin was by her side, sleepily leaning his head against his mom.

"Tam! Here . . ." Jake took his little girl, who was wrapped in a blanket, from Tam. Caitlin's body was warm.

"Jake, I need you to take them," Tam said, stepping into the foyer. She looked at Cass, then quickly looked away.

"Hi, Daddy," Justin said in a sleepy voice.

"Sure, sure. Come on, Jus."

"I'm sleepy, Dad."

"Come on. Let's get you in bed."

"Here, Jake, let me help," Cass said.

Jake put his hand on his son's shoulder and walked the kids back to their bedroom, his head spinning with questions. Cass followed him. Together they tucked them into their beds, speaking in hushed tones, their hands moving sheets and blankets and comforters into position, exchanging glances full of questions.

Jake's mind raced. Why had Tam brought them

over? What was going on? When he and Cass got back to the foyer, Tam had gone out to her car and retrieved two suitcases that Jake guessed were filled with clothes.

"I'll bring the rest tomorrow," she said, and tears glinted in her eyes. "Here's Cloud." She handed Caitlin's special pillow to Jake. "She needs it to sleep."

"Why are you here, Tam? What happened?" Jake asked.

She shook her head. "Just take the kids."

Jake's heart pumped hard. "I'm happy to do that. When do you want them back?"

Tears streamed down her face. "I need you to take them permanently."

"Tam!" Jake began. He couldn't imagine Tam giving up the kids. Couldn't imagine it!

But then the light in the foyer caught what looked like a bruise on the side of her face, and he saw it, and their eyes locked. Tam ducked her head and turned to the door.

"Tam!" Jake said, reaching out and touching her elbow gently. "Tam . . ."

She pulled away. She touched her face with her hand, which was visibly shaking.

What could he do? What could he do for her? "Tam, stay here. Or go with Cass."

"Yes, come home with me," Cass offered.

"No, no. I can't." It was somewhere between a sob and a scream.

Jake quickly grabbed a spare key off a shelf unit near the door. "Tam, here," he pressed it into her hand. "Take this. You can bring their stuff anytime tomorrow. And if you ever need a place to stay, a place to get away, you're welcome here. You understand, Tam? No pressure. No strings. I'll sleep on the couch."

His ex-wife looked at him. She nodded quickly, and before he could say anything more, she left.

Jake stood in his foyer, his heart drumming. He turned toward Cass, who looked as shocked as he felt. "What am I supposed to do now?"

Chapter 16

"So how's Mr. Mom?" Moose jabbed him in the shoulder as he sat down in the chair next to Jake's desk.

Jake shook his head. "The last few days have been crazy."

"I'll tell you what's crazy: You're crazy, letting that broad dump the kids on you."

"No, man, it's not like that."

Moose dismissed him with a wave. "It's nuts. Look, here's the deal. I got Juan to agree to meet me. He's got some information for me and I want to show him some faces. I need backup. Can you do it?"

He'd already had to cancel a Tuesday night bar assignment. Couldn't leave the kids. "Sure. Where and when?"

"This afternoon, at three. At the picnic tables down off Palmer Place. The ones by the creek."

The kids' school got out at 3:15. "Make it two o'clock," Jake suggested.

"No can do. It's three. You in?"

"Yeah, sure. I'll be there."

Jake tapped his pen on the desk as Moose walked away. What was he supposed to do? Sighing, he picked up the phone. He'd have to call for a favor. Cass showed up as he was ending the call.

"Life's a little complicated, right?" she said, catching the gist of his conversation.

"I feel like going over there and throwing Chase Westfield up against the wall and telling him if he ever touches Tam again I'll rip his arms off," he said.

"Stay away from Chase, Jake. Confronting him will only mean trouble."

And she was right. Of course she was right. But as he drove to meet Moose, he kept thinking about alternatives. And one came to mind.

By pre-arrangement, Moose would meet Juan at the Palmer Place park, positioning their discussion at the picnic tables near the creek, down from the parking lot. In the middle of the week in December, there'd be no one there. Jake would stay in the parking lot, watching from a distance.

So when Jake came walking down the hill and sat down next to Juan, Moose's eyes flared in surprise. "Afternoon, gentlemen," Jake said. "How's it going?"

"Apparently, not according to plan," Moose said, sarcasm dripping in his voice.

"I had a couple of questions for Juan, here," Jake said. "First of all, is this the guy you know?" He gestured toward the pictures of Cesar

Cisneros spread out on the table. Some were surveillance shots; one was his DMV photo.

"Yeah, man. That's him. That's the guy that sold me that coke."

Jake nodded. "Good, good." He cocked his head. "Did you ever re-sell some? I mean, pass the favor on to someone else?"

Juan glanced quickly at Moose, unsure of what to do. Then he looked back at Jake. "I might have."

"You know this guy?" Jake pulled a DMV photo of Chase Westfield out of his pocket and placed it on the table in front of Juan.

Moose kicked Jake under the table.

Juan shifted in his seat. His hands twisted together. "I seen him." He looked at Jake. "He's somebody isn't he?"

"Where have you seen him?" A tremor ran through Jake and he realized he was sweating.

Juan dropped his head in his hands. Then he put his hands back on the table and leaned forward, his eyes intent on Jake. "Look, I bought a little from Cisneros. One day, he tells me he'll give me extra if I help him out. I deliver a package to a guy in a limo. It wasn't him, but his driver. He had a uniform on. Later, I see that same driver on the news." Juan pointed to the picture of Chase. "This is the guy who got out of the car he was driving."

After Juan left, Moose and Jake sat in Jake's car. "Hey, next time you're gonna pitch a changeup, signal the catcher, okay?" Moose said.

Jake grinned at him. "Sorry. It was kind of spontaneous."

"What were you doin', anyway, showing him that picture of Westfield?"

"I just got to thinking, Westfield's all hooked up with the casino. We think drugs are going down there. We saw Westfield there with the owner. And we know Westfield was a major player in getting approval for casinos in general, and that one in particular. What if he's benefitting from delivering on that?"

"And what if he's married to your ex-wife and you don't like him?"

"That's beside the point. What I'm saying is we could have more than a random shooting going on. We could have drugs and prostitution at the casino, and ultimately, political corruption."

Moose frowned. "Why you got to make things so complicated?"

Wednesday night. December 7. Cass slid into her good black stretch wool pants and a shimmery white top, then added a sweet little gray tweed knit jacket she'd found on sale at Nordstrom. She checked the mirror. Satisfied with what she saw, Cass zipped on her short black boots. When her doorbell rang, she was ready.

"You look great," Travis said.

Travis had arranged a surprise date. On the

way, he started telling her about some crazy stuff going on at the police station. She had to admit, she only half-listened. Her mind kept flipping back to her partner. Watching Jake juggling his kids and his job was painful. He'd missed connecting with a source, forgotten a meeting with the Assistant U.S. Attorney, and been so preoccupied even Craig had commented on it.

"And here we are!" Travis said.

Cass blinked. He'd parked at the exclusive, members-only Severn Yacht Club. The old white building, so elegant, sat right on the harbor. Beyond the building, she could see masts rising. "Very nice!"

"Take a good look around," Travis said as they went inside. "I had to pull strings to get us in."

What was he thinking? Cassie's stomach clenched.

Travis ordered wine, a nice Virginia white, and grilled oysters as an appetizer. "Do you know what you want?" he asked Cass.

What *did* she want? Cass avoided his eyes and looked instead at the server. "I'll have the seared scallops and shrimp."

"Excellent choice," the young man replied. "And you, sir?"

"Zarzuela," Travis said, handing the menu to the server. The Catalonian shellfish stew was a house speciality.

Apparently, small talk was on the menu as well.

Travis began telling Cass about life in Georgia, growing up as the son of the local judge. Cass listened and commented appropriately. She couldn't help silently comparing Travis's childhood with Jake's, whose hard-drinking autoworker father had made life miserable. Jake had overcome so much!

The entrees came, and Cass found herself asking Travis questions, urging him on in his life story. Somehow, it was more comfortable than sharing her own thoughts.

Afterwards, when they were finished with their meal, Travis retrieved her coat and said, "Let's take a walk on the docks."

The temperature was in the 40s, the night clear and still. The full moon hung in the eastern sky, the man in the moon a witness to Cassie's anxiety.

Travis engaged in small talk as they strolled, pointing out different boats and telling sailing stories. And then he stopped in front of a sloop with a dark blue hull. She recognized it as a Freedom 38, a classy cruiser much newer and larger than *Time Out*.

"Let's take a look at her. We have permission," Travis added to Cassie's raised eyebrows. "It belongs to someone I know." He stepped onto he boat, unlocked the companionway, and flipped on the salon lights.

Cass followed him down the ladder. "It's beautiful." The dark red cushions looked great against the perfect teak. A new stainless steel stove swung on its gimbal, next to the galley sink. Ports were clear and tight . . . there was no water damage around them. Someone had cared for this boat.

They looked at the head, the V-berth, the storage compartments, and then returned topside. Then Travis said, "Cass, do you know why I asked you out tonight?"

Her stomach tensed. She shook her head.

"We met a year and nine months ago tonight. March 7."

"Oh," she said, weakly. She hadn't been keeping track.

"Cass, I've been single for a long time. Nine years. And it's really been fine. But since I've gotten to know you, I find I'm less satisfied alone."

She got the feeling he was picking his way carefully across a minefield. A swirl of emotions began in her head, like a pinwheel shape of a hurricane chugging across a weather map.

"We have fun together. You're a terrific person. I miss you when we're apart. I love working with you, and I love sailing with you."

"Cass, I've put some money down to hold this boat. I may buy it." He dropped to one knee and pulled out a small box and opened it. Inside a ring glittered. "Would you marry me and allow me to give this boat to you as a wedding present?"

Chapter 17

Cass seemed to be acting oddly, Jake thought, the next time he saw her. He couldn't quite put his finger on it.

Nor did he really have time to think about it. Between work and the kids he was really busy. Really, really busy. *Mi vida loco*, he thought to himself. My crazy life. Trying to juggle the kids, do the laundry, and keep food in the refrigerator while still doing his job was killing him. Figuring out this case required him to be available at virtually all hours. He and Moose had to do surveillance, watching the gang members' houses, their hang-out places. And not just during school hours. Sometimes he had to work late into the night.

He'd spent two hours on the phone one night just trying to line up babysitters for a 9 p.m. to 1 a.m. assignment. Finally Beth, the young woman from church, had bailed him out. Still, Jake didn't want to leave the kids with sitters all the time. Justin was stressed, Caitlin was whiny. With all the upheaval in their lives, he didn't need to be abandoning them.

Moose had asked him why he didn't hire a full-time nanny. "This is only temporary," Jake explained. "Tam will want them back. About the time I have it all figured out, she'll say she's worked it out with Chase and I can bring the kids back."

"Women!" Moose had responded, cursing softly.

In fact, Tam did call him, but not about returning the kids permanently. She called on a Thursday and asked him if she could have the kids for the weekend. Chase was going out of town, and she wanted to take them shopping, and to the movies and then to her mother's. And although the notice was short, the plan was okay with Jake; the kids needed time with their mom. As long as they weren't around Chase.

So he agreed to meet her on Friday at a local playground. The kids loved the pirate ship and the rope ladders and multiple slides. It was clear Tam just wanted to pick them up and run, but reluctantly, she agreed to let them play. "Fifteen minutes," she said, and off they went.

Jake could tell Tam felt awkward, standing alone with him as the kids played. At four in the afternoon, the place was empty except for them. He squinted at his ex-wife in the bright sunshine and tried to keep his jaw relaxed, his voice low. "So how's it going, Tam? Now that the kids are gone?"

Tears immediately came to her eyes. She tried to brush them away, but more sprang up.

"Tell me about it."

She shook her head.

143

"Tam," Jake said, moving closer to her, "when you brought the kids over to me that night, and left them with me, it nearly broke my heart."

Tam kept her eyes glued to the kids on the play equipment.

"As much as I love having the kids, I knew that something terrible was happening, or you would never, ever have let them go," Jake continued. "Tell me, Tam. What's going on?"

Normally, Tam would have brushed him off, irritated at the personal question. She would have told him it was none of his business. Tossed her head and stalked off. For some reason, this time she didn't. "He means well," she said, her voice tight. "I honestly think he means well." She looked at Jake and he could see the sorrow turning her eyes liquid. "He can be the most wonderful, kind, generous, romantic person. He sent me flowers, just the other day, because it was the third anniversary of when we met. He always seems proud of me in public. He says he loves me. But . . ." she hesitated.

"But there's another side to him," Jake suggested.

Tam nodded and looked down quickly. A tear fell on her coat.

Beyond her, Jake could see the kids happily playing, climbing up the slides, jumping on the pirate ship plank. "Tam," he said, "does Chase use drugs?"

She glanced at him sharply, as if to challenge that question, but when their eyes met, she quickly looked away. "He's under so much pressure, from his job. And it just gets to him. He can't help himself. I think once in a while, he uses something to relax. And sometimes, I just make him mad."

"And he's hit you." It was a statement, not a question.

Tam took a deep breath. Tears began running down her cheeks.

"Talk to me."

"The first time it happened, I was shocked. I mean I never, ever expected it. He just got angry. It had been a bad day. I said something and he slapped me."

"Once? Twice?"

"Just once. Afterwards, he was so sorry. He couldn't figure out what had gotten into him. He apologized and the next day, he sent me candy and an expensive necklace. Of course," Tam continued, her voice hoarse, "I forgave him. After that, it began happening more often. It was the stress, the stress from his job. I'm sure of that. And you. He doesn't like you. Then there were the kids. He just found me an easy target. It was like, whatever was inside only came out by hitting me." Tam began to cry softly, ducking her head and using a napkin to catch her tears. "What is wrong with me?" she sobbed. "Why can't I have a decent marriage?"

"Tam, don't blame yourself. This is not your fault!"

"I make him mad. I don't mean to. But sometimes, it just happens. You know, I can feel the tension building in him. I try to please him. But it doesn't work. It never works. Eventually, he just loses it. Oh, gosh! Why do I feel so crazy?"

Jake felt his anger building, but he knew he had to work to keep his feelings off his face and out of his voice, or he'd scare her off. "Tam, people like this, abusive people, they don't stop being abusive on their own. They need counseling. He's going to keep hurting you, Tam. I think you need to protect yourself. I think you need to get out of there."

More sobs. "I can't! I can't do that!"

"Why, Tam? Why not?"

"Where would I go? What would I do?" Tam's blonde hair half-covered her face. Her eyes were red and puffy, her cheeks blotchy.

"You could go back to teaching. And your parents would help you."

"But I can't imagine . . . two divorces? Two? I can't fail at this again!"

Jake swallowed. How should he respond to that? "I'm not talking about divorce, Tam. Just separating for a while, until he can deal with his anger. Just to keep yourself safe."

"I'm so afraid!"

"Of Chase?"

"Of being alone," she whispered.

Right after their divorce she had lived with a guy for a while. Then less than a month after she kicked that guy out, she met Chase. He took a deep breath. "Tam, you don't deserve to be treated badly. You should be honored and loved. You're a wonderful person. The kids love you. Whatever Chase's problems are, he needs to work those out. He shouldn't be taking his anger out on you. It's not right, Tam. But the only way it will stop, is if you make it stop by walking away."

That brought more sobs.

"Just until Chase gets help."

Tam had soaked the tissue she was holding. Jake reached into his pocket and handed her his clean handkerchief. "Look at it this way, Tam: Do you think what he's doing is right? No, it's not. So you'd be helping him to stop doing this wrong thing if you put an end to it."

Tam nodded. "I know, on some level, you're right, Jake." She took a deep breath. "It's time."

The fifteen minutes was up. Jake called the kids. "I want you to know, Tam," he said, "that I pray for you. Every day. I pray for you, and the kids, and Cassie, and some of my other friends. And if you need to, you can come stay at my place. With the kids. I'll move out."

Hope formed in her eyes. "You would do that?"

"In a heartbeat."

"So she admitted he's hitting her. That's great, Jake. I can't believe she told you that. She's opening up." Cassie and Jake were walking through Heritage Mall on Friday night. She was helping him buy clothes for the kids for Christmas.

"She even described the abusive cycle," Jake said. "I'm amazed that she opened up, but she did."

Cass nodded. "That's the first step. Recognizing the abuse."

"She is so thin!" Jake shook his head. "She looks haunted."

"What do you mean?" Cass looked over at him.

Jake shifted his packages to his left hand. "Satan's aim is to destroy every child of God. He hates God that much. He either tries to channel you into sin, or get other people to sin against you. When that happens, and sin gets hold of you, I think you get that haunted look. Tam has it."

Cass looked at him oddly, with tears in her eyes.

"What? What'd I say?" he asked.

She shook her head and didn't respond.

Jake puzzled about that. "One good thing—I talked her into going to the kids' play."

"You did! Amazing!"

"Turns out Chase is out of town that weekend."

148

Jake turned a corner and glanced at Cass. "She needs Jesus, Cass. We all do. She just doesn't know it. Like I didn't know it for so long."

They finished their shopping. He teased her about buying something for Maria, but reddened when she caught him buying Manny a new Ravens jersey. For once, Jake found shopping fun. Then he drove her home.

Jake pulled up in front of her apartment, but Cass hesitated getting out of the car. She was beautiful in a girl-next-door kind of way, dressed in a burgundy turtleneck sweater and jeans, her face lit from the side by a streetlight nearby. She had her hand on the door handle but something was holding her back.

"Thanks for helping me today," Jake said. Outside, night had fallen, its chill dropping like a curtain.

"Sure!" she responded.

"Let me ask you something," he said, softly. "Why'd you tear up when I was talking about Satan and sin and all that?"

She looked away quickly and dropped her head, then looked back at him, her eyes soft. "Because you sounded so much like Mike."

Jake felt a rush of emotion. "Whew. That's quite a compliment."

"You've changed, Jake, so much." Cass looked down again, her hands now folded in her lap. "I need to tell you something."

She lifted her head and her eyes met his. What was he reading in them? "What's that?"

He had to wait for her response.

"Wednesday night," she said finally, "Travis asked me to marry him." Her eyelids trembled.

A tremor passed through him. He cleared his throat. "That's great, Cass. So, did you say 'yes'?"

Her eyes searched his face, as if looking for his real opinion, and he fervently hoped she wouldn't find it. Cass. Married. Settled. It would be good for her. But he was losing her! Losing Cass. Nausea swept over him, like he had just taken a major gulp of seawater.

"I told him I'd give him an answer soon," she replied. "I think I'm going to talk to Trudy first. And Dad."

"Good idea," Jake agreed. "That's smart."

She nodded. Cass gathered up her things. "Goodbye, Jake."

"Yeah, thanks again!" His throat was so tight he had to cough the words out. "See you Monday."

She walked up the steps of her apartment, and he waved to her as she reached the door. Then he backed slowly out of the parking space. Cass. Married. What would he do without his partner? He said out loud, "I think it's time to get out of Dodge."

Chapter 18

Jake tossed and turned, flipped his pillow, and finally sat up. Why this? Why now? The clock read 1:35. For two hours he'd tried to sleep, but Cassie's words kept flashing like a lighted billboard in his mind. Travis had asked her to marry him. Marry him!

Should he have spoken up? Was she really in love with Travis?

Irritated, he got up. He picked up a book and tried to read, clicked on ESPN and tried to watch a basketball game, and then threw a sofa pillow across the room in frustration. Finally, he made coffee, got dressed, and headed for the office. The kids were at Tam's. He could do what he wanted. What he wanted was to get his mind off Cass. And the only way he could think to do that was focus on his other obsession.

The normally busy FBI building was shrouded in silence, dimly lit and sleepy at 2:30 in the morning. Jake spoke briefly with the security guard as he entered, then took the elevator to the sixth floor bullpen where he kept his desk. He waved to the on-duty agent across the room, and booted up his computer.

Was Chase in on the cocaine being delivered to the casinos? Was he getting any kind of kickback from advocating for the casinos in the legislature? What could he, Jake, learn about casinos and public corruption?

Politicians seeking to lure the big money gaming venues to their state often touted the jobs and tax revenues to be had by allowing casinos. Chasing gambling money had become a shell game, pitting one state against the other.

Chase had advocated strongly for the casinos, but even if casinos were bad, advocating for them wasn't criminal, unless a politician took a kickback from a casino owner for influencing who got the license or was paid for his vote, somehow.

To prove any of that, Jake would have to get access to Chase's finances, personal and political. And he had absolutely no legitimate grounds for doing that. But some of the information, political contributions for example, was public.

For the next three hours, Jake pursued every avenue of investigation he felt he could ethically pursue. At 5:45 in the morning, his stomach complained loudly that it had been empty for far too long. Jake left the building and drove to a nearby IHOP, where he ordered a large breakfast and mulled over what he'd learned, making notes on a small pad he always kept with him. There, between a bite of eggs over easy and pancakes, he had a sudden thought. The Fourth Man. Who was the Fourth Man Jake had seen with Chase and Garza and owner Sam Fico at the casino? Could he be a link?

Fortified, he went back to his office. He resumed work on his computer, searching online news images about the casino for the identity of the Fourth Man. That soon proved frustrating. Then he had another idea. He shut down everything, waved to the on-duty agent, and left the building. Twenty minutes later, he walked into the Lucky Leaf Casino.

Inside the casino, it was not 7:20 on a Saturday morning, it was Whenever. The lights, the noise, the atmosphere remained relentlessly stimulating. Jake nodded to the security guard when he walked in, refused a mixed drink offered by a server in a skimpy dress, and sat down in front of a slot machine.

Unlike the old one-armed bandits, the computerized slot machines were programmed, he'd learned, so that the house always won. The payouts were carefully calculated.

But tell that to the poor souls clunking coin after coin into the machines. Jake's plan was to play for a little while, and then see what he could learn. Pictures of the casino's grand opening hung on some of the walls. Maybe he'd see the Fourth Man in some of them. Or maybe he could spot him in person.

Twenty minutes later he got up from the machine. He walked over to the bar and ordered coffee. He strolled around, casually looking at pictures on the wall. He chatted with a few people, observed several more. On the way back to the men's room, he finally spotted what he wanted: On the wall hung a newspaper story about the casino, with a picture of the casino owner, Sam Fico. Next to him stood the Fourth Man. His name was in the caption: Frank D'Angelo.

Jake looked around. He was alone. He pulled out his cell phone. He filled the frame with the picture, being careful to include the caption. He snapped one shot without flash, and then took another, from forty-five degrees, with flash. As the flash fired, a man walked out of the men's room.

Their eyes met. His were bright blue. It was the man from his church. Jake shoved his cell phone into his pocket and walked right past him.

Jake left the casino a short time later. Now he had the name of the Fourth Man. But would it lead anywhere?

He drove back to the office and began researching again. Frank D'Angelo was a builder, a developer from New Jersey. But what was he doing in Maryland? Had he been part of the casino project?

At first, he couldn't find it, but Jake kept digging, and two hours later, his digging paid off. That's why he didn't hear Cassie until she was right next to his desk.

"Is this how you spend your time when your

kids are gone?" she asked, smiling. "At the office?"

Jake felt blood rush to his face. "What are you doing here?"

"I forgot something, a book I wanted to show Travis." Cass sat down. She tilted her head. "So, what are you working on?"

He shrugged. "I just had some thoughts about the case and I wanted to pursue them."

She didn't let him get away with it. "Danny's case? Something about the drug dealers?" Cass grinned. "C'mon, Tucker, spill it. What are you up to?"

"Look, I just got curious about some stuff, all right?"

"So tell me."

He did. The whole story. His investigation into casino corruption, his early morning visit to the casino, finding the Fourth Man, and yes, even seeing the man from his church outside the restroom. And then, just now, discovering an investigation in Atlantic City into a subsidiary of D'Angelo's company called Shady Creek Foundations. The concrete company had been fined and the CEO, D'Angelo's wife, held criminally liable for contract violations, including shoddy construction, which had caused a partial collapse in a parking garage in Atlantic City. With this background, why was D'Angelo involved in casino construction in Maryland?

"So this guy, who you also think may have

155

mob connections, sets up his wife as CEO of a subsidiary. Then she takes the fall when a building collapses?" Cass asked. "And now the guy gets contracts in Maryland?"

"That's the way I see it."

"And how is this connected to the assault on Danny?" Cassie asked.

Jake hesitated.

"The appropriate answer is, 'It isn't.' " She shook her head. "Jake, you're going after Chase Westfield and you know it."

"Who is going after Westfield?" Craig Campbell walked up behind them.

"Why is everybody here? It's Saturday!" Jake exclaimed. "Look, I'm not going after Westfield. It's just that, well, I think there's something shady going on and he's part of it. We think the gangbangers who shot Danny are small-time drug dealers. We think these guys are delivering drugs to the casino. Looking into that has made me realize there's a lot more going on."

"Like what?"

"We've seen Westfield there and he was crucial to getting the casino approved to begin with. So is he involved in the drugs? In something else? Is there corruption associated with the casino? Did he profit personally from its approval?" Jake gestured. "Now there's this: A guy with possible mob connections is a casino contractor. How'd that happen?"

Craig listened. He frowned. He raised his eyebrows. He crossed his arms. And then he spoke. "I think you're chasing rabbits."

Jake exhaled. "No, I'm not." He felt his heart begin to pound. "There's something with the casino. Maybe it's just drugs, or maybe it's more. Why did Cisneros make an unscheduled stop to deliver what looked like a box of fish to the loading dock? The casino wasn't on his route list. Moose asked the company later. The casino doesn't have an account with them. And why did the guard at the door accept a package from a gangbanger? What's the connection between the politicians and all of this?"

"And you have what proof that Westfield or any other politician is involved?"

Jake's face flushed. "Nothing yet. I'm just getting started."

Craig shook his head. "Look, Jake, this is way too personal. Even if you're right, you can't investigate that. You're too close to the guy! No jury would buy your objectivity. Because the truth is, it is personal with you!"

"So we're going to let this guy get away with this stuff?" Jake stood up.

So did Cass. "Jake, wait . . ."

"No!" He lowered his voice, but every word came out like a bullet. "Chase Westfield is a dirty politician. Are we going to let him get away with corruption?"

Craig Campbell stood toe-to-toe with Jake. "You cannot pursue this line of investigation. That's an order. You think you have something on it, refer it to the public corruption squad. Let them take it." He warned Jake with his forefinger. "You solve the assault on Danny. You got nothing on that, then work your other cases. I don't want you near the casino. Or Chase Westfield. You got that, Jake?"

Chapter 19

Jake drove blindly away from the office. Furious. He'd never been so angry with Craig. And Cass had seemed to agree with him!

He had to get his mind off of it. He drove to the gym trying to relax, trying to let go of the frustration that gripped him like a glove. He couldn't even pray.

Jake changed his clothes and worked out for an hour, the weights pulling both sweat and anger from his body. Then he ran on the treadmill. While he was showering, a thought occurred to him: Go back to Ninth Street. Go back to the place where Danny had been shot.

Why? He had no idea. But he drove to Ninth Street and parked half a block down from where he'd found Danny. Then he just sat and tried to re-imagine the scene from that night.

And then he saw it.

Jake got out of his car and walked to where red spray paint on the asphalt marked the place where Danny had parked his car. Just in front of that spot was a storm drain. Jake thought, if Danny had been crouched down, looking under his car, someone might have thought he was looking in the drain.

Jake glanced around. He didn't see anyone. He

pulled the flashlight out of his pocket and got down on the ground, and shined it in the drain. There it was: a remnant of tape. Someone had taped something in the drain. When they'd retrieved it, some tape was left behind.

Thank you, God, Jake thought. He stood up and brushed himself off. He went back to his car and called the on-duty evidence response team. No way was he collecting that tape himself. Not with Craig on his case.

So, he thought as he waited for ERT, if someone was using the drain as a drug drop, and they saw Danny crouched down near it, they might have thought he was stealing the drugs. That would make shooting him logical.

Jake saw some guys walking into the cemetery. They began hanging out near where he and Manny had looked in the crypt. He wondered who they were and what they were doing there. He could see four men, sitting on tombstones, talking and smoking.

One guy weighed three hundred pounds, easily. A short man, he looked like a fire plug. Even from fifty yards away, Jake could tell he dominated the conversation, gesturing with his hands, playfully shoving another guy, all the while smoking a big, fat cigar.

Jake made note of their descriptions as best he could—he was too far away for a photo. Besides the fireplug, the others were of average height, average build. One had a limp when he walked. One's neck looked like it was covered in tattoos. Otherwise, he couldn't see anything remarkable.

Maybe one or more of the five cars parked along the street belonged to them. Jake glanced in his outside mirror. No ERT in sight. He had time.

He called ERT first and told them about the guys hanging out in the cemetery. "Better have some backup," he told the techs.

Then Jake got out of his car and walked down the sidewalk next to the cemetery. Holding his cell phone like he was texting, Jake made a note of the make and color of the cars parked there, and their tag numbers. As he passed the area where the guys were hanging out, he put his phone in his pocket and himself on high alert.

But they didn't seem to notice him. He crossed the street, ducked down a side street and circled back to his car.

By the time he got back to Ninth Street, ERT was there, along with a surveillance team, and the gangbangers were gone.

Ninety minutes later, ERT had collected the tape fragment and done another sweep of the area. They even opened the manhole cover and crawled down in the sewer. But the techs found nothing else, and they left.

Jake checked his watch: 5:30. He'd been awake for nearly thirty-six hours. But he had one more job to do: Drop off Manny's Christmas present. He'd seen the boy wearing a Ravens jersey bearing the number of a player later arrested for domestic assault. He'd bought him a replacement.

Manny wasn't home but his mother accepted the package for him, thanking him in her broken English and placing it under the small, artificial Christmas tree near the couch where Manny slept. She had her graying hair pulled back in a bun, and had a worn housecoat pulled around her. On her feet were ragged pink slippers. The right one had a hole in the big toe.

Jake started to leave. Then he stopped, reached into his pocket and pulled out a wad of twenty-dollar bills, money he'd intended to use to buy himself new running shoes. He pressed the cash into the Latina's hand. "Merry Christmas—may God bless you."

Tears filled her eyes.

Jake slept. Finally. And Tam managed to get the kids back to Jake in time for Sunday's three o'clock rehearsal, which was a good thing, because it was a dress rehearsal. Beth, the woman he'd considered asking out, was working on the play and had helped Jake with the kids' costumes, which was also a good thing, because he didn't know one end of a needle from the other.

They looked cute, though, and watching the

rehearsal, Jake almost forgot his fight with Craig and the frustration that had saturated his soul like black ink filling a blotter.

On Monday morning, though, it all came back.

Moose showed up about then. "What's up?"

Jake took a deep breath. "Hey, I was up where Danny got shot on Saturday. Guess what? I found some tape in a storm drain."

"Tape?"

"Like someone had taped a package there. I don't know if ERT missed it the first time or if it was left after Danny was shot."

Moose nodded. "That's progress."

"And I saw some guys hanging out in the cemetery. Want to help me track them down?"

"Sure! What are we doing about the casino?"

"Nothing," Jake said. Moose raised his eyebrows. "I can't go near it."

"What if we find proof there's drugs going in there. I thought that's where we were headed."

Jake wrote down some tag numbers on a piece of paper. "Yeah, well, things change. Check these out, will you?"

"You got it."

After Moose left, Jake walked over to the window overlooking the traffic on the Baltimore Beltway. The remnants of rush hour had things all jammed up. Sort of the way he was feeling. Then he sensed someone's presence and smelled a familiar perfume. Cass.

"Hey," she said, moving close enough that her sleeve brushed his. "What's going on?"

Jake hesitated, still stung by Saturday.

"Are you mad at me?"

Outside, a horn blared. He could hear it all the way up on the sixth floor. "Honestly? A little. Yes." He turned toward her and when he did, he felt his anger melt.

"I'm sorry, Jake. I just agree with Craig. For your sake, you know? And the sake of your case. If Chase is guilty, you don't want him getting off because his defense attorney frames the case as a personal vendetta."

"I know." He took a deep breath. "I'm just frustrated."

"I get that." She nodded her head. "Things will get better soon. Are we all set for the play on Saturday?"

"Yes, absolutely."

"Tam's still coming?"

"So far."

Later that week, Jake got the report back from the lab on the tape found in the sewer. Investigators analyzed the silver "polycoated cloth tape," duct tape, and identified the chemical components in its backing and adhesive, paying particular attention to the elastomer to which sticky resins and other materials were added. They cataloged the tape's exact color, thickness, width, and reinforcement construction, in particular the warp yarn offset from the machine edge. And they estimated the tape had been affixed for approxi-mately four weeks, based on dryness and other degradation. Which means it had been there when Danny was shot. Why hadn't the first ERT found it?

Still, most of the information in the report would be useful only by comparison to another sample of tape. So Jake needed to find drugs packaged with tape from the same roll. Then he'd be closer to identifying the person who shot Danny.

He couldn't help but think, wouldn't it be great if a package delivered to the casino used that tape? Or a package found at Chase's house?

On Saturday, the night of the play, the stars seemed unusually bright to Jake, the sky itself unusually dark. The kids had to be at the church at six, the play was at seven-thirty. Cass had taken the kids so Jake could pick up Tam. Her car was in the shop and she'd asked for a lift and that was fine with him. He wanted the time to talk to her, to encourage her. Tam needed to get strong enough to confront her husband, to stand up to him. He was praying for that.

Tam slipped into his car like a teenager sneaking out on a date. "You okay?" he asked her.

"Let's just get away from here."

"He's gone, right?"

"Yes. He's in Connecticut, at a fundraiser." Tam crossed her arms. "It's the only time I feel peace, now, when he's gone." She looked over at Jake. "How are the kids?"

"They will be so excited when they see you," Jake said. "It's a surprise."

He walked her into his church, wondering if anyone would recognize her as the senator's wife, and if that would come back to haunt them. But it was a big church and he'd just have to take that chance.

Cass had saved them seats up front. She'd invited Travis but he'd declined, and Jake was frankly happy about that.

The play was everything a children's Christmas play should be: Sweet, charming. Wonder, innocence, and transcendent mystery merging in a captivating drama. There were angels with aluminum-foil halos and shepherds who couldn't keep their crooks to themselves. One of the Wise Men tripped on his robe and the sheep kept waving to their moms. The children's sweet voices filled the room with song.

Justin, a shepherd, read part of the Christmas story from Luke, and Caitlin was an angel. Out of the corner of his eye, Jake saw Tam staring at the stage, transfixed, tears in her eyes. She'd been raised in a church, but they'd never gone once they were married. Probably because of him, he thought now. How he wished he could do those years over!

When the final curtain fell, Justin took no time at all to race into the audience. "Mom!" His face was shining.

Caitlin was right behind him. "Mommy, Mommy!"

Jake caught Cassie's eye. She winked at him. "Good job," she mouthed silently.

And then, beyond her, Jake saw something that made his heart stop: A man with bright blue eyes wearing a dark overcoat was staring at them.

It was the man he'd seen at the casino, coming out of the men's room when he took the picture of the newspaper article about D'Angelo. Was he connected with the casino? With Chase?

Jake's throat closed. He redirected his attention to the kids. "All right, let's get out of here, guys! How about some ice cream?"

"Yay!"

Jake hustled them all out of the church and they drove in two cars to a restaurant where they got ice cream. And Jake forced the man in the topcoat out of his mind.

After ice cream, Cass followed him back to his apartment. She'd volunteered to help the kids get ready for bed while he took Tam back home. He wanted time alone with Tam, to gauge her reaction, and Cass had picked up on that. What a friend.

Tam looked over at Jake in the darkened car during the short drive to her house. "Thank you,

Jake. Seeing the kids up there, I don't know, it just brought me back."

Jake smiled. "I'm glad, Tam. I really am."

"I know I need to make a change. Thank you for helping me see that."

"Take care of yourself, Tam," he said, and she got out of the car and walked up her front walk.

Jake had just returned to his apartment when his cell phone rang. He automatically checked his watch. It was 9:26. He picked up the phone.

"Jake," Tam said, "I did something stupid. I left my cell phone in your car. It's in the back seat, where Justin was playing with it."

Across the room, Cass was just putting on her jacket to leave. Jake caught her with his eye. "Okay. No problem. Can I bring it to you tomorrow?"

Panic edged Tam's voice. "If Chase calls me and I don't answer, he'll be suspicious. I need it tonight, Jake."

"Okay, okay. Hang on." Jake put his hand over the phone. Cass was looking at him expectantly. "Can you stay for another twenty minutes or so?"

"Sure," she said.

"Okay, Tam," Jake said into the phone. "It's no problem. Cass will stay with the kids. I'll bring the phone over." He hung up the phone and grabbed his jacket and turned to Cass. "She forgot her cell phone. I'll be back in twenty."

"Got it."

Chapter 20

Jake sped through the night, Tam's cell phone in his pocket. When he got to Tam's house he parked and ran up the front stairs two at a time. The house was dark. That surprised him. He rang the bell. No answer. He rang it again. What was up? Tam was expecting him. Why wasn't she answering the door? He rang the bell a third time. Still no response. He looked through the wavy glass next to the door. And then his heart jumped in his chest.

"Tam!" he yelled. He tried the door. It was locked. He put a shoulder to it. It didn't budge. Then he spied a stone planter, an urn-shaped vase on the step, and he picked it up and smashed in the window nearest the doorknob. Reaching through the broken glass he fumbled with the locks until he'd freed them, and the door swung open, and he raced in.

Tam lay on the floor in a pool of blood.

"Tam! Tam!" he said, his heart pounding. He touched her neck and it was still warm, there was still a pulse. But her head! Someone had bashed in her head.

Tam moaned. Jake grabbed his cell phone and dialed 911. "I'm an armed FBI agent. I need an ambulance with advanced life support and police." He gave the address, and then he put the phone down and bent over his ex-wife.

Her face was bloody and misshapen, her blond hair red and sticky. Her skull was crushed in on the right side and her blouse was ripped. And as he looked at her, the whole world seemed to withdraw. He felt like he was in a tunnel. "Oh, God!" he cried. Jake took her hand in his. "Tam, I'm here. The medics are coming. I'm here, Tam." He spoke calmly, but all the while he felt like his hearing was off and his vision impaired.

Tam gasped and reached up and tried to grab his neck. Her fingernails cut into his flesh. He took her hand and tried to comfort her. "They're coming. Hold on, Tam," he said. His heart raced. "God help her!" He was barely aware of the sirens screaming on the street outside, of cold air pouring in through the open front door, of vehicle doors slamming and the clank and creak of equipment as the medics arrived.

As he focused on Tam, her eyes fluttered open and her lips moved. "Jake, Jake . . ."

"They're here, Tam, they're here." He heard a choking sound as she tried to speak and he bent closer to her.

"Jake . . ."

"Sir, we'll take over."

Gently, Jake let go of her hand, stood, and took a step back. His hands were wet with her blood and there were splotches of red on his clothes and he realized he was shaking all over. He took a deep breath.

"You the agent?" a male voice said.

Jake turned toward the cop standing next to him. "Yes, sir." Flashing red and blue lights reflected into the foyer.

"Anyone else in the house?"

"I don't know."

"Bobby, check it," the first cop said to his partner. "You have your creds?"

"Yes," Jake said, "in my pocket." He reached for his credentials and handed them to the cop.

"Did you call this in?"

Jake turned. Another man, a detective dressed in a suit and a topcoat, flashed a badge at him. "Yes, sir. Jake Tucker, FBI Baltimore."

The first cop handed Jake's creds to the detective. "I'm Detective Bruce Kilgore. I'd like to ask you a few questions."

The detective took his arm and they moved further into the house. Jake's eyes remained fixed on Tam. The medics were working hard on her, taking vital signs while they strapped her to a board and stabilized her head. A uniformed officer snapped pictures.

Detective Kilgore captured Jake's attention. "Why were you here?"

"She was with us tonight, me and the kids and a friend of ours." Jake told the story, once, twice, maybe three times, and it was like he was in a dream. Everything was surreal: the medics, the smell of the blood, the cops, and Tam, lying on the floor, Tam who'd been so alive, so animated just a few minutes ago, Tam who'd been waiting for him.

"What's your relationship with her?"

"I'm her ex." Then Jake remembered Cass. "I need to make a call," he said to the detective, "to a friend who's with my kids."

"Make it quick." He stayed right next to Jake.

He called Cass and said there'd been a problem and he'd be home as soon as he could. While he was talking to her he saw two other plain-clothes cops arrive, and they looked around at the scene, frowning.

Cass assured him it was no problem for her to stay. "What's going on?" she asked.

"I'll explain later," he answered with a tremor in his voice. Chase did this, he thought. Chase had to be the one. Jake turned to Detective Kilgore. "Her husband . . . there's a history of abuse," he said, and Kilgore looked at him oddly. "The senator . . ."

"Senator Westfield?"

Jake nodded. "He was abusing her." His voice trailed off, as suddenly, the action around Tam seemed to shift into slow motion. He saw them lift Tam on the backboard onto a gurney, strap it in, and raise the gurney to its normal height. He saw them moving Tam out the front door, down the sidewalk and into the ambulance. And in his mind, Jake was urging them on. Help her. Help her. Please, don't stop. Please!

The detective's voice droned on. He was asking Jake questions and his questions seemed repetitive and Jake was losing track of what he was saying. What? Why was I here? I was here because . . .

He couldn't take his eyes off Tam. "Where are they taking her?" he asked.

Detective Kilgore frowned.

Through the open front door Jake could see the doors of the ambulance slam shut. His eyes widened. His heart jolted. Then there was a ringing in his head and the sound of a train bearing down on him and then his throat closed up. Get a grip, he told himself. He took a deep breath, and shuddered.

"Are you all right?" Kilgore asked.

Jake stared at him blankly.

"You're bleeding."

He looked down. Blood from a cut on his arm was running down his hand and dripping onto the floor. His head spun. He closed his eyes.

"Medic!" Kilgore called out to a crew member from a second ambulance "Can you see to him?" he asked nodding toward Jake.

"Here sir, let me see that," the paramedic said, snapping on a fresh pair of gloves.

A cop with a digital camera walked over, and

when Kilgore nodded, he began shooting pictures of Jake. "Raise your head a little bit, sir," he said and when Jake did, the camera flashed.

The medic bandaged the four-inch wound. "There you go, sir. I'd recommend a tetanus shot."

But Jake didn't hear the rest. His mind went back to the early days, when he and Tam dated, to their marriage, to a trip to the beach, to Justin's birth, and Caitlin's, and then to the arguments that began to devour their love. "I'm sorry, I'm sorry," he mumbled under his breath.

"Agent Tucker?"

Jake snapped back to the present. Detective Kilgore was saying something. Another person, an evidence tech asked to see his hands. "Sure," he said and he held them out and the tech swabbed blood samples and took fingernail scrapings and it was bizarre, so bizarre!

"We are going to need those clothes."

Jake looked down. His tactical pants, his jacket, his sweater, even his gun pouch were blood-stained. It was all evidence now. "I live ten minutes away."

"All right. I'll send someone with you."

Once more he gave Kilgore contact information, once more he urged him to question Chase, once more, in his head, he saw Tam's bloody body. Oh, God, how did this happen? He shivered.

• • •

How long was the drive back to his apartment? In real time, ten minutes. Tonight, however, was anything but real. Heaviness weighed him down as if his flesh were iron. His heart felt like lead. One of the cops had volunteered to drive his car, and he had agreed and was sitting in the passenger seat. The other cop was following in a patrol car.

They parked and he sat, trying to gather the strength to push open the door, walk to the building, go upstairs. He glanced at his watch. Nearly eleven.

"Sir? This is the right building?"

"Yeah," Jake responded.

And then the cop's radio triggered. "Eight thirty-one. She's DOA."

Jake didn't hear any more. DOA. Dead on arrival. He looked at the cop. "That was her, wasn't it?" The cop didn't respond, but Jake knew. Tam was dead. Dead!

Somehow he got up the stairs and let himself into the apartment. Cass was curled up on the couch, but she sat up when she heard him. "Jake? What's going on?" she said. "You're covered in blood!"

He opened his mouth to respond but nothing came out.

"Sir? Are your clothes in your bedroom?" the cop said.

Jake nodded. He started to move, then turned to the cops. "The kids are asleep," he said softly. "We need to be quiet."

He and one cop went back to his bedroom, and the officer watched while Jake took off his bloody clothes. The cop collected them, and put them in evidence bags.

"If that's all you need from me, I'm going to shower," Jake said.

"Yes, sir. We'll be leaving then. Detective Kilgore will be in touch."

When he emerged fifteen minutes later, dressed in sweats and drying his hair, both cops were gone. Cass sat on his couch waiting, for him. She rose. Concern filled her face. She touched his arm. "Jake, what happened?"

Jake opened his mouth. His throat closed up.

"Tell me what happened."

The tone of her voice told him she already knew. She'd been talking to the second cop.

He said, "She was so happy. She seemed so open, you know?"

"I know, Jake."

"When I got there, she didn't answer the door, and so I looked, and," his voice broke, "she was in there, on the floor." He looked away, seeing it again in his head. "I broke the window, and opened the door," he said, his voice sounding strange even to him, "and there was blood everywhere, blood all over. She died, Cass. She

176

didn't make it!" he said, and sobs shook his body.

Cass put her arms around him. "Oh, Jake," she whispered, "I'm so sorry."

He pulled her to his chest, desperate for the closeness.

"I'm so sorry," she said, a sob catching in her throat.

They stood holding each other, shrouded in a fog of grief, and he knew he needed her at that time more than he'd ever needed anyone in his life. Cassie, Cass. She was the only thing holding him in this world. He needed her, needed her touch. "He killed her, Cass!"

She pulled back a little. Her eyes ranged over his face. She stroked his cheek with her thumb, tenderly wiping his tears away. And her hand felt warm, comforting. "Oh, God!" he whispered, "She's dead! Dead!" and he closed his eyes.

She slid her hand around behind his head, pulled him toward her, and kissed him on his cheek, a tender kiss of affection and care. "I'm so sorry," she whispered.

His heart stirred. He turned his head and his lips found hers, and he felt thankful that she didn't turn away. Her lips were warm and responsive and he could taste the salt of his tears and the salt of her tears as they mingled together. The smell of her perfume filled his nose. *Oh, Cass!*

They parted. She led him to the couch. "Sit

down," she said and then she snuggled up next to him, leaning against his chest, her head on his shoulder.

He held on to her like an anchor. "I can't even pray," he said hoarsely.

"I'll pray for you," she responded, and she did, through tears and sobs.

He drew her close and they spent the rest of the night there, on the couch, holding each other. He was so grateful she didn't make him talk, so thankful he could just feel. And the world kept turning and dawn began to break.

Tam was dead. Dead. How was he ever going to tell his kids?

Chapter 21

Jake sat up with a jolt when he heard Caitlin's feet hit the floor. Cassie jumped to her feet, and smoothed her clothes. The two adults looked at each other, shocked by the change in their world, shocked that they were together, dreading the conversations that would follow.

"Daddy!" Caitlin cried as she ran out into the living room. She had on a pink-and-white nightgown and her blonde hair was tousled.

Jake swept her into his arms. "Hey, Punkin." When he looked over her shoulder at Cass, he had tears in his eyes.

Caitlin squirmed to get down. She ran to Cassie and hugged her legs. "Cassie, did you come to play with us?"

Cass glanced at Jake. She squatted down and hugged the little girl. "Yes, honey."

By the time Justin was up, Cassie had bacon and eggs and pancakes cooking. Jake worked alongside her in silence, making coffee and pouring juice. Confusion muddled his thinking. Images played over and over in his mind. His feelings were all over the place: anger, sadness, grief, fury, sorrow . . . and guilt. A sharp sense of guilt.

The kids were in the living room. "Cass," he said.

She turned to him. She had braided her hair and she looked fresh and beautiful to him, like a rose blooming in winter, and he wanted to kiss her again. "Thank you for being here with me. Thank you for staying," he said softly.

"I didn't want you to be alone, Jake. We've been friends for too long."

"Travis . . ."

"Don't worry about it."

He nodded and started to respond but then the kids came back and they sat down to eat breakfast. And Jake couldn't eat. He just pushed the food around on his plate and drank coffee. After the meal was done and the dishes put away, Justin asked if they could watch TV, and Jake said no, there was something he had to tell them, and then carefully, as if walking on ice on a half-frozen lake, he told them about Tam.

His heart seemed to stop as the word came out. As the information sank in he saw a dark cloud cover Justin's face and a scowl appear. Caitlin frowned and asked some questions. Where was she hurt? Who hurt her? Could she go see Mommy?

Jake answered gently and carefully. Out of the corner of his eye, he could see Justin processing everything. Then Caitlin was quiet. She crawled up on Jake's lap and put her thumb in her mouth, a habit she'd given up four years earlier. He held her close. He could hear her sniffing and when he stroked her face he felt tears.

He kept his eye on Justin. Finally, the boy reacted. Justin's face got red and his eyes narrowed and he suddenly exploded. "Why did you let her die?" he yelled and he raced over to Jake and shoved him, hard. "I hate you!"

"Whoa! Whoa! Justin!"

"Justin, stop!" Cass said, and she moved quickly to intervene. But the boy was gone. He raced back to his room, slammed the door and then they heard the sound of things breaking.

Caitlin started howling. "Cass, take her," Jake said as he handed her the little girl. He jogged back to the bedroom. The door was locked. "Jus. Jus. Justin! Open the door," he commanded, but the boy didn't respond. He looked at the lock, checked the doorframe for an emergency key, and didn't see a quick way in. So he took half a step back, raised his leg, and kicked in the door. He'd have to explain that one to the landlord later.

Justin was throwing all of his toys off the shelves and onto the floor. His lamp, his favorite remote-controlled car, and his soccer trophy lay broken on the floor. He worked furiously, sweeping books off the shelf with one arm, his face the picture of rage.

"Justin, stop!"

The boy looked at him, his blue eyes, so like Tam's, flashing. Then he yelled, "You left us!"

Jake's heart twisted. The boy was barely six

when he and Tam were divorced. What had he thought happened?

"You left us and now she's dead! Why'd you do that? Why'd you leave? I hate you!"

"Wait, Justin. Wait. I didn't want to leave. I wanted to stay with you." Grief welled up in Jake's chest. What a mess he and Tam had made of it! His chest felt like it had iron bands around it. "I wanted to stay. It just wasn't working and your mom thought she'd be better off . . ."

Justin came at him again, slamming his body into Jake, pummeling him with his fists. "You left!"

"Justin, Justin, wait!" Jake grabbed his son, and took him in his arms, feeling his boy-strength. And the kid fought—crying and yelling all at the same time, anger and grief erupting in a volcanic rage. Jake just held him, absorbing his blows, tears running down his face. "Justin, stop. Listen to me." But he wouldn't stop and finally Jake just started praying, out loud, and asking God to help his son. And then the struggling slowed and gradually stopped. The boy grew limp in his arms, and his tears wet Jake's chest, his sobs wracked his body. And Jake just held him, like Cass had held him, an anchor in the storm.

The phone rang, but he knew Cass would get it. He stroked Justin's hair and murmured in his ear. "I love you, Jus. And I loved your mom. She was a good mother and she loved you so much.

She was caught, Justin, in a trap, and she didn't know how to get out. But she loved you."

"Chase killed her, Dad," Justin sobbed. "Chase did it."

"And the police will figure that out, son. We just have to give them a chance."

Time seemed to crawl. The storm raging in Justin slowly began to calm, and they were able to return to the living room. Jake sat on the floor. Justin curled up next to him and rested his head on Jake's thigh. Caitlin sat on the other side, playing with her My Little Pony toys. And one pony's mommy was lost.

The doorbell rang and Cass answered it. Craig Campbell and his wife had come, and Jake felt a wave of gratitude. While they talked, Cass disappeared. Later he would discover she'd cleaned up the mess in Justin's room, even fixing his car with a little tape. The Campbells offered to take the kids back to their house to play for a while. The kids wanted to go, so Jake let them. And when the apartment was quiet, he sat down on the couch and dropped his head in his hands and wept.

Cass sat down next to him. She put her hand on his shoulder, a comforting touch. "Is Justin okay?" she asked.

"I never expected that reaction," Jake admitted, blowing his nose. He looked at Cass. "You know, if I hadn't encouraged her to come with us last night, if I hadn't been so pushy . . ."

"About trying to help her?" Cassie put her arm around him. "Jake, this isn't your fault."

"Look where it got her," he whispered.

Chapter 22

The day of Tam's funeral, Jake woke up feeling heavy and sad. The images of Tam bleeding and dying played in his mind over and over, nauseating him. He went through the motions of getting the kids breakfast and getting them dressed, trying to stay upbeat for their sake.

Chase had arranged for the funeral, which would be held at Annapolis's largest Catholic church. If Jake had it his way, Tam's husband would be behind bars, not at the church.

Cass came over to help get the kids ready. What a friend. Travis came with her—he had volunteered to drive them. That was nice of him, Jake thought.

While the kids were brushing their teeth, Cass asked him, "You doing okay?"

Jake shook his head. "I don't know how this is going to go down. Chase is going to be there." He set his jaw. "They still haven't arrested him."

"Don't interact with him unless you have to."

The press had camped outside the big, cathedral-like church. Travis let them out right in front and they waded through the photographers and reporters, shielding the kids as much as they could. A few minutes later, sitting inside, Jake kept reminding himself of Cassie's advice. He felt like a pit bull on a short chain. He hoped the chain would hold when Chase showed up.

The pews were filling with people he knew— Tam's parents, her sister and other relatives, and FBI people—a lot of FBI people, including Craig and Moose.

But then, a hot flood of anger washed over Jake as Chase and four men walked down the aisle. They approached the white coffin in the front. He could see Chase speaking with the priest as he laid his hand on Tam's coffin. His heart pounding, Jake had to force himself to stay still.

Cass leaned over. "That's all staff. Does he have any family?"

Jake shrugged.

Then Chase, in his black suit, stark white shirt, and carefully arranged face, turned. He spotted Jake. Their eyes met momentarily. And he came to where Jake and the kids were sitting. Jake braced himself. "The children should sit up front," Chase said, "with me."

It was all he could do to keep from exploding out of his seat and decking the guy. He felt Cassie grab his belt, warning him not to react. "No," Jake said. It came out like a snarl and Caitlin snuggled closer. Fortunately, Chase gave up and Cassie's grip on Jake's belt disappeared.

During the service, Cass moved over, pressing her shoulder hard against Jake's. Her touch refused to let him slide into the black anger in his

186

mind. Finally it was over. They drove to the cemetery for a short graveside service. Someone had arranged for a reception at the church afterwards, but Jake wasn't going. The kids had had enough. So had he.

After Tam's death, the holidays became a green-and-red tinseled blur to Jake. Cassie was gone. She and her dad and Travis had chartered a sailboat in the British Virgin Islands for a week. She'd volunteered to cancel, to stay home and help him out, but Jake said no. He'd be okay. Maybe.

Tam's parents had asked Jake if the kids could spend Christmas with them. The kids seemed so excited about that he finally agreed. He took them over on Christmas Eve and made arrangements to pick them up on the 26th. Then he drove home in the dark, by himself, his heart shredded.

Trudy saved him, as she so often did, by inviting him to spend Christmas with her. With Cass and Jim gone, she'd be lonely, she said. He'd be doing her a favor. She made Southern Maryland stuffed ham, pineapple stuffing, roasted winter vegetables and yeast rolls. His appetite was off, but she didn't seem to notice. She shared with him some things she'd been reading, a new discovery in the book of Second Corinthians, an insight into Isaiah's heart, and in doing so, she managed to transport him further into his grief, forcing him to see it, but also helping him bring it into the light.

"You know, you wonder sometimes, what's the point?" Jake said, sitting in front of the fire in the evening, stroking Jazz the dog's soft head. "It all seems so futile."

"That's what old Solomon says in Ecclesiastes. 'Vanity! Vanity! All is vanity.' He goes through eleven chapters of groaning about the futility of life."

"I haven't read that book," Jake said.

"Ecclesiastes? You should," Trudy responded. "It's very interesting. Here he is, wiser than any man, rich, able to indulge all of his senses, powerful, and yet, he's depressed. Everything's meaningless."

"And that's it? He never sees the point?"

Trudy smiled. "You'll have to read it and find out. It's better when you discover it on your own."

She went to bed and Jake sat up with Jazz at his feet, the fire popping in the fireplace. Meaning-less, meaningless . . . Jake took a deep breath and dove into Ecclesiastes. What could the old book have to say to him?

"Fear God and keep his commandments, for this is the whole duty of man. For God will bring every deed into judgment, with every secret thing, whether good or evil."

Jake rolled the final verses from Ecclesiastes over and over in his mind on his first day back at work. Bring Tam's murderer to judgment, Lord. Bring justice for Tam.

"Hey, guy," Cass said softly, as he hung up his coat in the office closet. "How are you?"

Jake took a deep breath. He hadn't seen her since she'd returned from her vacation. Her hair fell softly around her suntanned face, framing her expression. Her eyebrows were slightly arched and her green eyes and those impossibly long lashes seemed to penetrate the shield he had so carefully put in place to guard his emotions. "I'm all right," he said.

"I've been praying for you. I prayed for you the whole time we were gone. I thought about you a lot, Jake."

He glanced down at the new ring on her finger. Cass had accepted Travis's marriage proposal while they were in the BVI. He shrugged, trying to diffuse the emotion he was feeling. "Thanks."

"What's been going on?"

"I've talked to the detectives three times. I've given them everything I know about Chase and Tam, everything I've observed, all that she told me." He sighed. "But you know how these things go. It takes forever, sometimes, to get what you need to bring charges. Especially when there's a high-level politician involved."

"How have the kids been?"

Jake looked up toward the ceiling, trying to shape his feelings into words. "Kids seem so resilient, so flexible, you know; but then again, it's hard to tell what's going on underneath."

"And you, Jake? What about you?"

He started to tell her about his anger and despair, the nausea that never went away, the nights he'd spent praying and searching the Bible and trying to understand what his reaction was supposed to be, how he was supposed to cope with his anger and grief, and his fears that he would never find joy and peace again. What did God expect of him? What was God teaching him? But before he could dive into his deep emotions, her cell phone rang.

"Excuse me," she said, looking at the number. "Hi, Travis. What's up?"

And Jake walked away.

Chapter 23

Jake fell into a routine. Get the kids up. Drive them to a before-school babysitter. Go to the office. Try to function. Pick up the kids at the after-school sitter's, make dinner, help with homework.

Merging his two jobs, agent and single parent, had become harder than he'd ever imagined. Every once in a while, Tam's folks would help out. They loved the kids, he knew, but it was awkward dealing with them.

And then there was work. The team investigating Danny's shooting needed to regroup. He had arranged a meeting with Moose and Cass, who asked if she could invite Travis. Of course, he had told her.

"Where are we, and what new ideas can we come up with?" Jake asked as the four sat down in an FBI conference room.

Cass started them out. "You found what may be remnants of a drug drop in the storm drain near where Danny was shot, right?"

"Right," Jake said, "but we need tape that matches what we found to really make that point."

"So getting an undercover cop to make buys, so we can try to match the tape, is the key. Which is why I wanted Travis to join us."

Jake turned to him. "Any progress on identifying a cop we can work with?" What had it been since he'd first asked for one? Six weeks?

To Jake's surprise, Travis reached into his pocket and pulled out a slip of paper and handed it to him. "Jaime Gonzalez. He's working out of Annapolis but I spoke to him about helping out up here. Give him a call and tell him what you're looking for."

"Will do. Thank you. I'll call him." Jake gestured with the paper. He saw Cass and Travis exchange glances, and he knew in that instant she had pushed her fiancé into connecting with the undercover cop.

He wanted to be thankful. Instead, he felt jealous.

"What about Cisneros?" Moose said. "We've seen him delivering packages to the casino. Juan says he's bought cocaine off of him. He says he sold cocaine to Westfield's driver. So we've got a cocaine dealer and the casino and a politician."

Stomach acid rose in Jake's throat. He coughed it back. "We're leaving the casino out of it. All we're doing is trying to find a package with matching tape, so we can put a dealer near where Danny was shot."

"A small-time dealer like Cisneros would roll on a big-time politician easy," Moose said. "We practically got a case there already."

Jake forced himself to be patient. "But not a

case that would close the shooting investigation. Besides, we can't go near Westfield, at least until he's charged with Tam's murder."

Moose shook his head.

Travis raised his eyebrows. "Chase has a solid alibi."

Jake's stomach clenched. "What do you mean?"

"I overheard the detective on the case, Bruce Kilgore, saying Chase was out of town the weekend Tam was murdered."

"I heard he came back early," Jake said, his face hot.

"It's true, he returned early, flying into BWI, but instead of going home, he went straight to a party hosted by one of the political elites in Annapolis. Sixty of the finest, most upstanding citizens in the state saw him there."

"That can't be." He stared at Travis, willing him to be wrong.

"He was there when he got the call about the murder. Chase Westfield is not a suspect."

"If he didn't do it himself," Jake said, standing up, "he had it done."

Travis shrugged. "They have no record of any claims of domestic violence from Tam, no indication that the marriage was troubled." He raised his hands. "All I'm saying is, if you're waiting for Chase to be charged, you're going to wait a long time."

Jake felt like his head would explode. His

hand still held the paper Travis had given him. He wanted to crush it. "The man is guilty, whether he did it himself or hired someone. He's guilty. I hope Kilgore has the brains to figure that out."

A few minutes later, the meeting adjourned. Moose and Travis left. Cass lingered. "Hey," she said, her green eyes fixed on Jake's face, "you okay?"

"Did you know about this?" His question came out sounding more aggressive than he intended.

"No, Travis didn't tell me."

"It's wrong. You know it's wrong."

"I know, Jake."

"Chase killed her. And they're letting him get away with it!"

"Maybe for now, Jake. They'll figure it out. Travis says Kilgore is a good detective. Give him time to uncover the truth."

Jaime Gonzalez looked to be about thirty-five, according to Jake's estimate. Short, dark-haired, brown-eyed, he looked Mexican. His fluent Spanish completed the picture.

"I'm from San Antonio," he told Jake when they met in Annapolis. The meeting place was about as unlikely as they come—he'd chosen an off-beat Thai restaurant just a block from the State House. They were seated in the back, off by themselves.

"How'd you find your way up here?" Jake asked.

"The Army sent me to Fort Meade. I liked the area and decided to stay."

Jake nodded. "Let me show you what I'm looking at." He pulled a map out of his pocket and spread it on the table. "I've marked the place where the initial contact was made here." He marked the map with an X where Danny was shot. "This is the bar," he put a Y on the map, "and this is the cemetery where a local kid has seen some activity that may be drug-related. We found the tape inside this storm sewer." He drew another X and handed Jaime a sheet of paper with some drivers' license photos of the men they'd identified, including Cesar Cisneros and Tiny Medina, the 350-pound fireplug Jake had seen at the cemetery. "We followed one of these guys around on his route, and he ended up here." Jake marked a Z on the casino.

Jaime met his gaze. "You think that's involved."

"I think maybe." Jake sat back. "But our main interest is in getting something on one of these guys so we can find out who shot Danny. We want packages with tape so we can match it to the remnant we found in the storm drain. Do you think you can help us?"

"Can I get some backup once in a while?"

"Sure."

"You got it, man."

Chapter 24

Jake tapped his knuckle on the wall. "He says he found some Christmas presents Tam had bought Justin and Caitlin. And he wants to give them to the kids. He says he feels bad that they've lost their mom, and he realizes he wasn't a great stepfather. He wants to give them the presents in person and say goodbye." Jake stood at the window in a quiet area of the FBI office, staring into the bright sunshine as if it would shed light on his dilemma.

"And what are you thinking?" Cass asked.

"That I have to do it. I don't want to, but I have to." Jake was breaking a rule he'd just made, talking this over with her. But who besides Cass would understand the dynamics of the situation? "I'm convinced Chase killed Tam, or had her killed, but I have no proof, and I think if I don't do this, I'll regret it somehow. That the kids need the closure." He sighed. "The counselor I'm taking them to recommended that I go along with what Chase wants."

Cass nodded. "Where would you meet?"

"He wanted them to come to the house. I said no. I don't want them to see where she was killed. And I refuse to let them see him in his big fancy office. Let the rest of the world think he's a big shot, not my kids. I suggested a restaurant."

"In public. Good idea."

Jake turned toward her. His eyes were weary. "We're going to meet Thursday night, eight o'clock, at Tuscany Gardens. The kids are off school on Friday."

Cass stood up and moved toward him. "I'll be there, Jake. We will—me, Craig, Moose. We'll back you up."

"No, I'm not worried."

"You're not going in there alone. We'll be there. No arguments."

Her subsequent phone call explaining that to Travis didn't go over as well. The detective had been planning to take Cass with him to BWI airport to pick up his mother, who was flying in just to meet her son's fiancée.

"I'm sorry, Trav. I'll come later that night. Or the next day. But I've got to do this for Jake."

He was not pleased and later Cass thought, maybe I am asking too much of him, to understand this friendship. Maybe I am too involved in Jake's personal life. She sighed deeply. Travis was a bit of a loner. He didn't have a lot of male friends, much less a friend of the opposite sex. There's no way he could understand her relationship with Jake. No way. So how could she explain it?

Chapter 25

"Now remember," Jake said to his kids on the drive to the restaurant, "you have to pretend you don't know Cassie, or Mr. Moose, or Mr. Campbell. Got it? Don't even look at them. They are strangers, okay?"

"Got it, Dad," Justin answered.

"Caitlin?"

The six-year-old was busy playing with a My Little Pony figure. "Yes, Daddy." She was humming a little tune as she played. "Can I wave?"

"No. You have to pretend. You're good at that, Caitlin. Just pretend you don't know them." And he prayed that she would.

The Tuscany crowd was thinning out when they arrived. As Jake walked in, he touched the gun riding on his belt with his elbow, reassuring himself of its presence. He had on a new pair of khaki tactical pants, a black shirt and his black leather jacket. His backup weapon, a snub-nosed Chief, was in an ankle holster. He couldn't imagine Chase would try anything in public, in front of the kids, but he was going to be prepared.

The restaurant was dark and smelled like pasta and cheese and oregano and garlic. Stock Italian music poured from speakers secured near the ceiling at the corners of the dining room. Jake noted the security camera watching the register area. Beyond it was a dark wooden bar. The bartender looked over at him, his face blank, as he wiped a glass with a white cloth. It was Moose. Moose was tending the bar.

Jake redirected his gaze as he felt Caitlin tugging at his pants. She'd seen the same thing. He touched her head, drawing her closer to him, silently reminding her to be quiet. He had just spotted Cass and Craig, seated at a table, eating dinner like any other couple, when Chase arrived, laden with wrapped Christmas presents, along with two other men.

Thankfully, Chase had never met Cass.

"Julie!" Chase said to the hostess. "How are you?" His arms full of gifts, he leaned over and gave her a quick peck on the cheek. "Okay if we use your back room?"

"No," Jake said. "Back there is fine." He nodded toward three empty tables just beyond Cass and Craig.

The hostess looked at Chase. "Whatever he says," the senator responded.

They spread out on all three tables and although the kids had eaten, Chase insisted on ordering a dessert tray. Caitlin, shy at first, was quickly softened up by the sweets and the gifts. Justin kept glancing between Chase and Jake. He wasn't buying Chase's loving stepfather routine, Jake could tell.

Caitlin ripped through the wrapping paper and began opening presents. Then Justin got into it. Once he'd opened a Lego pirate ship, even he seemed to relax.

Chase's two goons, one of whom was Garza, stood over by the wall, just watching. Every once in a while, from across the room, Jake could hear Moose's voice as he joked with a bar patron.

It took almost an hour. Then it was over. Jake felt relieved. Cass and Craig were just paying their bill as Jake helped the kids put on their jackets. Chase insisted on helping carry the gifts to Jake's car. It was a clear night and it seemed colder than the twenty-eight degrees the bank time-and-temperature sign said. The kids' breath made frosty streams of white in the darkness as they crossed the parking lot. "Look, Daddy, I'm smoking!" Caitlin said.

"Smoking is stupid," Justin said.

Jake sighed. Then he saw Moose emerge from the restaurant's kitchen entrance. He disappeared into the rows of cars.

Jake opened the tailgate of his SUV. He and Chase loaded the back with the gifts and the kids buckled up in the back seat. Chase went to the side and leaned into the car to say goodbye to the kids. Jake watched him carefully. Then he and his two companions got into their car and drove off. Jake breathed a sigh of relief as their taillights disappeared down the street. Thank God.

Jake climbed into the SUV. His gun pack caught on the seat belt and he took it off and put it in the front passenger seat. Then he started the car and slowly pulled out of the parking lot. Glancing in his rear view mirror, he saw Cass in her Cabrio right behind him.

He took a deep breath as he pulled onto the street. Another hurdle overcome. He wasn't sure he could even be around Chase without getting into a fight, or at least arguing. But he'd kept his temper and Chase had too, and now all he wanted to do was get the kids home and get them to bed. It was after nine-thirty for crying out loud.

It had probably been a good thing to let them have that last visit, to let them get those gifts from their mom, he thought. He had to remember they were kids and the complexities of the adult world had not yet overwhelmed them.

"Daddy," Justin said from the back seat, "do you think Mommy really bought that stuff for us?"

"Sure, Jus. Why?"

"She always told me she hated guns. But I got a dart gun."

It was a Nerf gun, and its darts were made of soft foam, but still. While Jake thought about that, the oil light on the dashboard flickered on and off. That was odd. He'd just checked the oil

201

a week or so ago. Still it had been cold and Jake remembered once in another car the drain plug had failed. He sure didn't want to drive this relatively new car with no oil in it. When the light came on and stayed on a block later, Jake knew he had to check it.

He waved Cassie on. She had something she was supposed to be doing with Travis. It was good of her to show up at all. She didn't need to hang around while he checked the car.

Jake pulled into a well-lit gas station. "I've got to check the oil, kids," he said, and he pulled the keys from the ignition and threw them on the SUV's center console as he popped the hood and stepped outside.

"I'm going to hide from Daddy," Caitlin said as she unbuckled and slid to the floor behind the driver's seat, covering herself with a blanket.

"That's stupid," Justin replied. He leaned forward and picked up his dad's keys. His hand brushed the strap of his dad's gun bag, the bag he was never, never, ever to touch. He wasn't even tempted. The consequences were too great. Justin looked at the keys and fingered each one, trying to remember what they were all for. He traced his forefinger around the SUV's remote and the red panic button.

"Jus, hand me a quart of oil from under the seat," Jake said.

Justin unbuckled, found the oil and handed it

to his father. As he slid back into his seat, h
 saw his dad's cell phone on the center console,
and he picked it up, put the keys in his lap,
unlocked the phone, and began scrolling through
the apps.

Chapter 26

Jake's breath looked white in the chilly night air and he stared into the engine of his SUV. Could he have lost a freeze plug? If so, the oil he was putting in would leak right back out. Should he have the SUV towed? Call a cab and get the kids home? Maybe he shouldn't have waved Cass on.

Out of the corner of his eye, he saw a late-model sedan pull up. He touched his side, and realized he didn't have his gun bag. He looked at the car. A young Hispanic woman had rolled the passenger side window down. There was another woman in the driver's seat and no one in the back.

"Excuse me, sir!" she said in accented English. "We are looking for . . ."

Wiping his hands on a paper towel, Jake eyed her carefully.

The girl looked down at a piece of paper in her hand, "Four one one three Taylor Street. Can you help us?" She looked back at him, her eyes big.

Taylor Street. Jake thought about it and started to respond, but then he saw her eyes flick to her left, and instinctively he turned, brought his arm up, and blocked a blow from a metal pipe with his forearm.

The blow sent a jolt of pain through his right arm. Adrenaline screamed through his body. He grabbed the pipe, but then someone grabbed him and pulled him backwards and he heard men's voices shouting in Spanish. "¡*Andale, andale!*" The young women in the sedan sped off, tires squealing as Jake drove his elbow into the person behind him.

When Justin saw the car pull up, he instinctively pressed the "lock doors" button on the remote. What was the woman saying to Dad? What did they want? When he saw a second car pull up on the other side of the fuel pump, fear gripped him. Panic followed when four men got out, pulled ski masks down over their faces, and ran toward his dad. "Dad!" he screamed. "Stay down," he commanded his sister. "Stay where you are." Hands shaking, he pressed Cassie's number on the cell phone.

Cass had seen Jake wave her on as he pulled into the gas station and she had hesitated, unsure what to do, but then she pressed the accelerator and continued down the street. The danger was over. Chase was gone. Jake just probably needed gas. Two blocks later, however, something had begun working at her. An uneasiness, a worry, a concern. Should she go back? A tug-of-war began in her gut. Go back or not? She was probably just imagining things. She really should get over to BWI, to meet Travis.

But something bothered her. Just as the impulse

to return grew irresistible, her cell phone rang. She looked down. It was Jake's number. She picked it up. "Hey," she began.

"Cassie, help, help!" Justin's high voice.

A flash of alarm raced through her body. "Justin, where are you?" She came to an intersection marked "No U Turn." Cass wheeled the car around anyway and slammed her foot down on the accelerator. "Are you at the gas station? What's wrong?" A cop put blue lights on behind her. Great. She might need him! "Justin?" she said into the phone. "Justin?"

"Cassie!"

"*¡Agarren los niños!*" Get the kids!

When Jake heard that, he exploded, lashing out with his legs, his arms. His fist connected with someone's jaw, his head smashed another's face, his foot landed solidly in a rib cage. He felt the blows of the metal pipe on his back, on his arms and he grabbed it, wrenching it out of someone's hands. He threw it as hard as he could and it clattered into the night. Then hands were on him, pushing him, forcing him toward the open door of a dark sedan. He bit the hand on his shoulder, dodged a blow to his head, and used leverage to resist the push to the car.

Justin watched wide-eyed as his dad fought the men. Hands shaking, he hit the panic button on the SUV's remote, and the horn started beeping and the lights flashing. The fourth man approached the SUV. The man tried to open the front seat passenger door first, but it was locked, and as he raised his gun to break the glass, Justin yelled, "In the back, Cat, in the back!" The gun came down and the window shattered. Justin grabbed his father's gun pouch and followed his sister into the cargo area, pushing presents aside.

Jake heard the SUV's alarm and the sound of glass breaking and all he could think of was his kids, his kids! He buried his head in someone's gut, butting him, hard. He had to fight. He had to protect his kids.

"¡*Socorro, socorro*!" Help! someone yelled.

And then he heard sirens, blessed sirens, and he felt the hands slip off him. Blood was pouring down from a cut over his eye, but he was able to see two men jump into a car.

"¡*Ponlo detrás*!" a man yelled. Put him in the back!

But the two remaining men were not enough to get Jake Tucker into that car and when Cassie's Cabrio—followed by the police car, its lights flashing—raced into the gas station, the men dropped Jake, dove into their own car, and tires squealing, raced away. And shots rang out in the night.

•••

"FBI!" Cass yelled to the police officers who had been chasing her. "We need that car!" She pointed toward the fast-receding taillights of the dark sedan. Later, she would wonder why they had listened to her at all. She was a woman in civilian clothes, driving her civilian car.

She ran toward Jake as the officer yelled into his radio for backup. "Jake, Jake!" He was staggering to his feet, covered in blood, his snub-nosed Chief in his hand, his breath forming a cloud around him. "Jake!"

"My kids . . . my kids . . ." He could barely get the words out, he was breathing so hard. "They took my kids . . ." Head spinning, he dropped to his knees. Blood ran down his face.

Then the cop yelled, "Hands up! Lemme see your hands! You, in the vehicle!"

Cassie's head snapped around. The second cop had his flashlight and gun trained on Jake's SUV.

"Wait!" Cass yelled. She left Jake and ran toward the SUV. "Wait!"

The cop stayed focused on the vehicle. Two little sets of hands had emerged over the back seat. "Kids?" the cop said, glancing at Cass.

"Justin? Caitlin?"

The two Tucker children clambered over the back seat and out of the SUV and spilled into Cassie's arms. "Cassie!"

"Here! Come here!" she cried, drawing them into a hug. "You're safe!"

"Where's Dad? Where's my dad?" Justin demanded, crying.

"He's all right. Look, Justin, he's all right. Just a little, well, bloody."

Chapter 27

Within minutes, Craig arrived on the scene, and Moose. Craig called in a surveillance squad working in the area. Meanwhile, the suspects' car had disappeared into the night. Confusion on the police radio hampered the chase. The chopper couldn't get there in time.

Jake sat on the ground, his arms propped on his knees, shaking all over while an EMT tried to sop up the blood from his face. All he could do was sit there, trembling with adrenaline, feeling naked and unprotected and intensely angry.

The attendant at the gas station had pressed an alarm button, which automatically locked the doors and called the police, as soon as he saw the men with ski masks. He was giving investigators his version of the story. He handed over the data file from his security cameras. A neighbor who saw the whole thing from his apartment window repeated over and over, "The guy wouldn't give up. It was unbelievable. He kept fighting and fighting."

"The guy" himself, Jake, furious that his kids had been threatened, kept insisting to Craig, "You find Westfield. You find him. He set this up. You find him, or I swear to God, I will."

"I don't want you near him, Jake. You understand? Stay away from him," Craig had replied. "That's an order." Privately, Craig told the others he had doubts about Jake's analysis. Why would Westfield order an assault? What would he gain from it? The attackers spoke Spanish. They could easily have been the friends of Renaldo trying to get back at Jake. Or members of 11th Street who had somehow recognized him. Or random thugs.

Gradually, Craig sorted out the scene. Cass would take the kids to an FBI offsite, where they'd be questioned. Young as they were, they were witnesses, and perhaps something they remembered would help find those who had assaulted their dad. When they were finished, she would take them to the Eastern Shore, to her Aunt Trudy's, a place far from their home, where even Jake thought they'd be safe. The lead man on the surveillance squad took charge of the crime scene. The squad would do a door-to-door in the neighborhood, oversee the inspection of Jake's SUV, maintain chain of custody for the security data and other evidence, and report back to Craig.

"Moose, you go with him to the hospital," Craig commanded.

"I don't need that," Jake protested. "I'm all right."

Craig squatted down. "You have to be checked."

"I don't want to."

"I know that. But you have to."

Jake started to say something and Craig interrupted him. "Your head, Jake. You've had several blows to the head. Did you pass out? Lose consciousness? That's the question. You have to be checked."

Craig stood up and turned to Moose. "Stay with him all night. Don't leave him."

At the ER, Jake was as twitchy as a rodeo bull in the chute. When it was all over, when the docs were finished stitching Jake up, when he'd been MRI'd, examined and iced, Jake told Moose he wanted to go back to his own apartment and sleep for a couple of hours before he went to Trudy's to see the kids.

Fine, Moose said. He drove to Jake's. It was 4 a.m. He'd sleep on the couch. But as they walked in, Jake turned to Moose, and said, "Go. I want to be alone."

Arguing didn't work. Invoking Craig's orders gained Moose no ground. Logic was useless. And when Jake got mad enough, when he'd had all he could stomach of Moose's excuses about why he couldn't leave, why he had to stay with Jake, he picked the smaller agent up by the shirt, threw him out the door, slammed it and locked it. He wanted to be alone. Alone!

And so he was.

The next day dawned sunny and bright. Moose had spent the night in his car, one eye on Jake's

Bureau car, parked in the apartment's garage, one eye on the door of the building. At 8 a.m. sharp, he sat up straight. Jake was walking out the door, dressed in a business suit. Where was he going?

Moose scrambled as Jake headed toward his Bucar. "Hey, Jake! How are you feeling, man? Where you going? Here, let me drive you." Jake's face was swollen and purple, he had a bandaged cut over his eye, both eyes were blackened, and his lip was puffy.

Jake stopped and looked at Moose. "I'm going to see my kids. Why don't you go to work and find out who did this?"

"Okay, man, but listen, why don't you just let me . . ."

But Jake was in the car, with the windows up and the doors locked. He had the ignition on and was pulling out of his space.

"Jake, man, wait!" Moose thumped on the side of the car as Jake drove off. Then he jumped in his car to follow him, but Jake knew the area a lot better than Moose, and in three swift moves, he'd lost him.

Frustrated, feeling guilty, Moose dialed Craig Campbell on his cell phone. The team leader was silent as Moose explained the situation to him. "I'm sure it'll be all right. He said he was just going to see his kids," Moose assured him.

Silence followed.

"I didn't understand the suit," Moose admitted.

"The suit?"

"Yeah, he was all dressed up: dark suit, white shirt, red tie. I think his neck was swollen; it looked like he couldn't get the top button of his collar buttoned. But hey, for a guy that got beat up last night . . ."

"Moose!" Craig said sharply. "Get down to Annapolis now! The Senate Office Building—you know where it is?"

"Yes, but . . ."

"Go! Now! Westfield's office! I'll meet you there."

Jake wheeled the car down the exit ramp for Annapolis. He hadn't slept all night. After getting home at four in the morning and kicking Moose out, he'd paced the floor of his apartment, back and forth, moving relentlessly, unable to shake the tension that gripped him. He hurt, big time. His face hurt, his jaw hurt, his hands hurt, his teeth hurt, his ribs hurt. And his anger was a hot ash in his mouth.

By 6 a.m. Jake had decided what to do. By seven, he was getting ready. At eight he walked out the door.

Losing Moose was easy. Then it was a quick twenty-minute drive to Annapolis. He pulled into State Circle. In front of him loomed the old Maryland State House Building, the oldest legislative building in use in the country. The cramped capital area had a chronic parking deficit but Jake was in his Bureau car. He pulled his car into a 20-minute space and grabbed the blue light from under the seat. He set it, turned off, on the dash. This wouldn't take long. The police would recognize the blue light and leave him alone. Checking his appearance in the rear view mirror, he straightened his tie. He touched his backup gun, a Glock he kept at home, with his elbow, and then he stepped into the bright sunshine.

The Senate Office Building was new, built of brick in a colonial design to match the historic State House. Jake had been here before on other business: a public corruption charge, a drug case. And he had also come out of curiosity when he'd found out Tam was dating a senator. He knew a lot of the guards from a seminar he'd given once on street survival. With any luck, someone he knew would be on duty this morning.

His cell phone kept going off. First Moose, then Craig, then Craig again. Jake turned it to vibrate.

Walking through the courtyard and into the Senate Office Building he saw he was in luck. There were three guards at the security point, manning the scanner, and he knew two of them. Now, he just had to get through quickly. He pulled his creds from his pocket, flashed the badge and made a pre-emptive strike. "Butch, man, good to see you. I gotta catch somebody before a meeting, okay? I'll come back and we'll talk," he said walking between the scanning devices.

"Tucker! What happened . . ."

But Jake had escaped. He was down the hall already. "I'll be right back!" he yelled over his shoulder. He heard Butch's voice behind him, talking to another guard, "No, he's okay, man. He's FBI. He's good."

He'd gotten across the great seal embedded in the floor and was walking down the hall lined with portraits and pieces of art encased in glass. He was taking the stairs, two at a time. Nothing was going to stop him. Nothing. He'd be in Chase Westfield's face in less than five minutes.

Craig Campbell recognized Jake's Bucar, and he pulled up behind it and jumped out. Touching the hood as he went by, he could feel the engine was still warm. He walked quickly up the brick walk and into the Senate Office Building. The guards at the front examined his creds. It seemed to take forever.

Butch walked over, saw he was another FBI agent, and said, "Hey, you know Jake Tucker? He just came through here."

"Where'd he go?" Craig asked.

The guard motioned down the hall to the right.

"You know him?" Craig asked.

"Yes, sir. We're friends."

"Come with me," the agent said, starting quickly down the hall. "Show me where Chase Westfield's office is."

Dark wood. There was something about dark wood that made offices feel rich, their occupants important. The dark wood, the brass plate, the leather furniture, the secretary in the outer office. Chase Westfield was a big man, a big, important man. Jake opened the door and walked in. The secretary looked up. Her eyes widened and he knew the sight of his bruised and swollen face was having its effect.

The door to the inner office was open. Chase was standing beside his desk with his back to the door, reaching high for a book.

Jake touched his gun with his elbow. He felt its weight on his hip. He set his jaw, and walked past the secretary, ignoring her cries of "Sir, Sir!" When he got to the door to Chase's inner office, the senator turned around. And all the blood drained from his face.

"What's going on?" Butch was out of breath, trying to keep up with Craig as they sprinted up the stairs and down the hall to Westfield's office.

"Nothing, maybe. I don't know. There's been some animosity."

"What happened to Tucker? My gosh, he was a

mess!" Butch gestured. "Third door here, on the right, sir."

The two men turned into Chase Westfield's office and skidded to a stop.

Chase Westfield dropped the book. He moved quickly toward his desk, for the panic button or the gun Jake suspected was there, and he tripped. Jake moved forward and caught him. He grabbed him by his jacket and backed him up against the bookshelves. Jake's eyes locked onto Chase's, which were wide with terror. The senator's skin was pale, pale enough he might pass out. Jake could see the veins popping in the man's forehead, could hear his breath coming shallow and fast, could feel the fear emanating from Chase in waves.

Chase was scared. Terrified. Of him.

As Tam had been of Chase. As he, Jake, had been of his own father.

Something in Jake's head clicked a warning. *The anger of man does not produce the righteousness of God.* He hesitated, but then tightened his grip. "Getting rid of me won't solve your problem," Jake said, spitting out the words. "One day every hidden thing will come to light. Every hidden thing." He shoved the senator harder against the bookshelves. "Worry about God, not me. But you touch my kids again . . ."

"Jake!" Craig Campbell's voice rang out.

Chapter 28

Jake let go of Chase. His heart was racing, blood screaming in his veins. He turned. "Boss," he said, nodding to Craig. He could hear running footsteps in the hall, guards responding to a silent alarm the secretary no doubt initiated. As Jake brushed past Craig, the guards arrived.

"Hold it!" one said, putting his hand on Jake's chest. Jake stood still, his blood pounding in his head. He heard mumbling behind him, and then the lead man, who was inside the senator's office yelled, "Let him go. False alarm."

Craig Campbell fell into step with Jake as they walked back through the halls of the Senate Office Building. "I told you to stay away from him. If you ever," Campbell said in a hoarse whisper, "disobey a direct order of mine again . . ."

Jake stared straight ahead.

". . . I will have you busted so fast." Craig continued, using words like "suspended" and "disciplinary action" and "on the bricks" but Jake didn't respond.

When they reached their cars outside, Craig took a breath, and then Jake looked him squarely in the eye, squinting in the bright sunshine. He had a great deal of respect for his squad supervisor. He didn't particularly like disobeying him. But sometimes, stuff has to happen. "I had to show him," Jake said slowly, "I would not be intimidated. I'm sorry. But I had to do that."

"You don't even know that he had anything to do with last night."

"Chase Westfield set that up. I'm sure of that. He killed Tam and he tried to have me killed. Bank on that. And my kids . . ." Jake's voice caught.

Craig ran his hand through his hair. He looked away, like he was trying to control his own temper, then turned back to Jake. "I have to admit," he said, "you know how to create a scene."

Jake's suit and his battered and bruised face formed a walking contradiction. The guards would have stories to tell their families at dinner that evening. "I don't think the senator was expecting me," Jake said.

Craig shook his head again. "I don't know what to do with you!"

Jake sighed. "I'm going to see my kids."

At that moment, Moose pulled up, and jumped out of his car. "I got here as quick as I could."

Campbell looked at his watch. "You're late."

"Yeah, man, the traffic . . ."

"You got lost," Jake said.

Moose stopped short. He looked down at his feet. Then he raised his eyes toward Craig Campbell. "What happened? What'd I miss?"

"Nothing," the squad leader responded and he

put his hand on Moose's shoulder and walked him back to his car. "I'm following you," he said to Jake.

"No, it's . . ."

"It's me or him," Craig asserted.

"Okay, you then. He's no fun. Too easy to lose."

Trudy's house, Jake thought, had become the Tucker family refuge, a place to relax, to be sheltered, to be loved. What grace!

Jazz, Trudy's Springer spaniel, greeted him at the door, with a wagging tail and excited barks as Cass let him in. Cassie's eyes scanned Jake's face, then looked beyond him to where Craig Campbell was getting out of the car. "Come in," she said.

Inside, the house smelled like cinnamon and sugar. Trudy was baking. Jake found her in the kitchen. "Hey," he said, giving her a quick hug.

"Jake! My goodness . . ." she couldn't finish her sentence. Her eyes ranged over the bruises and cuts on his swollen face.

Jake saw tears fill Trudy's eyes. "I'm sorry to dump this on you."

She quickly wiped them away. "I'm glad to help."

Cass heard them speaking and came into the room. "Jake! How do you feel?" She hugged him gently.

"I'll live."

"Why are you so dressed up?" Cass said, eyeing him.

He just shrugged. Craig rolled his eyes and shook his head slightly. Cass acknowledged him with a slight nod.

"Where are the kids?" Jake asked, petting Jazz on the head.

"Daddy!" Caitlin burst into the room and grabbed her dad's legs.

At the impact, both grief and relief flowed through him. The kids were safe.

"Cassie said you'd come!"

Jake picked her up. He winced in pain as he did it. "Hey, Punkin!"

The little girl looked at him warily. "Daddy, you sound funny." She traced the bruises on his cheek with her finger, and his swollen lip, and felt the knot on his forehead. Her voice grew quiet. "Are you gonna die like Mommy?"

His heart twisted. "No, Punkin. I'll be fine," he said, putting her down. "Where's your brother?"

Justin was, in fact, standing at the door, half-hidden by the doorjamb. Jake spotted him. "Come here, son!"

"Jake," Cass began, and she touched his arm. But he had already begun moving toward Justin.

The boy refused to meet his eyes, refused to look at him, and at first, Jake was afraid the kid was reacting to last night, frightened and withdrawn. "Jus, what's up?" he asked, squatting down to the boy's eye level, wincing again with the pain of it.

"Jake, Justin needs to talk to you about something," Cass said. "Calmly."

Calmly. Okay. He could do that. Jake took Justin to the sunroom, his favorite room of the house. Outside the big wall of glass a cardinal was pecking at an orange Trudy had hung from a tree branch. Smaller birds flitted at a feeder. A fire crackled in the fireplace. "Okay, buddy, what's going on," Jake asked. He took his jacket off and eased himself to the floor, leaning back against the couch. He couldn't believe how sore he felt. The pain pills the ER doc had given him rattled in his pocket. He had refused to take them. The last thing he wanted was to be doped up.

Justin wouldn't look him in the eye. He was still standing, staring at Jake's backup gun in the holster on his side.

Jake followed his gaze. "What's up, buddy?" he asked again, keeping his voice soft. "You get scared last night?"

Justin took a deep breath. Then his eyes, blue like his mother's, met Jake's. "I know where your FBI gun is, Dad. I . . . I took it."

"What?" It came out a little sharper than Jake had intended.

Tears filled Justin's eyes. He turned away.

Cass, standing in the doorway, cleared her throat, warning Jake with a look.

"Tell me about it, Justin," Jake said softly.

"The man, he was coming, breaking in the car,

and I yelled at Caitlin to get in the back. And I took your gun." He began crying.

"Yes," Jake prompted.

"I . . . I took your gun." Justin sobbed.

Jake looked at Cass, who said, "We found it, Jake. It was in the cargo area of your SUV. The pack, everything."

Jake nodded. Gently he touched his son, turning him around, bringing his chin up so they could look at each other. He took the handkerchief out of his pocket and handed it to the boy, who blew his nose loudly. "You took the gun?"

Justin nodded.

"And then what?"

"We hid in the back. I unzipped the pouch and I took it out, Dad. I had it in my hand."

Jake took a deep breath. It was forbidden, absolutely forbidden, for the kids to touch his gun.

"I kept the safety on, Dad. I was only going to use it if I had to."

So many evenings they'd worked together taking apart the disabled gun Jake had gotten for Justin, putting it back together, practicing cleaning it, practicing holding it, going over the rules. "Guns are not toys," he had said over and over. "You never point a gun at anyone unless you intend to use it. There's only one reason to use a gun," he'd instructed them, "just one reason." At times he had wondered if the boy was even listening.

Justin's shoulders heaved with his sobs. Jake

realized he was probably almost as scared now as he had been last night. "Justin," Jake said, "what's the one reason to use a gun?"

The boy closed his eyes, as if he was recalling a catechism. "To defend yourself or someone else," he said, "against a deadly threat." He looked at his dad.

Jake nodded. "So what were you doing last night?"

"I wasn't going to let them take my sister," the boy repeated, sobbing. "I had to protect Caitlin."

Jake wrapped his arms around his son and pulled him close. He buried his nose in the boy's hair and smelled his shampoo. He kissed the top of his son's head. "Justin, when I told you never to touch my gun, I had no idea," Jake's voice caught in his throat, the emotions of the last twelve hours finally catching up with him, "I had no idea you'd ever have to do what you did last night. I never expected that." He felt the boy's head burrow into his chest. "I understand, and I'm not angry."

The sobs came, then, deep, wrenching sobs as the boy shook in Jake's arms. He looked over at Cassie. She was wiping her eyes. "It's all right, Jus," he said softly, "you did the right thing."

"I'm sorry, Dad, I'm sorry."

"I'm sorry, too, Jus. The main thing is, we're all okay. You took care of your sister. I'm proud of you."

Chapter 29

Surrounded by his kids, Jake began to relax, and then he grew sleepy, and, unwilling to leave them, he lay down on the floor. The fire was so warm. An hour later, when Cass peeked in, all of them were asleep. Jake lay on his side, his head on a pillow from the couch. Cat was snuggled up against his chest and Justin was against his back. Even Jazz was asleep, her head resting next to Jake's leg.

Cass stood looking at them, captured by the scene. When she lifted her eyes and looked past them, to the big wall of windows that looked out onto Trudy's side yard, she saw big puffy flakes were drifting from the sky, turning the world into a snow globe.

Trudy came up beside her and put her hand on Cassie's shoulder. Then Cassie turned and looked into her aunt's wise, gray eyes, and she spontaneously hugged her.

The two women left the room and moved into the kitchen. Craig was sitting at the table, working on his laptop. "I love you, Aunt Trudy," Cassie said. "Thank you for taking care of all of us. Me, Jake, everybody."

"What else do I have to do," Trudy said, smiling.

Cass shook her head. "I hope you don't mind.

I've got to go. Travis is going to be really annoyed. I'm supposed to be meeting his mother."

Trudy nodded.

"Will you be okay?"

"Of course, honey. They're no trouble."

Craig stood up to say goodbye to Cass. "I'll stay here until Moose arrives or you get back. One of us will be here."

Cass nodded. "You'll be well taken care of. Still, you call me if you need me," Cass said to her aunt. Giving Trudy a peck on the cheek, she tore herself away.

The visit with Travis and his mom, in comparison to the storm around Jake, felt to Cass like sailing on a dead calm day. Mrs. Lowery was 70 years old, white-haired, and had the same startling blue eyes as Travis. She spoke in a soft Georgia accent. In her prim, shirtwaist dress, she seemed like someone out of a movie. Aunt Bea, maybe, but thinner.

"Mah Travis says you're with the FBI," she said, holding out a thin-skinned, blue-veined hand. "Ah nevah thought of doing something like that, something so daring." She smiled sweetly.

"Well, mostly it's just paperwork," said Cass. They were having a regrettably late lunch in a tearoom in downtown Annapolis. Before her, on a porcelain plate was a quartered sandwich, half cucumber, half thinly sliced smoked turkey and provolone with raspberry mayonnaise. Mrs. Lowery, unable to decide, had ordered the same.

Travis, looking oddly uncomfortable, sat across from Cass. He had ordered roast beef on a bun, cole slaw, and fruit. A small pot of tea sat in the center of the table. His irritation at Cassie's tardiness was barely masked, and her brief explanation had done little to assuage him. "Mom taught school," he said, trying to get a conversation going, "for thirty years. Elementary school. Music."

Cass nodded. "That's wonderful, Mrs. Lowery. I'll bet you influenced a lot of lives."

"Oh, my, yes. How I loved my students! And you know, they were just darlin' back then, just darlin'. Not at all like the hoodlums teachers have to deal with today."

Cassie felt like she'd shifted into low gear and was drifting up to a stoplight. How she'd get through the rest of the day, she didn't know.

Jake slept for nine hours. When he woke up, his head felt like it was in a vise. He got to his feet. It was dark outside. He staggered into the kitchen, where Trudy was sitting, reading a book at the table. "Well, hello," she said, smiling.

He dragged out a chair and sank into it. "What time is it?" He dropped his head into his hands.

"Nine o'clock. We thought it would be best if you just slept. The kids were so good, playing quietly so they wouldn't wake you up."

He glanced around. "Where is everybody?"

"Your friend Moose is outside, just keeping an eye out, he said. He's staying the night. Cassie should be back soon. She needed to go to Travis. The kids are asleep."

Jake shook his head. "I've invaded your peace and quiet again. I'm sorry."

Trudy smiled. "I'm glad you're here. Let me get you something to eat."

He touched his jaw. His whole face ached. "I don't know if I can eat."

"A milkshake? Fruit smoothie?" she asked.

"Yeah, okay. Anything cold."

While Trudy was pulling things out of the refrigerator, Jake turned the book around to see what she was reading. It was called "When God Weeps" by Joni Eareckson Tada and Steve Estes. He flipped it open. *God cares most—not about making us comfortable—but about teaching us to hate our sins, grow up spiritually, and love him,* he read silently.

Hate our sins. Including anger?

A few minutes later, as Trudy put a tall glass filled with a vanilla milkshake in front of him, he realized how hungry he was. He sipped it and the cold felt so good on his throat. "Thank you," he said. "That's perfect."

Trudy brought him more ice in a zippered plastic bag and then sat down across from him. Her good gray eyes roamed over his face, inspecting the damage. When they got to his eyes, he looked away. "So who do you think did this to you, Jake?" Trudy asked softly, bringing him back.

"Chase Westfield. Tam's husband."

"I thought the attackers were Latinos."

"He paid them. That's what I mean. It was a hit."

"And that's why you went to the Senate Office Building?"

Jake nodded.

"What were you going to do?"

He picked up a spoon and started playing with it. "I just needed to confront him." Jake replayed the scene in his mind.

"Did you hurt him?"

Jake shook his head. "No. I wanted to, but something stopped me." He raised his eyes and met Trudy's. "So is this it? Is God finished breaking me now?"

She cocked her head.

"You know, your vision. The pot breaking and all that. I got custody of the kids, Tam's dead, I got jumped. You think God is done with me?"

There was more inquiry than bitterness in his voice. This "walk of faith" as Trudy called it was new to Jake. He'd only been at it a couple of years.

"It's hard to tell," she responded softly.

"I just don't know how long she's going to be able to live on her own," Travis said. He was sitting

230

across the table from Cass at a cafe at BWI, having just seen his mother get through security for her flight back to Atlanta. It was the Monday after Jake's assault and Travis just seemed to need to talk.

Cassie's mind, though, seemed to wander.

"I mean, she's not all that frail, but still, she's 70! How much longer will her health hold out? And then what? I can't really see her moving up here. She's lived in Atlanta all her life. So do I move down there? What would you think of that?"

"Of what?" Cass's attention snapped back. What had Travis said?

"What would you think about moving to Atlanta, temporarily anyway, to care for my mother?"

Leave Maryland? Cassie couldn't even imagine that! Leave Trudy? Leave her dad? Stalling for time, her eyes drifted to a nearby table where a copy of that morning's *Baltimore Sun* lay abandoned. She began to read the headline, which was upside down. And then her eyes widened as she understood the words.

"Travis!" she said. "Did you see that?" Cass stood up, grabbed the paper and shoved it in front of him. "Look at this! Three murders!" Baltimore might be Murder City but to find three Hispanics dead in one day was remarkable even by Baltimore standards.

He seemed annoyed that she'd changed the subject. "Oh, yeah. I heard about that this morning."

"And you didn't tell me?"

The murdered men had been found in two different places: an alley in Glen Burnie and inside a dumpster in south Baltimore. All three had been shot in the back of the head. A ballistics test would be conducted to see if the crimes could be linked.

Cassie's head spun. Jake had been assaulted by four men, presumably Hispanic. Three Hispanic men were dead. Was there a connection? Had Travis thought of that?

Travis took a big drink of his coffee. "I'm not going to solve that problem today."

"Are you assigned to this?" she asked, gesturing toward the newspaper.

"I'm talking about my mom." He stretched his neck.

Guilt flooded Cass. Still, she couldn't let it go. "Trav, do you think these guys might have been the ones who muffed the assault on Jake? Do you?"

He shrugged. "I have no idea." He leaned back in his chair, stretching his legs forward, bumping into hers as he did. "Why would you even think that?"

Cass just stared at him.

Travis sighed. "Look, Cass, it's Pete Brown's

case. Pete Brown and Chuck Thomas, actually, because two of the victims were found together. I can ask them to let me know what they find out." He glanced at his watch. "If there's any connection, we'll figure it out sooner or later."

Cassie's blood pounded in her temples. That's right, she thought. Don't get excited, Travis. Be methodical. Trim those sails. It'll all work out. She bit her lip to keep from saying anything more.

"So, how's Jake doing?" Travis asked. He looked away as he said it.

"He's okay," Cass said, swallowing her hot drink as it scalded her tongue. "He's angry. Craig's assigning him to desk duty. That's not sitting too well with him."

Travis nodded. "Your friend sure has a temper. Maybe the night he attacked Renaldo, other guys saw him. He created quite a scene. That's not such a good idea when you're in the middle of an investigation."

Jake *attacked* Renaldo? Cass thought. "You think Renaldo had a part in assaulting Jake? We've questioned Renaldo. He was working that night. His boss confirms he was there."

"But his friends could have followed Jake."

"Yeah, but here's the thing," Cass said. "Jake was driving his personal vehicle when he left the restaurant. He had to have been followed.

And unless the gang has figured out where Jake lives . . ."

Travis shrugged. "Maybe they just happened upon him at the gas station. Saw him and recognized him."

"I'm still betting on Chase," Cassie said. "He has the most to gain from Jake being out of the picture."

"I don't know," Travis said, shaking his head. "I'm having a hard time seeing a Maryland state senator doing something like that."

Cass forced herself to shut up. *Really, Travis? Really?*

Chapter 30

Cass wasn't going to let the possibility of linking the three dead gang members and Jake's assailants go. She contacted the detectives on the triple murder case, obtained crime scene and autopsy photographs of the dead men, and sent them, along with images from the security cameras at the gas station where Jake was assaulted, to West Virginia. The Bureau's new Next Generation Identification system might be able to help.

Maybe.

The problem was that the gas station security footage was grainy. Plus the faces of the attackers were obscured by ski masks. Could they tell anything by body measurements?

Cassie had reluctantly resumed work on Danny's shooting. Moose had completed his assignments early and had asked for a couple of days off. He'd been evasive about his plans. What was he doing?

Cass eventually found out.

"I looked at that gas station video over and over," Moose told her over coffee one day. "Did you see Jake land that right on that guy's jaw?" Moose pretended to throw a punch. "It was incredible. The guy's head jerks back. So meanwhile, I'm thinking, Jake broke that dude's jaw. I'm bettin' on it." Moose drank his coffee. "So I checked all the hospitals, all the urgent care clinics, and I'm comin' up with nothin'. Then I get a brilliant idea: I spend two days in D.C. makin' the rounds. Sure enough, I find a guy showed up at the emergency room of the Washington Hospital Center at midnight the night Jake was hit. Broken jaw. Just like I said."

"Good for you, Moose!" Cass said. "What was his name?"

"Mr. Fake ID," Moose said, grimacing. "He said it was Jose Noriega. Noriega, no less! The general. I'm thinkin,' not quite. The address he gave is bad, too. The hospital figures he's an illegal alien. But they patched up his jaw. Wired him up. And he's gotta come back to get the wires off. When he does, they're gonna call me and the D.C. cops. Then we'll see what battle Gen. Noriega's been fightin'."

"That's great, Moose. Good work!"

"Lemme tell you somethin' else. Yesterday, I'm drivin' down Ritchie Highway, right? And I pull off. I just felt lucky, y'know? Lucky. Sure enough, there's new graffiti on the wall there, down by that liquor store on the corner near the bar."

"What's it say?"

"Three RIPs. Together. Midget. Tony. And Lonestar. Marked with the Los Bravos logo."

Cass cocked her head. Three RIPs? At the same time. "Did you run those street names?"

"I did. Guess what. At least two of them may be a match with the three Hispanics found dead last week."

"Yes!" Cass exclaimed. "I knew it!"

Cass couldn't get Moose's information out of her head as she drove home that night. Three new RIPs. She wondered what to think of the graffiti. The traffic was heavy on Route 2 as she moved toward her home. Seeing a convenience store, she pulled in, remembering she needed eggs, bread, and milk.

In just a few minutes, she'd gathered what she needed and stood in the checkout line. Overhead, a television hung from the ceiling blabbered on. It was annoying, to have televisions jabbering all day everywhere. Even if it was the news. She averted her eyes, but then something caught her attention. Senator Chase Westfield was having a press conference.

Her eyes locked into the TV. Something was weird. He was standing on a podium addressing reporters, talking about his domestic violence initiative. But something was different.

"Can I help you?"

The clerk's voice jerked Cassie's attention back. "Oh, yes. Sure." She tumbled her purchases on to the counter and glanced back at the tube.

"That'll be $8.37," the clerk said.

"Okay." Cass pulled a twenty out of her wallet

and handed it to the young woman. What was different about Chase?

"Your change, ma'am?"

"Sorry." Cass shoved the change into her blazer pocket and picked up the bag with her food in it. As she turned to leave, Chase was ending his conference, turning away from the podium, exiting to the rear. And that's when it hit her. Garza. Chase's ever-present assistant was not with him.

All the next day that observation bothered Cass. She didn't tell Jake. He was just beginning to really feel better, according to Trudy. No sense getting him agitated. So she searched for more information. The Maryland General Assembly was back in session, and despite the tragic murder of his wife, Senator Westfield was back on the job serving his constituents, according to the press.

But what about Garza? She called her dad's old friend, Len Boyette, editor of the *Bay Area Beacon*. After listening to her, Len suggested their capital reporter could ask around. A few days later, he called Cass and told her they'd found out that Garza had accepted another position outside politics. That was Westfield's story, anyway.

"He got canned." Moose took a big bite of his barbeque sandwich after making his pronouncement.

"You know that for sure?" Cassie asked.

"If you leave to take another position, you don't draw unemployment," Moose said, his mouth full. He took a big swig of his Pepsi.

"You know he's drawing UI?"

"A woman I used to date works for the Maryland State Employment Service."

Cass laughed. "Okay, so Jake gets mugged, three thugs get murdered, and Garza gets canned. Can't be coincidental."

"Chase tells his buddy Garza to get someone to take Jake out, because Jake knew about the abuse, and he was the main person pointing a finger at Chase for Tam's death."

Cass agreed. "And not just that—if Jake was on to something about the casino, and Chase knew it, that would give him two reasons to want him gone."

"Right. But hey! Maybe getting rid of Jake was Garza's idea, not Chase's. But his boys blow it. So he offs them and then gets fired himself."

"You could be right." Cass restlessly drummed her fingers.

"The question is, why didn't Garza's guys just shoot Jake? Why were they trying to get him in that car? Why were they trying to get the kids? And then, too, why wasn't Garza killed? If his boys blew it, why wasn't he executed too?" Moose asked.

"Because Chase isn't the cold-blooded murderer we'd like to think?"

Moose frowned.

Cass checked her watch. She was late to meet Travis. "I've got to go," she said, rising. "You're doing a great job, Moose, finding all this stuff."

Moose stopped chewing. "Thanks."

"Jake will be back tomorrow," Craig told Cass the next day at the FBI office. "He's accepted my terms. Grounded, at the office." He was playing with a pen in his hand. He looked like his victory wasn't truly satisfying.

Cass smiled. "And convincing him was only slightly easier than getting Attila the Hun to wear perfume."

"He's made his peace with it."

"He's bringing the kids back, too? Putting them back in school?"

"Yes. For now, anyway. He's thinking about moving," Craig ran his hand through his hair, "he just doesn't know where."

Jake, moving? Why hadn't he mentioned it to her? She kept her voice casual. "Somewhere closer to the office?"

Craig looked at her oddly. "No. He's thinking of transferring. Maybe somewhere out West."

Cass blinked.

Chapter 31

For the next few weeks, Cass and Moose beat their heads against the brick wall of Danny's shooting. No leads. No information. Even Jaime, the undercover cop, had not begun to crack the case. He'd bought some dope, but so far, none of the packages had tape that matched what they'd found in the storm drain.

Meanwhile, Jake stayed in the office. The swelling in his face had gone down and the bruising was yellowing. He seemed weary. Who could blame him?

"You know, it seems like nothing's going right now," he said to her when they passed briefly in the hallway. "Chase hasn't been charged with Tam's murder, nobody seems to know who knocked me around, and we don't even have an arrest on Danny's shooting. Is anyone in this town guilty of anything?"

"It's frustrating, I know, Jake," she replied. "Be patient. Something will break soon." She checked her watch. "Hey, you want to go for a run in a little while?"

He shook his head. "No, Cass. Thanks, but no."

A week later, Cass had a message on her cell phone. When she returned Travis's call, he asked to meet her at a coffee shop. Now.

"What's going on?" she asked, slipping into the seat across from him.

He looked up, but didn't smile. There'd been a distance between them since his mother's visit. Cass had felt it.

"Listen," Travis said, glancing around, "you know I can't talk about this." He tapped his finger nervously, then looked into her eyes. "You need to tell your friend to get a lawyer. A good lawyer."

Cassie's heart thudded. She started to say, "Jake?" but Travis held up his hand. She leaned forward. "What's going on?"

No one was around them. No one. Still, Travis was cautious. "I overheard something. I understand the prosecutor expects an indictment."

It took a minute to sink in. "Against him?" Cass said, horrified.

Travis just looked at her, but she saw the answer in his face.

"That's ridiculous!"

"They think they have motive, means, and opportunity." Travis looked down. "Look, I can't tell you more. But the prosecutor, he thinks he's got it nailed."

Cassie felt like she was going to throw up. Jake? Charged with murder? Come on! "Who's the prosecutor?"

Travis gave her a name, then added, "He's an ambitious guy, looking to cement his legacy. He thinks this is the one that can do it for him. I'm sorry."

"Oh, Lord," she said softly.

Jake walked into Craig Campbell's office. What was up? Craig said he wanted to see him right away. Maybe they'd identified the men who had attacked him. That would be good news.

Cass was already sitting in one of Craig's office chairs. She met Jake's eyes and quickly looked away. That was curious. "What's going on?" Jake asked.

"Sit down," Craig responded, motioning toward a chair. He left his desk, crossed the room, and shut the door. Then he sat back down in his chair and motioned toward Cass. "Go ahead."

Cass looked at Jake. He saw something terrible in her eyes—fatigue? Grief? What? Had Trudy died? Her dad? He gripped the arm of his chair.

"Jake," she said, "I've gotten word . . . I've heard the grand jury is meeting today on Tam's death."

Jake raised his eyebrows. "Oh, yeah?" Curious, he leaned forward.

She nodded. "They may be bringing an indictment."

"Yes! Finally."

"But it's not against Chase, Jake."

What was he reading in her eyes? His heart started pounding. "Then who?"

Her face twisted in pain. Now there were tears. "You, Jake. That's what I've heard. I'm sorry," she whispered.

He blinked his eyes in disbelief. "No." He sat back. An indictment? Against him? They thought *he* did it? Jake felt like the room was receding. Cass was talking, but he couldn't understand what she was saying. There was a loud buzzing in his ears.

He blinked again and tried forcing himself to hear Cass and Craig, to understand their words but he couldn't, he couldn't. He stood up, unable to sit any more. Sweat popped out on his brow.

". . . and we're going to stand by you, Jake. We know you are innocent . . . the best lawyer . . . it doesn't matter how much . . . we'll be there . . ."

Nausea swept over him. And then anger, in a hot wave. What happened to Chase? What happened?

His squad supervisor was saying something. What was Craig saying?

"Are you all right?"

"That scumbag!" Jake exploded. "He couldn't kill me. So now . . . that son of . . . He's convinced them that I did it! Me! I had nothing to do with Tam's murder. Nothing!"

They let him vent, nodding soberly. Then Craig said gently, "You understand if you are indicted, what will happen?"

An agent charged with a felony could be fired,

even before the trial. No presumption of inno-cence, no waiting for the legal process to play out. Fired.

The best he could hope for was administrative leave without pay. "Yeah, I know all about that! I know! You don't have to tell me." Jake gestured angrily. Chase Westfield had killed his ex-wife. Now, he was coming after him. And the legal system was going along with it. The Bureau was going along with it!

Jake saw Craig's lips moving again but the drumming in his ears and the fog in his head would not let the words pass through. An indictment . . . losing his job, oh, God!

Finally, Craig and Cass stopped talking. Jake's chest was on fire. "Look, I didn't do this . . . I didn't kill Tam."

"We know," they said in unison.

"How can we help you?" Cassie asked, her voice catching in her throat.

"I should have ripped him apart!" Jake yelled. "I can't believe the detectives are buying his story. He's got to be paying them off!"

"What will you need, Jake?" Cass reiterated softly. "Help with the kids? A recommendation of a lawyer? Money?"

What did he need? What would he need? Time to think, that was it. Time to think. He closed his eyes and shook his head. An indictment. Oh, God, no! Jake turned to leave.

"Jake!" Craig stopped him with his voice. Jake turned around. "Don't go near Westfield, you understand? I don't care how angry you are."

"I'm not!" Jake said in a voice that surprised even him. "You don't have to tell me that!"

Cass rose to her feet. "Can I come with you?"

"No!" Jake replied. "No. Leave me alone!" And he walked out.

"Where will he go?" Craig asked.

"I don't know," Cass said. Misery filled her voice.

"Is it safe for him to be by himself?"

"I think if either of us tried to push it, he'd be furious," Cass responded.

Craig nodded. "I think you're right. He won't kill himself, right?"

Cass had to think about that. "I don't think he'd do that to his kids. It's just so unfair!" Cass said, rising suddenly and turning away from Craig. "Of all the people. He was trying to help her, trying to . . . it's so unfair!" She brought her hand up to her mouth. She didn't want to cry, she never cried at work, but this was so unbelievable! Her voice stuck and tears began to fall.

Craig said, "Look, Cass, I'd better go tell the boss. He does better if he's not surprised." He hesitated. "You going to be all right?"

She nodded. "Yes."

"You stay in here as long as you need to." Craig put his hand on her shoulder. "We need to pray, big time."

Jake left the FBI office, got in his car, and sat, dazed. "God, what are you doing to me!" he said, and he hit the steering wheel with both hands. He started the engine, drove out of the parking garage, and headed for the only place he could think of—the park where he liked to run.

The air seemed unusually cold that day, raw and bitter, the kind of cold that made his muscles feel brittle and stiff and his bones ache. Jake changed into sweats in the restroom and ran, slowly at first, down the path. In the park, he could forget about life. The oaks and poplars, though bare now in their dormancy, were thick and underbrush grew wild and untamed. The path, dirt covered with mulch, wound through the woods in gentle curves and mild ups and downs except for one long descent down to a creek, and then an equally steep climb back up on the other side.

He was alone in the woods, as he usually was on these late winter days. His feet made soft rhythmic sounds as he ran. His breath came easily, his heart felt strong, and it would have been a great run, an almost perfect run, had it not been for the infor-mation that Cass had conveyed and the feeling of doom that saturated him as surely as a soaking rain. An indictment. Against him! A tremor ran through him.

As he ran he prayed. God, I need your help. Why is this happening? How can I defend myself? What is going on? I just want to raise my kids and do my job. God, where are you?

Jake prayed and ran, prayed and ran. On the long hill down, he thought of his kids, and what would happen to them if he were convicted. He stumbled, and almost fell. On the long stretch up, on the other side of the creek, with his lungs burning and his head about to burst, he tried to map out his defense. He couldn't come up with much. God, help! What should I do?

Nearing the top of a rise, he heard it.

Humble yourselves, therefore, under the mighty hand of God so that at the proper time he may exalt you.

Humble yourself . . . under the . . . mighty . . . hand of God . . . and he will exalt you. His feet beat out the rhythm. Humble yourself under the mighty hand of God and he will exalt you. Humble yourself.

Chest heaving, he reached the summit and he heard it again, and this time the Voice was so clear he dropped to his knees. *Humble yourselves, therefore, under the mighty hand of God so that at the proper time he may exalt you.*

"I believe," he said, his breath coming hard, his head bowed. "I believe that you are God. I believe you are good." Sweat dripped off his brow and exploded in the dust. "I believe you love me. I believe you love my kids. I believe all things work together for good for those who love you and are called according to your purpose. I believe, I believe, please help me, Father God. Please help me." His tears fell in hot splashes. His heart hammered in his chest. *Humble yourself* . . . "Help me!"

There, in the path beneath the trees, bowed to the ground, the sun on his back, he knew deep inside he had to give it up once and for all: the anger, the hatred, the frustration, the grief. The control.

"Help me, Father," he sobbed. "Help me. I can't do this!"

Chapter 32

Cass saw him when he got back to the office, as he was packing up his personal items and cleaning up his desk. "Jake, are you leaving?"

"I'm going home early," he said softly, "to pick up the kids after school."

She couldn't hide the pain in her face. "Can I bring you guys dinner?"

He grimaced. "I think I just need to be alone with the kids tonight. No offense."

Cass nodded. "Let me know if I can do something, Jake." She started to leave and then turned back. "Will you call me, later?" she asked, tears falling from her eyes.

He promised he would.

It was nine forty-five before her phone rang. Cass was in her apartment, pacing the floor, her stomach tight, her head aching. She had gotten a call from Travis, who said simply, "Heads up" and she knew exactly what that meant. The grand jury had seen enough evidence to bring Jake to trial. Now he would be arrested, charged . . . "Oh, God," she cried out, "how can this be?"

She had confided in Moose. He was like a puppy, the way he followed Jake around and she sensed he'd be a help. Then she'd called her Aunt Trudy and her dad and asked them to pray, and her aunt reminded her that none of this was a surprise to God. He had a path through every field of suffering, even if she, Cass, couldn't see it She didn't think she had the faith to see it, but surely her dad and Trudy would. She would cling to that hope.

When she tried explaining that to Travis, he had no idea what she was talking about.

She had just poured herself a cup of tea when the phone rang. It was Jake. Her heart jumped at the sound of his voice. "How are you?"

"I'm all right."

"And the kids?"

"Okay. I picked them up from school and took them to the park. We went to dinner and I helped them with homework."

"Are you going to tell them?"

"I did. I had Justin read us the story of Joseph. You know, when Potiphar's wife lied and accused him and he ended up going to jail."

Cass trembled.

"We talked about how hard it must have been for Joseph, and how unfair, but that eventually he decided God meant it for good. Then I told them what I'd heard, about the grand jury, and what that was going to mean."

"Oh, Jake," she exclaimed. "How did they react?"

"Justin was mad. He cried. He was so frustrated."

"And Cat?"

"Caitlin . . . I don't know. She was real quiet. I

251

think it's all way beyond her right now." Jake paused. "Afterwards, they asked if we could camp out. You know, sleep in the living room. I think that's their way of saying they want to be close to me tonight."

"They're scared."

"Yes." He hesitated. "Me, too."

Jake scared? Cass took a sip of tea. Her hand was shaking. She felt cold.

"So we made a tent out of sheets in the living room, and put sleeping bags on the floor. I laid down with them until they fell asleep. Then I got up to call you."

"Thank you. I just needed to talk to you." Her voice cracked.

"Look, don't get stressed out. This isn't your problem. It's going to work out, Cass."

But it's so unfair, she wanted to say, but she held her tongue. "Listen," she said, taking a deep breath, "I did some research this afternoon, talked to some people I know, and I've got a list of the best, most aggressive defense lawyers in Maryland. And we don't need to confine ourselves to them. We can go anywhere." She hesitated, waiting for a response. "And don't even worry about money. We'll get it. We'll do whatever it takes." He still remained quiet. She frowned. "Jake?" She pressed the phone to her ear.

"There's this guy at church, Josh Willis. Craig knows him."

"I know who you're talking about. Jake, he's not the kind of lawyer you need. He handles DUIs and speeding tickets! You need an aggressive criminal defense lawyer, one with a track record!" She kept talking, hoping he'd agree. "Do you know what I mean, Jake?"

He sighed audibly. "Cass," he said, "this whole thing is overwhelming to me. I have no clue how to get through this, no idea what's going to happen. None whatsoever. I only know that God knows what's going on, and that I need to follow him. I need a lawyer who understands that, who will pray with me and for me. As best I can figure, that's Josh Willis. So that's who I'm going with."

"But Jake . . ."

"I have got to do what I think God's telling me to do. Period."

There was no point in arguing. It would just keep them both up all night. So Cass backed down. She tried to regroup, to think of something positive to say. "How can I help you, Jake?" she asked.

"If it's all right with you, I'd like to give you some legal authority with the kids—the right to pick them up from school, authorize medical care, that sort of thing, in case I'm detained for a time. I'd like you to back me up, with the kids."

"I can do that, Jake. I'd be glad to do that. They can stay with me if they have to. But what about Tam's parents?"

Jake hesitated. "If I'm indicted, things with them might get sticky. They're fine, Cass, with the kids, but right now, I'd rather you be the primary guardian."

"That's fine. I think Trudy or my dad will back me up, too."

"I'm going to type that stuff up right now, papers that you need to have with you. I'll leave them in the cabinet where I keep my guns. I'll include the addresses and phone numbers of the school, the babysitters, the doctor, Tam's parents, and so on. Just in case. And I've put your cell phone number on my fridge where the kids can see it. They know to call you if something happens." Jake stopped. "I have no idea when the arrest warrant will be served. I'm thinking I'm going to shortstop that tomorrow, go down to the police station and say I've heard a rumor, and see if I can turn myself in. That way, I can deal with the initial garbage while the kids are in school."

"Yes, that makes sense," Cass said. She sagged against a wall as her eyes filled with tears. Jake arrested? How bizarre was that? "Do the kids know what might happen?" She moderated her voice, unwilling to have him hear the emotion she was struggling with.

"I told them about it briefly. It just would be better if they didn't see it."

"I agree."

"But we've decided that whatever happens, we're going to believe that God means it for good."

"Oh, Jake," she almost cracked. "Jake, I just can't . . ."

He cut her off. "Just pray, Cass, okay? Pray."

"Yes. Okay."

"All right. Tomorrow morning I'm going to take the kids to school, then go by the police station. I'll call you after that. If you don't hear from me, pick up the kids, will you?"

When she hung up the phone, the tears fell, cascading down her cheeks in salty streams until she was sobbing, gasping for breath, her ribs aching. "Please, God," she whispered, "please help him!"

The next morning, the kids were getting ready for school. Jake could hear Caitlin brushing her teeth. He was tying his tie when he heard a knock at the door. He paced over to it, started to look through the peephole, then turned as Justin hollered out a question from the back. Answering Justin, not thinking about what he was doing, Jake opened the door.

A sea of blue. Cops.

"Jacob Tucker?" a uniformed officer said. In his hand was a piece of paper.

Dread flooded through Jake. Almost panic. "Oh, no. Wait." He held up his hand.

"Dad?" Justin said, emerging from the hallway.

The cops surged forward. "We have a warrant for your arrest," the lead cop said. "Put your hands behind your back."

"Daddy!" Caitlin screamed.

"Can you hold on?" Jake said.

"I said, hands behind your back!" The lead cop grabbed Jake's left arm.

Anger flashed through Jake. He wanted to punch him! His face burning, he said, "Kids, it's okay." He heard the ratcheting of the cuffs going on, felt the cold metal against his wrists, felt fear and anger rising in his chest like a black tide.

Justin grabbed the cop's arm. "He didn't do it! He didn't . . ."

"Justin!" Jake said, trying to move toward his son.

The cop shook the boy off. Caitlin screamed as her brother fell to the floor.

"Hey, take it easy!" Jake yelled. "He's a kid!" His head began pounding.

"He didn't do it," the boy sobbed. He began to get up.

"Justin!" Jake twisted against the hands gripping his arms. "Justin! Go back to the bedroom, and stay there with your sister. Go! Now!"

A cop moved toward the boy, but when she put her hands on his shoulders to guide him back to his room, Justin jerked away from her, dropped his head and, still sobbing, put his arm around Caitlin and retreated.

"There's a gun in an ankle holster on my left leg," Jake said, fighting to be calm, "and one on my belt." He felt the cops remove them. "Let me call someone for my kids."

"We've already called child protective services," one cop responded. "They'll be here shortly."

CPS! No! "I've got someone. If you'll just let me . . ."

Just then Caitlin came back, and she burst through the ring of cops and threw herself on him grabbing his leg. "Daddy! Don't let them take you!"

Jake shook. "Caitlin, it's all right."

"She got away from me, Dad," Justin said, crying. He tugged at his sister's arm. "C'mon, Cat!"

Why did his kids have to see this? Why?

"Get these kids outta here," a cop snarled.

"Can I talk to them for a minute, please?" Jake said, his voice shaking.

"Look, buddy . . ."

Another voice. "Let him talk to them. For crying out loud."

"We got our orders," the belligerent cop responded.

"He's not going to do anything. Have some heart. Let him talk to his kids."

And so they relented. He had three minutes.

257

Jake dropped to his knees and his kids hugged him. He told them to be brave, told them to remember, God meant it for good, told them Cassie would come and take care of them, told them he'd see them very soon. Tonight, maybe. And as he was finishing, he heard a voice at the doorway.

"Special Agent Robert T. Carter. FBI. What's going on here?"

The cops shifted uneasily.

Jake struggled to his feet and turned to look at Moose, who was wearing tactical pants and his FBI raid jacket with the giant orange letters. Good old Moose.

"He's under arrest," a cop snarled.

"For what?"

"That's none . . ."

Jake interrupted. "Special Agent Carter," he said, "I'm going with these officers down to the police station to take care of some business. Would you please tell the squad supervisor I'll be in late?"

Moose nodded. "I will."

"And call my partner?"

"Yes, sir." Moose glared at the cop nearest Jake. "Which one of you is in charge?"

The lead cop acknowledged he was.

Moose pulled a small notebook out of his pocket, and made a point of writing something down—the cop's badge number, Jake figured.

"He's a federal agent," Moose said, nodding toward Jake. "You watch how you treat him or you're gonna find yourselves in deep kimchi, you got it?" Moose reiterated his point, then he walked over and bent down toward Justin and Caitlin, both of whom were still crying. "Kids, how about if Uncle Moose takes you to school today?"

Jake took a deep breath. Uncle Moose. Thank you, he said silently.

"Let's go back in your room," Moose said.

Caitlin looked at Jake, but before he could say anything, Justin put his arm around her and guided her away. "C'mon, Cat," and he led her off down the hall.

"We'll see you later today," Moose said to Jake, over his shoulder.

"All right, let's go," a cop said, recapturing Jake's attention, and they jerked his arm, and Jake heard his life slipping away, like rain on a tin roof sliding into a cistern.

Chapter 33

Where had Moose come from, Jake wondered as they rode to the police station. The whole thing was bizarre. After being walked out of his apartment building, handcuffed, he'd been greeted by the flash of press photography. The press didn't hang out in front of his building. The cops must have called them. And suddenly he saw the plan. Someone had purposely chosen early morning to pick him up, when the kids were home, just to rattle his chain. There were lots of other ways and other times that could have happened, but whoever it was chose the circumstance that would be most difficult for Jake. And they'd notified the press to put more pressure on him. They were trying to break him down, right from the start.

Arriving at the police station, he saw more photographers. The murder of a state senator's wife was high profile. The idea that her ex-husband, an FBI agent, had done it was raw meat in the shark-infested waters of the media. There'd be film on TV by noon. Jake made a mental note to keep the kids away from the TV, away from the newspapers, away from the radio and the Internet.

The next time he saw the kids—when would that be? He took a deep breath as the doors swung open and the desk sergeant looked up. Welcome to my world, he seemed to say.

Surreal. It was the only word Jake could think of that described the next hours. Like a Picasso painting, all warped and out of whack, eyes and ears misplaced and faces distorted. He'd been on the other side, arresting people for years. Now, to be the one in the cuffs, the one being fingerprinted, and searched, having a mug shot taken. It was bizarre. Disturbing. Infuriating. Unbelievable.

Jake's mouth felt like cotton. His heart would not settle down into a normal rhythm. He felt like he was in a thick fog. *Humble yourself under the mighty hand of God.* And he breathed silent prayers and tried to focus—focus on hearing God in the middle of the insanity. Are you there, he asked silently. Are you with me?

Nothing. No response. Just the hard cold steel of a jail cell permeated with the sickening odor of sweat, urine, and fear.

Eventually, an officer took him to an interview room and Bruce Kilgore and another hardball detective tried to grill him.

You and your ex had problems, huh? When was the first time you hit her? She provoked you, didn't she? Made you mad. We all know, women can be like that. What'd she say to you that made you so mad?

But he refused to talk to them without his lawyer and they gave up. When Josh Willis

261

walked through the door it was like seeing an angel emerging form a cloud. Finally, some help.

Jake figured they intended to keep him overnight, just to tighten the screws down on him some more. Try to force a plea bargain. But the judge set the arraignment for late that afternoon. The judge, a gray-haired woman in her sixties who looked at him over her reading glasses, could release him after posting bail, or lock him up. What was he charged with? First-degree murder. How did he plead? Not guilty, your honor. Was he a flight risk? A danger to the community? The prosecutor said "yes" and "yes" but Craig Campbell and two other agents showed up to testify to Jake's reliability. When the gavel came down, Jake was ordered to post a $200,000 bond, and stay in the state of Maryland, and he was free.

Free. The word had never meant so much to him. At first, he wasn't sure where he was going to get the money to pay the bondsman—$20,000 up front—but Josh said it had been taken care of and within an hour, the two were walking out of the courthouse, into the cold February evening, Jake rubbing his wrists and silently thanking God.

Josh drove him back to the apartment in his battered Subaru station wagon. It was six o'clock. As he walked in, Cass and the kids were cleaning up the huge mess left by investigators. There were papers and objects all over the floor, drawers pulled out and even the cushions had been taken off the couch. Once again, he felt violated and anger welled up in him.

But the kids, seeing him, bubbled over with joy and he couldn't stay mad. They grabbed onto him and he gathered them in his arms and tears came to his eye. His kids. This is what it was all about. This is what mattered.

"Kids," he said, standing up and brushing himself off, "this is Mr. Willis. He's a lawyer and he's helping me. This is Justin," Jake said, putting his hand on his son's head, "and Caitlin." He picked her up.

Josh, who was in his late thirties, had dark hair and blue eyes. He was a bit portly, soft, like he spent more time with books than he did in a gym. But he had a quick smile, and, with four kids of his own, an easy way with children. He bent down and shook Justin's hand and then Caitlin's.

"He didn't do it," Justin said firmly. "It was Chase Westfield. He's the one."

Josh smiled. "We're going to figure it out. Don't you worry."

"And this is Cassidy McKenna."

"Yes, we've met," Josh said, extending his hand to her.

Jake realized in a flash it was Cass who had covered the bail bondsman's fee. His eyes connected with Cassie's. What a good friend. Then he looked at the mess in the apartment.

"They took the computer, Dad!" Justin said.

"We'll get it back," he replied. "There's nothing in there."

"My book report is," Justin said. "My book report, on the lighthouses." He'd been studying the lighthouses on the Chesapeake Bay, memorizing their names and learning their history. It was part of his obsession with the Bay and boats and the wildlife, and Jake wasn't really sure what to think about it, until Cass made a comment about how being on the water was like being in a whole different world. And Jake guessed that Justin would find a whole different world more comfortable than the one in which he'd seen his parents divorced and his mother killed. Maybe that was it. Maybe it was a form of escape.

"We'll work it out, Jus. I promise."

"I'll ask the police to put all unrelated documents and files on a jump drive," Josh said. "They will do that."

"Thanks," Jake said.

"Listen, I'm going to head out," Josh said. "I'll call you in a couple of days."

"Thanks, Josh. I really appreciate your help."

"We'll just keep praying. God's got a plan in all this."

Jake nodded. "I believe that."

Later, after they'd straightened up the apartment and put the kids to bed, Jake and Cass sat in the living room, exhausted.

"They took my guns," Jake said. "What's up with that? She wasn't even killed with a gun! They can't just come in and take everything!"

"It's miserable, isn't it?"

"Thanks, Cass. For putting up the money."

"It's no problem, Jake. Whatever it takes. I've got that life insurance from Mike and I can't think of a better use for it."

"I'll pay you back."

She waved him off. "We can talk about that later. Let's just focus now on beating this thing."

"Where'd Moose come from? That's what I was wondering."

"He told me he'd woken up in the middle of the night and couldn't get back to sleep. And he just kept thinking about you and the kids. On impulse he drove by here before work and saw the cop cars and the press and came on in." Cass smiled. "I told him it was a God-thing."

Jake shook his head and grinned. "It was so cool, the way he announced himself. 'Special Agent Robert T. Carter, FBI.' The cops weren't sure what to do."

Cass laughed, and then she got serious. "So what's next, Jake? What do we do?"

He stretched his legs out and slumped down, resting his head against the back of the couch. What was next? "I guess I'll have to look for another job."

"Another job?"

He shrugged. "I've got to support the kids! The bureau's not going to keep paying me. They could even fire me. I'll have a lot of time on my hands, waiting for the trial. Forty-five days, maybe sixty. That's a long time."

"It isn't much time when it comes to figuring out who really killed Tam."

Jake sighed and sat up. "I know. And the reality is, without the real perpetrator, I look pretty guilty."

"Jake!"

"I'm sorry! I do. Ex-husband. Messy divorce. Fights over custody. And I'm an agent. They love taking down the feds."

A miserable silence fell between them.

When he looked up, Cass was crying. "Hey, hey," he said, giving her a hug, "where's my tough little partner? My female agent friend?"

"I'm an agent, Jake, not a female agent," she said, smiling through her tears. It was a standing joke with them. She was an agent, a full-fledged agent. No modifier needed. "I'm sorry. It's you. It's the kids. It's Tam. It's the whole thing—it's just so wrong."

"Whoever said life would be fair?" Jake said softly. After her husband had been killed she'd been so reserved, so controlled he'd accused her of refusing to grieve. Now, every time he turned around she was teary. What had changed? "Trust God, Cass. Just trust him. We'll get through this."

"Look," she said, forcing herself to straighten up. "What can I do for you?"

"I want a gun," he responded. He'd been threatened, beaten up, his kids nearly abducted. You better believe he wanted a gun.

She grimaced. "Jake, no. That was a condition of bail, right?"

He sighed his acknowledgement.

"You can't risk it."

Jake shook his head. But he knew she was right.

"Moose and I want to help. Unofficially, of course. Craig hinted it would be better if he just didn't know about it."

"Okay."

"I called Trudy and my dad and both of them want to help. Money, babysitting . . . whatever you need."

Humble yourself. There were different ways of being humbled, Jake was finding out. "I'm very grateful for that," he said. He stood up. "I'm not sure what I'm going to need."

"We'll just play it by ear. But you're not in this alone, Jake. The people who love you, we're standing with you."

He turned and hugged her. "You're a great friend, Cass. A great friend. But you have your life, and a fiancé, and a job to do and a wedding to plan. I don't want to mess up any of that."

"Don't worry about it."

Chapter 34

Half a week later, he sat in Josh Willis' office, located in a low-rise office park outside of Annapolis. It was a sunny Tuesday morning. Outside the office window, sparrows flitted in the bushes.

Not even a sparrow falls without God knowing it, Jake thought. He had to believe that. He had to believe God knew and God cared. The God who cared for Hagar in the wilderness was surely aware of his situation. Surely.

Josh had a file in front of him. His desk was modest, purchased at a chain office supply store. The credenza behind him was filled with pictures of his family. His wife, Jake knew, had put him through law school, working as a teacher. Now she stayed home with their kids, three boys and a girl. Two of the boys were twins.

There were three chairs, cloth, not leather, arranged in front of the desk. Clearly, whatever money Josh made he chose to put elsewhere. Jake was in the leftmost chair, a position he chose so he could easily look out of the windows that formed the corner of the room. Cass sat next to him and Moose beyond her. They'd come to hear the prosecutor's evidence and form a battle plan.

"Okay, basically what they have is this," Josh began. "You and Tam were married for eight years, and divorced three years ago. You contested the divorce and fought over custody of the kids. She married Chase Westfield two years ago. They have a housekeeper, Consuela . . . Consuela," he repeated, searching for her last name, "Consuela Hernandez who will testify she heard violent arguments between you."

Jake swallowed.

"Violent?" Cass demanded. "What does she mean by 'violent'?"

Josh scanned down the witness's statement. "On numerous occasions, she heard shouting and angry exchanges between the decedent and Mr. Tucker. Several times, Mrs. Westfield was in tears after he left."

Jake took a deep breath.

"The senator will testify he was concerned about Mr. Tucker's history of violent behavior."

"Violent behavior!" Cass exploded.

Jake closed his eyes, his heart drumming.

". . . and ordered his wife not to allow him to come to the house. In fact, on December tenth, he told her not to see Mr. Tucker at all, he was so concerned for her safety."

"That's bull," Moose snapped.

"What else?" Jake said.

"An Anne Arundel County police officer says he saw Mr. Tucker parked on Magnolia Lane, watching the Westfields' house, around midnight on . . ." Josh recited the date.

Rudy Glass. He knew somehow that would come back to haunt him.

"Let's see," Josh leafed through the papers. "If you take the stand, they'll go after your character. They're going to try to prove a history of violence. You were involved in an arrest last November? You roughed up a thirteen-year-old?"

Jake sighed. "It wasn't exactly like that." He explained the circumstances under which he had tackled Manny. Josh nodded.

"And then there was that incident at the Senate office building. You breached security . . ."

"No way!"

Josh continued. "Your landlord will testify he had to replace a door in your apartment that you had kicked in."

"Because Justin had locked the door!" Cass said.

Josh looked back at his notes. "Let's see, you beat up a guy named Renaldo."

Jake rolled his eyes.

"And were subsequently in a violent altercation with four men at a gas station."

"They attacked him!" Cassie's eyes were flashing with anger.

Josh continued. "The night Tam was killed. She'd been with you . . ."

"And me, and the kids," Cass interjected.

". . . even though her husband had told her to stay away from you."

Jake worked to keep his voice steady. "She wanted to see the kids in the Christmas play at church. Chase was out of town, her car was out of commission, so I gave her a ride."

"And then went back to her house, by yourself."

"That's right. She called me . . ."

"I heard the call," Cass said.

". . . she called me to say she'd left her cell phone in my car. She was concerned that if Chase found out, she'd be in trouble." The memories of that night came flooding back, like deep, dark water, overwhelming him, drowning even his anger. Tam was dead. Dead. He heard his own voice telling the story, but he was lost somewhere far away in his emotion.

"You had Tam's blood on your clothes," Josh said, reading again from the paper, "and scratch marks on your neck. The techs found your DNA under her fingernails, and when the detective asked Tam who hit her, she said your name."

Jake glanced at Cass and her eyes were glistening. Tears! Tears again. "Yeah," he acknowledged. "I was talking to her and she was trying to talk back."

"The detective at the scene said you mumbled, 'I'm sorry, I'm sorry.' "

"I was sorry I couldn't help her! Sorry I hadn't gotten there sooner! Sorry I couldn't protect her!"

"According to the medical examiner, the victim's wounds were consistent with being hit by a statue found in the foyer. Your prints were on it."

"Yes! I moved it so I could get closer to her!"

Josh pursed his lips. He pushed his chair back. "Would you two please excuse us?" he said to Cass and Moose, standing up.

"Sure," they mumbled and filed out.

Josh sat back down, leaned forward and looked at Jake, his eyes searching and probing. "Is there anything, anything you need to tell me? Anything at all? Because the only way this will work is if you are completely and totally honest with me."

Jake took a deep breath and looked Josh straight in the eye. "We did argue, but I never, ever hit Tam. And I didn't kill her. It happened just as I said. I found her that way." He wiped his hands on his pants leg. "I don't know who beat her up. But in all my life, I never, ever hit her, or pushed her, or intentionally hurt her. Or any other woman, unless I was in the process of arresting her as part of my job. Never. I didn't kill Tam." He shook his head, remembering the night. "I was holding her and she grabbed for me, and scratched my neck. But she wasn't trying to defend herself; she was just trying to touch me. I didn't kill her, Josh. I didn't."

Josh narrowed his eyes as he looked at Jake's

face, and then he nodded. "I believe you." He sat back. "But we have a lot of work to do."

For Cass, life became the pursuit of two goals: Pursue Danny's shooter, and help Jake with his defense. So when Moose came in with evidence linking the two, her face lit up.

"Look here!" Moose said, handing her a sheaf of papers. "The ballistics on that triple murder. Two of the three victims were shot by the same gun that shot Danny!"

"Awesome," Cass said, scanning the papers. "This is great! Now we just need the gun."

"Well, that's the trouble isn't it," Moose said. "We need the gun. We're still three or four steps away from tying Chase to Jake's assault."

"And even farther from linking Chase to Tam's murder." Cass frowned. "You headed over to the lawyer's office?"

Moose nodded. "Four-thirty."

"Me, too."

Jake had asked them to meet him at Josh's office. "We need to brainstorm. My defense is pretty thin. If we can link Chase to Tam's murder, I'm off the hook. That's why I asked you two to come." He looked from Cass to Moose.

"How about Tam's parents or her sister?" Cass asked. "Have they been interviewed about Chase? Tam's marriage?"

Josh looked at his notes. "According to investigators, the Andersons and Tam's sister had no knowledge of any problems in Tam's current marriage."

Jake rolled his eyes. "They're either lying or Tam hid things well. Josh, hand me a legal pad, would you? Let's see what we can do to break Chase."

Chapter 35

Jake's lawyer pulled a blank pad out of the credenza behind his desk and handed it to Jake. "All right, here's what we've got," Jake said, and he drew a line down the middle of the page. He labeled the two columns, "Chase Did It" and "He Hired Someone."

"If Chase did it," Jake said, "we need to figure out how to break his alibi. We need to know when and with what. We need to know when he flew into BWI, on what flight, and how he got to the house where he spoke. We need to know who drove him. We need to know what car. Who saw him." He scribbled on the legal pad as he spoke.

"And if anyone saw that car near the Westfields' house that evening," Cass said. She pulled out her own small notebook and began taking notes.

"What else?"

"Did Chase own any guns?" Moose asked. "What about the threats he supposedly received? Were they threats against his family?"

"Shouldn't the detectives have been asking these questions?" Josh asked.

"They should have, but they may not have.

Sometimes," Cass explained, "the easy explanation seems the best and they stop looking. Besides, nobody wants to get on the wrong side of a state senator."

"All right," Jake said. "Now, we need to establish a timeline. Everything, from the time he landed at BWI to the time he arrived at the house to when he spoke, when he left, what time he was," Jake's voice cracked, "notified of the assault on Tam."

"I'd say about the second it happened," Moose said, sarcasm dripping from his voice.

Jake cleared his throat. "We need a good, solid timeline."

Josh interrupted. "Some of that timeline must be on the security tapes."

Jake raised his eyebrows.

"The house where Chase was speaking has a security system." He looked down at the papers on his desk. "That's part of the reason detectives cleared Chase. They have him on the tape."

The room fell silent. Then Cass spoke. "Let's get a copy of that tape."

"I've already asked for it," Josh said.

Cass continued. "Okay, so what if he had it done—if he hired someone to kill Tam when he was conveniently out of town." She told them about the connection they'd found between the thugs who beat up Jake and Danny's shooting.

"Assuming he was behind the assault on you," she said to Jake, "then Chase has some contact with violent criminals."

Jake shook his head. "I don't think it was a hired killer. Here's the thing: A hired gun, even if he's just a thug, is not going to risk a personal confrontation. He's going to shoot from a distance, from across the room, at least."

"Or sneak up behind and strangle her," Moose suggested.

"Unless Tam knew the guy and let him close to her."

Jake shook his head. "Think about it: Tam's face was bashed in." He stood up and gestured to Cass who, responding, stood up with him. "Her killer picked up something heavy, probably that statue in the foyer," he said, pretending to do so, "and slammed it into the side of her face, here," he motioned toward Cassie's face, "and here." He turned to Josh. "That's not something a hired gun would do. It's too personal. Plus, it's messy. That close, she might fight back." His throat squeezed shut and he sat back down.

Cass continued to speak, but Jake found himself imagining the scene, seeing Chase hit Tam, seeing her drop to the floor, seeing the ugly, bloody mess of a bashed-in head. Grief washed over him in a black wave.

"Jake?"

Jake raised his head. "I'm sorry." He ran his hand through his hair. "Okay, what else?"

Ten minutes later, they were done.

He had so much to think about, Jake hardly knew where to begin. Defending himself, taking care of the kids, planning for contingencies. So when he got a phone call from Craig a week later asking him to come in to the office, apprehension gripped him. Was this it? Was he fired?

All he had ever wanted to do was be an agent and take care of his kids. Now, both goals were slipping through his fingers like sand.

He walked in and found the Special Agent in Charge, Brian Burnett, sitting in Craig's office. "Boss," he said, nodding a greeting as he sat down. He braced himself.

"How are you doing, Jake?" Burnett asked.

"All right, sir." Jake's stomach rolled with tension. Would they ask for his creds here and now? He had worn his best suit, like he was dressing for his own funeral.

Craig sat at his desk, not making eye contact. The pictures on the wall behind him seemed to swim as Jake looked toward them. He fought the urge to leave, to run away from what had been his life before they took it.

Craig began talking. Jake had trouble following what he was saying. His mind was ping-ponging around all the possibilities.

Then Burnett took over. The SAC reached into his breast pocket and drew out an envelope. It was thick and Jake could see it held an FBI official return address. So this was it. His letter of dismissal. He took a deep breath.

"This is for you," Burnett said and he handed the envelope to Jake.

But it felt odd in his hand.

"Go ahead. Open it."

He did, expecting to see a sheaf of official papers separating him from the FBI. What he saw was money. A huge wad of bills and checks. Hundreds, no, probably thousands, of dollars. Jake's face grew hot. He looked at the boss.

"It's coming in from all over the country," Burnett said. "Everyone wants to help."

The agent fraternity. Jake blew out a breath. "I don't know what to say. I didn't expect this."

Craig nodded. "There will be more and we'll pass it along as it comes in."

He looked at the two men. "I had no idea how I was going to pay my lawyer," he said. "This is huge."

"There's something else," Burnett said. "I've spoken with the Director. You're being placed on administrative leave. Without pay, unfortunately, but . . ."

"But I'm not fired?" Jake asked, incredulous.

"No. Not unless, of course, things go badly."

Jake looked from Burnett to Craig and back again.

"The boss went to bat for you," Craig said, "and the Director bought it."

"Thank you, sir. Thank you. This is a huge relief."

Burnett nodded. "The Director wouldn't do that for just anyone. I told him I was absolutely convinced of your innocence. So get through this and get back to work."

Sunday morning, early, Cass heard her phone ringing. It's Jake, she thought to herself, jarring herself awake. What's wrong?

But it wasn't Jake, it was Travis. "Hey," he said, softly. "Guess what? It's snowing."

"Is it?"

"How 'bout that sail?"

Oh, yes. A sail in the snow. That's one reason she'd left her boat in the water over the winter. Cass walked over to the window and looked out. The snow was just beginning to fall, big, puffy flakes descending in a lacy curtain. One more touch of winter on this mid-March day. "Have you heard a forecast?" she asked him.

"Perfect. High of thirty-eight. Winds east at ten to fifteen. Snow showers on and off all day. No accumulation expected."

It would mean changing gears, skipping church, but it was something he'd been looking forward to, something he thought would be romantic. "Okay, Travis." She glanced at her watch. "I'll need an hour."

"Meet you at the marina, then, at eight. I'll bring the food."

By the time Cass got to the marina, Travis had the companionway open, the diesel engine warming up, and the sail cover off. He kissed her and she stowed her gear and together they cast off, Cass at the helm, Travis handling the lines.

The sky overhead was leaden, the clouds low and heavy. The snow was coming harder now, the flakes melting as they hit the water. But the wind was perfect and the temperature reasonable. Cass was comfortable in her heavy parka, gloves, and knit hat. "You look cute," Travis said, and then kissed her cheek.

The waters of the Bay were gray, reflecting the sky, and *Time Out* was the only boat in sight. Emerging from the channel, Cass turned into the wind and Travis put up the mainsail, lifting the white canvas into the gray sky. Then he let out the jib, and the two sails caught the wind and heeled the boat comfortably to starboard. Cass cut the engine and the silence surrounded them. Thomas Point Light was visible in the distance, the octagonal white building nearly blending in with the increasing snow. "Let's head north, Cass suggested as she swung the boat around, and Travis agreed, trimming the sails for that course.

For all the years she'd lived near the Bay, Cass had never sailed in the snow. It was beautiful, in its own way, different from any other experience. The gray of the Bay and the curtain of snow, the white sails and the leaden sky merged at times into a seamless landscape, and the sounds seemed muffled and distant. With no other boats visible, the feeling was magical. At least, it should have been.

Travis moved to sit on the edge of the cockpit right behind Cass. And he put his arm around her and pulled close, his head next to hers, his voice in her ear. "You are beautiful," he said softly, "and I love you."

Cass looked over the side and saw the water slipping by, slipping by like her life. She was here, with Travis. But was she, really? Where was her heart?

She fought it, for the rest of the day. Fought the intrusive thoughts of Jake. Fought the voice in her head that told her she was making a mistake. Fought the fear of change and the embarrassment of admitting the truth.

Until finally, she had to.

Chapter 36

That night, Jake sat in his living room. The clock read 10 p.m. The kids were asleep, but he was wide awake. Wide awake, his stomach in turmoil. Upset again, after eating half of a hamburger and a little bit of salad. He couldn't remember the last time he'd been able to eat an entire meal. Even Justin had noticed. And yes, he was losing weight. A lot of weight.

Trudy had given him the book he'd started reading at her house, *When God Weeps*. He picked it up. A dozen pages in, he heard a soft knock on his door. Who in the world would be knocking on his door this late? He looked through the peephole and saw Cass. His heart jumped. He swung the door open.

"Hey," she said, stepping into the apartment.

"Cass! What are you doing here? Is something wrong?" Jake closed the door as she began stripping off her outer clothes. Then she held up her left hand. There was no ring on her finger.

Jake blinked. "What happened? What did you do? Cass, come in, tell me about it."

"You have any coffee?" she replied.

"Sure. Of course." He fixed her a steaming mug while she kicked off her shoes and hung up her coat. Then they sat down on the couch. She sat cross-legged, her back to the arm so she could face him.

"So what happened?" Jake repeated.

"It snowed today, you know?"

Jake nodded. "Yes, I saw it. The kids and I played in it."

"Travis and I went out for a sail. So here I am, on what was supposed to be this romantic sail with my fiancé, and all I could think about was the trouble my partner was in."

Jake groaned and dropped his head. "Oh, no."

Cass continued with her story. "He knew something was wrong with our engagement. I guess I did too, on some level. For instance, I just couldn't get around to setting a date!

"So we went out to dinner tonight and we talked about it. And it was all very civilized," Cass stood up and paced away, as if the story demanded physical action. She turned toward Jake, her cheeks red, her long hair falling around her face. "Travis said he'd noticed my preoccupation and wondered if this was the right time to be thinking about getting married. He suggested maybe we'd better wait until your situation is resolved."

Jake stood up. He walked over to the window looking out onto the street. "Wow, I'm sorry," he said, turning toward Cass. His words were stilted, set upright in rows, as if keeping them in line would still the wild pounding of his heart. His eyes searched her face, and for a moment, he thought about taking her in his arms and kissing her, telling her he loved her. He loved her!

But he couldn't! His mind raced. What would be the future in a relationship with him? Nothing. There'd be no future, not if this trial went badly. And how could he hurt her that way? After what she'd been through when Mike died?

No, she was better off without him. "Maybe," he said, "you'll get back together. After this is over." His words sounded stiff even to him.

Cass looked down. "He says he loves me. But honestly, I don't think it would work."

"Was he upset?"

"No. Resolved is probably the right word." She shrugged. "It wasn't just your problems. I had another issue as well."

"Oh? What's that?"

"He says he's a believer, but doesn't go to church. And his faith, it just isn't a big part of his life." Cass frowned. "He's such a good guy, I guess, I just figured . . ."

"He was a Christian in his own way."

"That's right! But when I was talking to him about faith and prayer and your situation, the conversation just kept falling flat."

"Because it doesn't make sense to him."

Cass nodded. "Yes."

Jake looked at Cass. The light was on her face.

She is so beautiful, he thought. And he knew in that moment he would do anything, anything to protect her from more pain. "Cass, I'm not going to tell you what to do, but he'd take good care of you."

"But maybe not in the most important way," she confessed.

"What do you mean?"

"The way you're handling all this," she gestured with her hands, stood up again, and crossed her arms. "I see Jesus in you, Jake. Like I did in Mike. I feel your faith."

Jake's mouth felt dry.

"I mean it." She reached out and touched his arm and a jolt ran through his whole body. "And for right now, I just want to concentrate on helping you."

Cass and Moose together decided the next step in solving Danny's shooting was finding the gun. And that meant working with Jaime Gonzalez, the undercover cop, and sometimes with Travis, which was awkward.

Jaime didn't want to go anywhere near the FBI office, or any police station for that matter. So when they met, it was in odd places—in a park, at a restaurant, in a car.

One night, Cass and Moose were waiting for him at the edge of a park in Annapolis.

Moose started going over Jake's case while they

waited. "Chase came into BWI on an American flight that landed at seven twenty-six. He had a limo pick him up."

"Have you found the driver?"

"I'm working on that. So he's picked up at seven forty-five, and it's thirty minutes down to Annapolis. So the security tape has him walking into Crawford's house at eight eighteen."

"So far, it fits," Cass said.

"At nine thirty, he's on the steps talking to the crowd, and at nine forty-nine, we see him at the bar." Moose looked up from his notes. "Are the time stamps set by the system or the individual cameras?"

"What are you saying?"

"Could the time stamps be wrong?" He scratched his chin.

"I don't know." Cass nodded. "Here comes Jaime."

The undercover cop slipped into the back of Cassie's car and tapped the seat. "Let's move, okay?"

Cass pulled out of the space and left the park. "Where to?"

"There's an old gas station just ahead on the right. Pull behind it."

Cass did, after first checking to see no one was following them. She parked and turned to look at Jaime. "How's it going?"

"Your boys in Eleventh Street are just that,

boys. They think talking big and smoking dope is hot stuff. You still in touch with that woman, Maria?"

"Yes."

"I don't think she's going to be much help. Because I don't think your shooter was part of Eleventh Street."

"Los Bravos, then?" Moose asked.

"Maybe."

"How 'bout this," Moose suggested. "How 'bout you put word out you need a gun, a nine millimeter, to be exact."

Cass caught on immediately. "If the guy who shot Danny and then killed those men thinks it's hot, maybe he'll be looking to get rid of it."

"And then maybe we will find our shooter."

"Sounds good," Jaime said.

"So we asked Jaime to put word out that he was looking for a gun. If we can get a match, it's progress!" Cass told Jake as they walked toward Josh's law office. She didn't tell him about all the dead ends they'd run up against, the frustrations and difficulties.

Jake opened the door to Josh's office and followed Cass in.

"I have two questions," said Josh after Jake and Cass sat down. Josh had squeezed a table into his modest office. Papers and photos and scraps of ideas lay spread out before them like a jigsaw puzzle—one they had no idea how to piece together.

"Go ahead," Jake said. He leaned forward.

"Why wasn't Tam's alarm on, and could she have interrupted a burglary?"

Jake exhaled. His dark eyes focused on the table as he reached back in his memory for that night. It was a month before his trial, and it sometimes felt they were no better off than they were right after his arrest. "I remember when I took her home, that she unlocked the door, stepped in, and immediately walked over to the right to turn off the alarm."

"But does that reset the alarm? Don't you have to do that every time?"

"I think so." Jake rubbed his head. "Even if she had reset it, knowing I was coming she probably turned it off again."

Moose burst in a few minutes later, his excitement buffeting the room. "Guess what I found out!" Moose said.

"What?" Jake asked.

"You know the whole 'Six Degrees of Separation' deal, right?"

Everyone nodded.

"Well, listen to this. Stoddard Hughes, the prosecutor, used to work for Bryan, Allen, and Holmes in Baltimore. So did a guy named George Hunicutt. George Hunicutt went to Columbia

Law School. He roomed with a guy named Greg Mason."

"And who's Greg Mason?"

"He's the stepfather of Jason Witherspoon."

Cassie's eyes widened. "Westfield's legislative aide!"

"Bingo."

"Good work, Moose! How'd you put that together?" Jake said.

"I got lucky."

"So Chase was in on which prosecutor was assigned? Is that what you're saying?" Josh asked.

"Seems obvious to me," Moose said.

Josh shook his head. "There may be a connection, but law is a small world, and even if there is some remote link, it doesn't go anywhere toward proving a conspiracy to falsely accuse Jake."

His logic dampened their mood.

"All right," Cass said. "What *do* we have?"

Over the next hour they reviewed the findings of their investigation. Josh was still waiting for the tapes from the night Tam was slain. Moose had the name of the limo driver who had picked Chase up that night and driven him to the party. And yes, according to his log, they arrived at eight fifteen. Cass had worked on the medical examiner's report: His finding was that Tam had been struck three times with a heavy object with one sharp edge—most likely the statue from the Westfields' foyer, found on the floor near her.

"And my prints were on it," Jake said.

Cass looked at him. "Because you moved it."

"Right!" Jake said, unable to mask the edge in his voice. "But here's the thing, if I wanted her dead, why would I call 911?"

The silence in the room concurred with his opinion.

Josh cleared his throat. "Let's go over the game plan as we have it now."

They would call character witnesses for Jake: Cass, Craig, Jake's pastor, and others. Cass would testify about the discussions they'd had regarding the possibility that Tam was being abused. They'd subpoena Tam's medical records. "She had an appointment with a psychologist," Josh said, "but she never saw him, so that's no help."

Jake nodded. "How about her emails and any journals she may have had?"

"I subpoenaed those and so far, we've gotten some emails but no journals."

"How about her friends?" Cass asked.

"That's part of the problem," Jake said. "Chase was isolating her. She didn't have any. That's why she confided in me."

Cass twisted her mouth and frowned. "Another parent at school maybe? A casual acquaintance?"

Josh sighed. "I went to talk to the school

principal. Honestly, they barely knew Tam. The kids' teachers didn't notice her connecting with any of the other parents."

The more they talked, the more discouraged Jake got. Their case was pretty weak, compared to what the prosecutor had put together against him. Outside, in the parking lot, Cass noticed his gloom and tried to cheer him up. It didn't work.

"We've got four weeks," Jake reminded her.

"We just need to catch a break!"

"I don't know, Cass." Jake ran his finger down the frame of the windshield of his car. Then he looked at her, squinting in the bright sunlight. "I think I've got to face facts. I think I could be headed for prison."

"No, Jake!" Cassie's anguish exploded. "Don't say that!"

He listened to her vent, trying to control the churning in his own gut. Finally he stopped her with an upraised hand. "I need a break, Cass. I need to get away, but I can't leave Maryland. So how about we go out this weekend on your boat."

"What?" Her eyes searched his face.

"How warm does it have to be?"

"I don't know—it depends on who is going out."

Jake was already checking weather on his iPhone. "Sixty. Sunny and highs around sixty both days this weekend." He looked up. "Is that warm enough?"

She nodded. "But why? Why now? You hate boats!"

"You're right, I do. But I promised Justin we could go out for a weekend some time in the spring. I'm starting to wonder—I'm thinking maybe we shouldn't wait." The look on Cassie's face told him she knew exactly what he was talking about. Closer to the trial would be unworkable; after the trial could well be too late. "So let's go, Cass. You, me, the kids, and your dad. As long as we stay in Maryland waters, it'll be fine."

"I'm not sure there's room on my boat." She frowned. "Someone will have to sleep in the cockpit."

"I will. I'll do that."

"It'll be cold overnight."

"It's okay. I can handle it." Jake closed his eyes momentarily. "I want to make another memory for the kids. And time's running out."

Chapter 37

Saturday morning, Jake parked his car at the marina where Cassie's boat was docked and began unloading gear. The kids had already scampered down the dock to where Cassie's sailboat, *Time Out*, was waiting. He was glad she'd gone along with his idea. The air was soft, the promise of spring was everywhere. It would be good to be outside.

Cass met him at his car and picked up a couple of bags. "Dad's got the engine running." Cass nodded toward the boat. "He was really excited when I called to invite him."

"Hey!" Jim Davison called out as Cass and Jake approached. "Hand some of that over."

They'd brought enough food for two days, and that, plus their sleeping bags, clothes, life jackets, and other equipment, soon filled the cockpit. Five people was a bit much on the Alberg for an overnight; it was a good thing two of them were kids.

"You think we have room for that?" Jake smiled as he nodded toward Cassie's laptop.

She sighed. "I know. I should just forget it for a couple of days. But I thought I'd bring it. I have a meeting Tuesday and if I have time, I'd like to go over some things."

Jake shook his head. "You always were so conscientious. That's why I wanted you as my partner. To do all the hard work so I could kick back."

"Oh really? I thought I was just a pretty face!"

"Well, that, too," he said, grinning.

Jake went below to put the last of the supplies in the food lockers and stow the kids' gear. He didn't like being below deck. The smell of the diesel always got to him. He quickly did what he needed to do and pulled himself up the companionway stairs. "Kids! Get your life jackets on."

The two kids scrambled to obey. Jake looked around the marina. It was quiet on this Saturday morning, just a few boaters preparing to go out. The sky was a brilliant blue and the sun warm. The water was still way too cold to go swimming, but the air temperature would make it a pleasant weekend, anyway.

Cass stood behind the wheel in the cockpit. "Go ahead, Justin," she said, nodding.

Justin moved forward, ready to cast off the two forward dock lines. Jake started to follow him. Cass stopped him. "He can do it!"

"All right."

Caitlin looked up at him. "I'm not scared this time, Daddy!"

"Good girl!" He looked at Cass. "You need me to do anything?"

Cass shook her head. "Just sit down."

So he did, next to Cat, and she put her arm through his and snuggled close to him.

"Okay, cast off, Justin!" Cassie called out.

Jake craned his neck to watch his son as he carefully unwound each dock line from the horn cleat at the front of the boat, and neatly threw each one onto the dock.

"Okay, Dad," Cass said.

Jim nodded and cast off the aft lines.

"One hand for the boat, Justin!" Cass said, as the boy moved back to the cockpit. Justin responded, carefully keeping a hand on the safety rails. Cass put the engine in reverse and the boat began to slowly back out of the slip.

"What kind of bird is that, Daddy?" Cat said, pointing to a swooping white bird with a black head.

"A seagull."

"I know, silly! But what kind?"

"I don't know," Jake responded. "You're going to have to ask Mr. Davison."

"That's a laughing gull," Cassie's father said. "Listen to him." Indeed, the bird seemed to be chortling.

"What's so funny?" Cat called out to the bird, then she giggled and buried her face in her dad's chest. He kissed the top of her head and stroked her hair. It was light brown, with strong red undertones, like Tam's before she'd bleached it.

Cass had *Time Out* well in hand as they moved down the channel toward the Bay. The boat rose and nodded with the gentle waves. Jim began showing Justin how to pull the fenders up on deck and secure them. A steady breeze was coming from the southwest. "Come help me find the channel, Justin," Cass said as the boy and her dad re-entered the cockpit.

Justin stood next to Cass, peering into the distance. Jim had the charts in hand. "We're looking for a green can," he said. "Green Can Number Three."

"There it is!" Justin cried, pointing to a channel marker.

"What side should we be on?" Cass asked him.

"Red, right, return," he recited. "We should keep the green can on our right—our starboard side—going out."

Jake marveled at his son. The kid had soaked up so much information about sailing and the Bay and navigation and wildlife over the winter. It was amazing. It was stuff Jake wasn't even interested in. Obviously, Justin was. At first, Jake wasn't sure how he felt about that. He'd expected his kid to be into football and baseball and guns, the same things he, Jake, liked. But no. He was more of a scientist. Jake had to adjust to that, but once he did, he found it pretty neat.

"Red nun, Justin. Where's the red nun?" Cass asked.

"Over there!" Justin cried out, pointing to the triangular buoy.

"Daddy, why can't we just go straight out?" Caitlin asked Jake. "Why is Cassie zigzagging?"

Before Jake could answer, Justin turned around. "Because there are shoals, Cat. Shallow places. And Cassie's boat draws three and a half feet. That means the water has to be that deep or we'll get stuck. So we're following the channel, the deep places, so we don't get stuck."

"Is that right, Daddy?"

Jake squeezed his daughter. "If Justin said it, I'm sure it's right."

Chapter 38

They sailed down the Bay on a good broad reach, sails held taut by the wind, the sea spray arching up over the gunnels every once in a while. Jim and Justin studied the charts, marking their position with an orange grease pencil. They used the GPS to keep track of their course and speed while Cass steered. They were sailing without the engine, and that made it a pleasant ride.

Jake had to admit that he actually felt relaxed. There was something different about being out on the water this time. He felt happy to be leaving all the trial stress behind. And he was with Cass.

By mid-afternoon, they were near the Point No Point lighthouse. "What's up with that name, Justin?" Jake asked his son.

"It's because there was a long stretch of the Bay with no navigation aids, Dad. And the sailors, they wanted another light so they could steer straight." Justin looked at him.

Jake smiled. "I'm glad you know all that stuff!"

They dropped sails and motored around the white caisson structure and Cass found a cove in which to anchor for the night. Safely at anchor, Cass hooked up the grill on the back rail of the boat and Jake pulled steaks out of the cooler. Soon the smell of grilling meat wafted through the cockpit. The air was cooling off now that the sun was down. A good dinner, and the kids would be ready for bed. It would be a good night for sleeping.

"This is like camping, only no neighbors," Jake said, as he and Cass cooked the food.

"I know. There's hardly anything more peaceful than this."

Jake nodded. Near the shoreline, a large gray bird took flight, landing about twenty feet up in a tree.

"That's a heron," Cass said. "It must be nesting up there."

"When their babies fall out of the nest, they just leave them and let them die," Justin piped up. "Mr. Davison told me heron rookeries stink."

"Heron what?"

"Rookeries, Dad. Where a bunch of them nest."

Jake ruffled his son's hair.

When the steaks were ready, they ate dinner, and while Jim and Cassie cleaned up, Jake put his kids to bed, first reading them the story of Paul's shipwreck, dramatizing it with his voice. Then he prayed with them. He tucked Cat into the V-berth, where she'd sleep with Cassie, and Justin into the port side salon berth. Jim would sleep in the starboard berth and Jake had gladly volunteered to take the cockpit. By the time he got back topside, Cassie's dad was up at the bow, looking out over the dark water, and Cassie was in the cockpit staring at her laptop screen.

"Can't get away from it, huh?" Jake gently prodded.

Cass sighed.

"What's this?" he asked, looking at a grainy video file.

Cass shook her head. "That's your case. The video from the night you were assaulted at the gas station. Don't go there, Jake."

"No, wait," he responded. "Look at this." He began playing with the file, choosing to stop the action and blow up a frame until it half-filled the screen. "I never noticed this before."

"What?" Cass said, angling the laptop.

"Check this out. Is this a tattoo? On the guy's neck?" Jake took Cassie's pen and pointed to a section on the screen.

"It's so grainy, it's hard to tell. I thought it was a shadow."

"No, look." He traced the outline with the pen. "It's a salamander. See?"

"I think . . ."

"Daddy?"

Jake jumped. Caitlin was right behind him, looking over his shoulder. Quickly, he turned the laptop away from her. "Cat! What's the matter? I thought you were in bed."

"That man looks like he's crying," Caitlin said.

"What man?"

"The one with the lizard on his neck."

"Cat, why are you up here?" Jake said, annoyed.

"Daddy, I heard something!"

"What?"

"That," Cat said, pointing toward the shore.

"It's a whippoorwill," Jim said, returning to the cockpit. "Listen, Cat." Everyone was quiet. The sound of a bird calling "whip-poor-will" repeated in the distance.

"It scares me," Cat said.

Jim looked at Jake. "C'mon, Caitlin," Jim said, "I'll tell you a story about it," and he took the little girl by the hand and led her back down below deck to her bunk.

"Thanks, Jim," Jake said, when Cassie's dad came back twenty minutes later. "I got frustrated. I really don't want the kids to see that video again. It was bad enough when they had to look at it before."

"We had to see if they could identify any of the attackers," Cass said.

Jim nodded. "What's the meaning of the tattoo?"

Jake sighed. "The salamander? Nothing in particular. But most gang members, certainly all the MS-13 members, have tattoos. They'll have MS-13 tattooed somewhere on their bodies, maybe the name of their clique. Sometimes they'll have three dots, that means the same thing, or a teardrop coming out of one eye."

"Jake!" Cass said suddenly.

He looked at her in the dim light of the cockpit. "Could Caitlin have recognized . . ."

"Of course not. The guys beating me up had ski masks on. If this one has a teardrop tattoo, it was covered." Jake ran his hand through his hair. "Let's get rid of that, okay?" He nodded toward the laptop. "Let's just enjoy the evening."

"Yes, of course," Cass said. She closed the laptop.

Jake started asking Cass's father about the days when he taught biology at the University of Maryland, and the research he'd done on the Bay, his oyster gardens and grass-planting missions. The diversion worked. Jake began to relax and before long, all three were yawning and ready for bed.

After Cassie and Jim went below deck, Jake stretched out in his sleeping bag in the cockpit. Millions of stars were out, piercing the black night sky with pinpricks of light. The breeze had died down. All Jake could hear was the occasional cry of a bird and the lapping of waves. The boat rocked gently and Jake lay still, allowing it to relax him. He prayed, then, for his kids, for Cass, and Jim, and Trudy, and then for himself, talking with God until his lids grew heavy and he fell asleep.

Periodically through the night, Jake woke up and looked at how the stars had changed on their courses. And it was comforting to him, somehow, like the rocking of the boat, and the soft snoring he could hear from below deck. When dawn's fingers began to stretch over the Eastern sky, he turned so he could watch the sunrise. And for the first time in weeks, he felt peace.

"Sleep okay?" Cass asked, as Jake stood in the cockpit and stretched.

"Yeah. It was a beautiful night."

"The cockpit's a little short for you."

"I might as well get used to close quarters," he said grinning at her, "and hard bunks."

"Jake, will you cut that out?" Cass said.

"Hey! Lots of people would like to live in a gated community!"

She rolled her eyes. "Do you joke like that around the kids?"

"Sometimes." Jake looked forward. Caitlin and Justin were on the foredeck of the boat, sitting on the deck. They were talking about something. Jake could see Caitlin's lips moving.

Jim was making breakfast down in the galley. Suddenly, Jake saw Justin turn around, an odd expression on his face. He looked at his dad, got to his feet, and began walking back toward the cockpit, with Caitlin right behind him. He was hurrying and tripped on a metal ring securing part of the rigging. Jake's heart jumped as Justin fell, but the kid caught himself and stepped into the cockpit. "Dad," he said, his face intense, "what were you and Cass looking at last night? On her computer?"

"Just some pictures, Justin. Why?" Jake's heart started thumping, but he didn't know why.

"Let me see them."

"No, son, I don't want you to . . ."

"Dad! Let me see them!"

"I said . . ."

"Why, Justin?" Cass said, putting her hand on Jake's arm. "Why do you want to see them?"

The boy looked from Cass to his dad. "Caitlin thought she recognized somebody."

"I did, Daddy!" the girl piped up.

Jake's jaw tightened.

"Jake," Cass said, "maybe just that freeze frame, you know? Without the whole video?"

His heart was beating hard now, and his face felt hot. He wanted to protect his kids! And yet . . .

"Please, Jake. I think it will be okay."

"All right," he said finally. The words were barely out of his mouth before Cass grabbed her computer from the salon, brought it into the cockpit and began booting it up. Within minutes, the video was on the screen. When she had frozen it on the picture Cat saw, she turned it toward Justin and carefully watched his face. The boy studied the picture. Shyly, his sister pointed her finger to the salamander tattoo, visible only because the man on the screen was reacting to

Jake's hard blow to his jaw. Then Justin turned to his dad.

"Dad, remember that time you couldn't come get us? You had to work because Uncle Danny got shot, and Chase sent us to that babysitter's house with those people we didn't know?"

How could he forget? "Yes."

"One of the guys there had that tattoo. On his neck. Just like that."

A jolt of emotion sent adrenaline surging through Jake. He swallowed hard and looked at Cass.

"Justin, are you sure?" she asked.

The boy nodded. "He's got three teardrops tattooed coming out of his eye."

Cass looked at Jake. "That's why Caitlin said he looks like he's crying."

Jake's mouth felt dry. "Caitlin?" he said.

The little girl nodded her head. "He has tears right here." She pointed to the skin next to her eye.

Cass looked at Jake. "There you go."

Chapter 39

To Jake, the trip back took forever. Cass and her dad called it a "beat." The wind had clocked around and was coming from the northwest, from just the direction they needed to travel. A chop had formed on the Bay, and Cassie's little boat bucked and lurched as it plowed forward.

It made him sick. It all made him sick. The boat, the waves, the sun beating down, the glare, but those elements were nothing compared to the thought of his kids spending the weekend with gang members. He tried to relax but he couldn't. Cass kept looking at him with concern as she stood at the helm fighting the rough ride. Jim, thankfully, had assigned himself the role of chief kid wrangler; Justin and Caitlin were happily looking for birds, unbothered by the lurching craft, oblivious to the implications of their recognition of the man with the salamander tattoo.

"It's especially rough right here," Cass shouted over the sound of the engine. "Whenever you have one body of water joining another," she said, pointing to the Patuxent River, which was joining the Bay, "you get confused seas. The currents get all mixed up and it makes the ride rough. It'll get better soon."

Jake nodded grimly.

"Try to focus on the horizon," Cass suggested.

He tried, but he still felt sick. In fact, he was about to lose it.

Cass saw the look on his face. "If you have to throw up," she shouted over the roar of the diesel, "go to the lee side."

"The what?"

"That side!" she said, pointing to starboard. "Downwind!"

Five minutes later, he took her advice.

After six hours of fighting wind and waves, they made it to the marina. Jake, his face white with nausea, helped tie up the boat. The evening sun was dropping down to the horizon quickly, and a chill was in the air. Ironically, with the setting sun the breeze had died down. Soon the Bay would be placid again. Jake got the kids to pack up their gear and he offloaded it. The dock seemed to swim whenever he looked down.

"Wasn't that fun, Daddy!" Caitlin said, as she stepped off the boat.

"Oh, yes," he replied, looking past her to Cass. "A whole lot of fun. Especially the throwing up part."

His daughter giggled.

Jim hefted his green duffle bag onto the dock and stepped ashore.

"Dad, can I get a seabag like Mr. Davison's?" Justin asked.

Jake looked at his son. "We can probably manage that."

"Thanks, Dad! Race you to the parking lot!" Justin said to his sister.

"No running on the dock!" Cass cried out. She shook her head as the two kids began race-walking toward land.

"If they could bottle that energy and put it into pills, I'd be the first in line," Jim said, smiling. "You all right, son?" he asked, clapping Jake on the shoulder. His eyes squinted as he studied Jake's face.

"I will be, as soon as the world stops moving," Jake said with a sigh.

Cass couldn't wait to call Moose and tell him about the salamander-tattooed man. She tapped in his number as she left the marina. Now they had a potential connection with Chase.

Cass wondered about that as she listened to Moose's cell phone ringing fruitlessly. Tam had refused to tell Jake who the kids were left with that weekend. All Jake knew was that the kids didn't know them, they'd never been to the house where they lived before and they spoke Spanish and smoked a lot. So who was the connection?

Moose didn't answer. In the end, she had to leave a message.

"Where's Moose?" Jake asked Cass. They were meeting at Josh's law office.

"I don't know! He's been out on leave for a couple of days." She looked over at Jake. "Meanwhile, I still haven't found Salamander Man."

"He wasn't in the tattoo database?" Jake said.

Cass shook her head. "No."

"What other resources do you have?" Josh asked.

"Nick, the bartender. Cass, we should check with him," Jake said.

Cass nodded. "And Jaime. He's an undercover cop who is working with us. And as soon as we finish here, I'm going to tattoo parlors to see if I can find out where he got his ink," Cass said. "I've dropped off copies of stills from the video we have with an Anne Arundel detective. I'll check with Nick and Jaime. Beyond that, it's going to take legwork and luck." Cass took a deep breath. "Can we look at the security tapes from the Crawford house again?"

Jake groaned.

"Please?"

Josh inserted a DVD in his computer and angled the screen toward Cass and Jake. Together they watched the grainy black and white images. People, dressed in Christmas finery, walked down the driveway of the large estate home and entered the front door. At 8:18 p.m., Chase, with his new assistant and two other men, walked up. Chase was dressed in a tuxedo. Switching views, other cameras saw him entering the home and standing on the interior steps to address the crowd. Time stamp: 9:30 p.m. There was a gap after that, but then another image of Chase at the bar at 9:49.

"You see?" Josh said. "He was there at the time Tam was killed." Josh said. "So what about my other theory? Could she have interrupted a burglar?"

Jake sighed. Every fiber of his being told him Westfield killed Tam. "I guess that's possible."

Josh frowned.

Just then, the door to the conference room burst open and Moose walked in. Josh's secretary was right behind him, looking helpless.

"Hey!" Moose said.

"Where have you been?" asked Jake.

"Up north," said Moose.

"Great time to take a vacation," Cass said.

Moose dropped a load of papers unceremoniously onto the table. He looked "You guys are going to love this."

What now? Jake thought.

"Look at this," Moose said, and he turned a copy of a microfilmed newspaper article toward them. All three leaned forward and read the headline.

"Bristol man kills self, family."

The dateline was from thirty years ago. The accompanying photograph showed a small one-story house surrounded by police cars.

"Let me read it to you," Moose said, picking up the paper. " 'Late Sunday night police were called to the home of Charles Westover in the three hundred block of First Street. Neighbors reported hearing shots fired shortly after nine p.m. When police arrived, they found Westover, thirty-nine, his wife Nancy, thirty-six, and their children John, six, Kelly, three, Susan, one, dead of gun-shot wounds. Charles Jr., nine, escaped injury by fleeing to a neighbor's house.' "

"This happens all the time!" Cass exclaimed. "What's the point?"

"Where was this?" Josh asked. "Bristol, Virginia?"

"Connecticut," Moose responded. "Bristol, Connecticut." Undeterred by Cassie's frustration, he continued reading. The story described how the family kept to themselves but had evidenced no serious problems before the incident. Charles Westover was a truck driver and his wife stayed home with their children. The neighbors described themselves as "shocked" by the incident.

When he was finished, Jake leveled his eyes at him and said, "I don't get it."

"I know! I know you don't. Because you didn't drive ten hours to Connecticut to check something out. But I did. And what my checking uncovered is that Charles Westover Jr.," he hesitated, "is now Chase Westfield."

"What?" Cass stood up.

Moose beamed triumphantly. "I was checking backwards, from his college days. I was looking at public records, newspaper articles, that kind of thing. I felt like there was something I needed to know, something that was back there, but I kept runnin' into a block, a wall I couldn't get past. Until I got lucky. I found an old librarian at the local newspaper and she put me on to something. Chase Westfield legally changed his name when he was eighteen."

"Because of what his father did," Jake said soberly.

"That's right! The old man seemed nice, but he was an abusive tyrant to his family and he murdered them all. His surviving kid wanted nothin' to do with his name. And the librarian remembered it, because it was a big story at the time. Thirty years ago, not too many quadruple murders went down."

"He could change his name, but he couldn't escape his fate." Jake shook his head, struggling to process this new information.

"What do you mean?" Josh asked.

"He was nine years old when this happened, the same age as Justin. His father was thirty-nine. Chase is now thirty-eight." Jake rubbed the bumpy spot on his skull. "Some people who've been abused as a child will repeat the abuse as an adult. Almost like they're trying to get control over what happened to them as a kid, by being the strong perpetrator this time, not the victim."

"Cops see it over and over," Cass said softly. "But let's not give him a pass." She looked straight into Jake's eyes. "Not every abused child makes that choice. Some choose a different life."

Jake felt his face grow hot. He stood up from the table and paced over to the window, his mind racing with thoughts of Chase's father, his own father, images from his childhood colliding like cars on ice. He had to force his attention back on their meeting.

"Unfortunately, this information, while interesting, doesn't implicate Chase in Tam's murder," Josh was saying. "It does nothing to refute his alibi!"

Jake turned around "It's good to know, though," he said, nodding at Moose. "I appreciate you chasing it down. It explains a lot. To me, at least." Jake began pacing. "How do we use it?"

"Let me go confront him with this information," Moose suggested. "Let me push him. See what happens."

The other three looked at each other, as if gauging each other's reaction. "Hold off on that," Jake finally said. "Let's just wait."

"Wait? For what? The verdict? Man, you don't have time to wait!" Moose said.

Jake reached down deep for patience. "I'm just not sure that's the right thing to do."

Chapter 40

"What if we drive the kids around the neighborhoods near Eleventh Street and see if they recognize the place they spent that weekend?" Cass asked. Her mission to check tattoo parlors had failed to produce anyone who would acknowledge inking a salamander on a guy's neck. Now she was talking to Jake, standing in the parking lot of Josh's law office where they were meeting—again.

Jake shook his head. "Cass, no! That's too stressful for them."

"We have to do something!"

"Let it go."

She exhaled her exasperation. "We have to find him! Or else . . ."

"Or else what?" Jake turned around. "I go to trial? That's going to happen. Get used to it!"

"That makes me sick!" Cass said.

He gripped his hand and released it, over and over. "I know, Cass. Believe me, I know." He opened the door for her.

They went inside and the minute Jake saw Josh's face, he knew something else was up. He braced himself.

"Before we get into your case, I got a letter," Josh said, gesturing with the paper in his hand.

"Tam's parents are suing for custody of the children."

Jake's eyes widened. He took in a sharp breath. "No!" he said.

"That's ridiculous!" Cass exclaimed.

The room seemed to spin. Jake heard a loud drumming in his ears. He felt anger and fear flash through him, then grief. He could lose the kids! Lose them!

Cass continued her rant. But then, Jake shook his head and held up his hand. "Stop, Cass. Stop." He looked her square in the eyes. "They're concerned about the kids. That's all."

"It's just not fair to pile on you this way!" Cass exclaimed.

"I'll deal with it."

Josh cleared his throat. "Do you want me to handle this or your divorce lawyer?"

"The divorce lawyer," Jake said, his chest tight. "Give me the letter."

The meeting with Josh was not fruitful. Back at the office, Cass was slamming drawers and shooting looks at agents who annoyed her.

In one way, she could see Jake's point—the grandparents were trying to protect their grandchildren. But she couldn't imagine Jake without his kids!

Or maybe she couldn't imagine herself without them.

She shook that thought off when Jaime, the undercover cop, called. She listened to his news and then phoned Moose. "I just talked to Jaime. He's making arrangements to buy a package of cocaine from Cesar Cisneros!" Cass told him. "He wants backup. Can you help me?"

"I'm right in the middle of something, Cass. Can you handle it?" Moose said.

Cass frowned. What was Moose doing? "Sure. I'll call a surveillance squad."

"And Travis. He said he'd help."

Right. Travis.

Jaime had arranged to meet Cesar Cisneros in an alley off of Willow Street, in a residential area near the location where Danny was shot. Cass scoped the place out, then met with the surveillance team in a shopping center parking lot three miles away. She gave them pictures of Cesar and Jaime, and described Jaime's car. She described the buy going down, and outlined possible complications, none of which Jaime expected to happen.

While she spoke with the squad, a light rain began falling. That would make surveillance a little more difficult. On the other hand, it might keep casual passersby away. "I'll be nearby," Cass told the squad. "I'll let you know where I end up." She checked their radio connections, and released them.

Cass knew she should retreat to some coffee

place, some cozy restaurant, or at least to some quiet, darkened street where she could listen to the radio traffic until the deal was done. But she wanted to be there, to watch Cesar Cisneros hand Jaime the package, to see who else came with him, and to add this information to their notes so they could once and for all get the guy who shot Danny.

Where could she watch the deal? A woman alone in a parked car at night, even on a neighborhood street, would look odd. A woman, a *white* woman, walking alone at night in that neighborhood would also look suspicious.

She should stay away. She knew that. She got in her car and drove away from the parking lot where she'd met the squad. She tried to think of a place up ahead where she could get a cup of coffee and sit in the car and listen. But when she came to the decision point—left to stay away, right to watch—she turned right.

What now? She was improvising, something Jake did all the time. Jake. This was really about Jake after all, she had to admit. If she could get Danny's shooter and close out that case, she'd gain time to work on Jake's case.

A cold chill ran through her. Jake, charged with murder! The idea of it sent panic racing through her. Jake in prison? For the rest of his life? No. No way.

The buy would take place in an alley off of

Willow Street. Cass checked her watch. Nine forty-five. She had forty minutes, forty minutes to make a plan and get into place. She glanced over to the passenger seat. On it sat her camera. Subconsciously, she'd known all along she was going to have eyes on the buy.

Seven blocks from the buy site, she saw a Goodwill store. She went in, bought some clothes, and then drove to the parking lot of a nearby gas station. Its restrooms had exterior doors. Grabbing the bag of clothes, she went into the women's room. Ten minutes later, she emerged, dressed as a homeless woman in sweatpants, a hoodie, and a plastic raincoat. Her face was dirty, her hair bedraggled, and no one—no one—would have recognized her. Well, maybe Jake.

She slipped back into her car, drove two more blocks and parked. She attached her ear bud to the radio and slipped it into her sweatshirt pocket, then threaded the wire up to her neck, under her hair, and into her ear. She checked her gun, then put her camera in the backpack and got out of the car.

Maple. Oak. Willow. Whoever named the streets in this neighborhood could not be called creative. Cass walked slowly down Oak Street. The rain, falling more heavily, was starting to soak her clothes. She flipped up her hood and walked faster. She'd seen a building, a garage, she thought would provide her cover. She checked her watch: With any luck, she'd be in place half an hour ahead of time.

But a noise behind her sent shivers down her spine. A car. In the alley.

She couldn't afford to be spotted. She picked a dark house, opened the back gate, and walked up the back sidewalk as the car went by.

As she neared the house, a motion-detector spotlight clicked on. A light went on in the house! Heart pounding, Cass ducked back toward the garage and behind some bushes. She heard a door open. "Who's there?" someone called out.

Cass remained still, hoping the homeowner didn't have a dog. Minutes later, the door shut. The light clicked off. And Cass crept back to the alley.

The rain began falling even harder. She had just gotten to the old garage behind an abandoned house near Willow Street when she heard another car coming. Cass shoved the sliding door of the garage and stepped in quickly. She heard scurrying. Rats.

She didn't dare turn on a flashlight. Forcing herself to forget about rodents, she saw that one of the windows in the garage facing the alley was broken out. Cass moved to it, and carefully watched. The car kept going, its tires swishing on the wet pavement. Two minutes later, two men came walking down the street.

They were dressed in work boots, jeans, and

jackets. Both had knit caps. Then a third guy appeared.

Cass aimed her camera through the window and took pictures. She accidentally bumped the camera against the window frame, making what seemed like a loud noise, but none of the men looked her way. The pounding of the rain on the metal garage roof must have drowned it out. One of the men had a package in his hand, and as he moved under a streetlight, Cass could see it was secured with duct tape.

Should she move out of the garage to get a better shot? She was considering this when a transmission in her earbud chilled her to the bone. The surveillance team had been delayed by an accident a block away.

Cass slung her camera over her shoulder. She radioed the team. "I've got eyes on them. You need to get down here now." Then she heard a noise in the alley. She looked. Jaime plus all three men were walking straight toward her.

Desperate, she looked around. The garage had a loft, and a ladder nailed to a side wall. She scrambled toward it and began climbing the ladder, her heart pounding. The door below began to slide open just as Cass stepped onto the boards of the loft. She turned off her radio and cell phone and laid down, praying the boards would hold, praying she was out of sight, praying, praying, praying.

She could hear Jaime's voice, making the deal, speaking in Spanish. She identified two other distinct voices, both Hispanic. She could hear her own heart drumming in her ears.

She felt movement across her legs! She jumped. The scurrying sound was unmistakable. Rats! Rats! She wanted to move. To jump up. To scream. To run!

But no way. Moving would get her killed. And Jaime, too. So she gripped her fingers on the boards and bit her cheek to keep from screaming.

She felt the cloth of her pants leg moving and she jiggled her leg. Then, hope! She heard Jaime finishing the transaction. Heard him leave the garage. The other men stayed, speaking quickly in Spanish. Her knowledge of the language was limited; even so, she picked up a name: Luis Molina.

Luis Molina. She repeated it to memorize it. Luis Molina.

Then she heard the garage door slide open. She heard the men's voices fade. She heard the door slide shut.

And then the boards on which she was lying collapsed.

Chapter 41

The candle on the coffee table in Jake's apartment flickered. The clock on the wall said he should be in bed, but he remained up, cherishing the time with his kids under the same roof, even though they were asleep. He sat up, thinking and praying, watching and waiting. For what? For hope to fall out of the sky?

His cell phone rang. Cass, maybe?

He looked at it. No, it was Craig. What would Craig want at 11:30 at night? "Tucker."

"Hey, Jake. Is Cass with you by any chance?"

He stood up. "With me? No."

"Have you heard from her tonight?"

"What's going on? What's wrong?" Jake's heart began beating hard.

Craig hesitated. "Oh, probably nothing. We had a buy going down tonight, that cop who's been helping us—Jaime. Cass was overseeing it. The buy went down, everything was fine, but no one's heard from Cass." He paused. "Don't worry. We'll find her. I'm sorry to bother you, Jake."

Jake clicked off his phone, sweating. He punched in Cassie's number. No answer. Then he tried texting, adding "911" as a signal that it was an emergency. Then his mind began racing around other options.

Cass? Missing? Where was she?

• • •

Darkness enveloped her, even with her eyes open. Cass tried to figure out her surroundings. Her right hand gripped a board. Her other hand found concrete.

Struggling, she sat up. And then she remembered. The garage. Jaime. A drug buy.

She hurt. Her ribs hurt. Her arm hurt. Her head hurt.

She heard scurrying and it all came back. The rats! Rats in the loft! She forced herself to her feet. She turned. Squares of light helped her locate the door. She shoved it open and limped out into the alley. Her camera banged against her side.

The rain still fell. Somehow, she had the sense to push the camera under her coat. Somehow, she remembered about where her car was parked. Somehow, she walked there, blood dripping from the side of her mouth. Willow. Oak. Maple. And then she saw her car. Around it stood members of the surveillance squad and Craig Campbell.

Jake raced to her apartment after he dropped the kids at school the next morning. "What were you thinking?" he asked Cass.

"I was pretending to be you!" she retorted. Her face was bruised, her right wrist was in a brace, and she walked with a limp.

"By being an idiot?"

"I had no idea the surveillance squad would get hung up! I wanted to get an eye on whoever came to get the drugs."

"We know what Cesar Cisneros looks like!"

"But we didn't know who would come with him," Cass said. "And that's what I got." She sat down on her couch. "Providing that fall I took didn't kill the camera."

Jake sat down next to her. "I had a hard time staying in that apartment last night. If it hadn't been for the kids . . ."

"I'm sorry," Cass said. "I didn't mean to scare everybody."

Jake shook his head in exasperation. "You did."

A moment of silence fell between them. Then Jake put his arm around her and momentarily pulled her close. "I'm glad you're safe."

She grinned. "You want to see something really creepy?"

"Sure."

Cass rose, retreated to her bedroom, and retrieved the knit pants she'd been wearing the night before. "Look." She stuck her fingers in the multiple holes in the legs.

"You ripped them when you fell?"

"Nope. Rats chewed them."

Jake uttered an expletive. "But they didn't bite you?"

"I was lucky."

"God protected you," Jake said. "What a night!

Listen, don't ever do that again," he said. "Please."

"I'm not planning on it," Cass said. "Let's get off that."

"Cass, honestly . . ."

"Seriously, Jake. New topic—have you figured out what you need to do to fight the custody battle with Tam's parents?"

Jake looked at her. "I'm not going to."

"What?"

"I'm not going to fight it. I'm giving Tam's parents custody." Even as he said it, his heart sank.

She exploded. "Why? Why are you doing this?"

"Because I think it's best for Justin and Caitlin."

"To lose you, too? They've lost their mother. Now they're losing you!" Cassie threw up her hands in disgust. "Why are you giving up? Why aren't you fighting?" she cried. "What's up with you, Jake?" She gestured violently. "Why don't you just give them to Chase?"

He turned away. His throat felt tight, like someone was choking him. He tried to respond to her but the words stuck. He stood up, walked to a window, and looked out onto the street. He heard Cass walk out of the room, heard her slamming dishes around in the kitchen, then heard her come back.

"I'm sorry, I shouldn't have said that. That was a low blow," Cass said, touching his shoulder. "Jake, I'm sorry. I just don't understand."

He turned to face her.

She put her hand on her forehead. "Wow, I thought my head hurt before!"

"Cass, I know you don't understand," he replied, his voice tight. He looked deeply into her eyes. "Here's the deal: I went to a park yesterday. I ran and I prayed. I've been praying and praying. I just believe not fighting them is the right thing to do." His dark eyes searched her face. "Please trust me."

Her eyes filled with tears. "I feel like you're just giving up! And I don't want you to!"

He reached over and took her hand. Oh, how he needed her to understand! "Cass, the trial starts three weeks from Monday. What's going to happen? I'm going to be in court all day. Probably talking to Josh at night. The press . . . who knows what they're going to do. Camp out in front of the apartment? They'll be at the courthouse for sure! And it'll all be on the news! I don't want the kids exposed to that! That's enough strain for an adult, much less a little kid."

"So get a babysitter. Or Trudy—she'd take them in a heartbeat. Why would you give up custody?"

"Because I'm hoping it's temporary. I called them. I negotiated a deal. I'll give them temporary custody. If by some miracle," he took a deep breath, "I'm cleared, I'll get them back. In the meantime, the kids have some privacy and stability."

Cass remained silent. Tears dripped down her face.

Jake squeezed her hand. "Tam's parents love the kids. I know they'll miss me, and you, but . . ."

"I can't stand this," she said and she threw up her hands.

If Cass thought escaping into work would help get her mind off of Jake and his kids, she was wrong. The next day she sat at the office, searching for information on the name she'd heard in the garage, Luis Molina. Then Travis called her. "Cass, it's Maria. She's disappeared."

"What?" Cass sat up straight. When was the last time she'd called Maria? A week, two weeks ago? She'd been so busy helping Jake.

"Frank Teller called me early this morning. Maria's gone along with all her stuff. It looks like she's just run away."

Teller was the state police officer in Montgomery County who'd, along with his wife, taken Maria in. "And there's no sign of forced entry or anything?"

Travis said, "No. This is trouble, Cass. If she comes back in this area, and the gang puts together the fact that she's been talking to us, she's dead."

"I've got to find her." Her heart was beating hard.

"Not alone. They probably have made you by

now as law enforcement. Especially after what Jake pulled with Renaldo."

Cass flinched. "I'll be careful."

"If you wait until tomorrow, I'll go with you."

"Okay, Travis, thanks."

But she couldn't wait. She was too anxious to find Maria. So she called the Tellers, the people Maria had been staying with, first, and found out all they knew, then she called the girl's cell phone and of course, had to leave a message. Did she dare go by her apartment? She'd stick out like a sore thumb in that neighborhood.

Well, it wouldn't be the first time.

Cass double-checked her gun, and set out for Glen Burnie.

As she drove, she went over the possibilities in her head. She should check Maria's apartment, or actually the cousin's; Renaldo's house; the mall; the fast food place where Maria had had a part time job. Where could she be, and why in the world had she left the Tellers' home?

Cass cruised through Maria's neighborhood. There was no sign of her. She drove to Renaldo's, to a house he had shared with five other men. She drove past the house first, then parked on a side street and simply watched the neighborhood for a while. The streets were quiet.

Then she left and looked at the mall, a coffee shop, a nail salon, and a few more common hangouts. She saw some girls who might have been some of Maria's friends, but by mid-afternoon, it was time to quit.

She called Jake later and told him about it. "Do you think she's gone back to that guy? Renaldo?" he said. "What's with these women?"

"I don't get it either," Cass said.

Then Jake changed the subject: "Hey, tomorrow's the day, if you still want to come."

Tomorrow? He was taking his kids to their grandparents' house tomorrow?

Cassie's heart dropped.

For Jake, the drive to the Andersons' house, with the kids in the back and Cassie in the front passenger seat, was the hardest twenty miles he'd ever traveled. He kept his voice upbeat, for their sakes, and talked about the plans Grandma and Granddad were making for them, all the while glancing in the rear view mirror, thinking, *this could be the last time I see them, this could be my last view of them.* He had already told them he wasn't going to visit them during the trial. He would call, but not visit. He wanted them to continue bonding uninterrupted with Tam's parents. If the worst should happen, they'd be better off.

Cass was keeping her face angled toward the right, toward the window, but he could tell by the redness in her cheek that she was having a hard time. She'd asked to come along, and that was fine with him. He wanted the Andersons to meet her because part of the custody agreement involved allowing Cass to have contact with his children. But he could see she was struggling. He wanted to reach over and touch her, to take her hand and let her know it would somehow all work out, but he restrained himself. In a lot of ways, he thought, it would be better for Cass if he just let her go, too. Like the kids. Just detach.

Jake pulled up in front of the Andersons' house. It was a two-story colonial in an older suburban neighborhood with tree-lined streets, quarter-acre lots, and an elementary school right down the street. As he threw his SUV into park, he realized his heart was literally aching. He touched his chest, took a deep breath, and then resolutely opened the door. "Get out on Caitlin's side, Jus," he told his son. He walked to the rear, and opened the lift gate. In the back were boxes and suitcases and backpacks with their clothes and toys and books.

The Andersons came out when they saw Jake's car. Mrs. Anderson was wearing tan slacks and a yellow sweater. She was a very petite, very young-looking sixty, with short, curly brown hair and perfect makeup. Her husband, Frank, followed her, dressed in jeans and a plaid shirt. Jake introduced them to Cass, and then everyone began carrying the children's things inside. When they were done, Cass said goodbye to the kids and Tam's parents, and walked back to Jake's SUV. The Andersons, likewise, gave Jake a moment alone with his kids.

"Do you have Cloud?" Jake asked Caitlin.

She held up the pillow triumphantly. She looked composed, standing there on the front porch. He grabbed his little girl in a bear hug, trying hard to choke down the lump in his throat. Oh, God, help me, he prayed silently.

Justin had taken some things inside. When he emerged from the house, Jake hugged him, too. The boy's face was troubled. He no doubt understood far better than Cat what this all meant. "You guys be good," Jake said, unable to trust his voice with anything more profound.

"We will," Justin said as he hugged his dad. "I'm gonna pray with Cat every night, I promise," the boy whispered in Jake's ear. "I promise, Dad. We're gonna be strong for you. We're gonna fight."

"You do that," Jake whispered back. "And I'll be praying for you. Don't forget that. I will be praying for you every single day. Be strong, son. I'm counting on you. And remember, I'll always, always love you. Nothing can break that."

The boy had tears in his eyes as Jake let him go, but Justin wiped them away quickly. "C'mon, Cat," he said.

The kids turned to go inside, and Jake touched

them one more time, his heart breaking. Then the front door began to close behind them.

Jake turned to leave.

"Jake!"

He looked back. Mrs. Anderson had opened the door just a few inches and was peeking out. "Jake," she said in a soft voice, "if it makes any difference, I don't believe you killed Tam."

He nodded. "Thank you," he said, his voice catching.

Chapter 42

When he got into the car and shut the door, it was like hearing a jail cell door shut. His life was gone, over, empty, changed forever. It felt like someone reached into his chest and tore out his heart. The pain of it took his breath away. He leaned his head back, his keys still in his hand. "That," he said softly, "was the hardest thing I've ever done."

There was no response. He turned his head. Cass was silently weeping, her hair framing her face, her shoulders trembling. A mound of tissues lay on her lap, some used, some waiting to be used. He touched her shoulder, but no words came to him.

He took a deep breath, inserted the keys, and started the car. Jake pulled into traffic, his neck so tight he could barely turn his head, Cass sniffling in the seat next to him. He drove, aimlessly at first, as if leaving the kids had so messed up his compass he couldn't find his direction. His attention wandered from the road to his kids to Cass to the upcoming trial.

"Hey," he said at the first traffic light. "It's going to be okay, Cass. Trust me. It'll be all right." He didn't sound convincing, even to himself.

"No, it won't, Jake." She looked at him, her

eyes red, her face swollen with grief. "Those kids will never be the same. They will struggle all their lives to overcome this. Losing their mom, losing their dad. I don't care how loving those grand-parents are, there is nothing that makes up for the loss of a parent."

Her voice trailed off and it was at that moment Jake saw into her heart, saw a piece of it anyway. She was finally feeling the full force of her own grief. Losing her mother, then her husband, and now it was all coming back. The ice dam was broken. Her love for his kids had breached it.

He spotted a coffee shop. Jake glanced right, moved into the next lane, and pulled in.

"What are you doing?" Cass asked.

"You need a cup of coffee," he responded, "and then we need to go somewhere we can talk."

She didn't protest. Jake parked the car and returned momentarily with two cups of coffee in his hand. Without discussion, he put them in the cup holders in the car and drove to a marina nearby on the Magothy River. Cass loved the water. Being near it would help her relax.

The day was bright, the sun warm on his back as he walked toward a picnic table next to the river. His stomach was tight, but he had to put his own grief on hold. He was on a mission now, a mission to help Cass. He put the cups of coffee down. Cass sat down across from him, facing the water.

"Promise me," Jake said, looking into her green

eyes, "you'll take the kids out sailing. They'll love it. Tam's dad will go with you. Or your dad will."

Her eyes filled with tears.

"C'mon, girl," he said. "Be strong. You can handle this."

"I hate it. It's so unfair." She tossed her head. "And here I am, sniveling, while you're the one hurt most by this. I should be comforting you! Instead, I'm . . . I'm lost, Jake. I don't know what to think or what to do. I don't know where God is. I don't know why he's allowing this to happen." A light breeze lifted up a piece of Cassie's hair and drew it across her face. She moved it aside with her hand.

"When I get scared, I ask myself questions. 'Do you believe in God?' Do you?" he asked her.

She nodded. "Yes. Of course."

"Good. So do I. Second, I ask, 'Do you believe God loves you?' I close my eyes and picture Jesus hanging on the cross. Yes, I say, he loves me. I know that. Do you know that, Cass? Do you see him hanging on the cross, dying there for you?"

Obediently she closed her eyes. "Yes," she said meekly, opening them again.

He was amazed. She wasn't arguing with him. He'd expected a challenge. "Okay, now, God exists and he loves me. So, does he know what's going on in my life? Yes. Does he care? Yes. Could he fix it? Yes. Will he?" Jake paused. "I don't know. You see, that's the trick, Cass. We don't know. Sometimes he intervenes, sometimes he doesn't. He heals me, he doesn't heal Mike. What's up with that? I've thought about this a lot, Cass. Here's the deal: I'm thinking maybe God doesn't care about fixing a situation as much as showing up in the middle of it. You understand?"

"I have no idea what you're talking about," Cass responded.

Jake ran his hand through his hair and tried again. "What if, what if me being rescued out of this situation didn't matter as much in eternity as, say, how I handled it? Whether I stayed faithful, whether I stayed true to what I believe, true to God. Trusted him to work. Gave up my need to control my life? What if that's what God cares about?"

"Fine for you. Be a martyr," she said, her temper raised at last. "Spend the rest of your life in jail suffering for Christ. But what about your kids? What about them? This is something they'll never get over, never! And they're not asking to be martyrs."

Jake sat back, glad to see the fire in her eyes. "Cass, listen. I've really thought this out. I have spent the last eight weeks with my kids, trying to make memories for them," his voice caught in his throat, "trying to show them how much I love them. But not only that, I've been trying to teach them to trust God, to go to him when they feel sad or lonely or afraid."

Jake took a deep breath, trying to get control of his emotions. Resting his forearms on the table, he ran his finger over the burn scar on his left arm, a permanent reminder, like Jacob's limp, of a touch of God in his life. Lifting his eyes to meet Cassie's he continued. "In the last couple of months we've taken hikes, gone horseback riding. I've taken Jus out in a kayak and Caitlin to a doll show. Every day we could we did something special. And every night we read Bible stories. Joseph. Abraham. Peter. Paul. Jacob. Jonah. And even Job. We decided our family verse would be Romans 8:28, 'And we know that for those who love God all things work together for good.' We memorized it along with a bunch of others.

"Cass, if this thing had played out like I wanted, if Chase had been indicted, they would have seen me as a tough guy who stood up for their mom. And that's fine. But because the table got turned, I can show them how a man handles fear, and injustice, and trusts God even when things are going badly."

"They're just kids!" she snapped, her eyes flashing. "And they're going to be miserable, because they've lost their mom and lost their dad."

"I know that they're already suffering," he said, his voice cracking. "But I'm hoping they'll eventually carry their hurt to God, ask him to heal it. I'm praying that they'll trust God and know that in eternity, he will make everything right."

"But what if they don't? What if they don't go to God?"

"Then that's their choice," Jake said, softly, "but I'll know I did everything I could."

Cass got up abruptly and walked to the edge of the Magothy River. The gulls were screeching and squawking, their white wings flashing in the sun. She folded her arms in front of her, hunching her shoulders as if she were cold.

Jake walked up behind her. "Cass," he said softly, "be strong. Trust God. This thing might not even go to trial. Anything can happen. But if it does, you know what it's like to lose a parent. Help my kids, Cass. Even if I'm not there, help them find God in the middle of all this mess. And help them hang on to him." And then he began to pray, and the words poured out, strong and tender, passionate and full of light. It was a holy moment, and when he ran out of words, he just stood there, holding her, unwilling to break the spell.

And then he felt her muscles relax, just a little, and amazingly she began to pray. The emotions spilled out from her heart like tears, the grief, the pain cascading in a torrent of anguished words. "I know you, God," she said tearfully, "but I don't know you well enough to handle this. Please help me."

Cassie's worry over Jake merged with her concern for his kids and became a knot of anxiety in her chest. The unanswered questions haunted her. Why hadn't they broken Chase's alibi? Why hadn't they found Salamander Man? What would happen to the kids? What would happen to *Jake?* Prison wasn't exactly a happy place for former law enforcement officers.

And what would happen to her? Losing her mom, losing Mike, and now, losing Jake, too? And his kids? She couldn't imagine it!

Back at work a few days after her fall, she finally got some good news. The lab said the tape on the package Jaime had bought from the men in the garage matched the tape in the storm drain! They had their connection! Now, how should they proceed? Cass sat in Craig's office, waiting for Moose. The three of them would decide.

Moose was late, and Craig used the time to talk to her about Jake. How did she think he was doing? What was his case looking like? Cass explained her perspective as best she could, fighting tears. Even Craig looked overwhelmed when she brought up Jake giving up his kids.

Then Moose walked in. "What's up?" he said. "Man, what happened to your face?" he said, reacting to Cassie's bruises.

"Took a little fall," she replied.

Moose grimaced. "I guess I'll get that story later. What's going on?"

Craig explained about the buy and the subsequent match with the tape from the storm drain. Moose responded with a low whistle. "Finally, we got something going. Awesome."

"So, are we ready to bring Cisneros in?" Craig asked.

"If we do, we gotta warn Jaime," Moose said.

"I talked to him about that," Cass said. "He wants us to bring him in, too, handcuffed, and let Cisneros see him. Like he's being arrested, too."

"Cool!"

"So, obviously, we're going to question Cisneros about Danny's shooting," Cass said. In her heart, she hoped Craig would add something about the drugs being delivered to the casino. Or Chase's driver. When he didn't, she brought it up. "I think we should ask him about delivering to the casino."

But Craig wouldn't go there. "Stay away from anything that might have to do with Chase. For now." He tapped his pen on his desk. "If you sense Cisneros didn't shoot Danny, offer him a deal on the cocaine charge if he gives us good information on the actual shooter. Let's see if he'll play."

Afterwards, Cass and Moose spoke. "Look, I got another lead the other night," Cass told him. She explained about the conversation she'd overheard in the garage, and the name that the men dropped.

Moose scratched his jaw. "Luis Molina." He looked at Cass. "You didn't find nothing in our databases?"

"Nothing. There's a handful of them around the country, according to white pages lookup. But no one by that name around here."

Moose nodded. "Okay, so he's an illegal, or from out of state, or he's using a false name."

"Who is he? That's the question we've got to answer." Cass cocked her head. "Where have you been?"

Moose grinned. "Atlantic City."

"Gambling? You had to go now?"

"Gambling on a hunch," Moose replied. "I'm thinking, this guy D'Angelo is virtually kicked out of Atlantic City, right? But Chase goes there. A lot. And I got some friends up there, so I went and started asking around."

"About . . ."

"Seems that Chase lost a wad of cash in the casino owned by a guy reputed to have connections to a crime family in New York. Westfield dropped enough cash that, well, he got a reputation, you know? Even my buddies in security knew about it."

"So he had a major loss. One he couldn't cover?"

"One he couldn't cover," Moose confirmed. "And I'll bet I know who covered it for him."

"D'Angelo," Cass said.

Moose nodded. "Which would make Chase owe him. Which might grease the skids for D'Angelo getting that contract for the casino."

"Now, how do we prove it?" Cass asked.

Chapter 43

Arresting Cisneros turned out to be easy—a couple of agents found him delivering fish on his route the next day. As planned, they brought Jaime in, handcuffed, at the same time, although they allowed Cisneros to get only a side view of him.

Now, sitting across from Cisneros in an interview room, Cass almost felt sorry for him. The man was visibly shaking. "Mr. Cisneros, I don't care about your immigration status," Cass said, leaning toward him. "I care about the quarter kilo you sold a suspect the other night. That was a nice paycheck, right Mr. Cisneros? More than you make delivering fish in a year, I bet." Cass tapped impatiently on the table in front of her.

A drip of sweat ran down Cisneros' face. "Look, I don't know what it is. I was told to deliver it, that's all."

"Told to deliver it? By whom? Who told you to deliver that package, Mr. Cisneros? How much did they pay you?"

His eyes pleaded with Cass. "Please, I have a family! I do what I'm told, and yes, I make a little cash, but what is it? I don't know. I just trying to work. To feed my kids. That's all."

Cass tended to believe him. His face, his voice,

his demeanor reeked of sincerity. "Who's the man you're delivering for?"

Cisneros closed his eyes. "He will kill me."

"He'll kill you? If you talk?" Cass stood up. "Okay, spend the rest of your life in jail. I don't know how that's going to help your family."

On cue, Moose took over. "I get it man. You're scared. Start with this: Were you alone the other night? When you sold that quarter?"

Of course they knew he wasn't.

Cisneros shook his head.

"Who was with you?"

Without making eye contact, he muttered, "Fresno and Teego."

Moose glanced up at Cass, then looked back at Cisneros. "Which of them is the boss?"

"No boss. Not them."

"Who, then?"

"The big boss, he is a rich white guy, that's all I know. I not see him!"

"I need a name!"

Cisneros' hands shook so hard his cuffs were making noise. When he spoke, his voice was so low, Cass could barely hear him. "They call him Smith. Señor Smith."

"Who is 'they'?"

"Fresno, Teego, and the others."

" 'Smith' isn't going to cut it! I need to know who he is, where he lives, what kind of car he drives." Cass ticked off the basics.

"I cannot tell you!"

"You're afraid."

"I have a family!"

Cass brushed her hair back behind her ear. "Cesar, we can help protect you. And your family. But you have to help us."

Moose held up his hand, then tapped his finger on the table. "Do you know a guy named Luis Molina?"

Cesar's eyebrows shot up. "I hear of a Luis. Drives a limo. Very nice."

"You've seen this limo?"

Cisneros nodded.

"Where have you seen this limo, Mr. Cisneros?"

Cisneros wiped his nose with his sleeve. "I see him at the casino."

"The Lucky Leaf Casino?"

Cisneros nodded.

"Were you there, gambling?"

The man didn't respond.

"Mr. Cisneros, have you ever been asked to make a delivery to the Lucky Leaf Casino?"

Cass looked at Moose, startled. Craig had said not to go there! Still, the question was a logical progression.

Cisneros looked at Moose, searching his face as if to gauge how much he knew. Finally, he nodded. "I work for fish company, *si*? I deliver restaurants, grocery stores . . . one day, I told to make one more stop. One more. To casino. Then more and more. Soon, every week."

"And what were you delivering, Mr. Cisneros? What was in those boxes?"

"I no look, but . . ."

"But?"

The man looked up at Cassie. "The enforcer? He watch me. I see him, a block, half a block away, watching me at the casino. I think therefore it is more than fish."

Cass stood up straight and walked away, her heart pounding. So they were right! Cisneros was delivering drugs to the casino.

"Who is this enforcer?"

"*Su nombre es la Sangre.*" His name is "the Blood." Tears came to Cisneros' eyes.

"This man scares you."

"One time, a man try to steal the drugs from the place where we kept them. And la Sangre, he shoot him! Right on the street! Pow! The man fall down, dead."

The hair on the back of Cassie's neck stood straight up. "Where did this happen, Cesar? Where and when?"

"By the cemetery. Ninth Street. In the fall." Cisneros looked from Cass to Moose. "The enforcer, he do that! And he kill me, too, boom! Like that, if I mess with him." He trembled. "If he find out I talk, he cut out my tongue and then shoot me. I know this!"

Cass and Moose exchanged glances. "We can

help you, Mr. Cisneros, but we need a name," Cass said, leaning over the table. "A real name, not a nickname. This la Sangre: What is his real name?"

"That all I know!"

"Then what's he look like?"

Cisneros looked up at Cass. "He have three teardrops here." He pointed to the corner of his eye. "And *la salamander* here." He put his hand on his neck.

Cass felt the ground shift under her feet. She caught her breath. Salamander Man! "How can we find him, Mr. Cisneros? Where does he live?"

Cisneros shrugged. "I don't know. He find me!"

"Un-flipping believable!" she told Jake over the phone a few hours later. "Cisneros pinned Salamander Man to Danny's shooting. Now all we have to do is find him!"

"Yes, that is the problem," Jake responded.

"But we're a giant step closer to solving Danny's shooting and the assault on you!"

Jake didn't respond. With the kids at their grandparents' house, he had decided to save money by giving up his apartment. He had moved into the house of an agent he knew, a recently divorced guy who was in the process of transferring to Houston. Jake figured he'd only need a place to stay for a month, one way or the other. The trial would be over then. If he was acquitted, he'd want to move anyway. Give the kids a fresh start. Stan, the agent, was rarely around, preoccupied as he was with making the most of his new single status.

"Jake?"

He pressed the phone to his ear. "Yeah?"

"Are you all right?"

"I'm sorry, Cass. My head is somewhere else." Jake was staring out of the window, watching kids get off a school bus.

"Don't give up, Jake," Cass said. "Please don't give up."

Moments after she'd hung up with Jake, Cassie's phone rang again. It was Maria! "Where are you?" she asked the young woman.

"I am in Glen Burnie."

"With Renaldo?"

There was a pause. "No. I am with Tomas now."

"With Tomas." The guy with Los Bravos? Tomas Bandillo?

"And Cass, there's something else."

"What?"

"I am pregnant."

Pregnant! Cass took a deep breath. "How far along are you, Maria?"

"Just two months. Tomas is so excited."

Cass tried to measure her words. "Where are you living?"

There was a long pause.

"Can we meet somewhere?" Cass suggested.

There was a pause. "I am getting off work in twenty minutes."

"Where's work?"

"The Mexican grocery store, La Bodega, on Tulip Street."

"Okay! I'll meet you there."

"I walk down a block."

"Okay!" Cass reached down and turned on her car's ignition as she clicked off the phone.

Twenty-two minutes later, Cass found Maria in Glen Burnie, half a block down from La Bodega. She pulled over and opened the passenger side door. Maria slipped in.

"Maria! How are you?"

"I am fine," the Latina said, buckling her seat belt. The only sign of her pregnancy was a slightly fuller face.

Cass drove them away from the area, to an elementary school in a quiet part of town. She parked behind it. "So tell me, how have you been?"

Maria began talking, telling Cass about the family she stayed with in Rockville and about missing her friends, and how Tomas tracked her down.

"How did he track you down? No one knew where you'd gone!" Cass said. She and Travis had made sure of that.

Maria's gaze shifted. Then she looked back at Cass. "It's true. He did not find me. I called him."

Cass blew out a breath.

"We talk and talk. And then we fell in love!" Maria said. "He even drove to Rockville to see me! And then, I get pregnant." She smiled. Clearly, that was a positive thing.

"But what about your music? College?" Cass asked.

Maria grew silent. "It's okay. I am happy." Her tone changed. She frowned. "But today, I am also worried. About Tomas. So I call you."

"What's going on, Maria?"

"Last night, a man come to our apartment. He want Tomas to help him with something. Tomas, he doesn't want to. He keeps saying no, no! But the man, he threaten him! He say, you help or else."

"Who was this man, Maria?"

The young woman shivered. "They call him la Sangre."

La Sangre. The Blood. Salamander Man! Cass tried to keep her voice level. "What does he want Tomas to do?"

"I think . . . I think maybe hurt someone."

"Who?"

"A traitor. One who talks."

"Where can we find this la Sangre?"

"I don't know. But I'm afraid he will hurt

Tomas! Cass, how can I help him?" Tears came to Maria's eyes.

Cass thought fast. "You need to find out if Tomas is making plans to meet this man. Then you call me, or Travis, you understand? Call right away. We will help you. But we need time." She hesitated. "Maria, this la Sangre, I have heard of him. He is dangerous!"

"I know!" Tears filled Maria's eyes. "He scares me."

Cass reached over and put her hand on Maria's arm. "In the meantime, if you find out anything else about this guy—a real name, where he lives, anything—you call me, okay?"

Maria nodded.

Chapter 44

After dropping Maria a couple of blocks from her apartment, Cass called Jaime. "Have you heard of this guy? La Sangre?" she asked the undercover officer.

"I haven't met anyone by that name or with those tattoos," Jaime responded, "but my guess is he stays in the background until they need a gun."

Cass pondered that. "Cisneros linked him to Danny's shooting. We also know a man with those tattoos was involved in the assault on Jake. And my guess is, he's the man who murdered at least two of the other three assailants."

"So you want him."

"Yes," Cass said, "I do."

"I'll push in a little bit."

"You're not in danger because we brought Cisneros in?"

"I don't think so. I'll be careful."

Cass clicked off her phone. Salamander Man, la Sangre, was the gang's enforcer. They had him connected with Danny's shooting and with Jake's assault. Could they connect him with Chase? Did Chase hire Salamander Man to kill Tam?

But Jake had pointed out that the way she was killed made it look personal. Still, maybe that was intentional, to implicate Jake.

But no one knew Jake would be at the house! No one! He was only there because Tam had forgotten her phone.

Cass put her thinking on hold. The clock on the dash read nine thirty. She called Craig first, and told him about la Sangre. "Jaime's on it, but I think his handler should know."

"I'll get in touch with him," Craig responded.

It was still not too late to call Travis. "Maria's back!" she told him.

"Where is she?" Travis asked. "With Renaldo?"

"No, she is with Tomas Bandillo now." Then she explained about la Sangre. "I told her to call me or you when she finds out if he is going to meet this guy. We need to get him into custody so we can question him! And we need to protect Tomas and Maria."

"Right." Travis said. "So is Jaime's cover blown?"

"I don't think so." Cass explained his pseudo arrest.

Travis remained quiet. "So how are you, Cass?"

That's when she remembered why she hadn't called Travis to tell him about the meeting between Jaime and Cesar, or her fall in the garage, or just about everything else that had happened in the last three weeks. She took a deep breath. "Fine, Travis. Just fine."

But of course, Jake wasn't fine, as a call from Josh the next day reiterated.

• • •

"I need you to help him rehearse," Josh told Cass. Without a last-minute breakthrough, Jake's future would rely on instilling reasonable doubt in the mind of jurors. Jake would have to take the stand, which meant presenting his version of what happened the night Tam died, subjecting himself to cross examination by the prosecutors, and hoping that the jury believed him, not them.

The prosecutors would try to push Jake's buttons. Get him flustered. Try to make him lose his temper and display the kind of aggression of which they were accusing him. Truth was not the issue. Getting a conviction was the prosecutor's end game.

"I need you to help role-play. I need you to be the prosecutor," Josh said. "Will you help?"

Of course she would.

Cass walked into Josh's office that evening wearing her trial suit—a black skirt and jacket with a fancy white silk shirt. Her hair was up in a French braid and on her feet were black power heels.

Jake's eyes widened. Man, he thought, she looks like a prosecutor!

Cass greeted Josh and then her eyes met Jake's. She gave Jake a quick hug. Unspoken thoughts rolled like thunder through his head.

"So, what do you say we get started?" Josh said.

He pulled an office chair off to one side. "Here's the witness stand."

"I guess that's for me," Jake said, sitting down.

Cass took a deep breath.

"I'll start," Josh said. He began asking questions, routine questions at first: *State your name, sir. Your occupation. Your relationship with the deceased. Tell us, Mr. Tucker, why you were at the Westfield residence on the night of December 10 last year.*

As he began telling his version of the night Tam was slain, Jake's mind slipped back in time. He went through the story, carefully, like he was walking on stones across a roaring stream. He wanted to get everything right.

But when Cass took over on cross examination, she got aggressive. "Did you know Senator Westfield had asked his wife not to interact with you?" she asked. "That he was concerned about you? Why exactly did you arrange that evening with her? To drive her to that play?"

He answered, but she began interrupting him. Misinterpreting what he was saying. Trying to catch him in inconsistencies.

No question about it, Jake got frustrated. Even angry. His hand tightened into a fist. He pounded the arm of the chair.

When he did, Josh corrected him. Coached him. Helped him reframe his responses.

After ninety minutes, everyone felt exhausted.

"Tomorrow evening?" Josh asked them both.

"No," Jake said.

"Yes," Cass responded.

Jake glared at her.

"We have to practice this until you don't get angry!"

Grudgingly, he agreed. And so they set the time: Eight the next evening. And the next. And the next.

Gradually, over the course of five days, Jake learned to control his attitude. Eventually, he learned to be thoughtful and direct, emotional but not angry. But every night, he would drive home to his rented room feeling sick to his stomach, exhausted and sad.

Jake had just gotten out of the shower on Saturday morning on what could be his last free weekend when his cell phone rang. The voice on the other end was Josh's.

"I just got a call from the prosecutor," he said. "Judge Bryan had a heart attack last night."

"You're kidding," Jake replied. The news buffeted him like a wave. He gripped the phone. Two days before his trial?

"He's in CCU at Johns Hopkins."

Jake had been counting on Judge Bryan, the man known for his decency and fairness. He'd been praying for him. "What happens now?" he asked.

"They'll find a new judge to hear the case. But there may be a delay."

"Who would the new judge be?"

"My guess is Caldwell. Or maybe Morganthal."

"Isn't Morganthal the guy from Severna Park?" Jake said. "He's retired."

"That's right. Comes back in to help out once in a while."

"He's a member of the Annapolis Yacht Club." Jake cleared his throat. "Would he have to recuse himself because he and Chase belong to the same club?"

"The Yacht Club? No, not necessarily. If there's a pecuniary connection, maybe. Or if they were particular friends. But just the same social club? No." Josh paused. "Well, that's about all I know right now. I'll call you back later when I get word."

Jake clicked off the phone and sat down heavily on the bed. "Lord, are you sovereign over this as well?" Of course he was, Jake reminded himself. Of course.

Four hours later, Josh called with word that Morganthal was indeed going to take the case. And later that afternoon, with the word that the trial was postponed until Wednesday.

"Morganthal!" Cass exploded when he told her. "Why him? He is the most . . ." She rattled off a few choice words about him. "Jake, this is crazy!"

The anger and fear in her voice resonated with him and he wanted to join her there, to say, yes, this isn't fair, this whole thing is a crock. Ridiculous! Absurd! Such a miscarriage of justice! In fact, it made him want to run! Get away! Instead, heart aching and hands trembling, he reached down deep. "Cass," he said, fighting to keep his voice steady. "God knew this would happen. He has a plan."

"A plan? What plan! Jake . . ."

"Cassie!" His voice was sharp. "Cass. I have to walk through this. Just pray, okay? That's all we can do, now."

Chapter 45

"We have to stay fresh," Josh warned them. He and Cass and Jake were in his office on Monday. The trial would start Wednesday, old Judge Morganthal, with his white hair, spectacles, and acerbic wit presiding. "So we're going to go over it all again."

"So if it's a five-day trial, how's it going to work?" Jake asked.

"They'll allow one day for jury selection and one day for opening arguments," Josh said, "although jury selection may not take that long. The prosecution has asked for two full days, then we get to start presenting evidence."

"And we'll get the weekend off?"

"Probably."

So he'd get one more free weekend out of the deal, Jake thought. One more.

They started going over the evidence. Again. The fears that Tam had expressed to Jake. What the kids had told him. The bruise Cass and Jake had both seen on Tam's face the night she brought the kids to Jake. The testimony they were expecting from her sister, her parents about how much she loved the kids, and how out of character it was for her to give up custody.

And the downside, too: how under cross examination they would probably testify to Jake's volatility, to the circumstances surrounding the demise of their marriage, to Tam's version of the arguments they'd had. *Humble yourselves, therefore, under the mighty hand of God . . .*

They reviewed, practiced, and debated until Jake could no longer sit still. He volunteered to go out and get lunch for them all. He left, and Cass and Josh began going over the security camera tapes from the Crawford party one more time. Nearly lulled into complacency, Cass yawned as the black and white images flickered on the computer screen. When she refocused, she saw something that made her heart jump.

"Hold on a minute, Josh," she said. "Stop!"

"What?" Josh sat up in his chair.

"Look at this. Look at this. Oh, my gosh. He's wearing a different jacket."

"What are you talking about?"

"Can we capture frames of this and print them?"

"I'm not sure."

Cass was on fire. "Look! Do you see what Chase is wearing?"

"It's a tuxedo jacket."

"Look at the cut. Look at the lapel. You see that?" The jacket, which appeared to be black on the tape, had a standard V-cut in the lapel.

"Yes."

"Okay, now look." Cass forced the computer to

track to the earlier images of Chase arriving at the party. She froze the frame, and it was clear: Chase had on a different jacket. This jacket's lapel was cut differently, in a double-V.

"I see. I see!" Josh said. "But what does this mean? Could he have mixed his up with someone else's? Spilled something on his and switched with someone?"

"Or gotten blood all over his and had to change?" Cass said. "We have to work out the chronology. We have to find out, did he own more than one tuxedo? Did anyone see him switching jackets? What happened to the bloody one?" She stood up. "It's time to put the heat on that maid."

"What are you going to do?" Josh asked, rising to his feet.

"Burn a duplicate disc for me. I'll take it over to some video guys I know and have them make stills for us. Then, I'm going to see Consuela the maid."

They had questioned her before, this Consuela Hernandez, in regard to her expected testimony about the conflict between Jake and Tam. She had said she was not working the night Tam was killed. She had gone home early. That, they suspected, was a lie. Now Cass was going to find out. This time, she'd invade the woman's home turf. And yes, she should have backup, but Moose was working on the connection between

Chase and D'Angelo and she was keeping her work on Jake's case low-profile.

Consuela lived in a 1940s house on Maple Street, a single-story bungalow with a real attic, Cass could tell from the outside, and a large tree in the front yard. A small, shorthaired dog yapped at Cass as she walked up onto the porch and rang the bell. Surprised to see Cass on her porch, Consuela invited her in.

Cass had spent some time pulling together scraps of information on the woman and she'd conscripted Moose to do the same thing. Now, armed with the information on the tux, she felt ready to confront her.

She began by placing a small, digital recorder on the coffee table. "I need to record this," she said in a relaxed, friendly tone. After saying who was in the room and where they were, Cass began: "Consuela, we're trying to piece together some things that happened the night Mrs. Westfield was killed, and, you know, we're having trouble with a few things. You told us earlier, you were off that night, right?"

The woman nodded. "*Si*. Yes." They were sitting in her living room, a tidy space dominated by a big screen, plasma TV against one wall and religious icons on another.

"But then we checked with the alarm company, and someone used your code to enter the house around nine p.m. We mentioned that, right?"

Consuela's face grew tight. "I told you, I had forgotten something. My purse. So I had to go get it. I was only there for a minute."

Cass glanced over to a small end table where the maid's handbag was clearly visible. Her keys were hooked onto the purse strap with a clip. "It would be hard to forget your purse, wouldn't it, the way you keep your keys clipped to the strap that way? I mean, as soon as you got to your car, you'd know you were missing them, right?"

The maid shifted uncomfortably in her seat, her eyes glancing toward the dining room, as if she were hoping someone would come and rescue her.

"Consuela, just out of curiosity, do you handle the laundry at the Westfields' house?"

"Oh, yes. Laundry and dry cleaning."

"That's a lot! I know Mrs. Westfield loved clothes. Did that create a lot of work for you?"

The woman sighed. "Sometimes, I not get it all done."

"Especially, I imagine, when they are traveling." Cass twisted her mouth like she was thinking. "Did you pack for the senator when he went to Connecticut to give that speech in December?"

"I don't know where he go. He tell me, pack this, pack that, pack my tux. And I do it."

"Which tuxedo did he ask for? Was it this one, with the V-cut lapels?" Cass showed her a picture. "Or this one with the double-V?" She placed the second picture down.

Consuela cocked her head.

"He has more than one, right?"

"Well, yes, but . . ."

"Consuela, I think you know something that you haven't told us. Something about that night." Cass leaned forward. "Now, we know you didn't hurt Mrs. Westfield . . ."

"No! No . . ."

"Of course not. Whoever killed her was physically strong and very angry."

"Yes, that's right. He is a strong man."

"Who is?'

"Her ex-husband. Señor Tucker."

Cass sat back, leveling her eyes at the woman, then let her gaze drift to the large picture window and the driveway outside. She relaxed her face. "That's a nice car out there in your driveway, Consuela. It's new, isn't it? I was thinking about buying a Nissan like that myself."

"Oh, yes, it's very nice." The maid smiled as she looked at the brand-new SUV, then Cass. "I got a good deal. Senator Westfield, he . . ."

"The senator helped you buy that?" Cass asked innocently.

Consuela's face clouded. "I . . . I mean . . . well, yes, he helped me. Well, he buy it for me, as a bonus."

"Quite a bonus." Cass shuffled some papers in

her lap as if she had information on the car. In reality, she didn't, she'd just noticed the vehicle walking in. And it didn't seem to fit with the neighborhood and a maid's salary. "Let's see, you bought it in January, right?" Instinctively, she'd noted the expiration date on the tags as she'd passed it.

"Yes, yes that's right."

"Mr. Westfield was very kind to you. There he was, grieving the death of his wife, intent on finding her killer, and he managed the time to help you buy a car. To buy it for you, in fact."

The woman reddened and Cass knew she had her.

"Did you know, Consuela, that withholding information in a criminal investigation can result in charges of obstruction of justice? And that can result in deportation?"

Consuela shook her head.

"Well, it can. Which would be really hard, you know, on your children, your family." Cass let her eyes drift to the pictures on a nearby shelf. "Oh, and your brother. Is that him?" Cass stood up and looked closely at the picture of a thirty-something Hispanic male. "I think I recognize him." She glanced back at Consuela. The woman's face was white. Returning her gaze to the picture, Cass said, "Ah, well, no matter."

She sat down again. "And you understand, Consuela, if you actually testify falsely, that's perjury, and that could mean jail time." She let that sink in. "Of course, there's still time to correct the record, to refresh your memory about what really happened that night . . ."

Suddenly Cass heard a back door slam and heavy footsteps approaching. Alarmed, she looked up. And a man with a salamander tattoo on his neck and three teardrops tattooed on his face walked into the room.

Chapter 46

Cass's heart jumped to her throat.

Salamander Man took one look at her, turned, and ran.

"Stop! FBI!" Cass yelled, and she took off after him, but by the time she'd reached the back door, he'd disappeared into the rabbits' warren of backyards, garages, and fences behind the house.

She picked an alley. Pulling out her cell phone as she ran, she called dispatch. "I need backup!" she told them and she gave them the address. "In the alley!"

"We're sending the county," dispatch said a moment later.

Cass grimaced and kept running herself, dodging trash cans and stacks of scrap wood.

But Salamander Man was gone.

She had to give up. With uniformed officers on the way, Cass returned to the house but the living room was empty. Consuela was gone! "Consuela! Consuela!" she called out, then she heard the sound of a toilet flushing.

Drugs? Was Consuela flushing drugs away?

Cass didn't care about the drugs; she cared about Jake and the guy who'd assaulted him. She raced toward the sound. Consuela was just emerging from the bedroom. "Consuela! Who was that man?"

The Latina avoided her eyes.

"Who is he?"

"My nephew. Why?"

"What's his name!"

"Alejandro."

"Where does he live?"

The woman shrugged. "He and his father, they fight, so he live here, there, everywhere. Wherever he can find a place. Why you want him?"

Cass didn't answer that question. "What's his last name?"

"Escobar."

"You have a phone number for him?"

"Let me look."

They walked back out to the living room. Consuela pulled a small, tattered notebook from a drawer and began leafing through it.

Cass was quite sure she was stalling. Through the front window, she saw the first patrol car arrive. She stepped out on the front porch, identified herself, and spoke to the officers. She described Salamander Man and gave them his name. Then she went back inside. Consuela had disappeared again.

A few minutes later, sitting outside Consuela's house in her Bucar, Cass made calls to Travis,

Craig, and then Moose. "I saw him! I've got a name. We need to get this guy! Alive."

Within a short period of time, the FBI had issued a BOLO—a "be on the lookout"—for Alejandro, and had notified TSA. He would not escape on a plane.

"Can we put surveillance squads on his father's house, and Consuela's?"

"They're on the way," Craig said. "He won't get far."

Then she called Jake.

"Good job, Cass," Jake said.

"We can connect Chase with Salamander Man through Consuela," Cass said. "Like you said, the night Chase wanted to meet to give the kids their gifts was a set-up."

"Yes, but," Jake responded, "it still doesn't prove Chase killed Tam."

"True, but Jake, we're going to push Escobar. We're going to make him talk!"

"Once you arrest him."

"Yes. Once we arrest him."

About six hours later, that became a real possibility.

Maria called Cass. "Tomas is meeting la Sangre at Nick's in an hour," the young woman said breathlessly. "Then, they are going to a club. Cass, I am afraid!"

"What's the name of the club?"

Silence.

"Maria?"

"I can't remember!" she wailed.

"We're on it, Maria. Stay where you are. If you remember the name of the club, call me."

Cass called Jake as she was sliding into her ballistic vest.

"Cass, be careful!" Jake said.

"I will!"

"Call me when you're done. I don't care what time it is."

Nick the bartender looked up in surprise as Cass, accompanied by half a dozen agents and uniformed cops, strode into the bar.

"Have you seen either of these men tonight?" she asked Nick, flopping two enlargements of driver's license photos down on the bar.

"Yes! They were here. They left fifteen, twenty minutes ago!"

Cass turned to her entourage. "All right, let's go."

Outside, a light rain had begun to fall. A car pulled up. Travis got out. "I'd like to do this with you," he said to Cass.

She nodded. "Yes, good."

"What happened to your face?"

Her bruises from her fall. "Long story," she responded.

Maria called. She had finally remembered the name of the club: Acapulco Nights. Located just over the Baltimore city line, it looked like anything but Acapulco. Dingy and dirty, the club sat one step down from street level in a nasty neighborhood.

Cass assigned a team to watch the rear. She and Travis and four others would go in through the front.

The smoke inside nearly choked her. The loud salsa music made her head throb. She moved through the crowd carefully, searching for Alejandro or Tomas.

"I don't see him," Travis said.

"Let's ask the bartender," Cass replied.

They had nearly made it to the bar when a commotion broke out across the room. Cass turned toward the sounds of men shouting, women screaming, and glass breaking. "Hey!" she shouted. "FBI! Stop!"

The sea of people between her and the fight seemed to swell. Were the people intentionally blocking her path? Cass kept one hand on her holstered gun as she worked her way toward the fight. Glancing over her shoulder, she saw Travis had fallen behind. "Hey!" she yelled. "Stop!" She saw a salamander tattoo and headed straight for it.

She saw Alejandro kick through a door. Cass pushed toward him, through the crowd. She felt someone touch her gun. She tightened her grip on it. Then she heard glass breaking. "Escobar!

Stop! FBI!" she yelled. She reached the door and saw it led to a back room. She moved in cautiously, pulling her gun from its holster and holding it in two hands. Cool air from a broken window hit her face. Was he gone? Or was it a ruse?

"I'm here," Travis said, coming up behind her. "Look! He went out the window!"

Maybe. Cass saw an interior door and nodded toward it. Travis walked over. As he put his hand on the doorknob, the door flew open, and Alejandro Escobar burst out.

Travis couldn't maintain his footing. He fell down backwards. Alejandro threw something at Cass, a jacket, maybe, temporarily blinding her. And by the time she had thrown it off, he was gone.

"Out the back!" she yelled into her radio. Then she pressed back through the crowd toward the front door. On the way, she spotted Tomas. "Tomas Bandillo! Come with me!" she shouted over the music.

He looked left, then right, his eyes wide. But she got to him and put a hand on him, and he gave in.

"Right behind you," Travis said breathlessly.

Cass glanced over her shoulder. "This is Tomas. Take him."

Outside, rain fell in sheets. Most of the arrest team members gathered in front, near their cars. "What do we have?" Cass asked.

"Bob and Jamison ran that way," an agent said, gesturing with her hand toward a side street.

Cass nodded. "Take him to the office!" she said to an agent, pointing to Tomas. Then she took off running in the direction of Bob and Jamison.

The darkened side street looked creepy in the rain. What stores remained open had metal security gates down. Garishly painted signs advertised "Boots $20" and "Pay Day Loans." Cass ran past them all, checking doorways and narrow alleyways. She wiped the rain out of her eyes with her sleeve, stopped momentarily in a doorway, and radioed the two others chasing Alejandro. "What's your status?"

Bob responded first. "I lost him somewhere around Claybourne and Twenty-second."

"I'm at Twenty-fourth and Montana," Jamison said.

"Okay, hold your positions. We'll work down toward you."

Cass called Travis on his cell. "Can you muster a team to move down Twenty-second and Twenty-fourth Streets, beginning from Abilene and going for about eight blocks?"

"Yes, sure," Travis said.

But after an hour of searching, the team still had not found Alejandro. "I think it's time to give it up," Travis said to Cass.

Give up? How could she? When they were so close. She took a deep breath, then shook her head. "No. We're not giving up. He's here, somewhere." She looked up at the three-story buildings surrounding them. "You take your guys that way five blocks," she said, motioning to her left, "and we'll go right. The uniforms should maintain the perimeter."

"My guys are soaked. I think he got away, Cass."

Her chin jutted out. "I'm not ready to end it. Not yet."

Travis's mouth straightened into a thin line. "We'll go one more round. But then, that's all I can ask of them."

Cass bit the inside of her cheek. "Let's go, then."

Twenty minutes later, she was walking down a pitch dark alley, when something other than rain hit her shoulder. She looked up. Alejandro was two stories up, on a fire escape, preparing to drop a metal box on her head. He's ditched the gun, she thought. He knows it's dirty and he's ditched it.

She moved aside quickly. The box clattered on the concrete. "Come down, Escobar! You're not going anywhere!"

But he thought differently and began climbing.

Cass radioed for help, jumped up, grabbed the fire escape ladder, pulled herself up, and began climbing toward the man. When he disappeared onto the roof, she climbed faster. Breathless, at the top she grabbed her gun again and peeked over the low roof wall. No sign of the man. But then she heard a noise.

"Give it up, Alejandro! We've got you!" she yelled. She could hear footsteps on the fire escape below her. Then she heard the man on the roof running, heard him splash through a puddle. She looked. He was headed for the next building. Cass holstered her gun and took off after him. Six feet from the edge, she tackled him.

Alejandro cursed and turned on her, hitting her hard in her face, sending flashes of light through her vision and pain through her head. Cass hit him back, hard, right on the nose, and red blood spurted. He tried to throw her off, tried to scramble away, but she climbed his back and got her arm around his neck, then wrapped both of her legs around one of his. Then she saw him make a move, and realized he was going for a knife!

Cass reached to block him. That's when Bob and Jamison caught up. The three agents over-powered him. Two minutes later, they had Alejandro Escobar in cuffs. Cass stood up, panting for breath. "Thank you," she told the other agents. Her eye was already swelling shut. "Now, help me get him down."

Chapter 47

"Jake, we got him." Cassie's call came at 2 a.m.

"Good job!" Jake said. He'd been pacing for hours. "Tell me about it."

And so Cass did, recounting every detail and every move she made. "So his full name is Alejandro Gonzalez-Fernando Escobar. We've got him on possession of cocaine with intent to distribute with more charges to come."

"Is he talking?"

"Not yet. And he would only speak Spanish, although I know he knows English. I saw him reacting to some of the things we were saying. Then he demanded a lawyer. Tomorrow, Jake. We'll get what we want tomorrow. We'll get him on your assault and Danny's shooting—that's two assaults on federal officers!—and, if we're lucky, we'll link him to Chase. We're going to do this, Jake. We're going to prove Chase set you up, and that he killed Tam."

"I hope so, Cass. I really do." Jake sat down on his bed. "Did you get Escobar's gun?"

"He ditched it."

Silence on the other end.

"We'll find it, Jake. We will. I've got people out there looking for it now."

376

• • •

Tuesday, the day before Jake's trial. The day slipped away like water over a mossy rock. Before Jake knew it, Cass was calling him late in the evening, frustration etching her voice. Alejandro was not cooperative. He had not provided them any information linking him to Chase. He pretended not to even know who his Tia Consuela worked for. Worst of all, they hadn't found his gun. Not in the streets. Not in the club. Not in Consuela's house. Not in any dumpster, storm drain, or sewer they could find.

Cass sounded so exhausted. And as Jake hung up the phone, the realization hit hard. He was actually going to have to stand trial for the murder of Tam. Tomorrow! The connection to Chase had not been made. He was going to have to stand trial, and he could lose his freedom, his kids, and Cass. All at once.

It would be a sleepless night.

Wednesday, 6 a.m. He was due in court at nine. Jake got up, showered, ate, and waited. Josh would pick him up at eight. He tried to read the Bible, but this morning, the words seemed to move around on the page and, frustrated, he finally gave up.

The Anne Arundel County Courthouse, constructed in 1824, sat on Church Circle in downtown Annapolis. Recently renovated, the historic old building with its brick exterior, tall entrance tower, and cupola represented the best of Georgian Revival architecture. Its new addition, not visible from the front, contained the most modern technology available.

Dread sat like a bad meal in Jake's stomach as he and Josh waded through a sea of reporters and entered the building. The structure, which sat near the Maryland State House and the Senate Office Building and just a few blocks uphill from City Dock, was familiar to him. But the familiar had become the feared: The historic old building could well be where he would experience the last of his freedom.

The hallway in the new addition was light and airy, aided by skylights and a high ceiling. In the courtroom, the judge's imposing bench was made of cherry, and his brown leather chair loomed high above the clerk's position. The tables for the prosecution and the defense, cherry as well, were just in front of the low, wooden "bar" that separated the front of the courtroom from the long, pew-like benches for the spectators. The jury box was off to the right, and next to it, a side door guarded by a deputy.

Jake and Josh walked in at 8:50. Jake's neck was tight, his breathing shallow, tension gripping him like a fist. Moving toward the front, he assessed the spectators quickly: Behind the prosecutor sat a mob of reporters, Tam's father and sister, and two of Chase's assistants. No Garza. Mrs. Anderson was probably with the kids, Jake thought. Behind the defendant's table Jake saw a dozen FBI agents, Cassie's dad and aunt, and a bunch of other people he didn't know, reporters most likely. Maybe some law students.

Then the door opened behind him and Jake glanced over his shoulder in time to see Danny and Lavonda Stewart walking in. Danny was using a cane, and Lavonda looked beautiful in a cream-colored suit. Danny gave him a little wave.

Jake's heart thumped. Such faithful friends. *God, help me remember that you're here, too,* Jake prayed silently. *Help me focus on you. Help me remember you are in charge. Help me trust you.* He touched the small New Testament in his right suit-coat pocket. Trudy had given it to him as a touchstone, a way to remind himself that God was fully aware of what was going on.

But as the proceedings got underway, Jake felt like he was having an out-of-body experience. He was on trial! Not in court as a witness, but as a defendant. How unreal! He swallowed hard.

The prosecutor came over to the defendant's table. "Last chance, Tucker: We'll do a plea—second-degree murder, thirty years."

Thirty years! He'd be almost seventy!

Josh looked at Jake, the question in his eyes.

"No," Jake said quietly. "I didn't kill her. I'm not going to plead to something I didn't do." He swallowed hard. The lump in his throat felt like a tennis ball.

Then the judge came in and everyone in the courtroom rose. Jake was asked to state his name. Yes, he did understand the charges and yes, his plea remained not guilty. His lawyer made a motion to dismiss, which old Judge Morganthal denied. There were some other largely administrative motions and decisions. And then jury selection began.

Cassie glanced at her watch. 9:05. She could only imagine what Jake was going through now. The preliminary instructions. Jury selection. A whole plethora of procedures, emotions and thoughts.

She wished she could be there. She wished she could be sitting on those benches, her eyes fixed on his shoulders, his neck, the back of his head . . . praying for him, supporting him. But as a potential witness, she'd probably be sequestered anyway. Besides, cracking Alejandro's resolve was more important.

Maria had taken a risk to turn Alejandro in, a huge risk, and Cass wanted to call her later and thank her. Alejandro thought he was in trouble for the drugs. But federal charges—assault on two federal officers, Jake and Danny—were also being prepared. As soon as they could get Cisneros to confirm Alejandro was the one he saw shoot Danny, they'd charge him.

Alejandro could be facing hard time. Who put him up to it? Why was Jake targeted? That's what Cass had to find out. But she was too close to Jake and would run into conflict of interests charges. So two other agents should arrive shortly to follow that line of questioning. Cass would consult with them, once they arrived. They were late already.

Twelve jurors. At the end of three hours, the panel was selected. Six women, six men. Six Caucasians, three African-Americans, two Asian-Americans, one Hispanic. Three were retired government workers, one was a schoolteacher, one a mom at home. Tall, short, heavy, thin, intelligent, simple, Jake's fate was now in their hands.

After jury selection, the court recessed for lunch. Josh walked Jake out. They fought their way through the gaggle of reporters to a waiting car and drove to a small cafe on the other side of Spa Creek. By pre-arrangement, Aunt Trudy and Cassie's dad would meet them there.

Entering the dark room, Jake slid into one side of a booth. Josh followed. Jim and Trudy joined them moments later. Jake introduced them, and then the waitress passed around the menus.

"The crab cakes are really good here," Jim said, then lapsed into some small talk with Josh.

Jake stared at the menu. What did he want? He

was having trouble concentrating. The server came back. When it was Jake's turn to order, he simply mimicked Jim.

Who cares about food, he thought. Jake took a big drink of water, crunching the ice. Josh and Jim were talking quietly about law and juries. Jake wanted to run away. He looked across the table and met Trudy's eyes, then quickly looked away.

"Will Cass come today?" Jim asked.

Jake groped for an answer. Then Josh chimed in. "The prosecutor may call her to establish Jake was with Tam the night she was murdered. Then again, he may use a young woman from Jake's church. He's got both of them listed."

Jake wished Stoddard Hughes would just call Cass. He could depend on her. Beth had never been to a trial, he suspected. Who knew what she'd say?

"Of course, I'll call Cass as a defense witness, but that won't be for a few days."

The food came and Jake tried to eat. But his appetite just wasn't there. "Look," he said to Jim and Trudy, "you don't need to sit through this whole thing. Especially tomorrow. Don't come tomorrow." That was when the medical examiner would present autopsy evidence. Who needed to hear all that?

"We want to support you, Jake," Trudy said.

"I know that. Thank you. But tomorrow . . ." He shook his head, unable to complete the thought.

●●●

Opening statements began when court resumed at one-thirty. As he listened, Jake felt himself sinking into despair. The prosecution had scheduled two days for its case—the whole trial should be over in twice that. Four more days and his fate would be set.

"The state will prove that this man, trained to kill by the Federal Bureau of Investigation, this man, Jacob Preston Tucker, broke into the Westfield home on the night of December 10, and brutally murdered his ex-wife, Tamara Lynn Westfield," Stoddard Hughes intoned.

Humble yourself under the mighty hand of God, Jake repeated over and over in his mind as blood pounded in his temples. Murder Tam? No . . . no . . .

One of the two agents who showed up to interview Alejandro was not who Cass expected. Meg Harrison had brought with her Angela Parker. Angela was a beautiful, petite, very feminine agent who could put a 230-pound guy on the ground before he could blink. Her maiden name was Jimenez. She was a native of East Los Angeles and spoke fluent Spanish.

Very smart, Cass thought, as she shook hands with both of them after they'd been checked in. Very smart. Alejandro may have met his match.

Chapter 48

Josh gave his opening statement, and then the witnesses for the prosecution began parading through the courtroom in a formidable line, like elephants linked with trunks and tails. First, the maid, Consuela Hernandez, who testified she had seen Mrs. Westfield when she left the Westfields' residence at 6 p.m. Then Beth, the woman from Jake's church, told the court she saw Jake with Tam at the church play. She didn't make eye contact with Jake the whole time. Maybe she was nervous. Probably she was, Jake thought.

The prosecutor then called the rescue workers who responded to Jake's 911 call and the detective and police officers who had arrived on the scene. The window by the front door had been broken, one officer said. The cut on Jake's arm was consistent with a cut made by broken glass.

We're not challenging that, Jake thought. He bounced his knee impatiently.

The prosecutor's witnesses droned on: Tam was found with her head bashed in, her blood was all over Jake, his skin under her fingernails, his name on her lips. The photos produced as evidence, enlarged and displayed on foam board, were all horrific, gut-wrenching. Jake hated having them there in front of the jury. Seeing

Tam bloody and battered brought back everything about that terrible night. He felt like he was going to throw up.

Jake forced himself to concentrate on what the prosecutor was saying. To sit there listening to the case being built against him. To keep from exploding in anger and refuting every point. It seemed the afternoon would never end.

"You understand, Mr. Escobar, why we are here," said Special Agent Meg Harrison, taking the lead. Angela sat to her right, her legs crossed, her pink blouse peeking out from under her jacket collar, her dark hair framing her face. She was not reacting at all to the Spanish spoken between the suspect and his lawyer, but Cass, standing on the other side of the one-way glass, knew she was taking in every word.

Cass had asked them to question Escobar first on Jake's assault. After all, time was of the essence in Jake's case.

"Where were you, the night of January 17?" Meg began.

Alejandro looked at his lawyer, smiled, and responded in Spanish, "With a woman."

"Really?" Meg responded. "What was her name?"

He couldn't remember. There were so many. He met her in a bar and they went to her home, an apartment, no a room in a house, over on Olive

Street. That was it. A room. They got there around eight, and he left at six the next morning to go to work.

"Where do you work, Mr. Escobar?" Meg continued. He answered her. "Arcap Construction."

She responded. "Oh, yes, I see. Interestingly, they show you out sick that next day, the eighteenth. And the nineteenth. They had to dock your pay. Did you notice your paycheck was short, Mr. Escobar?

"And this—a man matching your description came to the Washington Hospital Center emergency room on the seventeenth around midnight. He had a broken jaw. Same tattoos. Broken jaw. What do you think about that, Mr. Escobar?"

He didn't respond.

"I see you're being charged with possession with intent to distribute. That's a serious charge, Mr. Escobar, a serious charge. But not as serious as, say, assault on a federal officer with the intent to kill, conspiracy to abduct, conspiracy to commit murder of a federal officer—all federal charges, sir, carrying heavy time, in federal prison. No. You like the idea of spending the rest of your life in prison, Mr. Escobar? Without the women?"

Alejandro's lawyer objected, without translating, as the agents knew he would, but the suspect had understood what Meg was saying. Cass could see that in his face. His eyes narrowed, his face flushed, and small sweat beads broke out on his forehead. From her vantage point, on the edge of the room, behind the interviewers, she had a good view of his anxiety.

But the man was stubborn. He was nowhere near the corner of Charles and First, at the gas station where Jake was assaulted. He didn't own a ski mask. He had never seen this agent, this Tucker. He knew nothing about an assault.

And his Tia Consuela? She provided him a room, that's all. A place to stay. Who did she work for? Who cared? She cleaned and cooked and let him sleep there. That's all. And she didn't bug him.

Yes, he paid her. One hundred and fifty dollars a week, room and board.

"What about these children?" Meg asked, showing him pictures of Justin and Caitlin. Have you ever seen them before?"

Alejandro recoiled.

"No, of course not," Meg affirmed. "You're not that kind of a guy. You love kids. But someone babysat them one weekend last fall, in October, and they saw a man with a tattoo like yours in the house. There's no crime here, we were just wondering . . ."

A puzzled expression overtook Alejandro, and Cass felt like he was really thinking. He recognized the kids; she saw it in his eyes. But what would be the risk, if any, of acknowledging that? He had to work that out in his mind before he responded. She saw him glance at his lawyer, then he said, "No. *No los conozco.*" I don't recognize them.

He was lying. Cass sensed that. Lying and now she knew he was putting up a high wall. No useful information on any front, no matter how innocent. He'd have to be broken down.

"You do understand that lying to a federal officer is a grave offense, right, Mr. Escobar?" Meg said. "Do you want to take a look at those children again?"

As his watch edged toward five o'clock, Jake tensed and relaxed the muscles in his legs. The afternoon had dragged by and he needed to move, to run, to get out from behind that blasted table. No one was more pleased than he was when the judge's gavel came down, adjourning court for the day.

"I'll take you home. Get something to eat. Then be at my office at seven-thirty so we can go over some of this stuff again," Josh said clapping him on the shoulder.

It was the last thing he wanted to do. Still, he had to comply. Jake glanced at his watch. He could just barely get a run in. That's what he needed more than anything. Then he'd call Cass.

Jake had a routine of calling the kids at six-thirty. He had just finished his run when it was time. Forcing himself to keep his voice upbeat, he keyed in the number. The kids' homework, their friends, their problems at school became his focus momentarily. The trial seemed far away, a different reality, a nightmare intruding on real life. "God, I miss them so much!" he said as he hung up the phone. His prayers had become a constant conversation. "Will I ever see them again?"

He tried to eat, then dutifully drove to Josh's. What could they say that hadn't been said?

Day Two. Thursday. Dreading the resumption of his trial, Jake hadn't slept well. He had tried calling Cass repeatedly the night before, but couldn't get through. She'd texted back that she was busy with the interrogation of Alejandro. Jake got that, but he was still disappointed. He wanted to hear her voice.

Josh picked him up late, at eight o'clock. One of his kids was sick. Reporters and photographers again mobbed the courthouse steps. Jake wanted to shove them away. Walking into the courtroom at eight-fifty, he automatically looked to see who was there. Jim, Trudy, Craig, Danny and Lavonda, and a bunch of other people Jake didn't know.

Stoddard Hughes looked every bit the prosecutor in his three-piece gray suit and starched white shirt and red tie. His gray hair clung to his head like a cap, and his eyes, dark and small, seemed designed to bore into people, penetrating their defenses and exposing the inner workings of their souls. "The state calls Dr. Albert Stockton to the stand." Hughes's voice rang through the courtroom like a bell.

The medical examiner's testimony would last all morning. Three hours. Three hours of blood and wound analysis, brain tissue slides, skull reconstructions. More crime scene photos. Spatter evidence. Autopsy records. Hearing the intimate details of Tam's death made Jake sick.

What must her dad be thinking? Jake wondered. He managed to sneak a glance back at him. Mr. Anderson was sitting forward in his seat, his mouth a straight line, his brow furrowed. And behind him sat Chase Westfield's assistants, taking notes.

Chase. Was he going to get away with Tam's murder?

Jake turned back to the prosecutor who was finishing up with the ME. By the time Josh rose to cross-examine, Jake was numb. The gruesome evidence, the photos of Tam's body, the awareness that jurors were watching his every reaction made his stomach roll.

Fortunately, Josh wasn't going to have a lot of questions for the ME. No point to that. They weren't contesting how Tam died, just who did it. Almost over, he told himself, as Josh approached the witness stand. He tightened his jaw against the nausea that rose within him. The bitter, bloody testimony was almost over.

Chapter 49

Early Thursday morning, Moose called Cass. "Hey," he said, "I got something."

"What?" Cass was busy outside the interview room where Meg would go after Alejandro again this morning. Moose had been following his own leads. Sometimes that was annoying, but Cass was beginning to see that sometimes his maverick tendencies paid off.

"Well, I was looking at the copy of those security tapes you gave me, and I noticed something in the background. There was a liquor delivery."

"Right, at nine thirty-three."

"Except I started wondering about that, because it looks like the delivery guy has a thick clip-board, with maybe a tablet on it. And he hands it to someone who signs it. Did you see that?"

"Yes."

"So that would produce an electronic record, right? Of the signature."

"As well as the time it was signed," Cass said, following his train of thought.

"So I found out who supplied the liquor and I went to talk to them. At first, they didn't want to talk, because, well, the senator and his crowd are good customers. But I finally convinced him. He looked it up, and guess what? The delivery was made at eight thirty-three, not nine thirty-three! That security cam was off by an hour!"

"What?" Cass pressed her free hand to her other ear so she could hear better. "Are you telling me the time stamp was wrong?"

"One of those time stamps was. Either the tablet was wrong or the camera was wrong. I'm thinking the camera didn't fall back—it was on Daylight Savings Time."

"So we don't know for sure that Chase was at that house at the time Tam was killed! Jake needs to know this! And Josh! Great work, Moose!"

The interrogation of Alejandro resumed at 9 a.m. and soon grew intense. An agent had taken the man's mug shot to the D.C. hospital and an emergency room doctor had positively identified him as the man treated for a broken jaw the night Jake was assaulted. The tattoos had nailed it. So Meg and Angela began pressing him again on the assault on Jake.

"So how did you break your jaw, Mr. Escobar?" He said he fell.

"Why did you go all the way to D.C. to get it fixed? What happened to your friends? Who shot them? Why were they killed?" Meg's questioning was interrupted by Angela, who said something softly to her, a prearranged tactic.

"Did they mess up, Mr. Escobar? Fail to complete the mission? Who sent you on that mission? Who demanded that you kill your friends?"

Parry, thrust, retreat, like a fencer Meg worked him. She was good, Cass thought, as she observed, and having a woman do the questioning was smart. The man's defenses were softening, his demeanor less belligerent. Cass sensed they were about to get their break, if they could just keep it up.

The trial resumed after lunch. Jake sat impassively at the defendant's table, a legal pad in front of him, his heart heavy. An expert on blood spatter evidence was continuing his testimony. Someone taller than Tam had hit her on the left side of her head with a blunt object, twice, then had beaten her, fracturing her skull, creating contusions on her brain. The blood spatters, the expert testified, indicated the blows were inflicted with great force.

"So the assailant would have had to be someone strong, correct?" the prosecutor said.

"Yes, that's right."

"Particularly fit, or just average?"

"I would say particularly fit."

"Like Mr. Tucker."

"Objection, your Honor!"

"Sustained." Judge Morganthal frowned.

Still, the testimony continued. The blood spatter

expert was followed by a DNA expert who was followed by the detective who heard Tam whisper Jake's name. A personal trainer from the gym where Jake worked out testified about his strength. Then an instructor from the FBI Academy explained the training agents receive in physical combat.

"And Mr. Tucker received this training, as a new agent?" the prosecutor asked.

"Yes, sir."

"And any refresher courses?"

"Our records show Special Agent Tucker was back at the Academy for a street survival course last year, sir."

"When, exactly?"

"March, sir."

"Ah, just a year ago." He gestured with the papers in his hand. "Are these the records, sir?"

The instructor affirmed that they were, and the prosecutor entered them as evidence. Then he resumed, "Would it be logical to assume, then, that an FBI agent of Mr. Tucker's size and strength, recently trained in hand-to-hand combat, would be able to overpower a hundred-and-thirty-pound woman with no such training?"

"Objection!"

"Establishing means, your Honor."

"Overruled."

And so Jake sat, and listened as brick by brick, the case against him was laid. The wall was growing higher and higher, his chances of destroying it slimmer and slimmer.

A deputy came in and handed Josh a slip of paper. Josh looked at it, and put it in his pocket. He glanced at Jake, then turned his attention back to the witness stand.

Jake focused there as well. Tam's father was testifying about the divorce and the child custody issues, and Jake began reliving those conflicts. Then Tam's sister talked about Tam's concerns about Jake. And even though Josh got both of them to admit on cross-examination that Tam never complained about Jake physically abusing her, and that they did have some concerns about Tam's marriage with Chase, it was easy for the prosecutor to counter the implication that the senator was involved in her death: Anne Arundel County police had no record of a complaint by Mrs. Westfield regarding domestic abuse. And sixty people had observed Senator Westfield at a party the night she was slain.

Chase would testify the next day, the crown jewel in the prosecutor's stellar case.

"See you at seven-thirty tonight, right?" Josh asked as he dropped Jake off after court adjourned. Josh had developed an eye twitch as his time to present the defense was getting close. He wanted to go over Jake's testimony and his defense yet again. Maybe they'd missed something.

Jake understood. There just wasn't a lot to work with. Josh wanted to have Jake's kids testify, at least Justin, about Chase's abuse. Anything to cast reasonable doubt on Jake's guilt. Jake had been adamantly opposed to the kids being involved, but even he was now wavering. Maybe just Justin. Maybe that would be okay.

They'd have to decide tonight. "Yeah, seven-thirty," Jake said, getting out of the car. He had been sitting still all day, trying to contain all of his anger and fear and frustration in one wooden chair and he felt like he would burst if he didn't move. "Thanks, Josh."

Jake walked toward the house. Inside, he looked around his small room. Suddenly, he couldn't stand to be confined in that small space. He called Cass again, hoping she'd be free for dinner. This time he connected. "How 'bout it, Cass? You need to eat, right?"

And yes, she did need to eat but she didn't have time. Alejandro was about to crack. She was sure of it. She had to stay, and she was sorry, she said, she couldn't see him. "Jake," she said, her voice tense, "I don't need to tell you how important this is. I know the connection between this guy and Chase is there. I know it's there. I just can't prove it. But I do want to talk to you. I have to talk to you. As soon as I can get free, I'll call you."

Frustrated, he clicked off the phone, flopped

down on his bed, and stared at the ceiling. "Where's this going, God?" he said. "Where's this going?" He got up, changed into shorts and his running shoes and headed out the door. In the back of his mind, he wondered how many more free runs he'd have.

Jake had to leave at seven to get to Josh's office on time. He called the kids at six-thirty and that did not go well. Justin had cried. Justin! He'd accidentally overheard his grandparents discussing what had gone on in court and fear was gripping the boy. Jake's attempts to bolster Justin's confidence were feeble, undermined by the doubts now plaguing him. He knew it and was angry with himself for not handling it better. Where was his faith?

And now, to top off the night, he was going to have to meet with Josh, sit again and go over more evidence. Josh, the DUI lawyer who now seemed clearly in over his head. "Where's Johnny Cochran when I need him?" Jake muttered to himself as he walked out to his SUV and jerked open the door.

As he started the car and pulled out onto the street, he realized, he couldn't do it. He couldn't go to Josh's. He couldn't stand to sit in that office and go over the prosecutor's case or even his own testimony one more time. Fear clawed at his gut. Despair was pulling him down like a fresh kill.

He needed Cass! He needed his kids. And he wanted to run. To just get away from this mess. Drive to where no one could find him. Run!

The air was chilly and the winds out of the northwest had flags flapping. A full moon was rising in the east. At the corner, Jake turned left, away from Josh's office.

Ten minutes later, his cell phone rang. He looked. Josh. He was late for their meeting. His lawyer was checking on him.

Jake clicked it off and threw the phone into the cargo area of the SUV. He heard it clatter as it hit the side wall. He took an entrance onto Route 50 West, toward Washington, D.C., Virginia, and beyond. His mind leaped forward. He could get on Interstate 95 south, then head west on 66. Within a few hours, he could be in the Blue Ridge Mountains, winding his way down into Tennessee.

He could see the mountains in his head, he could taste the freedom.

But he could feel the tension of it, too. He'd be a fugitive. Cass would forfeit the bail money she'd put up. He'd definitely get jail time.

One exit short of the Maryland line, he pulled off Route 50 and turned around, his heart pounding, his hands sweating. "God, help me!" he cried out, as loneliness and fear swept over him in a wave. "God, please help me."

Chapter 50

Jake drove back toward Annapolis slowly, in the right lane. Every successive mile felt like another step further into the spider's web. Soon, he would be wrapped up tight.

He needed hope. Without knowing why, he drove to the marina where Cass kept her boat. He parked, questioning his own sanity. Then he stepped out into the cool, dark night.

The marina was about as close to Cass as he could get. And maybe, as close to God.

The moon was a luminous disk of silver light hanging in the sky. The breeze seemed to go right through Jake. He shoved his hands in his jacket pockets to warm them as he walked down the dock.

The boats were gently moving in their slips, their halyards clanking against masts like nautical wind chimes. Jake paused next to *Time Out*, Cassie's boat. He put his foot on the gunnel and rocked the boat. After Mike died, Cassie had taken a leave of absence from the FBI. Jake had searched for her and found her working on the boat, restoring it. Then their lives had taken another dark turn. He was assaulted and left for dead, with a serious head injury.

Impaired with seizures, unable to work or even

to drive, he had fallen into a deep depression. After he'd walked away from a rehabilitation hospital, Cassie found him and insisted there was hope.

Without Cassie, without those seizures, he wouldn't have met Aunt Trudy. Without Aunt Trudy, he wouldn't have found God. Without God, he would be dead. They were links on a chain God used to draw him close. Could prison be a link as well?

Jake took a deep breath, shivering in the chill. He walked on down the dock. There was no one out but him. The creek on which the marina was built stretched into the distance, black and deserted. And Jake stood at the very end of the dock, staring into the night, as if its dark mysteries held a key to his own heart, to God, to Providence.

By nature and by training he was geared up to be assertive, to take control of a situation, to be in charge. Now, he was utterly helpless, at the mercy of twelve jurors.

But no. God was sovereign. He believed that with his whole heart.

Jake stared over the water. The moonlight tipped the waves like frosting. "I can't do it, God," he said out loud. "I can't fix it, and I can't run away from it. I can't." Somewhere in the dark, a fish jumped, making a plopping sound. A marker light blinked, red, red, red in a 4-second cycle. Jake leaned against a piling. "God," he prayed, "I need some hope. I need some encouragement. I need . . ."

"Jake?"

He jumped. He'd been so lost in his thoughts, he hadn't heard her footsteps. He wheeled around.

"Jake? What are you doing?" Concern edged Cassie's voice. She was dressed in a dark suit, her hair braided, her face illuminated by the moon-light.

Jake's voice froze. He couldn't answer.

Cass came close. "You're shivering! Jake, how long have you been out here? What are you doing here?" She reached out for him, taking his hands in hers. "Your hands are freezing cold!"

Her hands were so warm, her eyes so clear. It was all he could do to keep from pulling her close. Jake swallowed, fighting his emotion.

"We couldn't find you. Josh called me a couple of hours ago. I went to your . . . to where you're staying and Stan hadn't seen you. We were all worried, Jake. We didn't know what had happened to you. You probably have a hundred messages on your phone."

"I'm sorry." He pulled away from her. "I just couldn't go to Josh's," he said. "I couldn't go over that stuff again." He shivered. "How'd you find me?"

Cass blinked. "I have no idea."

It was God, Jake thought. *Thank You.*

She touched his arm. "Josh said it was a pretty rough day in court."

"Sitting there, listening to all the testimonies about the crime scene, the autopsy," Jake gestured in frustration. He looked at the blinking beacon across the channel, and tried to focus on it, to use its rhythm to slow his own racing emotions. It didn't work. "It's all mounting up, Cass, all the evidence against me," he said, turning toward her. "They're making me out to be . . ."

". . . guilty," she said, softly.

He flinched at the word. That was his worst nightmare. Hearing the jury pronounce him guilty. Guilty. Of what? Of trying to help Tam?

Cass's touch brought his attention back. "Where's your faith, Jake?"

He didn't respond.

"Is there a God? Of course there is," she said, reciting his own catechism back to him. "Does he love you? Yes, he died for you. Does he know what's going on with you? Of course he does. Could he save you? Yes, absolutely. Will he? Who knows? But God loves you, Jake," she said, moving close to him. "God loves you. Receive that. And believe it."

Her eyes were soft, her face open to him.

"God loves you," she repeated, "and so do I. No matter what happens, I love you."

The words exploded in his heart. "What?" he said.

"I love you, Jake. I realized when I was with Travis, that all I could think about was you, not just because you're my friend, but because I love you."

"No, no!" he said, and he backed away from her. He was nearer to the end of the dock than he realized and his heel went off the boards. Cass reached out, grabbed his belt, and pulled him back from the edge.

He didn't think he could breathe. "No, Cass. You're just caught up in all the emotion."

"That's not true."

Jake looked at her, forcing himself to say what he absolutely did not want to say. "Look, Cass, I appreciate you, you know . . .

Cassie's eyes looked like they were catching pieces of moonlight and throwing them back to him. Beautiful eyes, capturing him, entrancing him.

"I love you. I love you. Are you listening, Jake?"

"Oh, Cass," he groaned softly. It was all he desired and yet he feared it. His eyes blurred with tears.

She pulled him close. "Jake! Listen to me. I love you. It's you I want. You."

"Cassie, no, no, we're not starting this," he said.

"It's already started," she whispered. "I've seen it in your eyes." And she kissed him.

Her lips softly pressed into his. Jake closed his

eyes. She turned her head slightly, and kissed him again and his emotions tore at his resolve like an avalanche ripping away a hillside. He felt the rushing of a cold mountain stream and the boiling of a hot spring all at once, the burning light of a thousand suns and the deep darkness of midnight. His whole body, mind, and soul became focused on this woman and this time and the incredible miracle of her touch. "Oh, Cass!" he murmured, and wrapped his arms around her and held her close. "Oh, Cass! I love you! I do! And I am so afraid of hurting you." He pulled back, breathless.

"Come on," Cass said gently, looking at him with those deep green eyes. "Let's get out of this wind." She took his arm, and they walked back to the parking lot, their shoes sounding a staccato rhythm to the ring of the halyards on the boats around them, his heart beating hard. "Let's take my car," she said. "Have you eaten?"

"Not since breakfast."

She made him call Josh. Then she called Trudy and her dad. "Yes, he's fine," she told them. "Just burned out."

Then she drove him to an all-night diner. As they entered, the warm smell of coffee and syrup and hot pancakes started diffusing the tension within him. Somewhere between the eggs over easy and the second cup of coffee, she reached across the table and took his hand. "I feel like

I'm in a dream," he said. "You have no idea how long . . ."

"When did your feelings change?" Cass asked, her eyes soft.

"Last fall. That's when I realized I loved you."

She raised her eyebrows. "Before Tam died?"

"Long before Tam died," Jake responded.

"Why didn't you say anything?"

"You had Travis. You seemed happy. Why interfere with that?"

"Oh, Jake."

"Besides, if I had told you and you didn't respond, how could I work with you any more? No, it seemed better just to stuff those feelings away somewhere. I was busy, remember, between my job and my kids."

"You are so crazy."

"Crazy? No, I just love you. I do. I think you are so smart and beautiful and spunky. But I wanted what was best for you. That seemed like Travis." His eyes fixed on hers. "I love you, Cass. I can't believe I can actually say that. I just hope I'll get the chance to show you." He reached for her hand and kissed it.

She blushed and smiled at him.

"But there's this slight legal thing I have to get through first."

"We're working on that! What did you think of Moose's news?"

He raised his eyebrows. "What?"

"Josh didn't tell you?" She relayed the information about the time stamp on the liquor delivery.

"The time was off?" Jake said. "That's incredible!"

"Moose sent a note to Josh. I'm surprised he didn't tell you." Cass frowned. Then she looked up at him. "But there's more."

"What?"

"We got Garza."

"What are you talking about?"

"Late this afternoon. Meg pressed Escobar . . ."

"Who?"

"Alejandro. Salamander Man." Cass leaned forward, her eyes bright. "Meg pressed him . . ."

Jake couldn't focus. "Cass, you look so beautiful . . ."

"Listen to me!" she said, laughing and tapping the table. "Listen. Meg pushed Alejandro until he admitted Garza was the one who had hired him to attack you."

"Garza? Westfield's assistant?" Jake felt his blood quicken.

"Right."

"Yes!" he said softly.

"So we've got somebody in L.A. picking Garza up and Moose is flying out there to question him." She smiled. "Moose insisted on going. He and Angela Parker. They're taking a six a.m. flight out of BWI. We may have our link to Westfield!"

"All right! Thank you, Cass, thank you." Jake shook his head, grinning. "You're unreal."

"Listen to this: Before he left, Moose said, 'Pray for me, Cass. However you do that.'"

Jake raised his eyebrows. "Wow."

They finished eating and Jake paid the bill. Outside in the dark parking lot he took her in his arms and kissed her again, inhaling the scent of her perfume, running his fingers through her hair, drinking in her presence like a tonic. And with total amazement, he realized just how much his whole life had changed in just an hour. Thank you, God, he said silently. Now, if it's not too much to ask, just give me some time with her. Please. "You've saved me," he said out loud.

"We're good together, Jake. You need me, I need you. We do things better together." She smiled.

And that, Jake thought, is the most beautiful smile in the world.

Court began at nine the next morning. Adjusting his dark blue suit as he sat down at the table, Jake tried to focus. But his heart was flying somewhere up around the ceiling and all he could think about was Cass. She loved him. She loved him! She looked so beautiful in the moonlight, her hair was so soft as he touched it, her skin so smooth. When he thought about the evening, he wanted to smile. After she had driven him back to his car, and each had left, presumably to go home, he had been surprised to see her following him.

Outside the house where he was staying, she had pulled up behind him and called him on his cell phone. "I don't want to leave you," she had said. And so she'd parked her car and climbed into his and they'd sat holding hands and just talking quietly, watching the moon and the stars make their nightly journey across the heavens, as excited as two teenagers, until finally Cassie's breathing grew heavy and he realized she'd fallen asleep, there in the passenger seat. And Jake spent the rest of the night wide awake, holding her hand, his mind whirling with thoughts of her.

"Hey," Josh said, nudging his elbow. "Jury's coming in."

"All rise!"

Jake snapped his attention back to the courtroom. Judge Morganthal entered. He had to focus, had to concentrate on what was going on.

Moose would be landing in L.A. by noon. Hopefully, Garza would be in custody. Hopefully, he'd have a lawyer assigned to his case. Hopefully, Moose would get in to see him. Hopefully, he'd be cooperative.

That was a lot of "hopefullys." Meanwhile, Jake would have to endure a lot of trial. Today, more evidence from the night Tam was murdered was on the menu. There would be little for Josh to challenge.

Motive, means, opportunity. They all lined up and pointed to Jake if you looked at them a certain way.

Judge Morganthal was droning on and Jake tried to listen to him. He was sixty-four, played golf twice a week, and had a reputation for embellishing his score. That much Jake knew. That, and the fact that he could be argumentative and difficult. He once threw out a case because a cop failed to recite the Miranda rights mantra exactly on the witness stand.

What was happening in California? What was Moose finding out?

There was no way of knowing. For now, he had to focus. Chase was taking the stand.

Chase Westfield's testimony sounded well-rehearsed. A prime performance. The state senator, elegant in his black tailored suit with his four-hundred dollar haircut and his perfectly manicured hands, had wept when he spoke of his wife. Her death, he said, was the greatest tragedy of his life.

Oh, really? Jake thought, but of course Chase's background, his childhood, his father's murder of Chase's mom and siblings, was irrelevant, unknown to the court or the jury.

For more than an hour, Chase talked about his love for Tam, his concerns about Jake, and the terrible tragedy of that last night. He was slick. He was polished. He was utterly convincing as a grieving husband. When he expressed concern for his stepchildren, Jake's kids, Jake wanted to kill him.

But Jake stayed quiet. Josh would cross-examine Chase after lunch. And as the court adjourned for ninety minutes, Jake knew he needed a miracle.

Josh escorted him out of the building. They went to a restaurant but of course, he couldn't eat. Not with his feelings for Cass and his fear colliding like asteroids inside. Josh must have been nervous, too. Their plates sat practically untouched.

Outside the courtroom, Jake saw Chase and his entourage. A priest stood near them, and Jake stiffened as he realized it was the priest who had officiated at Tam's funeral. What was he doing here?

Inside the courtroom, on the left, sat Jim Davison and Trudy, and four agents, including Craig Campbell. Jake nodded to them and took his seat at the defendant's table in the front.

"All rise," the bailiff said as the judge returned to the bench.

Judge Morganthal called for the jury. Once they were seated, the court came to order and Chase took his place in the witness stand.

Josh began his cross-examination. He started

with questions about Chase's work, about his marriage, about what drew him to begin his domestic violence initiative. Then Josh started getting personal, pressing him on arguments Chase and Tam might have had, and tensions with the stepchildren.

"Objection, your Honor! Irrelevant," the prosecutor claimed over and over.

Jake figured Josh was batting about .500, with the judge overruling about half of Hughes's objections.

But no matter how hard Josh pressed, how personal he got, Chase wasn't breaking. His calm demeanor, his timely tearfulness, and even his sly humor as he poked fun at Josh played well with the jury. And Jake's frustration grew.

After a while, Jake couldn't watch. He stared at the legal pad in front of him. Chase was too slick for Josh, too practiced at the art of projecting an image. Just listening to Chase's voice grated on Jake's nerves.

And then a motion to his right caught his eye. A man dressed in a suit walked down the courtroom aisle and opened the gate in the bar separating the spectators from the front. He crouched down next to Stoddard Hughes, handing the prosecutor a note. Then they were whispering.

Jake's eyes narrowed. What was going on?

"Senator, did the arguments with your wife

ever become physical?" Josh was asking. "For example, did she ever push you?"

Jake saw the man pull a document out of his inner jacket pocket and unfold it. And as Hughes's eyes scanned the page, his face turned red. He muttered something under his breath.

"Mr. Hughes?" Judge Morganthal said sharply.

He's annoyed, Jake thought. Hughes was looking at Chase, and Jake saw their eyes meet. Jake's heart began to pound. What was in that note?

"Your Honor, sir," Hughes said, pulling his eyes away from Chase and looking straight at the judge, "may I approach the bench? Along with the counsel for the defendant?"

Josh turned, and Jake saw a confused look on his face.

"Yes, Mr. Hughes," the Judge said.

The impeccable Mr. Hughes accidentally kicked the table leg as he got up, tripping and nearly falling, his hand slapping hard on the table as he caught himself. Then Jake saw Chase, still on the witness chair, half rise. He saw him glance to his left, toward the side door, just to the right of the jury box, where a deputy stood guard. He's going to run, Jake thought.

Why would he run?

Jake looked toward the bench. The prosecutor handed the document, whatever it was, to Judge Morganthal. Then Jake heard the judge say,

"Gentlemen, in my chambers! Court will recess for fifteen minutes." The gavel came down.

Jake rose. Josh turned, looked at him, and shrugged.

Chase stepped down from the witness stand. He turned and locked eyes with Jake and in a flash, Jake knew. He saw the guilt in Chase's eyes and the fear. He had the look of a feral cat. Chase glanced left, then right, and moved toward the door. Stop him, Jake urged silently.

Stop him. Jake couldn't take his eyes off Chase. He began moving in Chase's direction. "Stop him!" he said out loud, and people turned toward him.

His words caught the judge's attention. "Deputy, keep Senator Westfield in the courtroom," Judge Morganthal called out.

But Chase kept moving. The deputy at the side door motioned for him to stop. Chase ignored him. His hand came up to push open the door, but it opened by itself, and Jake saw Cass standing on the other side. Cass, in her black skirt suit and white shirt, her hair in a French braid, her eyes sharp. She held up her hand. And then Jake saw the senator spin toward the deputy, jerk the gun out of his holster, and turn toward Cass.

"Gun!" Jake yelled. "Gun!" and he began charging toward the door. "Gun, Cass!" He heard screams and out of the corner of his eye, he saw a deputy moving toward him from his left.

Jake pushed forward, but the deputy tackled him and he went down, banging his head against the prosecution table. And then Jake's whole body jumped as a gunshot reverberated through the room. "Cass!" he yelled.

Spectators screamed. The deputy twisted Jake's arms back. "No, help her! Help her!" Jake said. Handcuffs clicked closed. Jake fought against the restraints, his heart drumming. "Cass!" Someone put a knee on his back.

"Medic!" a voice shouted.

Jake's stomach heaved. Cass!

And then, an eerie silence fell over the room. What was happening?

"Let him up," a voice said with authority.

Cass? Cassie?

He sucked in a huge breath as the pressure came off his back. Someone grabbed his collar and pulled him to his knees. He raised his head, blood dripping down the side of his face, his chest heaving. He blinked, and his vision began to clear, and there she was, Cass, moving toward him, her cheeks flushed with exertion, her green eyes intense.

"Uncuff him," she said without taking her eyes off his. He heard the clinking of the keys, and then the cuffs came off, and a hand helped him as he staggered to his feet.

"Cass," he said hoarsely. She reached out for him and steadied him. As he put his arms around her, he felt the body armor she was wearing under her clothes. "Oh, good girl," he said, inhaling the scent of her hair. "Good for you." And the pounding of his heart slowed and the sounds around him began to fall into place. It was Cass. She was okay.

"Jake, you're bleeding," Cass said.

"What happened?" he asked, pulling a hand-kerchief from his pocket and pressing it over the wound above his ear.

"I saw him go for the deputy's gun and I took him down," Cass said, her voice shaking. "We were on the floor, fighting for the gun. When he pulled the trigger, he shot himself."

"Oh, Cass!" He put his arm around her. "That was so close! Where's he shot?"

"In the gut."

Deputies were clearing the courtroom as EMTs arrived. Jake saw Craig flash his creds and stay near where Chase lay just beyond the open side door.

Then Jake saw the bailiff emerge from the judge's chambers, look over the scene, then motion that the judge could follow. "Young man," Judge Morganthal said, pointing to Jake, "don't go away. Let me through. Let me through!" he barked, walking toward the crowd gathered around Chase.

"What was the message to the prosecutor?" Jake asked Cass. "The one that guy brought in?" He realized his heart was still pounding.

"Moose got to Garza. When he found out all he could be charged with, including murder one, he flipped. Agreed to testify against Chase. He was with him that night, saw the whole thing. Chase came back to the house, found Tam talking on the phone to you, and went ballistic. Killed her with a statue they kept in the foyer, then changed his shirt and jacket and went back to the party."

"So the time stamp on the video was wrong."

Cass nodded. "Yes."

He held her closer. "Just like you said."

Josh joined them. "Wow. I've never had anything like this happen." He shook his head. "I've never even heard of it."

"You read the note?" Jake asked.

Josh nodded. "Amazing."

"That's not all," Cass said. "We arrested Consuela. She admitted the senator gave her a black trash bag that night and told her to put it in the dumpster at her house. She wondered about it and looked inside. It was a black tuxedo jacket. It had blood on it. She had it dry cleaned and gave it to a relative. We've checked that out, too. And we got a magistrate to issue an arrest warrant for Chase."

"Thank you, Cass. Thank you."

"You need to let an EMT look at your head," Cass said.

"Yeah, yeah, I will," he responded. He saw Craig hovering around Chase Westfield.

Seconds later, Craig jogged over to them, his eyes wide. "Westfield just confessed to his priest and the judge heard it!"

"He confessed?" Jake responded.

"Yes, a deathbed confession! You're going to be cleared, Jake. Cleared!" Craig clapped him on the shoulder, then hugged him.

And ten thousand tomorrows suddenly fell into place.

"Thank you!" Jake said, overwhelmed. He turned and took Cass in his arms. "Thank you!"

Suddenly, the judge, who had been bending over Chase, stood up and strode toward the bench.

"Your Honor, should we release the jurors?" a deputy asked.

"We have something to do first," the judge responded. "Have a seat, Mr. Tucker, at the table, along with counsel. Mr. Hughes?" he bellowed. Then he commanded the bailiff, "Close that door, and bring the jury back. And Mrs. Tabor."

There was a pause while deputies went to retrieve everyone. Jake sat down in his chair, well aware that Cass was right behind him, in the first row of spectator seating.

"You need medical attention first?" Josh asked

him, staring at Jake's blood-soaked handkerchief and shirt.

"It'll be all right."

"Come to order!" Judge Morganthal said, as Mrs. Tabor, the clerk, sat down at her seat. "We're back in session. Mr. Hughes, would you like to say something?"

"Yes, your Honor," the prosecutor said, rising to his feet. "The state would like to withdraw the charges against Jacob Preston Tucker."

"All of them?"

"Yes, sir, all of them."

"Every one."

"Yes, sir."

The judge nodded. "Mr. Tucker? Is that all right with you?"

Jake stood up, grinning, his heart pounding in his chest. "Yes, sir."

"All right then," the judge said, banging his gavel, "case dismissed. You're free to go." He gestured with his hand. "Better see to that cut."

Jake turned around and grabbed Cass, lifting her over the bar. He hugged her. "Thank you."

She grinned. "You know, this kind of changes things for me. I thought you were about to be convicted. It was that whole prison romance thing that was attractive."

He laughed and kissed her hard.

Josh cleared his throat.

Jake turned and grabbed the lawyer's hand.

"Thanks, Josh, I really appreciate all you did."
Then he said, "We need to thank God." And he
took both of their hands and prayed.

An EMT walked over to Jake. "Can I look at
that head wound, sir?"

"What's going on out there?" Jake asked,
nodding toward where Chase lay.

"He didn't make it."

Chase Westfield. Dead. Wow.

"Can I take a look at that cut?"

"Got a couple of butterfly bandages?"

Craig came back while the EMT was working
on him. "We're celebrating. My house. Okay?"

Jake nodded. "Sure!" He thanked the EMT.

"Sir," a deputy said to Jake, "could you leave
this way?" He directed them toward the back,
away from the area where Chase's body lay.

And so Cass and Jake and Josh walked out of
the courtroom and into life. "If there's press
outside, do you want to talk to them?" Josh asked.

"No," Jake responded automatically. They
emerged onto the portico of the old building, into
the bright sunshine, and were immediately
mobbed by reporters, photographers, cameramen.
Jake began to push his way through them.
Suddenly, the sea of newsmen parted, and
Caitlin and Justin came running up the steps
towards him. Tears came to Jake's eyes and he
swept the two kids up into his arms. Cameras
flashed all around him.

Tam's mother said, "Frank called me and told me to bring the kids down. They need to be with you."

"Thank you."

A newswoman stuck a microphone in his face, and asked, "How does it feel to be exonerated, Mr. Tucker?"

"Great," he said, his voice hoarse with emotion. "I'm thankful. Very thankful to God. The truth came out. Just in time." As he was speaking, he saw Travis working his way through the crowd, a serious expression on his face. Jake saw him motion to Cass, and Cass responded. They moved near a pillar, just beyond the mass of reporters, and as Jake watched, he saw Cass focusing on Travis. Then her expression turned to anguish, and she covered her face and bent toward the detective. And Travis gingerly put his arms around her, looking at Jake as he did, as if to say, she needs you.

"That's it, for now," Josh said, on cue, moving Jake and the kids away.

Cass turned and saw him, and came to him.

"What happened?" he asked her.

She shook her head, grief written on her face, and he leaned down. "What happened?" he asked again.

"They killed Maria," she said, biting her lip. "They killed her and Tomas."

"For talking to us?"

Cass nodded. "I think so."

Jake took a deep breath, and put his arm around her, and drew her to his chest. He leaned down and gently kissed Cassie's head, just behind her ear. "I'm sorry, Cass. It's never perfect, is it? Not in this life."

"I thought I was going to save her, but she died to save you," she said.

"I'm so sorry."

Cass looked up at him, tears in her eyes. "God's in control, isn't he? It's hard to believe that sometimes."

"C'mon," Jake said, taking Cassie's hand. "We'll believe it together." He grabbed Caitlin's hand and Cass reached for Justin. They walked away, Jake, Cass, Justin, Caitlin, two J's and two C's in a very fallen world. A flock of pigeons took off from high in the pillars of the building, and from somewhere, a pair of mourning doves called.

Acknowledgements

My heartfelt thanks go to my husband, Larry, who has diligently pursued all the jots and tittles necessary to produce this book. Who knew publishing would become a cottage industry, and that our home in the woods of Virginia would be that cottage? Thank you, Larry, for focusing on the details I tend to gloss over, and for your constant encouragement.

My beta readers are simply the best. They caught many mistakes in the manuscript draft and asked so many good questions. Because of them, Cass wears more than a white shirt and khaki pants, and Jake finally kisses her *on the mouth*.

I appreciate so much my agent, Janet Grant of Books & Such Literary Management, and the rest of the "Bookies." Janet has the business smarts I lack, and I lean on her with every book.

God has put it on my heart to write, a tremendous privilege and a joy. May my words honor Him and bring readers closer to the One who loves them beyond measure.

Please visit my website, www.lindajwhite.com for information on events, to inquire about speaking engagements, and to sign up for my occasional email newsletter.

Center Point Large Print
600 Brooks Road / PO Box 1
Thorndike, ME 04986-0001 USA

(207) 568-3717

US & Canada:
1 800 929-9108
www.centerpointlargeprint.com